Chag Sameach!

Open this book and let the pages inside
inspire a smile
ignite Jewish pride
teach a lesson or two
enlight and discover
take it all in - from cover to cover.
As you enjoy the Chag from beginning to end
And spend time with family and friends
Remember your Oorah family who cares
And will keep in touch throughout the whole year.

- Rabbi Chaim Mintz

Little Star

732-730-1000 · OORAH.ORG · THEZONE.ORG · TORAHMATES.ORG · JEWISHLITTLESTAR.ORG

D1095938

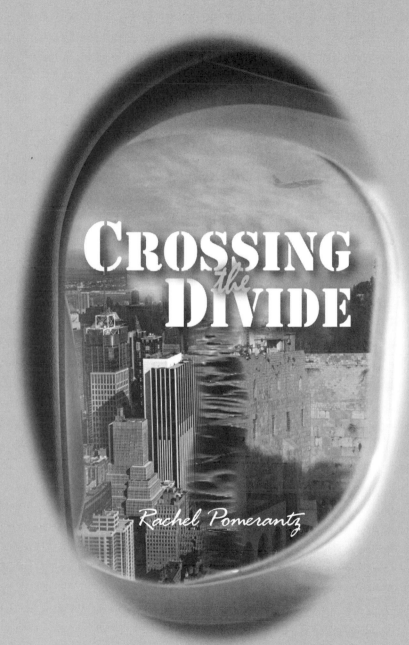

CROSSING *the* DIVIDE

Rachel Pomerantz

Hamodia
Treasures

First Impression 2007
© *Hamodia* Treasures

ISBN 13: 978-0-9791155-4-7
ISBN 10: 0-9791155-4-X

Published by Hamodia Treasures
207 Foster Avenue
Brooklyn, NY 11230

Distributed by Israel Book Shop
501 Prospect Street #97
Lakewood, NJ 08701
Telephone: 732-901-3009
Fax: 732-901-4012
www.israelbookshoppublications.com

Cover Design: F. Levovitz
artisticgraphics@aol.com

Printed in Canada

Preface

It is with pride that **Hamodia** **Treasures** presents its first published novel, *Crossing the Divide*, by Rachel Pomerantz.

Where should a Jew live? In a "great city, filled with scholars and scribes"? (*Avot*, 6, 11) In Eretz Yisrael, where the holiness of the very soil compensates for dangers and hardships? In one of the outlying communities, where every individual counts? There are as many answers as there are Jewish families.

In this novel from **Hamodia** **Treasures**, we follow several families as they try to make *aliyah* from America to Eretz Yisrael, facing obstacles that range from the more amusing forms of culture shock to the life-threat of terrorism.

Crossing the Divide, originally serialized in *Hamodia* Daily under the name *Inheritance of Our Fathers*, treats the adventures of young people as they try to find their proper place. The wrench of leaving their families, the disagreements and social adjustments, the financial challenges all become catalysts for self-knowledge and growth. Each family must find its own personal, and occasionally surprising, answer to the question, "Where should we live?"

Responding to our readers' many requests, we present the entire story between the covers of this book, so they can revisit its unforgettable characters and share their adventures with family and friends. New readers, of course, will find the ups and downs of life as experienced by the Lerner and Wahrhaftig families, their friends and neighbors both timely and timeless.

Hamodia **Treasures** was established for the purpose of publishing literature of the highest quality for the discriminating public, culled from columns that first appeared in the pages of our daily editions. We trust that you will derive hours of enjoyment from these selections.

Chapter 1

Bombshell

Mimi Lerner was just pulling a cookie sheet covered with brownies out of the oven when her husband walked in the front door. "Hello, Benny, what's new?" she called as she put the hot pan down on a towel on the counter. When Benny reached the door of the kitchen, she gave him a nod, then picked up a knife and began slicing the cake into bars.

Benny cleared his throat. "Mimi?"

"Yes?" She remained bent over her work, trying to keep the cuts straight and parallel.

"Mimi, I think we should move to Israel."

"You what?" squawked Mimi, swinging around with wide-open eyes.

"I didn't expect you to jump at the idea, but I also didn't think you'd take it quite so hard," said Benny, pointing to the knife in Mimi's right hand.

Mimi laid the knife on the counter behind her and wiped her hands on her apron. "That sounds better. It was all a joke, wasn't it?"

"About moving to Israel? No, I wasn't joking about that at all. I really think we should. I've been trying for a few days to figure out how to broach the subject, and I finally I decided to just blurt it out."

Mimi turned back to her cake so that Benny would not be able to read every expression on her face. "This is Chaim Ozer's idea, isn't it?" she asked quietly. Her high school friend Ella Wahrhaftig had spent Shabbos with them the week before, together with her husband Chaim Ozer. They had flown in briefly from Yerushalayim for his younger brother's wedding, but his parents' house had been full over Shabbos, and Mimi had offered to ease the strain by inviting them. She hoped that wasn't a mitzvah she would now have to regret for the rest of her life.

"Chaim Ozer? No, he doesn't have anything in particular to do with it. It's this *ba'al teshuvah* couple for whom my mother is making *sheva berachos* tonight, the Millmans."

"I thought you hadn't spoken to the *chassan* for years — since before we were married." Mimi had been recovering from the flu the night of the Millman wedding, and had let Benny go alone because the connection seemed so distant. The *chassan* had been a Shabbos guest of Benny's parents for a year or two, before the boy went off to Yerushalayim to study in a yeshivah.

"I did manage to exchange a word or two with Michael after the *bentching*. He congratulated me on my marriage and on the children. I asked him where they were planning to live. Do you know what he said?"

Mimi, realizing that Benny was waiting for her to look at him, turned around slowly and met his eyes.

Benny continued. "He looked at me in surprise and said, 'In Israel, of course. Isn't that where every Jew lives if he has a choice?'"

The doorbell rang, rescuing Mimi from having to give an immediate answer. "Oh, that must be the baby-sitter!" The next few minutes were spent on giving instructions, writing down emergency phone numbers and packing up the brownies in aluminum foil. Not until they were in the car on their way to her in-laws' house did Mimi have to deal with Benny's bombshell.

"Family," she said, with a tone of finality. "That's why."

"Why what?" asked Benny.

"Why we don't move to Israel. My parents are a few blocks away. Your parents are in Flatbush. All our brothers and sisters are all over the Greater New York area."

"We lived in Lakewood for four years. That was more than a few blocks away."

"Lakewood is practically a suburb of Brooklyn; think how often we ran back and forth. Besides, we were living in Lakewood so that you could learn in the *kollel* there," Mimi said.

"Because learning Torah is such an important mitzvah that it is considered in some sense equal to all the others. For that, we were willing to give up for a while on the convenience of being next door to our families. Living in Israel is also considered in some sense equal to all the other *mitzvos*. Maybe for that we should also be willing to give up on living near our families. It's not as if either of us is an only child, solely responsible for caring for our parents as they grow old."

Mimi smiled. Sometimes Benny sounded very talmudical. "We would miss all the *brisos* and *bar mitzvos* and weddings," she said. "We surely couldn't fly back for all of them. You don't even know how you would support us there. You have such a good job here, with time in the evenings for a *Daf Yomi shiur*. From what I hear of Israel, you would have to take two or three jobs just to make ends meet, and then they still wouldn't."

"Chaim Ozer doesn't have two or three jobs. As I understand it, he just learns Torah, pretty much straight through, from six in the morning to eleven at night."

Ha! So Chaim Ozer did have something to do with it. "Maybe Ella holds down the two or three jobs. If anyone would be capable of it, she would. Or perhaps they subsist on manna from heaven. All I know is, for us to survive that way would require a miracle, and one isn't supposed to depend on miracles. Oh, speaking of the Wahrhaftigs, I forgot to tell you. Your mother called and asked us to pick them up on the way. Apparently she was short of a *minyan*, and managed to persuade Ella that coming tonight was a mitzvah that no one else was going to do."

"Wish you had told me earlier. I should have turned up 45th Street." Benny turned left and began to go around the block so that he would be going the right way in order to pass the Wahrhaftig house.

Mimi felt a rising sense of panic. She wanted to scotch this suggestion so thoroughly that Benny would never bring it up again, but arguments that seemed completely conclusive to her did not always carry enough weight with Benny. She surely didn't want to discuss it in front of Ella and Chaim Ozer. They would take Benny's part. They had gotten married with the understanding that they would live in Israel. "What about the army? Since you work, you would have to serve."

"So, I'll serve in the army. What's so awful about that? Since we already have two children, I think I would go straight into the reserves."

"If there's a war, the reservists fight too."

"So, I'll fight. It might be less nerve-wracking than sitting here chewing my nails the way I did during the Gulf War. Chaim Ozer says that over in Yerushalayim they were much calmer than their families here, because they knew what was going on."

"Benny, it's dangerous over there."

"Mimi, it's dangerous right here in Boro Park. Do you go out alone at night? In Israel you could roam the streets alone until midnight if you felt like it." He pulled over to the curb in front of the Wahrhaftig house. A curtain on the first floor, which had been pulled to the side, fell back into place.

"We won't talk about it any more right now," said Mimi firmly.

Mimi sat beside Benny without speaking, as they waited to give their friends a lift to the *sheva berachos*. Though she had requested silence about Benny's new proposal, her thoughts were racing. What should she say to him when they could talk privately again?

The front door of the Wahrhaftigs' home opened. Chaim Ozer and Ella emerged from the house, bundled up in coats and scarves against the winter chill. Mimi, glancing at the back seat, said, "Oh, I have to take out one of the children's car seats. Press the button to open the trunk." She got out, opened the back door, and unsnapped the catch that secured the seat belt. She was just starting to drag the heavy car seat out of the car when the Wahrhaftigs reached the curb.

"Let me take that," suggested Chaim Ozer.

Mimi released it gratefully, stepped aside as he pulled it out of the car, and lifted the door of the trunk so that it could be put in easily. Ella slid into the back seat on the curbside, Mimi got into the back on the street side, and Chaim Ozer took the place next to Benny.

"Brrr," said Ella, when they were all settled and Benny had started the car. "I'd forgotten how cold New York gets in December."

"On the other hand," said Mimi with an edge in her voice, "the houses are well heated. Once you get inside, you can unknot your muscles."

Ella laughed. "Still the local patriot, I see. Remember how we used to argue the relative merits of living in New York or living out of town?"

Ah, this was a subject to which Mimi could relate. "I surely do. I remember that when you first came to stay with us at the beginning of high school, you would be offended that perfect strangers didn't all say 'Gut Shabbos' to you in the streets."

"Those first few months were terribly hard," Ella reminisced. "To go from being a graduating eighth-grader in a small day school to being a lowly ninth-grader in a huge high school was one of the most humbling experiences of my life."

Part of the shock had surely been the switch from being the daughter of the local Rosh Yeshivah to being a boarder with a very ordinary family; but, of course, Ella would never admit that part of it. Just as Mimi never said out loud what a shock it had been for her when Ella had joined their family. She had known Ella's mother as Rebbetzin Gutfreund, and perhaps she had even been introduced to Ella once or twice at weddings, but she had never had to relate to her until the day that Ella's parents brought her to Mimi's house to live.

"I would never have guessed it from the way you walked into the building on the first day of school. I was nearly shaking with nervousness, even though I knew nearly a third of the girls in our class. You sailed in as calmly as if you had been going to the school for years, although you didn't know a soul."

"It was sheer bravado," admitted Ella, "but I didn't realize that I had pulled it off well enough to fool you as well."

"That's interesting," said Chaim Ozer to his wife. "You often told me how scared you were, and you never told me what a brave front you put up. Do you think it helped?"

"Can't tell you," said Ella with a shrug. "I never tried the experiment of creeping into a new place with my eyes on the floor."

"You must have been doing something right, since you were put in charge of organizing our class booth for the Chanukah bazaar." Mimi, of course, had been somewhat jealous of Ella's rapid rise to a position of responsibility, though she never doubted that Ella's organizational talents had justified the promotion.

"I'm sure at least part of it was due to trying to make the outsider feel welcome," suggested Ella. "I considered it thoughtfulness on the part of the teacher."

"Who is this couple we are going to gladden this evening?" asked Chaim Ozer, changing the subject.

Mimi wondered if that was intentional. Chaim Ozer was very sharp, not only about *Gemara*, but also about people. Did he realize that she was on edge? She didn't want anyone other than Benny to know that.

"I don't know the *kallah* at all," said Benny, "except that I know she is also a *ba'alas teshuvah*. The *chassan* was working for an advertising agency in New York when he started getting interested in *Yiddishkeit*. My parents were one of the families he used to come to for Shabbos and Yom Tov. He is about my age, so when I was home from Baltimore for vacations we talked a lot."

"I would think he would know a fair number of people in Boro Park," said Ella. "Your mother sounded absolutely desperate for a *minyan*. "

"There are a couple of weddings tonight in the community. Also, when my mother was making up the list, she thought that she would have at least the two fathers. It turned out that his parents already went back to Pittsburgh, and her parents are worn out from all this unaccustomed partying."

Ella nodded. "I already learned that a while back. If I make *sheva berachos* for a couple like this, I make sure to have a *minyan* without counting on the family. The idea of a week of parties after the wedding is too strange to the parents. In Yerushalayim there is no particular problem drumming up enough people, because I can always get extra guests from his yeshivah."

Ella, like Benny's parents, did a lot of mitzvah entertaining. Mimi's parents never had guests outside of their family. Of course, their family was pretty big by now. If several of Mimi's siblings came with their children, there might be more than twenty people around the dining room table. Still, after she had gotten used to always seeing new faces at her parents-in-law's house, she found her own family holiday meals a little dull, and she occasionally caught Benny yawning when he thought no one was looking.

They were drawing near to the Lerner home, and Mimi spotted

a parking space. "Benny, how about that space there?"

Benny shook his head. "No, it's so cold that I'm going to leave you all off at the curb in front of the house, and then start looking for a place to park."

Should she loyally volunteer to stick with him until he parked? But then they might resume the discussion of moving to Israel. She got out with Chaim Ozer and Ella when Benny stopped the car in front of his parents' home. She still hoped that, seeing how opposed she was, he would drop the subject entirely.

Was it really a coincidence, as Benny claimed, that this idea came to him just when their friends were here on a short visit from Yerushalayim? Was this not another instance of her life being changed to match Ella's ideas of how things should be done?

When the Wahrhaftigs and Mimi rang the bell at the home of her parents-in-law, Benny's brother opened it. Mimi explained that Benny would join them as soon as he succeeded in parking the car on the crowded Flatbush streets. She said nothing, of course, to indicate that the chill that had brought her in early was not the nip in the air, but rather a cold fear of the unknown that had seized her ever since Benny dropped his bombshell about possibly moving to Israel. The three new arrivals divested themselves of their wraps in the vestibule. Chaim Ozer entered the dining room, where the long table was opened out to full length, while Mimi and Ella went to the kitchen to hand over Mimi's brownies.

Mimi's three sisters-in-law were slicing, mixing, and arranging in various parts of the large kitchen. Mrs. Lerner was just sliding a pan of roasted potatoes into the oven to reheat. She gave Mimi a peck on the cheek, with an apologetic glance at her floury apron to indicate why it wasn't accompanied by a hug.

"What can we do to help?" asked Mimi.

"The most useful thing you can do at the moment is go cheer up the poor *kallah*, who is sitting all by herself at the ladies' table in the living room. I absolutely refused to let her help out here in the kitchen, which is where she would really like to be."

Mimi and Ella went back through the hall to the living room, where the bride indeed looked lonely. Mimi was just about to make the introductions when the young woman gasped, "Rebbetzin Wahrhaftig! What are you doing here?" and jumped to her feet. In a moment the two women were embracing, laughing and talking all at once.

"Trudy! Why didn't I know? I had heard that you went home to get ready for the wedding a month and a half ago, but I had no idea it would be just when we were in New York!"

"We were a little late getting off the invitations to Israel," apologized Trudy. "We didn't imagine anyone would come from Yerushalayim."

"I presume it will be waiting for us when we get back. Well, at least we got to the *sheva berachos!* Wait, just let me tell my husband so that he won't feel like such a stranger here."

Mimi, seeing that she was superfluous, returned to the kitchen and reported to her mother-in-law. "Ella and the bride turn out to be old friends from Yerushalayim. They don't need me at all. Can I help Tzippy cut the salad?"

During the meal, Ella took the place of honor at the bride's right hand, with Mimi on her other side. Mimi and Ella exchanged a few words about the children now and then, but most of Ella's time was devoted to the young bride. Ella was a fountain of practical advice about how to manage in Israel on a limited budget, and Trudy was determined to pump her for every last detail. Should Mimi herself be listening? No, it was surely unnecessary. Now that it was clear to Benny that Mimi did not want to go, he would drop the idea, right?

Actually, Mimi could not have taken in all of Ella's advice, anyway, because she was running back and forth to the kitchen to help her mother-in-law. Benny's sisters, of course, had been helping out at affairs like this since they were little, and each had her specialty.

It had taken Mimi almost a year to find a niche of her own, putting away or washing up whatever was no longer needed, and keeping the counters clear for the serving trays. Mrs. Lerner, whose attention during the main part of the meal was totally concentrated on providing plentiful, warm food with a minimum of delay, was always grateful when she looked around after sending out the last of the desserts and discovered that her kitchen was not in shambles.

Usually, Mimi enjoyed the hustle and bustle in the kitchen. One of the first things that had attracted her to Benny was his description of his parents' free-and-easy style of *hachnasas orchim*. A variety of Shabbos guests and miscellaneous celebrations like this one were all served out of this same kitchen. Tonight, however, Mimi could not enter into the fun of the occasion. Her thoughts were focused on Benny's bombshell.

"Where should I put this?" It was Benny himself, coming in from the dining room with a tray heaped high with nearly empty serving dishes. Glancing around, Mimi realized that, in her distraction, she had been falling down on her job. There wasn't a clear inch of counter space anywhere in the kitchen.

"Just stand where you are for a second," said Mimi. She picked up one of the trays that Tzippy had filled with spirals of ice cream cake.

"Wait!" protested Tzippy. "I was about to put a brownie on each plate."

"Too late," said Benny, setting down his tray in the vacated spot. "You can serve the brownies separately."

"Nonsense," said Tzippy in her best older sister tone. She was perhaps a year his senior. Taking the tray of cake from Mimi, she thrust it at Benny. "Just hold this in the air while I set out the brownies." Mimi began frantically consolidating the leftovers on the tray Benny had put down, cramming them into the refrigerator before one of his brothers or brothers-in-law showed up with another tray.

Benny said to Mimi, "If I collapse in the line of duty, tell them that you and the children expect a pension." Then, dropping his aggrieved tone, he added, "Wasn't that an amazing coincidence, the bride knowing the Wahrhaftigs?"

"Uhn-huhn," agreed Mimi without much animation.

"Chaim Ozer made up a *gematriya* on the Hebrew names of the bride and groom, more or less on the spot. It was a cute one, too."

In a desperate effort to make conversation, Mimi asked, "Where are they planning to live?"

"In the Shmuel HaNavi section. There are a lot of small old apartments there, and they seem to have gotten something pretty cheap."

"Okay," announced Tzippy, "I'm done. Get these out to the men before the ice cream melts."

Mimi took the smaller tray that Tzippy had made for the women's table and set off for the living room. In the doorway she passed Ella, who had filled up a bag with used paper plates and was taking it to the kitchen. As Mimi handed out the cake, she said to the bride, "My husband tells me that you have an apartment waiting for you."

"I've never actually been there," admitted Trudy. "Michael picked it out after I had already left for the States to get ready for the wedding. He says it used to be on the border, and you can still see bullet marks from the Six Day War."

"Oh, my," said Mimi, shivering slightly.

"A couple of my friends have volunteered to clean it up before we get there, but I really don't care so much what it looks like. What's important is the location."

"You like that neighborhood?"

"No, the neighborhood isn't important either. I just mean that it's in Yerushalayim."

On the way home, after they had dropped off the Wahrhaftigs, Benny and Mimi drove several blocks in silence. Mimi was in turmoil. What in the world had made him come up with this idea of moving, when their life was so nearly perfect? She would almost have said that it was perfect, except that they didn't own their own home. They could hardly have saved money while Benny was in *kollel*, but now they were putting some away, and in another two or three years they would be ready to make a down payment and qualify for a mortgage.

"Benny," she finally burst out, "You have to count your blessings."

"I did," said Benny. "There were seven, or, to be more precise, eleven, if you add in *Birkas Hamazon*."

"You know I wasn't talking about the *sheva berachos*. I was talking about our life. We have health, children, *parnassah*, family, and friends. Why put all that in danger?"

"*Be'ezras Hashem*, we'll have health, children and *parnassah* in Eretz Yisrael."

"As you heard me say before, I would much rather stay here with our families. Unless this idea is extremely important to you, I don't think that there is much to discuss."

"It's very important to me."

"Since when?"

"Just like I told you. Since Michael's wedding."

"Benny, we've been married for more than four years. During that time, we've always spoken as if we intended to live in New York, or perhaps in one of the suburbs, for the rest of our lives. Someone gave you a different idea, and now you tell me that within a week it has become very important to you. How can you treat me this way? I've always expected more consideration from you, and you don't usually disappoint me."

That comment made Benny pause. When he spoke again, it was in a more conciliatory tone. "I'm not trying to be perverse. Do you remember that picture in our dentist's office? It usually looks like a stack of cubes, but sometimes if you look away and look back, the picture inverts and the cubes all seem to be hollow. The two-dimensional picture is just the same, but the way we see it can change very drastically and very suddenly."

Mimi remembered the picture. She had not noticed the inversion effect on her own, but once Benny had told her to look out for it, she had seen the picture the other way occasionally. She always found the switch unsettling. "So maybe you should look away and look back again," she said.

Her husband sighed. "You know, you still haven't given the idea of moving to Israel serious thought."

"I don't know how you can say that," objected Mimi. "I've hardly been thinking about anything else all evening, and I assure you that my thoughts have been totally serious."

"But your thoughts have all been along the line of 'Oh dear, how can I talk him out of this?' Have you once stopped to consider what our life would be like if we lived in Israel?"

It would be horrible, she thought, but she did not want to say that. "What do you want me to do?"

"I just want you to think about it, maybe talk it over with your parents or your sisters."

Her mother's blood pressure would shoot up to the sky. Her father could probably have a heart attack on the spot. "I think that would be causing them needless anxiety."

"Okay, then don't discuss it with anyone. Just think about it yourself. I'll drop the subject for the moment, so that you won't have to waste energy on thinking of arguments to give me. I'm only asking you to give the idea a chance."

The subsequent silence lasted until he had parked the car near their house and turned off the motor. It was Mimi who broke it. "Benny?"

"Yes, Mimi?"

"Why do you want to move to Eretz Yisrael?"

"Because there is more *kedushah* there. Because Hashem is closer to us in Eretz Yisrael."

"Good morning! Everybody up!" Mimi sang out as she crossed the children's room to the window, where she pulled up the venetian blind. To her own ears, her accustomed morning heartiness with the children had a false ring to it. She knew that she had lain awake much of the night, and would like nothing more at the moment than to crawl back under the covers.

Shimon, nearly three, stretched and yawned without opening his eyes. Tamar, the baby, looked at her mother and gurgled.

"Shimmy, dear, '*Mo-deh ...*'"

Shimmy began to murmur along with his mother, "*Mo-deh a-ni le-pa-ne-cha, ...*" with a light sprinkling of mistakes. When he had finished the waking-up *tefillah*, he opened his eyes and sat up in bed. Mimi scooped up Tami and held her in one arm while she led Shimmy down the hall with her other hand. She set Shimmy to brushing his teeth while she changed Tami on the bathroom's changing table.

Mimi glanced at her watch. The whole point to waking the children up so early was to have them downstairs for breakfast when Benny returned from shul. Otherwise, between his job and his *shiur,* they would see him only on Shabbos. She had fifteen minutes left.

As she reached for the diaper cream on the shelf above the changing table, she thought again how convenient this table was. Mimi had spent a year in seminary in Israel after high school, and from what she remembered, it was rare to have a bathroom that wasn't cramped. Mimi sighed. That was the kind of comparison that Benny was asking her to avoid, but she couldn't avoid it.

Mimi took the children back to their room and chose their clothes with less than her usual attention to color and style. She was still putting on Shimmy's socks when she heard Benny's key in the lock of the front door. She decided to skip the shoes for the moment; after all, they had wall-to-wall carpet everywhere, except in the kitchen. She carried the baby downstairs, with Shimmy padding beside her. Over the banister she could see Benny putting his *tallis* bag on its usual shelf in the living room.

"Tatti!" called Shimmy in surprise when he got to the bottom of the stairs and saw his father. Only then did Mimi notice that Benny hadn't called out his usual "Good morning!" as he came in. Benny swooped up his son and gave him a hug that should have made up for the neglected greeting — a hug that Shimmy returned with all the strength he had, burying his face in his father's shoulder. After a tender glance at Shimmy, Benny rested his bearded cheek on his son's silky hair and looked up at his wife.

That was the first moment when Mimi realized that she might actually move to Israel.

Chapter 2

Announcement

Mrs. Adler, Mimi's mother, looked up the Wahrhaftigs' number in the Brooklyn phone book. She sat for a moment with her hand on the receiver before lifting it and dialing. A child answered. "Hello, is Ella there?" she asked.

"Just a moment. Ella! It's for you!"

"Hello?" That was Ella's voice, crisp and cheerful as usual.

"Hello, Ella, dear. This is Aidel Adler. I picked up a few little things for you to take back to your children, and I wondered when I could bring them over."

"It's terribly sweet of you to remember them, Mrs. Adler, but I wouldn't think of letting you come to me. I'll come over to you. "

"No, really Ella, I insist that you let me come. You have a plane to catch tonight, and I know that you came back from your mother's yesterday so that you could finish up your shopping today. Please let me drop by. If you aren't in when I come, I'll just leave the things with your mother-in-law."

"Under no circumstances. You took care of me for four full years, and there is no way I'm going to let you come here to bring me presents for my own children."

"I lived with your grandmother for three years when I came

over from Hungary."

"So, if I were my grandmother, I might let you come to me, but I'm not. Just sit tight and I'll be right over."

Mrs. Adler put down the receiver with a sigh. As usual, Ella had gotten her own way.

The doorbell rang fifteen minutes later, while Mrs. Adler was still collecting the gifts that she had bought on several different occasions and stored in different places. She had now put them together in one large shopping bag, but she was secretly hoping that Ella would open it.

"You look lovely, dear," said Mrs. Adler, as she kissed Ella on the cheek. "A little vacation has agreed with you." She had always thought that Ella worked too hard.

"I don't know how all this frantic rushing about can be called 'vacation,'" said Ella with a laugh, "but it has been wonderful seeing everyone. All of Chaim Ozer's family, of course, were at the wedding, and two of my sisters came to my parents' house to see us there with their families."

"Where did your mother put everyone?" asked Mrs. Adler.

"The neighbors absorbed the overflow, the way Mimi and Benny took us in for the Shabbos of the *sheva berachos.*"

"Here, sit down on the couch." Once her guest was seated, Mrs. Adler headed for the kitchen, filled a tray with refreshments, and brought it out to the coffee table. "How is your mother?"

"Still as youthful and energetic as ever. All the boys are off in yeshivos, so only my two youngest sisters are living at home right now. My mother is teaching high school, and running all sorts of *chessed* projects as she manages the house. She cooks with the phone on her shoulder."

Mrs. Adler pushed forward the shopping bag. "Do you want to look these over? If some of them are the wrong size, they could still be exchanged."

"I don't worry much about sizes," said Ella. "What's small for one will soon be big enough for another." Mrs. Adler was just beginning to feel disappointed when Ella added. "However, I will surely open it up to give you the pleasure of hearing me say 'ooh' and 'aah!'" She reached into the package. The first dress to come out was intended for Ella's five-year-old. "Oh, this is lovely. It will be just perfect for Leah'le for Pesach."

"I bought two others just like it for my own *eineklach*," said Mrs. Adler with pleasure.

After they had gone through the clothing piece by piece, Mrs. Adler carefully refolded everything and Ella rose to go.

"Do take care of yourself over there," said Mrs. Adler. "I worry about you sometimes. The newspapers make it all sound so frightening."

"Occasionally, if there's a terrorist bomb nearby, we get a little edgy ourselves; but most of the time we are very calm."

"I'm just so grateful that our own children live nearby."

Ella's voice took on a slightly pained note. "Mrs. Adler, you don't quite mean to put it that way, do you? After all, Eretz Yisrael is the Holy Land."

"All right," said Mrs. Adler meekly. "I'm glad that I don't have your mother's worries."

Mimi was sitting in her mother's kitchen, sipping tea and nibbling on a piece of strudel. Tami was being dandled on Mama's knee, and Shimmy was playing with a fire engine on the floor. Mimi was ostensibly here to pick up some cakes her mother had baked for them, but she was taking her time over it because she enjoyed being with her mother.

"Ella left last night," Mama said.

"I know," murmured Mimi.

"It sounds as if she is constantly rushing from one thing to the next. A bit like Malka."

"Malka has a lot of responsibilities. Now that she has been made assistant principal on top of her teaching it takes even more time. And it's not as if she has a small family," Mimi pointed out.

"I understand all that," Mama was saying. "Still, I always feel more relaxed with you and Reuven. The older ones, though wonderful children, are so very sure of themselves and so very busy. I treasure quiet moments like this one."

Mimi, feeling terribly guilty that she hadn't told her mother about Benny's plan, did not know what to say. Tami began squirming uncomfortably. Mama held her out and said, "I think she needs to be changed. I'll watch Shimmy while you take her upstairs."

"Thanks, Mama."

Mimi pulled a pad out of the diaper bag and laid Tami down on the bed in the blue bedroom. This had been her room for two months, between her sister Leah's wedding and the arrival of Ella at the beginning of high school. It was small, too small for them to use now when they stayed over, but she had always been fond of it. It was, after all, the first room she had ever had all to herself.

By the time she had finished diapering Tami, Mimi was more certain than ever that they should not move to Israel. Leaving Mama here with only Malka and Leah to talk to would be like putting herself in a situation where she had no one to speak to except Ella ... Mimi cut that thought short as uncharitable. She would cross that bridge if, and when, she came to it.

It was three full days before Mimi was ready to broach the subject of Israel again. She and Benny had been uncomfortable with each other for days. She had been full of forced heartiness with the children, and quiet and withdrawn with her mother and sisters when they called. In a sense, talking with Benny about the routine business of life had been the easiest, because there had been no need for pretense or for keeping secrets.

She knew now that she might actually go. She might actually move to Israel, because her husband's wishes and her marriage were more important to her than seeing her family, or having a large house, or living in a familiar culture. She thought Benny was equally conscious that he might not move to Israel. If she were too firm in her opposition, he would abandon the idea. That was how she understood the silent plea she saw in his eyes now and then.

She hadn't been able to do what he asked of her — to consider what their life might be like if they moved to Israel. However, by admitting to herself that she might be there in a year or two, she was in a sense giving the idea a chance. Perhaps she should speak to her parents and her sisters? Give them an opportunity to say whatever they had to say while the issue was still very much undecided? She would have to go with Benny, or otherwise she would just be caught in the crossfire. For that, she and Benny would have to talk some more.

Mimi decided that Friday night would be the best time for such a discussion. She turned down an offer of a guest in order to leave the evening open, and mentioned to Benny that she would like to speak to him after the children were in bed. He seemed more tense than happy at the suggestion. Thinking back over their previous discussion of the subject, Mimi could see why he wouldn't be anxious for more of the same.

On Shabbos evening, right after the soup course, Benny took the children up to their room and said *Shema* with Shimmy, while Mimi kept the Shabbos table from being deserted. She usually welcomed these few minutes as a chance to relax after a very strenuous day, but tonight she was too concerned about what, exactly, she and Benny would say to each other. When he returned, she popped up to get the main course, while he sang one of the Shabbos evening *zemiros*. Mimi served the chicken, and they ate in silence except for "Please pass the salt."

It was Mimi who finally said, *"Nu?"*

"Nu, what?"

"Nu, when are you going to say *'Nu?'"*

"It is only with superhuman self-control that I have avoided saying *'Nu?'* for the last ten minutes," admitted Benny, "but I remind you that I was honor-bound not to bring up the subject."

"All right, I said *'Nu?'* Now tell me something."

"About why I want to move to Eretz Yisrael? I *daven* very fluently, right? I've been doing it since I was six. The phrases slide out by themselves, without any need on my part for the least thought: 'Break the yoke from our necks, and lead us upright to our Land... Raise a banner to gather our exiles, and gather us together from the four corners of the Earth...' After what Michael said, I began to feel like something of a hypocrite. I *daven* as if I can't wait to get to the Holy Land, but in fact I have always planned to stay right here."

"But, Benny, that's all talking about the days of Moshiach, not about now!"

"But my heart is telling me to take my family now, and await Moshiach there."

"Then everybody will be doing it. Our families and our friends will also go. We won't be alone."

"We won't be alone if we go now either. We have each other."

Mimi suppressed a retort about that not being what she meant. She wasn't trying to argue the case; she was trying to find out what had caused Benny to change. "That was what made everything seem different? Paying attention to all the references to Eretz Yisrael in the *tefillos?*"

"No, it wasn't just that. Something else happened before that. I had asked Michael an ordinary question, about where he was going to live. I've already quoted the answer to you, 'In Israel, of course. Where else does a Jew live if he has a choice?' It suddenly hit me: We have a choice, and we should make that choice now."

"We didn't exactly decide to live in New York because of its large Irish Catholic population. We chose it because it's the largest Jewish community in America," Mimi pointed out.

"But first of all, because our families are settled here. What hit me was that I was somehow seeing my role in life and my responsibilities in raising our children in rather narrow terms, without considering the impact we would have on the broader course of Jewish history."

"Benny, the two of us are fairly ordinary people. Whatever we do, it is not likely to change Jewish history very much."

"We may not be influential, but we are representative. It's the same reason that one goes out to vote on Election Day, even though few elections are actually decided by one vote."

"I'm not following your train of thought. What's the connection between leaving my family to move to Israel and voting on Election Day?"

"It is in personal decisions like this, where to live and what to do, that ordinary people like us can make an impact. I feel that it's an important time for us to exercise that power."

"Why?" Mimi started collecting the plates. Neither of them had been very hungry. All the tension in the house was taking its toll.

"Because I think we are approaching a critical point, both with respect to the relations between Jews and Arabs, and also in the cultural struggle between the secular and religious camps among the Jews. Demography is going to make a difference in these conflicts, and if we want to be counted we must be there, not here."

At that Mimi's temper snapped. She had already picked up the plates to carry to the kitchen, but now she banged them down with a clatter of forks and stamped her foot. "I do not want to be counted. Not in some dumb census."

"Mimi, I'm not blind to the fact that there would be a lot of practical and emotional hardships."

"Well, you certainly seem to be blind to the problems." Mimi felt a sudden wish for reinforcements. "I think we should raise the possibility with our families, so that they can say what they have to say while the question is open."

Benny winced. "Will you speak to your mother tomorrow night?"

"No, I think we should both go over on Sunday, after you get back from your *shiur*. That will give me time to get a baby-sitter. We will hear what they have to say about this."

Mrs. Adler twitched the white lace tablecloth she had laid over the coffee table, to straighten out a fold. If Mimi and Benny had made a special appointment, they must have an important announcement to make, and Mrs. Adler was wondering what it might be.

She brought out the plate of Hungarian pastries she had spent all afternoon baking. She had made the deep-fat-fried "roses" that Benny loved so much. For Mimi, she had baked apple strudel. Mrs. Adler was very proud of her strudel dough. When she had finished stretching it, one could read a newspaper through the dough, it was so thin. She had only been eighteen when her parents had sent her out of Hungary in 1956, but she had had time to learn to bake.

The doorbell rang. "Papa," she called out to her husband, who was in his study. "The children are here. Come." She went to open the door.

"Welcome, darling," she said to Mimi, giving her a warm hug.

"It's so nice to see you, Mama," murmured Mimi, returning the hug and clinging for a moment longer than usual.

"Come in, Benny, come in," continued Mrs. Adler, bustling them over to the couch. "Sit down, and I will bring the tea so that we can talk comfortably."

Mr. Adler came in. He greeted Mimi affectionately and shook Benny's hand. "*Wie gehts?* Sit down, sit down. How's the job? How's the learning?"

"Everything's fine, *baruch Hashem*. We have a big project on at work, and the *Daf Yomi shiur* is in *Pesachim*."

When Mrs. Adler returned with the tea tray, the others were talking about cute things that the *eineklach* had done or said in the last two weeks. Mrs. Adler got regular reports on this subject by phone from Mimi. There was some clinking and stirring as the tea was poured and passed around. She took a first sip of her tea and looked at the children. Mr. Adler did the same. Mimi looked at Benny, who cleared his throat.

"We—uhh—came to tell you something."

Mr. and Mrs. Adler looked at him expectantly.

"Uhh, perhaps you would want to set down your teacups first," Benny said. He set the example by putting down his own. Mrs. Adler shot a glance at her husband as she set down her cup and saucer. Mimi continued to sip her tea and watch her husband quietly.

"We are thinking, or rather, I am thinking, of moving to Israel. Mimi is not yet convinced."

Good heavens, I should hope not! Mrs. Adler thought. *What in the world was Benny talking about? Her little girl should move to the other side of the ocean?*

Her husband looked equally astounded, but he managed to put his surprise into words: "Where would you go? What would you do? How would you manage?"

"I hope we'd settle in Yerushalayim; I think Mimi would be most likely to find a community she would be comfortable with there. I would try to line up a job in computers before we got there."

"Then this is not a transfer?"

"No, I would be starting fresh."

Mrs. Adler found herself paralyzed. She could not think of what she could or should say. Mimi set down her teacup and reached out a hand to her mother, who grasped it gratefully. It was like an anchor holding her fast in a sudden storm. Might they have to separate?

A silence fell over the group, as Mr. Adler exhausted his questions and Mrs. Adler could not formulate any—at least none that she wanted to ask in front of Benny. Once the children were gone, a thousand questions and worries would pop up to torment her. She would speak to Mimi by phone tomorrow.

Her son-in-law cleared his throat and glanced at Mimi before turning back to them. "We told my parents we would be over soon. I'm sure we'll have many more talks about this before the question is settled. All we wanted to do this evening is to open the topic for discussion."

Mrs. Adler nodded stiffly.

Benny leaned forward as if to rise.

"Wait," Mrs. Adler found her voice at last. "At least have a piece of cake. I spent all afternoon baking."

Benny relaxed against the sofa. Mimi dropped her mother's hand and served herself a piece of strudel. "This is delicious, Mama," she said. Benny took one of the "roses" and nibbled at it politely. He swallowed the rest of his tea and stood up briskly.

Mimi also got to her feet. "I'll call you tomorrow, Mama," she said, kissing her mother on the cheek.

As soon as the door closed behind them, the questions indeed boiled up. How serious was Benny about this plan? How firmly was Mimi opposed? If they went, when would they go?

Mimi's older sister, Malka, called around noontime the next day. Mimi had spent an hour on the phone with her mother in the middle of the morning. By the end of the conversation, both were in tears. Mimi had given Mrs. Adler permission to discuss the matter with her other children, and Malka had probably been first. "Mimi, what is this Mama tells me about some crazy plan to flit off to Israel?"

"I don't think Mama used quite those words."

"Of course not. She spoke very bravely and loyally about how the children must make up their own minds and do what is best for them, and so forth, but her voice was quivering the whole time. Mimi, you are going to break her heart."

Mimi bristled. "First of all, nothing has been decided as yet. Second, as Mama correctly said, it's something Benny and I have to work out between ourselves, with a minimum of outside interference."

"Then why did you decide to tell us?"

"I wanted to hear your opinions. I didn't want it to be a sudden shock if we should decide in the end to go. Let's even say that I felt the need for outside support. None of those is a reason to jump on me or on Benny."

"I didn't mean to jump on you, I was just worried about Mama. She sounds so miserable."

"I'm perfectly aware of that. I spoke to her for an hour this morning. Mama is one of the main reasons why we may stay here."

Mrs. Adler was waiting for her husband when he came home from work. She had calmed down somewhat in the course of the afternoon, and it was no longer obvious that she had been crying. She sat down across the coffee table from her husband. "I spent the whole morning talking to Mimi and Malka and Leah. I still don't understand what has gotten into Benny, because Mimi definitely doesn't want to go. What should we do, Papa?"

"I don't see that there is much for us to do, Mama," said Mr. Adler. "You know that I don't like interfering. They mean to talk to us some more before making up their minds. We can think about it so that we won't look quite so much like a pair of fish next time."

"Like fish, Papa?"

"Wide-open eyes and open mouths with nothing coming out."

Benny was having a pretty miserable week. Telling his parents had been easier than telling his parents-in-law, as he had expected; but in the case of his parents, the follow-up after the formal announcement was directed at him. His various siblings all phoned. His older brother, Tzvi, made a quip about how a green army uniform would match his eyes. Only Tzippy seemed to think it was a good idea.

His father met him after his *Daf Yomi shiur* the next day and gave him a long talking-to about the promises he had made in his wedding contract, and the importance of a dependable income for *shalom bayis*. The worst, though, was his mother. Definitely the worst.

She called him up at work in the morning and made an appointment to meet him for lunch in a small kosher restaurant near his office. Benny was already tense when he walked through the door and saw his mother seated at one of the small tables.

"Hello, Benny," she said as he joined her. "Would you like to order?"

He slid onto the vinyl-covered bench across from his mother. He extracted a menu wedged between the napkin holder and the ketchup, but nothing appealed to him. "I don't think I'm very hungry," said Benny glumly. He wasn't hungry at all. "Besides, I have the lunch Mimi packed for me back in the office. She won't like it if I bring it home uneaten."

"Well, I'm on a diet," said Mrs. Lerner, "but they won't think much of us taking up one of their tables if we don't order something." She glanced over the menu card. "I'll have the green salad and a Diet Coke," she volunteered.

"I guess I'll have a Coke and a hot fudge sundae."

"I thought you weren't hungry." said his mother.

"For a hot fudge sundae I can work up an appetite."

"I don't think they sell hot fudge sundaes in Israel. At least, not in the *frum* places."

"I know," admitted Benny. "Maybe Mimi could learn to make it."

"Well, that does bring us straight to our topic," said Mrs. Lerner.

Benny braced himself. "What is our topic, exactly?"

"Mimi."

"Oh."

The waiter sauntered over and Benny ordered for his mother and for himself.

"You know as well as I do," Mrs. Lerner continued, "that Mimi has been pretty sheltered. That year she spent in Israel was the big adventure of her life, and I understand that she was excruciatingly homesick."

"She was," agreed Benny. "But then she didn't have me and the children. Now her home is where we are."

"I understand the Adlers perfectly," Mrs. Lerner forged ahead in her lecture without pausing. "They both suffered so much, both during the war and afterwards. It is natural that they wanted to protect their children as much a possible. However, I think you have to realize that it makes her more vulnerable than someone who had a rough-and-tumble childhood."

"Like me, you mean."

"For example. Now Benny, you and Mimi have a beautiful marriage. It is a pleasure for your father and me to watch. And the children, of course, are dolls."

With that many concessive clauses, the "but" was going to be a doozy, Benny realized.

"But ..." His mother paused. "But it is just when things are going well that one is in danger of getting overconfident. Life seems to be just about perfect except for one thing, so you try to get that one thing too ..."

"And risk losing everything else," Benny finished for her.

"Precisely. Benny, moving to Eretz Yisrael is a lovely dream. Your father and I had some yearnings in that direction when you were all little, but for us there was never a time when it was really possible. I think you're right that if you ever want to go, the time is now while the children are still adaptable and you're not encumbered with a house. However, I just don't see Mimi in the pioneering role. The dream will turn into a nightmare if it ruins your marriage."

"I wasn't planning to tie Mimi up and drag her onto the plane. We won't go unless she wants to."

"Let's not be naive, Benny. You know about the concept of forcing a man until he says, 'I want to!' You exert psychological pressure just by moping."

"Mom, I'm twenty-six years old. Are you sure 'moping' is the word you wanted to use?"

"All right, by exhibiting symptoms of mild depression. I don't care what you call it, just as long as it is clear what I'm talking about."

It was clear, all right. As clear as an ice-cold mountain stream.

Walking back to his office, his shoulders slumped, Benny remembered how visionary, how noble, how altruistic he had felt when he first got the idea of moving to Israel. He had imagined that he would be strong for both of them, would soothe Mimi's fears and help her through the adjustment phase, until she, too, would agree that they had made the right choice. Now, within a few days, his parents and parents-in-law had reduced him to a pulp. How had they managed it?

Benny took a deep breath and tried to get a grip on himself. What had happened over this week was that he had lost his confidence that he could, indeed, be strong for both of them. At the moment, he didn't even feel that he could be strong enough just for himself.

Was his confidence really lost or just temporarily mislaid? He squared his shoulders and tried to focus on the positive side of the situation. He and Mimi had done very well at looking out for each other's welfare for more than four years now. What steps could he take to make sure that Mimi would be happy, genuinely happy, in Israel?

First of all, he would have to be sure that their life was not too rugged. If both members of the couple were enthusiasts, they would probably put up cheerfully with a lot of hardships, but not in a case like this where one was gung-ho and the other was hanging back. Second, there had to be some way for Mimi to keep in touch with her family —telephone calls, visits for special occasions like her brother's wedding. Third, he would probably have to spend more time than he now did helping with shopping and running to government offices. It all added up to one thing in his mind: He needed a good, solid job.

Benny walked a few more paces, remembering the conversation with his mother. "Sheltered," "vulnerable," "homesick," and finally, "I just don't see Mimi in a pioneering role." Once more he ran through the list of reasons for moving to Israel that he had given to Mimi. By the time he reached the building where he worked, he had come to a decision. He would not ask Mimi to move to Israel unless he had a good job ... and he was going to start looking for one.

Chapter 3

Between Light and Darkness

Jerusalem — City of Light

He was angry; he was steaming, boiling, roiling with fury. He had been out of work for seven months already. The bills had piled up and he was beginning to get letters from lawyers. The tax bill in his left pocket was already crumbled and creased. If he didn't arrange payment by tomorrow, they were going to sue him. The bill from the electric company only arrived yesterday. He was supposed to pay one thousand four hundred shekels within two weeks. Pay? Pay with what? Was Allah going to rain down golden dinars from the heavens?

He had one last hope. Maybe the hotel where he had worked a few years ago would take him back.

"...Who distinguishes between light and darkness, between Yisrael and the nations, between the Seventh Day and the six days of work. *Baruch Atah Hashem ... hamavdil bein kodesh lechol.*"

Ella watched Chaim Ozer set down the wine cup. Leah'le, who was struggling to hold the lighted candle high, winced as a drop of wax dripped onto her hand. Their guest, Elisha Sheinfeld, steadied the candle and handed Leah'le a napkin to wrap around her hand. Chaim Ozer took the *Havdalah* candle from their daughter and extinguished it in the wine that had spilled from his cup.

"*Gut voch!*" Chaim Ozer wished his family and his guest. "*Gut voch!*" they all answered. Ella hoped that it really would be a good week. With all the tension between Israel and the Palestinians, she worried a bit right after Shabbos. During the whole day they hadn't been able to hear the news, and who knew what might have happened?

"Thank you very much for having me," said Elisha. "I really appreciate it."

"We're glad that your cousins thought to give you our address. We hope you're having a successful year in yeshivah."

"Do you have *chavrusos* for all of the sessions?" asked Chaim Ozer.

Elisha nodded. "Americans, all of them. Some of my friends go out of their way to get set up with Israelis, so that they'll be forced to use Hebrew. I didn't try."

"Why not?" asked Chaim Ozer.

"Because I'm mostly here to learn, and I do that better when language isn't a problem. If I decide that I want to stay in Israel, then I will have to do something about improving my language skills."

"Are you thinking about it?"

"Am I thinking about it? Sure. How could I be here," Elisha made a sweeping gesture that took in the entire neighborhood, "and not think about it? Yerushalayim is very special, and the yeshivos are the very best, but..."

"There is always a 'but,' isn't there? What is yours?" asked Chaim Ozer with a smile, his eyes crinkling a bit.

"I've been thinking of going into *chinuch*, and that would be almost impossible if I stayed here. You know how intolerant children are of accents. If I want to go into teaching, I should go back to the States and marry a girl who is also interested in teaching. We would spend a few years out of town and either work our way back to New York or decide that we like it there."

"I've heard worse 'buts,'" said Chaim Ozer with a nod of approval.

Elisha looked pleased. "You never had any 'buts' about coming here, did you?"

"Not really. It was the natural thing to do."

Ella, always practical, turned to him and said, "Listen to that rain outside. You aren't going to walk all the way back from Mattersdorf to the Mir. We'll give you money for the bus."

"I have a better idea," said Chaim Ozer. "I'm learning with someone at the Mir tonight. We can take the bus together."

Elisha put on his coat and gave four-year-old Shloimi a ride around the room on his shoulders while he was waiting for Chaim Ozer to get his things together.

"I'm ready," said Chaim Ozer, pulling on his coat.

"Take these," said Ella, handing each of them a plastic cover for his hat, "and these umbrellas." The family's name and address were printed neatly in block letters on the tape Ella had stuck on the umbrellas when she brought them home from the store.

"If I am going by bus, I really don't need all that," protested Elisha.

"Nonsense—it's half a block from here to the bus stop, and another block or so at the other end. You could get soaking wet."

"All right," said Elisha, turning to his host. "I have to return to my apartment to get my *sefarim*. I'll also get my umbrella and then return this to you in the yeshivah."

As soon as they were out the door, Ella ran the water for the children's baths and started straightening up. She had once calculated that more than a hundred objects were moved out of place for Shabbos, and now she had to return each one to its place. It was a matter of pride with her not to leave over a mess until the next morning.

Motzaei Shabbos baths were a quick in-and-out affair. Soon, the children were in bed in their sleepers and Ella was sailing through the dishes. Windblown raindrops splattering against the windowpane reminded her that Chaim Ozer and Elisha were probably still out in this downpour. However darkly the newspapers might paint the political situation, she was still glad to be living in Yerushalayim, where her major worry in sending her husband and guest out into the night had been that they might get wet and catch cold.

The rain was pelting down. The street was deserted. No one wanted to be out in this weather. He was still holding the knife inside a plastic bag so that no one would see it. It had been a stroke of luck, snatching this knife without being noticed. He rubbed at the handle with the plastic of the bag, hoping to wipe off any fingerprints. Not that it should matter. He was planning to take the weapon with him, as proof that he was the one who had done this deed. They would have to help him. They would want to help him.

The man walking in front of him was struggling with his umbrella. The gusts of wind kept turning it inside out. Finally, the man gave up and furled it, turning up the collar of his black coat and jamming his hat on as tightly as possible. The way he was dressed, there was no doubt at all that the man was a Jew.

He grasped the hilt of the knife inside the bag and quickened his step to catch up with the man in front of him. When he was only one pace away, he pulled the knife out of the bag. Just as he was bringing it down with all his force, his victim turned to glance over his right shoulder. The blow connected and the man sprawled forward onto the dark, wet sidewalk.

Ella was drying her good silver and putting it away in the felt-lined chest in which it was stored during the week. The doorbell rang. She laid aside her dishtowel and went to answer it. Two large men in uniform were standing on the mat. "Mrs. Wahrhaftig?" one of them asked.

"Yes?" She hadn't the slightest idea what they could be doing here. The Wahrhaftigs didn't own a car, so it couldn't be some parking violation. Besides, for that the police would simply leave a ticket.

"May we come in?" The older of the two spoke for both of them. "We're from the Police Department."

Ella was getting uneasy. Not only did this problem, whatever it was, merit the attention of two policemen, but apparently it was going to take some time to settle. "Please do. Can I get you something to drink?"

"No, thank you. We are here on urgent business. Is your husband at home?"

"No, he went out a couple of hours ago. He should be home soon."

The two men gave each other significant looks. "Did he take an umbrella?"

"In this weather? Of course!" Ella's unease continued to grow.

Why were they questioning her about Chaim Ozer? She was sure his papers were all in order.

"Why don't we all sit down for a moment?" suggested the other policeman.

"Can you tell me what this is all about? I'm getting very worried," said Ella as she took one of the seats around the large dining table that dominated the living room

"Someone has been injured and we're trying to establish his identity."

Whoever it was must be injured badly if he could not answer these questions himself. Ella's eyes widened in fright. "And you think that it might be my husband?!"

"That is one possibility. Do you have a picture of him, Mrs. Wahrhaftig?"

A picture? Ella jumped to her feet. The albums were full of pictures of the children, but few of Chaim Ozer and herself. She stood paralyzed, fighting her panic, trying vainly to think which album might hold a picture of her husband. Then she remembered. She took a few strides to the mirror-lined cabinet where she kept their silver objects. Sliding open the glass door, she pulled out a portrait of herself and her husband as *chassan* and *kallah*.

Her hand was shaking so badly that the silver frame slipped out of her grasp and crashed to the floor. *Control, Ella, control, or terrible things will happen.* Control? she echoed. *What control? Everything is out of control!* Ignoring the shards of broken glass, which would have sent her scurrying for broom and dustpan on most occasions, she scooped up the picture in its frame and thrust it toward the policemen. They bent forward to examine it.

"Does he still have a beard like this?" asked one of them.

"It is fuller now." Ella sank back into her chair, waiting to hear if her whole life was about to shatter into fragments like that glass.

"Then the injured man is definitely not your husband."

Her personal relief was tempered by her concern for the man who lay there wounded. "Is he badly hurt?"

The policemen looked at each other again. "We didn't say this before because we didn't want to alarm you unnecessarily, but the doctors don't know if he will make it through the night."

Ella felt weak and dizzy. Something was bothering her, something she was missing. If it wasn't Chaim Ozer who was hurt, what had brought them to her? They surely weren't going from door-to-door throughout the *chareidi* community frightening all the housewives out of their wits. Nor did they show any signs of leaving. They were going to give her a moment to recover, and then they were going to ask her more questions. Why her?

"You found our umbrella! Oh, no! Oh, no!" She burst into tears.

"Try to be calm, Mrs. Wahrhaftig. We need your help. Yes, we found a black umbrella with your name and address a meter or two from the injured man. We weren't sure that there was any connection, but I gather now that there may be."

"Oh, oh, oh!" Ella, still sobbing into her hands, tried to take control of herself. She plucked a tissue from the package on the table, blew her nose, and wiped her eyes. "There were two umbrellas," she said in a low voice that was the best she could force out at the moment. "My husband took one, and I gave the other to our Shabbos guest, Elisha Sheinfeld." She stumbled over Elisha's name and started to sob again.

"The injured man carried no identification." It was a statement that was also a question.

"Of course not. He had walked over to our house on Shabbos. He had no umbrella either. Umbrellas are not for use on Shabbos. That's why I gave him ours." Ella helped herself to another tissue.

The older policeman looked at the younger. "That *dati* doctor said it was strange that he was carrying an umbrella if his pockets were empty. He didn't think that the umbrella was connected to the victim at all."

The younger policeman said, "We're still not sure, Grisha. Maybe her guest just happened to lose the umbrella near the scene of the crime."

"Crime?!" Ella seemed to be the target for one shock after another. "You mean he wasn't hit by a car?"

The older policeman made some motion intended to silence his companion, but the younger man didn't pick up on it. "No, he was attacked by an assailant."

The older man made a face as Ella burst into tears again. Then he said gently, "Mrs. Wahrhaftig, as Nachum here said, we still don't know if the injured man is your guest. Can you describe him and tell us what he was wearing?"

Ella choked back her tears and gave a wan smile, "Dark hair, glasses, black hat, black suit, white shirt, clean-shaven, and medium height. That could describe a thousand other yeshivah students in this city."

"The victim was wearing a tie."

"Green, blue, and gold paisley?" asked Ella, watching his face closely.

The policeman nodded sadly, "I'm afraid so."

After another predictable burst of tears had subsided, he asked, "I gather that he is single. Is he Israeli, American, or from somewhere else?"

"American."

"Do you have his parents' phone number?"

Ella looked at the clock. It was nine-thirty already. "I can get it for you in three hours." She would call Benny Lerner and ask him for his aunt's phone number.

The policeman looked disappointed in her. "Mrs. Wahrhaftig, I don't have to tell you that this is an emergency. If there is any chance that his parents can get here before..." He broke off. "We want them here as soon as possible."

"No, it is just that it is still Shabbos over there, and my friends won't answer the phone. Neither will his parents." Then she had an idea. "I'll give you the name and number of his Rosh Yeshivah. He will know how and when to contact Elisha's parents!"

After the policemen left, Ella sank down again in her chair, sobbing for a bright young life shattered to bits. The shards of glass glinted at her feet.

Nachum was pacing restlessly in the waiting room at Hadassah Hospital on Har Hatzofim. The chairs were all empty, except for one in the corner, where a *chareidi* man was swaying back and forth as he read from a small book. It occurred to Nachum to wonder what he was doing here. There were no scheduled operations at this hour.

He looked vaguely familiar, though Nachum could not say from where he knew him. He didn't have *chareidi* acquaintances. Maybe it was just that, as Mrs. Wahrhaftig had pointed out, there wasn't much to distinguish one *chareidi* man from another.

Remembering that conversation finally helped him make the identification. He walked over to the man. "Are you Rabbi

Wahrhaftig?"

"Yes, my name is Wahrhaftig. How did you know?"

"Your wife showed us your picture when we were trying to identify the man who was stabbed. If they were to let you into the recovery room after the operation, would you be able to identify your friend?"

"His face is undamaged?"

"Except for some bruises and scrapes where he fell."

"Then if it is indeed Elisha Sheinfeld in there, I should be able to identify him. You're waiting here for the identification?"

"No, I am waiting for the knife. If it remains in the wound, it is only removed on the operating table."

"Tell me, how badly is he hurt?"

"One lung is injured, he has probably lost a kidney, and there is injury to the spinal cord."

Elisha's friend shuddered. "And the doctors say...?"

"He lost a lot of blood before anyone found him. He's much too weak for the major surgery they have to perform. They don't know what will be."

"I'm going back to saying *Tehillim*. If anyone needs me, for the identification or for anything else, I expect to be here." Rabbi Wahrhaftig retired to his corner and bent over his book with redoubled fervor.

The swinging door to the anteroom opened and a nurse motioned to Nachum that he should come forward. He pulled out a large plastic evidence bag, but did not yet break the seal. "Have you got it out?" he asked.

She nodded. He opened the zip-lock seal. The door to the operating theater opened and out came a gowned nurse, a mask over her nose and mouth, holding the knife by the tip between a gloved thumb and forefinger. Nachum spread open the mouth of the bag, and she lowered the knife in gently so that the blunt side of the blade lay along the bottom of the bag, just as he had requested. He squeezed out the excess air and resealed the bag. "Thank you, that was perfect. And the hilt?"

"We grasped it only with instruments. Excuse me, I have to get back in there."

Nachum turned to the other nurse, the one who had called him. He jerked his thumb over his shoulder to the outside. "There is a guy out there saying *Tehillim* who will be able to identify the victim, if he makes it through."

"One way or another, we'll need an identification." She pushed open the door to see whom he was talking about.

Nachum passed her and crossed the waiting room with quick steps. The *chareidi* in the corner, seeing what he carried, gave another shudder.

Nachum drove his patrol car through the dark Yerushalayim streets toward the Russian compound. Someone had roused one of the forensic evidence experts out of bed, and he was supposed to be waiting there to see what he could get from the knife.

Two hours later, Nachum was still pacing up and down, waiting once again. By now the fellow who did this could be in Amman, if he had equipped himself with a passport and money before he set off to attack a Jew.

The door opened and Micha, the forensic expert, came out. "I sent all the photographs off to the databank by e-mail and put the knife in the safe. There were two clear prints, right thumb and forefinger, on the blade near the hilt. There were a few more smudged prints on the haft, but the surface was so rough that I doubt we can make any positive identification from them. The clothing fibers on the blade were probably from the victim; they usually are. Bring me samples from his coat, pants and shirt tomorrow and I'll check."

"I have them right here," said Nachum, pulling out a smaller evidence bag containing a few swatches of cloth. "Sorry about the omission. I was so focused on the fingerprints that I forgot to hand them over."

Micha looked them over with a practiced eye. "Hmm, maybe not all of the fibers are from the victim. I'll put these in the safe and tell you tomorrow."

Nachum said, "We are trying to keep this criminal, who might turn out to be a murderer, from crossing the border. It would help if we knew what color coat he was wearing."

The other man sighed and turned back toward his microscopes. "I don't necessarily do my best work at two in the morning."

"Neither do I," said Nachum, "but we can't always choose our times."

Micha came out again in fifteen minutes. "All right. Some of the fibers are of brown wool and don't match anything from the victim. However, the attacker will probably change his coat. If there are fibers on the blade, that should mean that there are bloodstains on the cuff of the jacket."

"Thanks, Micha, good work. I'll let you go now."

As Nachum walked out toward his cruiser, he lifted his cell phone and dialed his partner, Grisha, who was at headquarters coordinating the search for the attacker. "All right, the fingerprints have been sent to the data bank for identification, and Micha also identified some brown wool fibers, which seem to have come from the assailant's coat."

"I'm ahead of you," said Grisha. "There is an identification for the fingerprints already, and I expect an address any moment. You and I will go together to make the arrest, and two others will come to stay behind and search the house. It's very peculiar. The fellow is a Jew, with no police record at all."

"So maybe the background of the crime is not political after all?" suggested Nachum.

"The victim is a little strange for that. An American yeshivah boy who has only been in the country for five months? How far onto the blacklist of organized crime could he have gotten?"

"Maybe he was smuggling illegal substances and didn't hand them all over?"

"Right, and Mrs. Wahrhaftig is the go-between. Put a lid on your imagination and let's wait for a few more facts," said Grisha with scorn.

Twenty minutes later, they were ringing the doorbell of a third-floor apartment in a Jewish neighborhood.

The two policemen got no answer to their first ring at the suspect's door. Nachum pressed the bell again, and this time he leaned on it. Two other policemen were waiting downstairs, to make sure the man they had come to arrest didn't try to escape through a window or out onto the roof. Putting their ears to the door, they heard a slight shuffling sound inside.

"Whoizzit?" came a bleary voice from the other side of the door.

"Police. Open up."

That seemed to have shocked the fellow awake, for he asked, much more comprehensibly, "What do you want?" He looked through the peephole, and what he saw seemed to satisfy him, for he unlatched the door and opened it. He was barefoot and dressed in pajamas, his hair tousled. "Do you know what time it is?"

"Three in the morning. May we come in?"

"Sure, why not? I love having guests at this hour. Make yourselves comfortable." He gestured toward the couch.

"We will stay here for the moment. Is your name Yitzchak Schwartz?"

"Yeah, Itzik Schwartz, that's me."

"Identity card number?"

"021283554."

Nachum and Grisha glanced at each other. If this guy was doing an imitation of an innocent citizen hauled out of bed in the middle of the night, he was doing an excellent job.

"You guys may enjoy standing, but I only got home from work two hours ago and I'm ready to drop," complained Itzik.

"What kind of work do you do?" asked Grisha.

"I'm a cook."

"Where?"

"The Palace Hotel."

The scene of the crime was nowhere near the Palace Hotel, but it was on a straight line between the hotel and the Damascus Gate. Nachum and Grisha exchanged glances again. If he really was a cook, and that would be easy enough to check, his fingerprints were probably on a lot of knives in the kitchen of that hotel. "Listen, Itzik," said Grisha, "we need you to sit down and make a list of all the people who were in the kitchen this evening, full names and phone numbers wherever possible. Take your time over it, but try to get everybody."

"May I use my address book?"

"Sure."

Itzik first wrote down a long list of first names. Then he began filling in details. Part way through he paused. "There are a lot of people here whose last names I don't know. Do you want only employees or outsiders too?"

"Everyone who was in the kitchen. Outsiders particularly. There was an outsider in the kitchen?"

"Ahmad. He worked for us a few years back, and came in this evening looking for his job back. When we didn't agree, he cursed us all roundly and stalked off."

"When was this?"

"Early in the evening. Seven or eight."

Nachum and Grisha exchanged glances for the third time. Nachum walked over and looked over Itzik's shoulder. Several of the names had phone numbers beside them already. Grisha said, "Itzik, we would like you to get dressed and come down to headquarters with us. Take your address book and you can finish the list there."

"Listen, if you want me to go, I have to wake my wife and tell her something. Can't you give me a clue?"

"We are investigating a crime, and there seems to be a link to your hotel kitchen. We have to find out exactly what happened there all evening." That would probably give Itzik a solid alibi. They were sure by now that he was not the person who did the stabbing, but for the books they would need an excuse to release him.

As they filed down the stairs, with Grisha in the lead and Nachum following Itzik, Grisha asked, "Any idea what this Ahmad said when he cursed you all so roundly?"

"I don't speak any Arabic myself, but Biton was born in Morocco, and he gave me the gist. Ahmad started with us, went on to all lawyers, added in the electric company and City Hall, and finished with all Jews, individually and as a group."

Nachum nodded. It sounded as if they had their suspect. Now they had to catch him.

By pumping Itzik on the way to the station, they managed to get the full name of the fellow in charge of payroll at the Palace Hotel. Telephone information provided an address for him, somewhere in Rechavia. They split up; Grisha took the cruiser and one of the men to try to get Ahmad's name and address, while Nachum rode in the lock-up wagon with Itzik and a driver. They all three squashed into the high front seat.

"Where's the fellow you went for?" asked Eli, the night-duty clerk, when Nachum walked in with Itzik.

"Here," answered Nachum, jerking his thumb at Itzik.

"Then why isn't he in handcuffs?" wondered Eli.

Itzik stopped in place. "Handcuffs? Handcuffs! Why should I be in handcuffs?"

"Didn't he arrest you?" This time Eli addressed his question to Itzik.

"What's going on here?" shouted Itzik, his face turning red. "I want my rights! I want to speak to a lawyer!"

"Thanks, Eli," said Nachum with a glare. "Calm down, Itzik. We didn't arrest you because we don't think you committed any crime."

"Give me back my list. You aren't getting another bit of information out of me without the consent of my lawyer." Itzik folded his arms and gazed defiantly at Nachum.

"All right, call your lawyer. I was trying to save you the money you would have to spend on his fee. Just get him down here quickly, because we have to catch the guy who really did this thing." He pushed the phone on Eli's desk toward Itzik.

"Actually, I don't have a lawyer," admitted Itzik.

"Okay, Eli, I guess you had better charge him after all. Then I can get him a public defender."

"Wait a moment," said Itzik. "I don't want to be charged with some crime I didn't commit. If you really aren't planning to arrest me, maybe I will cooperate. Why do you need this list I was making?"

"To give you an alibi and find out who the suspects are," said Nachum.

"Can you tell me what the crime is?"

"Sure," said Eli. "Attempted murder."

Itzik's eyes opened wide. "Murder?"

"If the victim survives, it will only be 'attempted,'" corrected Nachum.

"So what does that have to do with my kitchen? I'm sure no one was murdered there on my shift."

"The murder weapon came from your kitchen and had your fingerprints on it," Nachum explained.

Itzik no longer looked angry. He looked very, very frightened.

Chapter 4

Identifications

Chaim Ozer looked up from his *Tehillim* as someone arrived from the outside. An American boy named Moshe, who was one of Elisha's *chavrusos*, had brought food and, more important, a *tallis* and *tefillin* for the morning *tefillos*.

"Elisha's parents have been told," Moshe announced, "and they got reservations on the midnight flight. Before they actually get on the plane, they would like to be sure it really is Elisha in there."

"You checked his apartment?"

"Long since. He never came back, never took his own umbrella or his wallet. It is pretty clear to everyone that it is Elisha in there, but it would be better to have a positive identification."

Chaim Ozer shrugged. "I can't rush them. They've been operating for six hours, and they won't let me see him until they are done."

The swinging doors opened and a green-coated surgeon came out. Chaim Ozer and Moshe hurried over. "He survived the operation, and we are optimistic that he will pull through the recovery period."

"Is there any permanent damage?" Chaim Ozer asked.

"If you are not a member of the immediate family, I cannot discuss the details. You will be called in to make the identification." The doctor vanished again.

A nurse summoned him shortly thereafter. He put the *Tehillim* in his pocket and followed her. Once they were inside the anteroom, she pointed down a corridor to some shelves. "Take a gown, a cap, and booties to go over your shoes. After you are dressed, go into the recovery room to see if you can identify the patient."

"Is he awake?"

"No, they are not trying to wake him up yet. When they get to that, they will call you in again. Familiar voices help."

Chaim Ozer donned the green gown and pulled the covers over his shoes. He fastened the gown over his beard. The worst part of the outfit was the green cap, which looked exactly like a woman's shower cap.

Only one bed in the recovery room was occupied. A nurse was standing nearby, watching the blips on various monitoring machines. The patient was lying on his chest, with his head turned away from the nurse. Chaim Ozer approached from that side. Even from halfway across the room, he could see that it was his friend Elisha, but somehow changed. Where the skin was not reddened by abrasions, it was quite pale. There was no movement at all, and, were it not for the blips, he would have wondered if Elisha were really alive.

He paused for a moment by the bed, looking down at his friend and *davening* for his recovery. Then he headed out to relay the message to Elisha's parents. The nurse told him to throw his used gown, cap, and boots into a laundry bin. He would take fresh ones the next time he was called.

Moshe telephoned the Rosh Yeshivah, who hung up quickly in order to relay the news to Elisha's parents. Then Chaim Ozer reached for the receiver on the public phone. He hesitated. Should he call Ella or not? It was now four-thirty in the morning. If she were asleep, it would be a shame to wake her; but if she were sitting by the phone, it would be a shame to leave her in suspense. He decided to call and let the phone ring twice. If she were awake, she could use the callback option.

The phone was answered after the first ring. "Chaim, is that you?"

"Yes, I'm here at the hospital. Elisha survived the operation. His parents are coming on the first possible plane."

Ella heaved a sigh of relief, then asked, "Is he badly hurt?"

"From what the policeman said, yes. But the doctors won't tell me much. Ella, have you been waiting all this time?"

"I've been sitting on the couch, dozing, with the telephone beside me. You don't know how rattled I was by those two policemen! I couldn't go to bed as if nothing had happened. I wouldn't have fallen asleep."

"I think you should get some sleep. You have to deal with the children, and with your pupils, tomorrow."

"Are you going to sleep at all?"

"Maybe later in the day. I want to be here when his parents arrive, since I'm the one who saw him last."

"All right, Chaim'ke." She yawned audibly. "I suppose you're right. If you're awake at seven-thirty, call in."

"*Be'ezras Hashem.*"

At five in the morning, the nurse called on Chaim Ozer to help waken Elisha. He again donned the hospital getup. The nurse called him off to the side and briefed him. "The patient is disoriented, traumatized, in pain. He may think this is all a dream, since he had no conscious preparation. We have to get him to reconnect with a very frightening reality, and he may prefer to remain in a haze. At first, we'll just call him by name and tell him to wake up. I understand that you were with him almost until the attack?"

"Yes, I was." Chaim Ozer thought sadly of saying *Havdalah*. For Elisha, it had marked a division between a normal, ordinary life and another, which began in danger and pain.

"So, if we see any signs that he hears us," continued the nurse, "try talking about what should have been his last pleasant memories."

"Tell me, can he move his legs?"

The nurse bit her lip. "No."

"Will he notice that?"

"Perhaps not immediately. Don't call his attention to it in any way." She led the way back to the monitoring station, where the machines continued to produce blips, punctuated by an occasional beep or buzz.

They positioned themselves on the two sides of the bed. The

nurse began. "Elisha! Elisha Sheinfeld! Wake up."

"Elisha? This is Chaim Ozer. I am standing beside you. Wake up, Elisha!"

For five minutes there was no response. Then, although his eyes remained tightly shut, he moved his head as if to listen. The nurse gave Chaim Ozer the "okay" signal, and he bent his head closer to his friend's. "Elisha, remember, you came to our house for *shalosh seudos*. Afterwards we all made *Havdalah*. A drop of wax burned Leah'le on the finger, and you gave her a napkin to hold the candle with. You gave Shloimi a ride on your shoulders while I got my coat on."

It seemed to Chaim Ozer that the corners of Elisha's mouth were turning up in a slight smile. "We went out in the rain. The wind turned your umbrella inside out, so you laughed and folded it up."

Elisha's eyes opened wide and his face contorted in fear. It seemed for a moment that he was going to scream, and then he lost consciousness again. Chaim Ozer and the nurse looked at each other in consternation. She beckoned him to the side. "I think something you said reminded him of the attack. Apparently he was aware of it. Go get your other friend, and we'll try something more neutral."

As Chaim Ozer left the room feeling like a failure, he heard her saying, "Elisha! Wake up! You're in the hospital. You have been in an accident. Your parents are coming to see you. You want to be awake to see your mother and father."

Chaim Ozer sent Moshe into the recovery room and slumped down in a chair, looking at his watch. It would be another half hour before it would be time to start *davening vasikin*. The door to the outer corridor opened, and Nachum came in, almost running. "Is he awake?"

"Elisha? Just barely," answered Chaim Ozer, sitting up straighter.

"Did he say anything about the attack? Did he see the man who did it?" asked Nachum eagerly.

Chaim Ozer sprang to his feet. "You can't try to talk to him about it yet. He isn't ready!"

"What do you mean, isn't ready? Someone made you an expert on psychology?" asked Nachum with scorn.

"He relived the attack before my eyes and lost consciousness because of it! I tell you, he isn't ready to describe all the details."

"Listen, Wahrhaftig, we have a criminal to catch, and we want to do it before he hurts someone else. We think we know who did it, and if we can get the address, we are planning to make the arrest soon, but all we have is circumstantial evidence. An identification by Sheinfeld would clinch the matter!"

The two men faced off, glaring at each other.

A green-coated doctor pushed through the doors leading to the recovery room. Chaim Ozer and Nachum, who had been glowering at each other silently until then, spun around and began speaking at once.

"It is very urgent..."

"It would be dangerous..."

"Whoa," said the doctor, holding up his hands, "One at a time. You first," he pointed to Nachum.

"We think we know who stabbed your patient. I want to bring in a police artist to make a composite picture of the man so that we can get him locked up. The evidence we have without that is very flimsy."

"Now you." He pointed to Chaim Ozer.

"Elisha is in very delicate condition. Just remembering the attack made him faint. He simply isn't strong enough for what they want to put him through."

"All right, I heard you both. Now I will go back and talk it over with the nurse." He pushed a button beside the door, answered the query from the intercom, and pushed open the door when it buzzed. Chaim Ozer and Nachum waited for his return with scant patience.

When he returned, he looked at Nachum and said, pointing to Chaim Ozer, "He is right, it is still too early. Leave a number where you can be reached. Once the patient's condition has stabilized, the nurse will ask him if he can deal with your artist. Remember, he was attacked from the rear. He may not have seen the fellow at all."

"Actually, I think he may have," admitted Chaim Ozer. "He looked terribly frightened."

"The blow was probably meant for his heart. The fact that it went in low, between the sixth and seventh ribs, instead of between the fourth and fifth, indicates that Elisha just may have seen his attacker. If Elisha turned suddenly, just as his assailant was attacking, that might be what caused the assailant to miss his target," Nachum suggested.

The doctor turned to Nachum. "We will get in touch with you when we think he can cooperate."

Nachum gave Chaim Ozer one last disgruntled glare, as if the whole thing were his fault, and stalked out.

As the doctor was about to leave, Chaim Ozer touched him on the arm. "Is he paralyzed?"

The doctor looked uncomfortable. "That is the sort of information I can only give to the patient's family."

"You don't have to tell me. I figured it out myself from the way that policeman described the wounds. Who is going to tell Elisha? I hope you aren't going to ask his parents to do it, because I think that they will be too upset themselves to do a good job."

The doctor looked Chaim Ozer up and down appraisingly. "Since you say that you already know, maybe we will press you into service. Perhaps you can say it in a way that will be consoling to a yeshivah student."

The arrest was to be made by Dani, one of the officers of the East Yerushalayim police station; Grisha had come along to collect evidence. They didn't actually have a search warrant, but he hoped that Ahmad's family wouldn't be sophisticated enough to ask for one. What he needed was to find that brown jacket with the bloodstain on the sleeve. If the blood was Elisha's and if the jacket was found in Ahmad's house, that would be pretty conclusive.

They had sent one man up to the roof and covered all the windows from below. Dani motioned for Mustafa, one of the Druse policemen, to stand near the door to translate if necessary. It was six in the morning, and dawn had not yet broken.

Dani rapped smartly on the door. When a minute went by without a response, he knocked a second time. This time, a woman's voice from the other side of the door timidly asked some questions. Dani didn't bother to get a translation. "Police! *Shurta!* Open up! *Iftachi!*"

There was a sound of motion on the other side of the door, but no further words. Dani rapped a third time. "If you don't open this door, we will have to break the lock," he warned, and called

Mustafa to translate that threat into Arabic.

There was another sound of motion, and then a man's voice in heavily accented Hebrew asked gruffly, "What do you want?"

"We want to get in," answered Dani. He rattled the doorknob for emphasis.

"Why?"

"Are you going to open the door or are we going to break it down?" asked Dani. He held on to the knob and put his knee up against the door, gauging its strength.

The bolt was drawn, and Dani managed to drop his knee in time to be standing in a dignified position when the door was slowly opened. The man in the doorway was tall and heavy-set. His eyes flickered from one policeman to the next and down to the reinforcements, waiting half a flight below. If he had had any thoughts of trying to make an escape, he seemed to abandon them, for he stepped back and allowed them to enter.

"Ahmad Zawidat?" asked Dani.

The man nodded a slow assent.

Grisha edged away from the group at the door and glanced quickly around the room. Where would the coat be hidden? The children's room seemed the most likely possibility. The door was ajar. Grisha pushed it open and slipped inside. The room contained two pairs of beds, with five children sleeping in them. During the day, the outer bed of each pair slid under the inner bed to create some floor space, but now there was barely room for Grisha to pass between the beds.

He did not want to awaken the children. Who knows what treatment they would expect from an Israeli policeman? Day after day the East Yerushalayim newspaper always managed to find a picture of an armed Israeli soldier to place prominently on the front page.

Grisha dropped to the floor as quietly as possible and peered under the beds. He could see nothing but the wooden boxes on wheels that were meant to hold bedding. Since the children had probably been asleep when Ahmad got back, it would not have been easy for him to hide anything there.

The first light of dawn glimmered in one of the windows. Grisha proceeded to the wardrobe. The most likely hiding place was behind some innocuous-looking stack of sheets or towels. The stand-alone closet was made of wood and looked rather beaten up. The doors probably creaked. He would open both doors quickly and step between them. Then if any of the kids looked up, they would see just the closet door. He grasped the two handles, pulled the doors open simultaneously, and froze in surprise. Two hostile eyes stared straight at him!

The man in the closet snaked his hand into his pocket, and Grisha lunged into action. He grabbed the man's wrist and pulled his empty hand out of the pocket while shouting, "Mustafa, Mustafa! Come help me! There's another man in here." Two of the children sat up in bed and began to wail.

Grisha, still holding tightly to the man's arm, started hauling him out of the closet as Mustafa, the Druse policeman, entered the children's room. Mustafa grabbed the man's other arm and together they brought him, struggling furiously, out into the light of the living room.

They clapped handcuffs on him, and Mustafa held him while Grisha slipped on a latex glove and put his hand in the man's pocket to see if he had been reaching for a gun or a knife. He found neither one; instead, his fingers closed around a slim, vinyl-covered book. Pulling it out, he discovered that it was an address book. If the fellow was really connected with a terrorist organization, this address book might be a real find! He opened a small plastic evidence bag, zip-locked it shut, and put it in his pocket. Of course, he was supposed to give the fellow a receipt for anything he confiscated, but he didn't have time right now. Perhaps he would get around to it when he got back to headquarters.

Ahmad's wife had been standing at the bedroom door, wringing her hands silently. Now she burst forth with a hot stream of expostulation aimed at her husband. The only word of it that Grisha understood was "Hamas," but that was enough to make him take interest. He hoped that Mustafa was paying attention to what she was saying.

Ahmad spit out two words that must have meant, "Quiet, woman!" for his wife broke off in the middle of her tirade. Four of the five children had awakened, and stood in a cluster at the door of their room.

"We're going to take you down to headquarters," said Dani, the policeman in charge of making the arrest, to his two prisoners.

"Let's go." He motioned toward the door.

The oldest boy ran forward shouting, *"Abu! Abu!"* He flung his arms around his father's waist. The other children followed. Seeing that the entrance to the children's room was clear reminded Grisha that he still hadn't searched the closet for that coat. He flicked on the light and began searching shelf by shelf. There weren't many piles high enough to hide a man's jacket, and he soon convinced himself that it was not there. The fifth child slept through the search.

Mrs. Zawidat had moved into the living room to disengage the children from their father. Grisha took the opportunity to search her bedroom and wardrobe as well, but did not find the brown coat.

He returned to the living room, where the hullabaloo was beginning to die down, and said to Dani, "Can you hold them here for a few more minutes? I still haven't found the coat." He was covertly watching Ahmad's face, which registered shock. He had been hoping that Ahmad would glance toward the coat's hiding place, but instead the suspect kept his eyes fixed on the door. Perhaps the coat was outside? Grisha quickly checked behind and under the well-worn couch. He pulled open the doors of the cabinets in the kitchen, but found nothing.

"All right, you can take them away. I'm ready to go," Grisha informed Dani. He took the other arm of Ahmad's midnight visitor and started walking him out to the police car. Despite the early hour, the streets were not empty. A number of people were hurrying to work. They gazed with undisguised resentment at the policemen leading their handcuffed prisoners to the lock-up wagon.

Grisha pulled a couple of plastic bags out of the locker in the back of the police wagon. "Dani, can you leave one of your men to help me? I want to look through the garbage cans for that coat."

Dani glanced at the crowd of Arabs watching them sullenly. "Are you sure one is enough?"

They agreed on two extra policemen, one to help Grisha search and one to stand guard. Dani left one car behind. As the other policemen drove away, the crowd began to disperse. Grisha stood watching the cars go, waiting until most of the bystanders had lost interest. Then he began the unpleasant task of transferring the garbage from the trash cans to the plastic bags.

At the bottom of the third can was a thick layer of newspaper, which Grisha pried up. Underneath was a brown wool jacket. Grisha raised it aloft in triumph.

Now that Grisha had found the coat, he called in Micha, the forensic evidence expert, to check if the fibers of the coat matched the fibers that had been found on the knife. There was indeed some sort of stain on the sleeve, so Nachum went back to the hospital for a sample of Elisha's blood. As long as he was going anyway, he took along the police artist.

Grisha paced back and forth in the anteroom to Micha's laboratory. If it turned out that he had sorted through all that garbage and the coat was not the right one, he was going to be very disappointed.

Micha came out and gave him a nod. "The fibers match. How much evidence do you have linking the suspect to the coat?"

"It was found in the garbage can next to his apartment building."

"That's pretty good, but not quite good enough. I think you should take me back there, and I will try to find some matching fibers in the apartment itself."

"If so, I had better take Mustafa or someone to translate. After what happened this morning, I don't think that Mrs. Zawidat is going to be very pleased to see us."

The streets of East Yerushalayim were full of children on their way to school, some in uniforms and some not. The men returned to the same apartment building and knocked on the door. Once again the door was answered, but not opened.

"*Shurta, iftachi,*" Mustafa called through the door. The answer was a flood of Arabic.

Mustafa persisted and the door was unlocked. After the upsetting night, Mrs. Zawidat had apparently decided not to try to send her children to school. Three were asleep again, and two were having breakfast in the kitchen in their pajamas.

Micha went straight to the couch and began plucking up fibers with tweezers. He ran his hand over the backs of the wooden chairs and collected a few tufts that had snagged on splinters. Then he began sweeping up dust from the floor. Mrs. Zawidat seemed to take this activity as confirmation that Israelis were crazy.

Grisha wondered just how much Ahmad had told her. Did she have any idea why he had been arrested? An announcement about the stabbing had been on the seven o'clock news, but the radio was not on and he doubted that she had listened.

Grisha pulled the Druse off to one side. "Mustafa, does she know what this is all about?"

"From what she said last night, I think she has a pretty good idea."

"Tell her that the boy who was attacked is still alive."

Mustafa went over to Mrs. Zawidat. There was a short exchange; then she looked up and raised her hands on high.

When Mustafa returned, Grisha asked him what she had said.

"'Allah be praised!' She was relieved that her husband would not be tried as a murderer."

After *davening Shacharis*, Chaim Ozer "suited up" for the third time and went into the recovery room. His friend was, as before, lying on his stomach. His head was turned to the side, and he was staring off into the distance. Chaim Ozer brought over a chair and sat down within Elisha's range of vision.

"How are you feeling?"

He closed his eyes. "*Baruch Hashem*, you shouldn't know from it. Besides all the pain, they've got me strapped down on my stomach, which is still upset from the anesthetic."

There were, of course, no straps. "Shall I leave or call a nurse?"

"No, stay. I want to talk." He opened his eyes again.

"There is a detective from the police department haunting this place, just waiting for you to say that. He wants to know if you saw the attacker."

"Yes."

"He wants to bring a police artist."

"Maybe later. It's still hard for me to focus. Will you tell me what happened? The nurse keeps dodging my questions."

"Yes, I'll tell you. First of all, you were stabbed three times and left for dead. You nearly did die. When you get out of here, you're not just going to *bentch gomel,* you're going to have to give a *seudas hodaah.*"

Elisha nodded in agreement.

"Do you know that it's morning? You can't *bentch gomel* yet, but you could say *Modeh ani* ..." Chaim Ozer donated his own yarmulke. Elisha's was probably in a mud puddle somewhere in Beit Yisrael. Then he helped him wash his hands. Elisha recited *Birkas HaTorah* in a very weak voice.

"I think that's enough for now. We can talk more later."

"No, Chaim Ozer, please. Please tell me what happened! Who found me?"

"Two yeshivah boys. The one who had been through a cardiopulmonary resuscitation course stayed with you, and the second boy ran for a phone. He called Magen David Adom, who alerted Hatzolah and the police. Hatzolah got there first. The guy who stayed with you said that you were lucky that your heart was still beating and that you were breathing, because in his course they had not taught them what to do if they couldn't turn the victim over on his back."

"Why couldn't he?"

"Beside the fact that you were bleeding from two wounds, the knife was still in the third." Chaim Ozer forged on. "Did you ever study *Chovos Halevavos?* The section where he asks you to imagine that you had almost died and a doctor saved you? Or that you had been blind, and an expert restored your sight? How grateful we should all be every day that we are alive, that we can think, that we can see."

"Learned it last year."

"Hold on to that idea, because some of the damage from your wounds is permanent. Are you ready to hear the details?"

"Haven't I been begging you to tell me? You think I can't tell that I was injured badly?"

"All right, the doctors think that the first blow was aimed at your heart but went low."

"The street was deserted, and I heard these quick footsteps behind me," said Elisha. His eyes were wide open and he was staring into space. "It made me a little nervous, so I turned to see who was coming. That probably threw his aim off." He closed his eyes and winced. "He struck me just as I saw him, and I don't remember any more than that."

"The second blow cut through your left kidney. The doctors said that there was no hope of saving it. You will have to get through life with only one kidney."

Elisha gave a slow nod of acceptance.

Chaim Ozer drew in a breath. Now for the hard part. "The third blow wedged between two vertebrae in your lower back."

Elisha stiffened, at least, as much of him as could still move. "And the spinal cord?"

"Almost completely severed."

Elisha assumed an expression of intense concentration. He held it for more than a minute, and then collapsed with a look of defeat. Tears welled up in his eyes. He had tried to move his feet and found that he couldn't.

What can I say to him? Should I say nothing, and wait for a cue from him? Chaim Ozer jumped up, went to the nurse's station, and brought back a box of tissues. He pulled out a few and handed them to Elisha, who wiped his eyes. He turned to Chaim Ozer with a look of despair and pleading intermingled.

He wants me to help him. What can I say that won't make him feel worse? "Elisha, as you were lying there on the sidewalk in mortal danger, the Accuser was giving every argument he could for ending your life right then and right there. He failed. The rest of us may wonder occasionally if we are just being carried along on the books in the hope that we will shape up eventually, but you can be absolutely certain that your *tafkid* is not ended, and that there are important things for you still to do."

"Without legs?"

"Yes, without the use of your legs, but with the use of your head and your heart and your hands."

Elisha stared off into space again. The expression of sadness on his face was heartbreaking. Finally he spoke. "Will you do something for me?"

"Of course. Just tell me what I can do."

"Will you learn with me something that will help? Once a week until my parents take me home. *Chovos Halevavos* or something else."

"Maybe *Sefer Iyov* with the Ramban's commentary?"

"Maybe. We can decide later. I want to say *Birkas HaShachar* now. Do I say, '... Who prepares a man's steps'?"

"Of course. It also refers to *hashgachah pratis*. Besides, even the blind say, '... Who opens the eyes of the blind.'"

Elisha began to *daven* with his eyes closed, reciting each word carefully, "Blessed are you, Hashem, King of the Universe, Who gives the cock intelligence to distinguish between day and night."

Chaim Ozer said, *"Amein."*

When Elisha reached, "…Who opens the eyes of the blind," he opened his eyes again.

At the phrase, "…Who releases the bound," he sighed, and again at, "… Who straightens the bent."

As he said, "… Who fulfills all my needs," he gave a tremulous smile.

After "… Who prepares a man's steps," he paused.

When he completed, "… Who gives rest to the weary," Elisha closed his eyes again, but his lips continued to move silently, until he reached, "Blessed are you, Hashem, Who grants loving kindness to Your people Israel."

"Amein!"

Chapter 5

Bite-Sized Advice

It was Sunday afternoon before Benny realized that the attack on Elisha would have consequences for him as well. Until then, all his attention had been focused on his cousin and Aunt Toby.

Benny had volunteered to drive his aunt and uncle to the airport. Of course, their own offspring came from all over the New York area to see them off, but the children all had cars filled with grandchildren, or were coming from another direction. The flight, which was due to leave around midnight, boarded at eleven, but until then there was a party of twenty-five milling around saying goodbye to the elder Sheinfelds. Aunt Toby's oldest daughter, Minna, was holding on to her arm. The women had red, puffy eyes. Some were still sobbing softly. There were always a few bent over, saying *Tehillim*. Elisha was the youngest of his aunt's seven children, the only one not yet married. Aunt Toby looked calmer than many of her daughters. Benny thought that it was probably because she was taking action. The others could only wait for news.

Benny pointed out to the family members that it would be hard for the Wahrhaftig family to function if they were being bombarded constantly by phone calls from abroad. Since he was the one who knew the Wahrhaftigs personally, he volunteered to call them regularly and pass on the news to his mother and to Minna.

He got home at one in the morning and fell into bed, exhausted. After *davening* in the morning, he called the Wahrhaftigs. Chaim Ozer answered.

"I'm glad to get you," said Benny. "How is Elisha?"

"Tired, weak, and wounded."

"Does he know that he will never walk again?"

"Yes. I was asked to tell him."

"How did he take it?" asked Benny heavily.

"He did his best to take it well."

Benny kept his regular Sunday morning learning schedule. After lunch, he sat down and said the whole *sefer Tehillim.* Since he wasn't used to it, it took him four hours. After he recited the special *tefillah* for a *choleh* at the end, he closed the *sefer* and kissed it.

That was when he first thought of the effect that the attack on his cousin would have on his own life. Although he was as interested as ever in moving to Israel, what would Mimi say? What would their families think? Setting aside the question of their families, he went to look for Mimi. She was downstairs in the laundry room folding the children's clothes and supervising them as they played on the floor.

"Mimi, could we talk?" he asked.

"Perhaps after the children go down for their naps?" she suggested. Benny nodded and went back upstairs. He called Israel again and was told that Aunt Toby had arrived and was now equipped with a cellular phone, which she would try to answer on the hour, going outdoors, if necessary, for this purpose. Benny passed on the news and the number of the phone to Minna and to his mother, resigning from his job as contact person. He returned to his *shtender* and reviewed the *Daf Yomi* until Mimi came to him. She sat down in a nearby chair. "What do you want to discuss? What happened to Elisha?"

"Not directly. I wanted to say that for me, the attack on Elisha doesn't make any difference. I'm still interested in moving to Israel. I know that you may not feel the same."

"I don't!" Mimi sounded very emphatic. "I think this was a very clear demonstration of what I said way back when. Israel is dangerous!"

"And I pointed out that America is dangerous, too. Neither is so dangerous that you have a one-in-a-thousand chance of getting killed; and if so, we aren't required to avoid living in either place."

"But it's different when Arab violence strikes someone in your own family, someone you know well. It makes it all so real!"

"It was real before. The pain and suffering of the victims and their families was very real, terribly real. We weren't sensitive enough, perhaps. I think that the lesson we should be taking away is that we should be feeling more sympathy and interest when we hear about a terrorist attack, not that we should be staying away from Israel."

"So, you still want to move?" asked Mimi again.

"I still want to stick to the agreement we made before this happened. You have already written to Ella about setting up a place for me to stay while I look for a job. I'll take this pilot trip. If I get a job on which we think I can support you and the children comfortably, then we'll move. If not, we'll stay here and look for a house to buy, either in Brooklyn or in one of the suburbs. If we go, we can take reasonable safety precautions, as other people do. I imagine that we'll soon get a feeling for which places are safe."

Mimi sat for a while, looking down at her hands folded in her lap. Then she looked up at Benny and said quietly, "Okay."

Benny felt a surge of joy. "You really mean it?"

"That was our agreement, and I'm willing to stand by it."

"Our families are not going to understand," said Benny ruefully.

"I don't think we have to discuss it with them. If we don't say anything more, they'll probably think we dropped the idea. We can make our own decision, just the two of us."

"I thought you wanted them involved?" Benny had the feeling that something important had just happened.

"I wanted us to hear what they had to say, but we've heard them out. They've gotten to the point where they're repeating themselves. From now on, we can work it out together."

Benny smiled. "Thank you for the vote of confidence. That's just exactly how I want to work it out."

They went on to discuss the details of the pilot trip: What to pack, how to organize his time, what gifts to bring to the Wahrhaftigs. Only when Tami awoke and Mimi went to fetch her did Benny notice how strange it was that he had called the Wahrhaftigs six or seven times in the last day, and had never mentioned that he was hoping to stay with them in a few weeks. Should he call back just to mention it? If he didn't, by the time Miri's letter arrived they would think that he had given up on the idea.

But after thinking it over he decided not to mention it by phone. Writing that letter to Ella was the first positive step in the direction of Israel that Mimi had made. Why should he short-circuit that by calling? Let the letter arrive, and let Ella answer it. This would give Mimi a part in the project.

Ella walked up the steps to the entrance of her apartment building pulling the double stroller behind her. The two older children arrived home in school buses. She wondered if she would have time to put in a load of laundry while heating up the lunch she had prepared in the morning, before work.

Ella stopped in front of the mailbox and felt around inside. There was rarely anything of interest, except a letter from her mother every couple of weeks. Let's see, a couple of requests for charity, and... Oh, how nice! A personal letter. The handwriting was only vaguely familiar, and she turned it over to see the return address.

Mimi Lerner. That was unusual. With a twinge of guilt, Ella remembered that she had never written a thank-you letter for that Shabbos she and Chaim Ozer had spent with the Lerners. She stuffed the letter into her purse. She would read it just as soon as she could, but for now she had better get that meal on the fire and that laundry into the machine. She unstrapped the two children, picked up the baby, and started urging her toddler to begin the long trek up to their third-floor apartment.

As she unlocked the front door, the phone rang. Ella dropped her purse on the hall table, shifted the baby to her hip, and picked up the receiver. "Hello, Rebbetzin Wahrhaftig? This is Trudy."

"Trudy! How nice of you to call. How are you settling in?"

"I want to speak to you about that. Could I come over this evening?"

"Hmmm. Once the children are asleep, I have to prepare a lesson for tomorrow. I can mark papers in the park, but to write out a lesson requires more peace and quiet. Could you come around six? I'll feed the children before that, and we can talk as I get them into bed."

"All right, I'll be there."

Trudy was about fifteen minutes late. Ella had already cleaned up from supper and was running the water for the children's bath. She was still wearing the *sheitel* in which she had taught. Trudy, when she arrived, wore a fringed kerchief, knotted on the left side.

"Does your husband know the Lerners' cousins, the Sheinfelds?" asked Ella immediately.

"I believe so," said Trudy. "I addressed several envelopes for wedding invitations to people by that name, and they surely weren't from my side of the family."

"Well, if it turns out that he does know them, you might let him know that Elisha Sheinfeld was attacked and very seriously injured, I'm afraid. Your husband can call us if he wants details about how to visit him in the hospital."

"I remember reading about such an incident in the papers, but I had no idea that it was someone Michael knew. You recognized the name from the newspaper?"

"No, we were much more involved than that. The Lerners had given him our name as possible Shabbos hosts, and he was eating *shalosh seudos* with us just before it happened." answered Ella. "He had no identification in his pockets, and they came looking for us because he was carrying an umbrella with our address on it. Chaim Ozer spent the night at the hospital, waiting for the outcome of the operation."

Ella recounted the whole story of that fateful *motzaei Shabbos.* "I still haven't replaced the broken glass from that picture, and something inside me has also changed. At quiet moments, I figuratively look over my shoulder, as if something might loom up to shatter my life as Elisha's was shattered. I'm used to planning months ahead, even years ahead, but that kind of planning has hidden assumptions, doesn't it? That everything will flow on smoothly."

"Planning months ahead?" commented Trudy with a sigh. "I hardly know how to plan next week."

"Come, sit down in the kitchen, and tell me what brought you here," said Ella solicitously.

"The problem," explained Trudy after she had been settled with a glass of hot tea and a plate of cookies, "is money."

"It so often is," agreed Ella, slightly distracted. She was listening for the change in pitch that would tell her that the bathtub was almost full.

"I wouldn't so much mind if we couldn't make ends meet," said Trudy, "but we can't even get them half-way around. Michael is getting only the basic stipend from the Religions Ministry for *kollel* students, and I am not working. Our income doesn't even cover the rent, without food, utilities, and transportation. The money we got for our wedding is evaporating quickly, and I don't know what we will do when it is gone."

Ella concentrated on her guest. "There are two things to be done in a budget crisis like that: One is to lower your expenses and the other is to raise your income. It sounds like you need both. When you have done as much as you can in both directions, then you have to *daven*, because none of your efforts will get you anywhere without *siyatta diShmaya*."

"Of course," agreed Trudy.

"Let's start with the expenses. Do you know that there is a rent subsidy for new immigrants?" Ella's sharp ear caught the expected change in the sound of the running water. "Excuse me, I have to plop the kids into the bath. I will give you some paper, and you can try to estimate your expenses for food, utilities, transportation, and so forth."

Ella came back twenty minutes later, having bathed the children and put them into their pajamas, to find Trudy chewing on her pencil and staring into space. "How are you doing?"

"Horribly. I have no idea exactly where all the money goes. I only know that it runs out too fast."

"Hmm, tell me, do you think your husband would be willing to cooperate with this budgeting project?"

"Oh, yes. He is as panicky as I am about this."

"Well, what you have to do is write down all your expenses for a week, and make a list of your major bills. Then we can sit down next week and try this again. In the meantime, try to think what you could do to earn some income. Look for signs on the bulletin board at the grocery store or on lamp posts. It doesn't matter if it's not what you want to do for the rest of your life; it's partly just to make you feel employable."

"My Hebrew is terrible. Who would want to hire me?"

"Someone who speaks English. We'll discuss all that when we finish trying to slash the expenses. Keep your eye out for 'Help Wanted' signs in English."

"You really think I could get work?"

"Pretty sure." She walked Trudy to the door and sent her off with a few more encouraging words. Then she went back to put the children to bed and to say *Shema* with them.

Only late in the evening did she finally have a chance to open Mimi's letter. She skimmed the lines, her eyes widening. Mimi was asking them to host her husband so that he could look for a job in Israel. Not, she said, that they had firmly decided to move. A lot depended on what kind of a job Benny could get.

Mimi Adler as a new immigrant? It was hard to imagine. Really, though, of course it could happen. Mimi would just need a little guidance; that was all.

Ella looked at the clock. It was already too late to do this topic justice. She would compose her answer now as she finished up her chores, and write it down tomorrow afternoon. She began to consider the question of what information the Lerners would need before they came: When to come, how to come, where to stay, what to bring, what to leave behind.

Only after she had been thinking about what, where and how for some ten minutes, did another question pop into her head. Why? She reread the letter, but it contained no clues, nor did it invite inquiry. There was no phrase like, "you will probably be surprised to hear this," or "you may wonder." Just a polite request for help with a project that was underway. It was a bit like coming across a smoothly flowing stream that had turned and was flowing uphill for a stretch.

The next afternoon, after she had served her husband and fed the children lunch, Ella sat down at her desk and took out her pad of notepaper. Chaim Ozer was taking a short nap before the second *seder* at *kollel*. Ella also wanted to take a nap, but she didn't want to put off answering Mimi's letter more than one day.

Dear Mimi,

Of course, your husband can stay with us. We will be delighted to have him. While we are on the topic of hospitality, let me thank you for hosting us while we were in New York.

If you do move to Eretz Yisrael, the best thing to do would be to stay in the immigrants' hostel at first. Let me explain. There are a lot of expenses in the first year, and you will find that you appreciate every penny of your savings. The rent at the immigrants' hostel is very, very low. It is also convenient to have an *ulpan* right there, since you will probably want to brush up your spoken Hebrew. I recommend Mevasseret Tzion, which is where we stayed.

What I would also advise is that you go straight from the plane to the hostel, living with what you brought in your suitcases and a little air freight. When Benny is settled in a job and drawing a salary, then you can order your lift over and look for an apartment to rent; I will be happy to help you. By then you should have some idea how much you can afford for rent and how much you need for other things.

The conditions in the immigrants' hostel are cramped. I believe that as a family with children, you will be entitled to one of the larger apartments with a small backyard. I think you would have about sixty square meters — not so bad if you are not encumbered with a lot of unnecessary baggage.

If your husband does decide to come on this pilot trip, it would be nice to have a little notice so that we can schedule our Shabbos guests appropriately. For the moment, I won't accept any houseguests for the few weeks after Pesach, until I hear from you again.

Please send my best regards to your parents.

Cordially, Ella

P.S. Please tell your mother that the dress she bought for Leah'le was a perfect fit and looks gorgeous. I'll try to write to her myself soon.

Ella folded the letter, prepared an envelope, and put both her letter and Mimi's on the table so that Chaim Ozer could look at them before he went back to second *seder*. Ella herself went to take a brief rest before the children got up.

She overslept, and woke up after Chaim Ozer had already left back to *kollel*. She saw that the letters were in a slightly different position than she had left them, and assumed that he had read them. She mailed her letter as she was taking the children to the park.

The children were in bed by the time her husband returned after *Maariv*. Ella was sitting at her desk in the living room, making up lesson plans for tomorrow.

"Did you mail that letter?" asked Chaim Ozer after he hung up his coat.

"Yes, on my way to the park with the children. Why, do you think any of my advice was wrong?"

"No, the advice was excellent. I just think that Mrs. Lerner may find it a bit overwhelming. If you have any more occasion to give her advice, I would advise you to divide it up into bite-size pieces."

"Was that bit of advice a bite-sized piece?" asked Ella.

"Of course," declared Chaim Ozer with assumed dignity. "You don't suspect me of setting a bad example on such an important issue, do you?"

"No, but seriously. What do you think I should have done?"

"I think it would have been enough to recommend the immigrants' hostel for the low rent, without the *ulpan* or the advantages to traveling light."

"You think she will worry about what to do with Tami while she is taking the *ulpan,* and how long she will have to live out of six suitcases?"

"Something like that."

"Mimi has to get used to the idea that if she wants to settle in Eretz Yisrael, she has to learn to live like an Israeli," asserted Ella.

"That's just the hitch, Ella. Who says that she does want to move to Eretz Yisrael?"

Mimi stared down at Ella's letter with stark dismay. She knew that Israelis sent their children off to kindergarten at some horrendously early age, but what in the world was she supposed to do with Tami while going to this *ulpan?* Sixty square meters! Was that much too small? Mimi had never gotten comfortable with the metric system, but Ella herself seemed to think that it would be a tight fit. And then she was supposed to live out of eight suitcases for months and months. No, six suitcases. Tami wouldn't have a ticket of her own yet, if they went at the end of the summer, so she'd have no baggage allowance.

When Benny came home that evening, the first question Mimi asked him was, "Benny, how big is sixty square meters?"

Benny stood in the hall, still holding his laptop computer in its case, as he made the calculation. "Let's see, a meter is a little over a yard, so a square meter is about ten square feet. Six hundred square feet is about twenty-four feet on a side. Okay, Mimi, imagine lining up four beds end-to-end. Then picture a square plaza, each of whose sides is as long as those four beds."

That did make it clearer. They would be able to get beds in the bedrooms. "Thanks."

"Why do you ask?" inquired Benny, putting down his computer and taking off his coat.

Instead of answering, Mimi handed him the letter from Yerushalayim. Some mild streak of rebelliousness impelled her to at least go on record as disliking the idea of living in such a small space. When he finished reading the letter, she said, "Won't we be rather cramped?"

"Well, you know, Israeli apartments are generally smaller than American houses. Perhaps after we live in this hostel thing, a real apartment of any size will seem luxurious."

"Maybe so," murmured Mimi, without any particular enthusiasm. She didn't even bother to tell him her reservations about the *ulpan.*

Benny stood with eyes narrowed in concentration as he made some mental calculation. "I suppose she's right about not bringing our things right away," he said at last.

Mimi had never even considered doubting that. Ella was always right.

Chapter 6

Pilot Trip

"Tel Aviv is now visible through the windows on the left side of the plane!" announced the pilot over the loudspeaker. Benny, who had a window seat on the right side, could still see only the blue water of the Mediterranean Sea.

He felt strange going off without Mimi and the children. It was very sensible, of course. His goal on this trip was to arrange as many job interviews as possible, and his family would only have been a hindrance. He just hoped Tami would still remember him by the time he returned, and that Shimmy would understand that he had had to go alone.

They flew lower and lower, and then began banking to the left to approach the one major runway. As the plane landed, there was a smattering of applause.

As Benny walked down the steps, he blinked a little as he tried to adjust to the mid-afternoon sunlight after the darker interior of the plane. Benny felt the usual wrench of inadequacy as he set his foot down on the asphalt. He should bend down and kiss the land, as so many *Gedolim* had done when arriving in Eretz Yisrael. If he were entirely alone, with no one else watching, he probably would. But he could not do it in this crowd of travelers walking so nonchalantly to the waiting buses.

Having brought only his carry-on bag, Benny exchanged some money, breezed through customs and soon found himself in a taxi passing through She'ar HaGai, the gateway to the narrow, winding valley that was the only way to get to Yerushalayim from the west. The tall slopes on either side of the highway were green, covered with cool-looking pine trees. He watched out, as always, for the bare hulks of the trucks disabled in the War of Independence, left as a memorial to those who had died in the siege of Yerushalayim. The places he passed still sounded exotic to him: Shoresh, Beit Meir, Telz-Stone, Abu-Ghosh — sprawled around its own little valley, Mevasseret Tzion along the top of the ridge, the long slope going down to the bend at Motza, Har Nof peeking over the brow of the hill. If he and Mimi were to live here, those names would come to sound perfectly ordinary.

When he rang the bell at the Wahrhaftigs' apartment, the door was opened by a little girl in long braids. "Hello," she said. "Are you the guest?"

"Yes, I am," said Benny, a little short of breath from carrying his bag up three flights of stairs.

"Leah'le, is that the guest?" came Ella's voice from somewhere in the periphery of the apartment.

"Yes, Ima," called Leah'le over her shoulder.

"Take him into the kitchen, sweetheart, and offer him some water. I'll be there as soon as I can."

Benny followed Leah'le into the kitchen, and was sitting down drinking a glass of water when Ella arrived, carrying a baby. "Sorry to leave you to the second team. I was in the middle of changing a diaper."

"I'm fine," said Benny, glancing towards Leah'le. "I was very well taken care of."

"Now, you're probably worrying about where to *daven Minchah*."

"No," said Benny. "Quite frankly, I hadn't gotten that far yet. I was still thinking about the possibility of a second glass of water, and wondering where I should put my suitcase."

"Well, here's the water," said Ella, refilling his glass, and setting down a few cookies on a plate in front of him. "There is still a fair amount of time. The sun doesn't set today until," she leaned over and peered closely at a calendar on the wall, "seven minutes after seven. We've been on Daylight Saving Time since before Pesach."

Benny finished his second glass of water and stood up. "I think I'll pass on the cookies for the moment."

"Fine, come put your suitcase in the boys' room, and then," said Ella with a determination that was not to be thwarted, "I will tell you where to find a *minyan* for *Minchah.*"

After *davening* both *Minchah* and *Maariv*, Benny caught a bus to the rehabilitation center where his cousin Elisha was hospitalized. The decor was decidedly dingy. The place gave the impression of an old hospital that had not made the grade; rather than being modernized, it had been shunted aside.

Elisha was pleased to see him. The muscles in his back had healed enough that he was able to sit up in a wheelchair, though he wore a brace that looked very uncomfortable.

"How are you doing?" Benny asked.

"Pleased that I am able to sit up. The ceilings in this place are decidedly dreary."

Benny glanced up and saw that, indeed, there wasn't much to look at above the bed. "It seems that Aunt Toby was sufficiently satisfied that she was willing to return to the States."

"With a little prodding from me. When Abba came for Pesach, he looked a little peaked, and I convinced her that three months without regular meals had been more than enough for someone his age. I have a whole staff taking care of me here."

He changed the subject. "What are you doing in Israel?"

Benny was slightly embarrassed to answer. Would it be taken as a lack of sensitivity that he was still considering *aliyah* after what happened to his cousin? "Looking for a job."

"Really? Thinking of moving to Eretz Yisrael?" Elisha asked.

"We're considering it."

"This is going to sound a little strange, but so am I," confessed Elisha. "I would like to come back."

It did sound a little strange. "How would you manage? You have no one here."

"I know, that's what my mother says. I tell her that that is a technicality which shouldn't effect the essential decision. I can't be the kind of bounce-around, keep-'em mesmerized day school teacher that I had planned to be. But I still hope to teach, and I think my best bet is to teach boys in the post-high school programs in Yerushalayim. I will have to learn some more first."

"I wish you success. But wouldn't you be afraid? If you were vulnerable before, you're much more vulnerable now." Elisha's plan sounded unworkable to Benny.

"I don't know. The social worker has been talking to me about Post-Trauma Stress Disorder. If I turn out to have it badly, if I'm always jumping when I hear footsteps behind me, then maybe I can't come back." He paused and gave Benny an assessing look. Apparently he decided to continue. "There is more at stake than just a career switch."

"Like what?" asked Benny, leaning back in his chair. Was Elisha worried about being a burden to his parents?

"I understand that I can get married and lead a normal life."

Benny sat up again. "Elisha, that's great news!"

"Right, it is, but finding a *zivug* is not going to be a simple matter under the circumstances." He gave the arm of his wheelchair a light slap. "I suspect that it will be easier here than in New York. Yerushalayim is full of special cases of one kind or another."

Benny tugged nervously at his tie. He was sorry now that he had worn it. In New York it had been standard dress for a job interview, and hadn't even particularly identified him as being religious. Only the yarmulke had done that. Here, or at least in this firm, it made him stand out. In all the hallways he had wandered through in search of the personnel manager's office, he hadn't seen a single other person in a suit jacket and tie.

Benny considered for a moment taking off the tie before he was called in to the interview, but embarrassment before the secretary stopped him. She had already seen him with the noose around his neck, and might comment to her boss about its later absence. It wasn't even a particularly conservative tie, bright reds and yellows. His sister Tzippy had given it to him for his birthday.

He had taken off his hat when he came in. There wasn't anything resembling a hat rack in the office, so the secretary had told him to leave it on a low bookcase in the corner. It went without saying that he hadn't seen a single other hat since he had stepped into the building.

In the business he worked for back home, the owner and half of the employees were *frum*. What would it be like to work in a place where he would be a definite outsider? Would he be ostracized at the water cooler? Would he be left out of decisions because he didn't go to lunch with the others? All that mattered, of course, only if he would actually get a job at a place like this.

"Mr. Lerner, Mr. Livneh will see you now."

Benny rose, picking up the attaché case containing copies of his résumé in English and Hebrew, the portfolio of computer projects he had participated in, and the lunch his hostess had insisted on packing for him. "Thank you," he said to the secretary, as he passed her desk.

Livneh was a rather burly man wearing a knit sport shirt. No formality for him. Benny slipped off his suit jacket as he sat down and draped it over the back of his chair. "Hot down here in Tel-Aviv, isn't it?" he said in partial apology for having brought the jacket at all. He rolled up his shirt sleeves to the elbow.

Livneh ignored all the by-play and reached out across the table. "Have the résumé?" he asked in Hebrew.

"Sure," said Benny, placing his attaché case on his knees and opening it. He saw with horror that something in the lunch bag had leaked. His crisp, neatly printed résumés were wet along the bottom edge! Fortunately, the Hebrew translations were in a plastic envelope. He slipped one out and closed the briefcase, putting the stapled sheets in the other man's outstretched hand.

Livneh flipped through the three pages quickly, returning to the first page and looking at Benny. "According to this, Lerner, you have only one year's experience," he said in a challenging tone.

"Hardly," said Benny. "If you will look again at that list of prizes and projects, you will see that I have been programming since I was fifteen, some of it professionally. This is my first year full time in an office. Until now I was a student."

Livneh looked at the section on education. "No B.A."

"Don't need it in New York for what I do."

Livneh looked up at Benny. "Yeshivah *bachur*, huh?" he asked, with a mocking twist to his smile.

"*Kollelnik*," returned Benny evenly. "Or at least, I was. Now, I work."

"They should all be put to work. In the salt mines," muttered Livneh. "Have you ever worked for the U.S. government or any other government?"

"No," answered Benny.

"Have you every belonged to any organizations that might affect your security clearance?"

"No," said Benny.

"If the computer division would be interested in hiring you, when could you come?"

"I would need to give two months' notice at my job, and a couple of weeks for moving."

"What kind of a visa would you get?"

"1-A."

"Temporary resident? Why?"

"So that I wouldn't have to go into the army right away," said Benny innocently.

"Never fails. Draft dodgers, every man jack of them."

Benny pulled himself up straight in the chair. He was sorry now that he wasn't wearing his jacket and hat. "Livneh, I was told by the official representative of the Israeli government to apply for a temporary resident's visa, and he said that he gives that advice to every American *oleh,* religious or non-religious. It would be hard enough getting settled in a new job, he told me, without the additional hassle of two months of basic training. Would you want your new employees to vanish just when they were getting broken in?"

"That's the real reason?"

"That's the real reason. At the end of three years, when I go over to a permanent resident's visa, I could be drafted."

Livneh gave Benny one long appraising look. Then he touched the intercom button on his desk. "I'll send you down to speak to the people in the computing section. They are the ones who have to decide if they want you."

Benny relaxed one notch. It was perfectly clear to him that Livneh could have just sent him away. Unsatisfactory as the conversation had seemed, he had somehow gotten through it.

On his way down to the computer section, he ducked into a rest room to try to repair the damage to his attaché case with a handful of paper towels. It was oil from the tuna sandwich that had leaked, and the whole lunch bag was contaminated with it. He couldn't put the bag back in the case, and he certainly couldn't carry it in his hand. If he tried to stash it somewhere, it might be blown up as a suspicious object. With strong pangs of guilt, he dropped the entire oily parcel into the trash can. What would his mother say if she saw him do that? Or his mother-in-law?

Both the envelope holding the Hebrew résumés and the folder of projects had proven to be blessedly impervious to tuna fish oil. Discarding all but the last three of the English résumés, he washed his hands with soap, and then managed to tear off the oily margin in such a way that the rest of the page remained clean. He stashed them in the attaché case and scooted down the stairs toward Room 218.

"You took the scenic route," commented the man seated at the computer console in English, without taking his eyes off the screen. He wore a white crocheted *kippah* with a blue border.

"Pit stop," explained Benny.

After saving his set and clearing the screen, the other man swung around to face Benny. "I'm Mitch Weissman. And you?"

"Benny Lerner."

"Sit down, Benny. Can I see your résumé?"

Benny opened his case, slipped one of the Hebrew résumés out of its envelope, and handed it over. Mitch gave just a glance and looked up. "Haven't you got this thing in English?"

There was a barely perceptible moment of hesitation before Benny replied. "I could fax it to you tomorrow morning."

"I wanted to look it over now," said Mitch, disgruntled. He began poring over the résumé in Hebrew.

Benny lifted the flap, pulled out the project folder, and laid it on the other man's desk. "These are all in English," he volunteered.

"What are they?" asked Mitch, not looking up from the paper.

"Documentation of various projects I have worked on."

Mitch put down the résumé and picked up the stack of projects.

"Ahem," Benny cleared his throat. "While you are looking those over, could you lend me a pair of scissors?"

"Sure," said Mitch, opening a drawer of his desk and pulling out a pair.

With the lid of the attaché case up between Mitch and him, Benny carefully straightened the bottom edge of two copies of his résumé in English, where he had torn off the tuna fish oil. It didn't look very polished, but if Mitch were not happy with three pages of single-spaced Hebrew, this would have to do. He set down the scissors unobtrusively on the table, put the English version of the résumé in his lap, and closed his attaché case.

Mitch reached for the Hebrew résumé and turned to the list of projects in the back to look up the one he was holding in his hand. Benny turned the English résumé to the same page and passed it across the table, "Here, you might find it more easily in this list," he said helpfully.

Mitch turned to the first page to see what he was holding and then looked at Benny accusingly. "I thought you said that you didn't have your résumé in English."

"That isn't the sort of final draft that I would want to leave behind in an application folder. I just thought you might want to use it now."

Mitch ran down the English list until he found the name of the project that had attracted his attention. "I see, written way back when. It's been a long time since I read a program written in PL/1."

"That's what they were using back when I started."

"Don't apologize to me," Mitch returned. "I did my first work in FORTRAN, with flow-charts and GOTO statements. The Dark Ages of computer programming." He turned back to the résumé. "Under your specialties you mention project management. What do you mean by that?"

"Dividing up a new project into parts for different people to work on, and arranging uniform standards for the information flow between the different modules."

Mitch grimaced. "That's what I was afraid you meant. Around here I do that. Are you applying for my job?"

Benny shrugged. "I'm applying for whatever job is open. Since yours is obviously not open, I must be applying for something else."

"It's not quite that simple in Israel. We don't have a lot of open jobs lying around. If we decide that we want you, then we will create an opening." He looked again at the section on work experience. "Why did they give a responsible job like that to someone new in the company?"

"I had experience doing project management from when I was working part-time. I was actually hired to replace the fellow who used to do it."

"What happened to him?" asked Mitch.

Benny grinned. "He came here."

Mitch swiveled his chair in the direction of the inner office and called out, "Rami!"

After a pause, a tall Israeli with a head of bushy black curls poked his head through the door and asked in Hebrew, "You wanted me?"

"I want you to meet Benny, here. If we should decide to hire him, he would be working with you on projects for the engineering division."

Rami looked Benny up and down and didn't particularly seem to like what he saw. He held out his hand rather reluctantly and Benny shook it.

"Take Benny in there and get him set up at a terminal. I'll join him in a few minutes, after I finish looking through this project folder. I want him to demonstrate one of his programs for me, and I have to decide which one."

Rami signed Benny onto a computer and showed him around the system. When they spoke shop, the tension between them lessened, but not so much that Benny did not have second thoughts about this job. To work side by side with someone openly hostile could be decidedly unpleasant.

Mitch arrived with a compact disk that he held gingerly, without touching the flat surface. "Here, install this one and let's see what it does."

Benny took the CD from Mitch, holding it just as carefully. Ah, good, it was one of his best efforts. He put it into the drive, found the install program, and set it running. Mitch pulled up a chair, but Rami chose to take a break and left the office.

When the demonstration was over, Benny signed off and took the CD out of the drive. He and Mitch went back to the outer office and Benny returned the CD to the envelope. "Okay, not bad. You can go back to Livneh now. I'll call down and tell him to give you a formal application to fill out. If we decide to offer you a job, we'll let you know by mail."

As Benny retraced his steps, he decided that the day had not been the unadulterated disaster he had expected when he first met Livneh and discovered that his résumés had been ruined. Of course, Rami's evident hostility was not particularly promising, but a lot of it was probably prejudice. Perhaps as they got to know each other it would soften.

Benny glanced at his watch. He was hoping to catch a three o'clock bus back to Yerushalayim, which would get him there in time for *Minchah*. On arrival in Mattersdorf, he would have to fend off questions about how he had enjoyed the lunch that he had been forced to discard.

When he reached Livneh's office, he heard loud laughter from behind the closed door. Someone was enjoying a good joke. The secretary buzzed her boss and then told him to go in. The door opened and Rami came out. He met Benny's eyes with a smirk that made Benny guess that the joke had been on him.

When Benny made his second visit to the rehabilitation center where his cousin Elisha was staying, he was pleased to find Michael Millman there. The Sheinfelds had been one of Michael's host families during his years in New York.

Elisha was sitting up without the brace and looked more comfortable than he had the last time. "*Yashar koach* for coming. This is really my day! Both of you, and also one of the policemen is supposed to show up soon with news of the trial. He's been dropping hints by phone that something is moving at last."

"What was holding it up?" Michael asked.

"Neither of the fellows they arrested was talking. They were both exercising their right not to incriminate themselves. The police have been trying to get one or the other to start plea bargaining, angling for a lighter sentence by cooperating with the prosecution. They were not well-motivated to cooperate, because they also fear retaliation from Hamas if they are labeled as collaborators. I've been learning a lot about the criminal justice system. Anyway, I got hints from the police that one of them is finally talking. I still don't know if it's Ahmad or Umar."

"Which is which?" asked Michael. "The story they had in the paper was kind of confused."

"Ahmad was the guy with the knife, the one who attacked me. Umar was the fellow they found hiding in Ahmad's closet when they came to make the arrest. They took them both in, but of course it's not a crime to hide in a closet. They charged Ahmad with attempted murder, and the other guy with conspiracy to commit murder. Enough of that for now. What are you learning in *kollel*?" This was addressed to Michael.

"*Kesuvos*. Kind of scary, what's written there. It all kind of hit home when I was getting married." Michael looked at his watch. "If I want to be back in time for my afternoon *chavrusa*, I'd better get a move on it. I'm sorry to have to go just when this is getting interesting, but you will have something to tell me on my next visit." He shook hands with Elisha and Benny, and took his leave.

"How did Michael know that you were here?" Benny asked.

"You forget that I was front page news. Besides, his wife knows the Wahrhaftigs."

"Any idea when you'll be coming home?" Benny asked.

"That depends on what sort of news Nachum has to give me. They would prefer for me to stay for the trial, although if necessary they can take a deposition. They had me do a composite drawing of the guy who attacked me as soon as I could, and it was a reasonable likeness of this Ahmad fellow. Then, when I was up to sitting in a wheelchair with a brace, they took me down to the station for a lineup, to pick him out of a group of eight men. That was horrible." Elisha shook his head ruefully at the memory.

"You weren't sure of the identification?" Benny asked.

"No, that was okay. I picked the right guy, though it would have been easier if he had been snarling instead of standing there deadpan. No, it was the traveling that was so difficult. I was on a stretcher in the back of an ambulance, but I felt every road bump and every rough spot in the asphalt. Finally, the medic made the driver crawl along at about twenty miles an hour. Fortunately, it is not so far from the hospital at Har Hatzofim to the police station. *Nu*, enough of that until Nachum gets here with his news. How is Tzvi?"

They spoke quietly for a while about family in Brooklyn, and Benny told him the current progress of his job search. "I have another interview tomorrow, some place in Bnai Brak that does software to order. It sounds similar to some of the stuff I was doing when I was free-lancing."

"Do you think they have enough work to provide you with a full salary?"

"That's one of the questions I'll have to ask."

A tall policeman came into the room and pulled up a chair.

"Got it!" he announced.

"Got what?" Elisha asked.

"Evidence for some convictions. Umar Fatchi, the Hamas operative, finally started talking a few days ago. He snitched on a number of Hamas activists, and the police have made some arrests. One of the guys turned out to have a bomb factory in his basement." Nachum paused and turned to Benny. "You have to realize that it's relatively easy to make an arrest, but much harder to get a conviction."

"But if you have an informant … ?" Benny asked.

"Who is to say that this Umar fellow isn't just trying to save his own skin by listing a lot of people with whom he has scores to settle? We need corroborating evidence. This stockpile of illegal explosives, with fingerprints all over them, is just the kind of break we needed. It shows the court that we're on the right track. The bomb squad is very excited, because the workshop used an unusual kind of timer that they have only seen once before. You know that every time a terrorist bomb goes off, they try to collect all the pieces they can find and look for identifying marks, whether the pieces are made locally or smuggled in, that sort of thing."

"So where was this from?"

"You remember that case during the Gulf War, when some terrorist tried to get his brother to plant a bomb in a vegetable store in Bnai Brak, but it blew up early and killed the brother instead? They think they can connect this workshop with that bomb."

"I hope the next time that Hamas tries to use that timer it also blows up in their faces," said Benny.

"I doubt that there was anything physically wrong with the timer," put in Elisha. "Bnai Brak got an extra portion of *hashgachah pratis* during the Gulf War."

"Well, they aren't going to build any more bombs in the workshop we raided. We'll have our collaborators in the town keep an eye on the location from now on."

"So what will the prosecution do now?" Elisha asked.

"They're going to try Ahmad alone and quickly. We'll have you called in early to give your evidence, and then you will be free to leave. The prosecutors tell me that they tend to believe Umar's story, that neither he nor anyone else in Hamas had anything to do with planning the attack on you. Ahmad did it in the heat of the moment. He only contacted them afterwards for help to pay his debts and a request for a false passport in case the police caught on to him." Nachum gave a few more details of the arrests. "I'll be in contact with you when we know something about the trial date," he said before leaving the room.

"I hope these arrests will forestall any terrorist attacks this group is planning," said Benny.

"So do I, of course," said Elisha. "Do you know that I've been studying with Chaim Ozer once a week?" It sounded like a non sequitur.

"What are you learning?" Benny asked.

"*Iyov.* The meaning of suffering. I think a lot about what happened to me." Elisha was no longer looking at Benny. He was staring at the wall in front of him.

"Of course."

"I could say that if the knife hadn't gotten wedged in my spinal cord, he would have pulled it out and they would never have caught him or these other fellows. I could say that, and it may be true, but all that was orchestrated by the *Ribbono shel Olam,* and I played only a passive part. I'm looking for a way to take my suffering and turn it into something positive."

"That's a life's work cut out for you right there," said Benny. He had always liked Elisha, but he didn't think that he had ever respected him as much as he did at that moment.

"I think that's why the idea of moving to Eretz Yisrael appealed to me right from the start," Elisha continued. "I wasn't yet thinking in these terms, but I believe that I was groping in this direction. If I could establish a branch of my family in Israel, that would have positive consequences for generations. It would give some meaning, at least for me, to all the pain and all the loss."

"*Hatzlachah*" exclaimed Benny. The plan, which had seemed so unworkable when Elisha first announced it, was now very real to him.

As he had been instructed, Benny got off the No. 400 bus on Chazon Ish Street in Bnai Brak. He managed to find the address he had written down — an apartment building on a dead-end street.

There was no sign pointing toward the software firm, but the street numbers matched, so Benny proceeded into the courtyard.

There were two entrances to the building. Benny tried the one on the right first, and there, on the door of one of the first floor apartments was the name of the company he was looking for. He knocked and someone called out telling him to come in.

The room was air-conditioned. There were two desks in what had originally been the living room of the apartment, each with a computer terminal. Trailing cords connected both workstations to a single printer. One of the desks was manned, and a client was sitting across from it wearing a jacket and hat.

The man behind the desk looked up expectantly when Benny came in.

"I have a two o'clock appointment. Benny Lerner," Benny explained.

"Naftoli Steinmetz. You can get yourself some water to drink from the cooler in the kitchen, and make yourself comfortable there," he pointed to the other desk, "until we finish."

The kitchen was obviously never used for cooking. There was an electric kettle and the paraphernalia for producing hot drinks on one of the two counters, beside the water cooler. The other counter was piled high with old monitors and disconnected computers. Old equipment was also stored on the top of the refrigerator.

When he returned to the main room, Benny settled himself in the proffered chair and began perusing his pocket *Gemara*. With all this running around, he had gotten several days behind in the *Daf Yomi*. At least in this office he didn't have to be embarrassed to open up a *sefer kodesh*.

"Why do you have to make sure the *shiur* will be labeled correctly? It's simple! We don't want someone dialing up a *shiur* in *shmiras halashon* and getting the *halachah yomis*. Can't you do some sort of test?" This was all spoken in Yiddish.

"If these were text files, nothing would be easier. Since we're talking about sound clips, it's a whole different story."

Benny picked up the thread in the *sugya* he was learning and managed to tune out the other conversation. In fact, he hadn't even noticed that the client had gotten up to leave until Naftoli called him over. "Are you on the *daf?*" he asked.

"My *shiur* is. I've fallen behind while traveling." Benny marked his place and stashed the book in his pocket. "I'm here in Israel looking for a job."

"So you told me on the phone."

"You get a lot of institutional clients?" Benny asked, indicating the door through which the "dial-a-*shiur*" administrator had vanished.

"We get some industrialists too, looking for a *heimish* firm." He took control of the conversation again. "Whether or not we might be able to take you depends on you. Are you good at what you do?"

Benny slid his projects folder across the table. "Here's my work. You can judge for yourself."

One evening toward the end of his stay, Benny managed to wait for supper until Chaim Ozer came home at ten. Ella had eaten earlier with the children and was now putting the baby to bed, so they had the kitchen to themselves.

"What are your plans for learning if you move to Eretz Yisrael?" asked Chaim Ozer.

"I was hoping to continue with the *Daf Yomi*," said Benny, "if I can keep up with it in Hebrew."

They ate for a few minutes in silence, and then Benny said, "You had something in mind when you asked me that question."

"That's true," admitted Chaim Ozer. "I would like to say something in praise of learning in depth, but without discouraging you in any way from learning the *Daf Yomi*."

"You know," Benny pointed out, "I spend most of my day at work. There isn't all that much time left over."

"I understand, but here in Yerushalayim there seems, somehow, to be a bit more time available for learning."

"But why in depth? I never expect to go back to *kollel* or to teach what I am learning. Perhaps, if more time materializes, I should spend it reviewing *halachos* or something else practical."

"Why do I think you should do some learning in depth? What you do in your job you really enjoy, right? You find it interesting and intellectually challenging?"

"Yes, I do."

"Well, it just seems to me unbalanced to have all your interest and enthusiasm poured out on your secular projects, while your Torah studies are at a more superficial level."

Benny thought that one over. There was something to it. "So why not take the hours I now use for the *Daf Yomi* and apply them to learning in depth?"

Chaim Ozer winced. "That's just what I didn't want you to suggest. I wish I hadn't said anything."

"Why not?"

"Because in no other kind of learning will you have the discipline, and the sheer volume, of learning a page every day, rain or shine, sick or well. It's like the difference between drawing a salary and freelancing. It's hard to be consistent when you're your own boss and what you're doing requires initiative."

Having freelanced as a programmer for years, Benny knew exactly what he meant. His problem had not been with finishing projects he had started, but with forcing himself to go out and look for new ones. "Assuming that I'll probably stick to the *Daf Yomi*, I really don't see myself having enough extra time for learning in depth. It's not the sort of thing you can keep up at the rate of one evening a month."

"At the moment, you don't even know if you're coming," Chaim Ozer pointed out. "There will be time enough to worry about it when you're here. Now that your trip is almost over, what do you think of the job market?"

"Not bad, but also not perfect. I'm pretty sure I could eventually land something in one of those little software places in Bnai Brak. I'd rather work for a bigger company, but I'm dubious about whether I can get a job in a secular firm."

"Why?" asked Chaim Ozer.

"Because I'm *chareidi*."

Chaim Ozer thought about that for a moment. "I imagine that it would be hard for a secular Jew to get a position in one of those software companies in Bnai Brak."

"I doubt that they get any secular applicants, but I suppose you're right. That doesn't mean that the situation is comparable. After all, the secular camp has the army, the air force, most heavy industry, most agriculture, and for the moment, most of the population."

"All that is good reason for us to be working as hard as we can."

"At what?" asked Benny.

"At whatever *Hashem Yisbarach* sent us down here to do."

"If we can figure out what that is," said Benny.

"If," agreed Chaim Ozer.

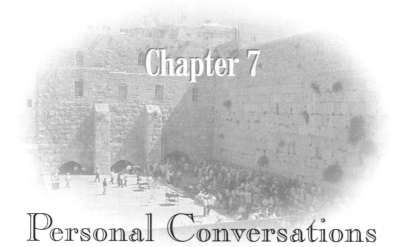

Chapter 7

Personal Conversations

"Hi, Reuven! What are you doing in town?" Mimi asked. Her brother had just picked up the phone at her mother's house.

"I had to come in to get a suit from the *shaatnez* lab. I have a ride back to Lakewood at 10:30."

"Could you come to us for supper? If Mama and Papa will give you up?"

"In fact, it turns out that Mama and Papa have a wedding in Queens, and I was going to go out for a pizza, so that would be great."

"Is Mama there? I want to come over and talk to her."

Reuven sounded newly tense. "Is it about this idea of moving to Eretz Yisrael? Has Benny had news about one of the jobs he applied for?"

"I want to talk to Mama first, and yes, that's the subject. If she wants to discuss it with you afterwards, that will be fine with me."

At about 8:30 in the evening, the doorbell rang. Mimi glanced at the kitchen clock. It was too early to be her brother Reuven. She had told him that they would eat when Benny came home at nine. She turned off the flame under the onions she was frying and went to peek through the little diamond-shaped window in the front door. The first thing she saw was a black hat at a jaunty angle, its owner looking out at the street. A moment later she realized that it was Reuven.

"You're early," she said after she had unbolted the door and yanked it open. It always stuck slightly.

"You said that Benny was coming at nine. I came now because I wanted to talk to you first."

"Well, of course you're welcome, but we'll have to talk in the kitchen as I make supper."

"The kids are in bed already?"

"'Fraid so." Reuven, her only unmarried sibling, spent a lot of time at their house and was a favorite with the children.

Reuven hung up his hat on the rack in the entranceway and followed her into the kitchen. "Smells good," he said, sniffing appreciatively.

"So far there's not much to smell except the onions." She turned the flame on again under the skillet. She checked to see that the boiling potatoes had enough water. "What do you want to talk about?"

"About *shidduchim*."

"*Shidduchim*!" Mimi turned around to face him, the spatula in her hand. "You've decided that you're ready to get married?"

"No, I haven't. I still think I want to wait. But..." He sat down at the table and seemed to find it hard to continue.

"But?" prodded Mimi, sitting down opposite him.

"But..." He took a breath and looked down at his fingernails, "but I always thought I would be able to count on you to help pick out the girl, and now... Now, Mama tells me that Benny has been offered a job. It looks as if you really are going to move away." The last was as close to a wail as one expects to hear from a twenty-year-old *yeshivah bachur*.

"Reuven," Mimi said earnestly, leaning forward and clutching the handle of the spatula with both hands, "you should never think that because we're moving, it means that Mama and Papa and you are one bit less precious to me."

"It seems to me that if you truly loved us, you could not bear to go!"

There it was. Reuven had blurted out the accusation that neither

Mama nor Papa had ever been willing to make. Tears filled her eyes, and one began to trickle down her cheek. She dashed it away with the back of her hand.

Reuven himself seemed startled by what he had said, and raised his hand to cover his mouth. "That isn't what I came here to say."

"I know," said Mimi, pulling a tissue out of the box at the end of the table and dabbing at both eyes. "But it's how you feel, and maybe it's just as well that someone finally said it."

"I surely didn't mean to make you cry, Mimi."

"That's not important." Mimi tossed the first tissue into the trash and took another. "Reuven, soon you'll get married, *b'ezras Hashem.*"

"Not to a girl picked out by Malka or Leah," grumbled Reuven.

"Mama will find you a girl and she'll do a good job. Mama understands people and she understands you. I'm not talking now about how you will find your wife, I'm talking about what will happen after you get married. You'll build a whole new world with you and your wife at the center. Of course, you'll still care about Mama and Papa and the rest of us, but your first responsibility will be to your wife and your children."

"If you're trying to say that you have to choose Benny over us, I know that."

"I'm trying to say something more complicated than that. When Benny and I got married, we had some dreams. One was to live on a pittance for several years so that he could learn in *kollel.* We managed that one with a lot of struggling. A second was to find a job for Benny that he would enjoy, and that would leave him time and energy to learn. That one fell into our laps.

"We had a third dream, to buy a house in a nice *frum* neighborhood and furnish it just to our taste. Every time another metal chair in our *kollel* apartment would break, we would talk about the sturdy wooden chairs we would buy when we finally had a choice." Mimi sighed wistfully and wiped her stinging eyes again. "Then Benny came home with a different dream, a dream of Yerushalayim stone and pine trees, a dream I didn't share." Mimi paused. The words had been pouring out, as if she were explaining the decision to herself as well as to Reuven.

"And then Benny lost interest in the old dream?" asked her brother.

"It wasn't only that. The old dream lost some of its luster for me as well."

"Because Benny didn't share it?"

"That was surely a big part of the reason," agreed Mimi, "but there was more to it than that. The old dream was a dream of varnish and silver. Silver tarnishes and varnish chips, whereas pine and stone renew themselves with time." Mimi gave an embarrassed laugh. "I don't think I'm really explaining myself very well."

"It is a bit poetical for me, but I think I understand."

"The last few months have been difficult, perhaps the most difficult since we got married, but we've got it more or less worked out. We're pulling together again. I'm sure that Benny understands what parts of the plan I will find most difficult, and he's trying his best to make it as easy as possible for me."

They lapsed into a silence that would have been companionable had it lasted, but it was broken by a loud "Brring" from above their heads. Both Mimi and Reuven looked up, startled.

"The smoke alarm!" he gasped.

"My onions!" cried Mimi. She sprang up, seized the handle of the skillet and ran with it to the sink, where she held it under running water. A burst of steam joined the smoke in the air. Reuven threw open the window and tried to clear the air, coughing as he worked.

"Mimi!" he called. "This is just getting worse! Could something else have caught fire?"

Dropping the skillet into the sink and turning off the water, Mimi peered through the thick haze in the direction of the stove. She didn't see any flames, only... "The potatoes!" She snatched a dishtowel off the rack as she ran toward the stove, knowing that the stubby plastic handles of the pot would already be hot to the touch. Wrapping the dishtowel halfway around the smoking pot, she grasped it gingerly and turned back toward the sink.

"Mimi! Now the towel is on fire!" shouted Reuven in despair.

Afraid the pot would burn her if she let go of the towel, she managed the three remaining steps to the sink and dropped the pot into the skillet. Then she threw the burning towel on the floor and began stomping on it. It was burning vigorously by this time, and she had a lot of trouble putting it out.

The smoke alarm was still clanging raucously from the ceiling. From the direction of the stairs leading up to the bedrooms she could hear first Shimmy and then Tami begin crying. Reuven ran to the stove and fiddled with the knobs, trying to turn off the two flames that were still lit.

"The corner of the towel must have caught fire from the front burner," she gasped when she finally extinguished the burning cloth. The haze of smoke around the stove was beginning to clear. She hoped they wouldn't all have to be hospitalized for smoke inhalation. Also... was that gas she smelled?

Her brother had turned off the front burner, but was having trouble with the back one. "Reuven, that's the wrong knob!" She ran back to his side and turned both knobs to the "off" position. For good measure she threw the switch turning off all the gas to the stove.

"Well, I suppose that's some small consolation," said Reuven.

"What?" asked Mimi.

"At least we didn't have a gas explosion, too."

"Listen, I'm going up to see if the children are all right. Can you shut off the smoke alarm?"

"Where's the switch?"

"I have no idea," admitted Mimi. "Maybe if you climb up on the table, you can find it."

Shimmy was sitting up in bed and Tami was standing in her crib crying as loud as she could. A few minutes later Mimi came part way down the stairs, a sniffling, hiccuping child on each hip. A bemused Benny, who had obviously just arrived, was staring through the kitchen door.

"Oh, Benny! I'm so glad to see you!"

"Why do I see Reuven's legs sprouting out of the center of the table?" he asked.

"He's trying to turn off the smoke alarm."

"The switch is in the fuse box." Benny went through the door into the kitchen and fiddled in the fuse box. The horrible noise cut off completely. Tami gave a sigh of contentment, laid her head on her mother's shoulder, and closed her eyes, but Shimmy was still wide-eyed and fearful. "Is it safe to bring the children down?" asked Mimi from the staircase where she had halted.

"First tell me what happened, so I'll know what the dangers are."

"I burned supper and the kitchen filled up with smoke."

"Smoke rises. There could be a lot in the bedrooms, too. I think you had better put on a coat, wrap the children in blankets, and go over to the Weinbergs' house until Reuven and I get the smoke cleared out of the house."

"Maybe we should call the fire department for advice," suggested Reuven, who had already scrambled down from the kitchen table.

Hearing the siren of an approaching fire engine, Mimi said, "That may be unnecessary. The neighbors must have called already."

Benny quickly opened the front door, before anyone would decide to take an axe to it. As the fresh but cold air billowed into the house, Mimi retreated a step or two. Two firemen came bounding up the front stairs, one of them holding a fire extinguisher.

"Step back! Where's the fire?"

"It's out already! It's out!" shouted Mimi, afraid that the firemen were about to spray foam all over her living room furniture.

"We had a kitchen fire," Benny explained, "but my wife put it out. The neighbors apparently called you because of all the smoke. We're terribly sorry about the confusion, and we thank you for coming so quickly."

The firemen went into the kitchen, looked over the charred remnants of the Lerner's dinner, and wrote a brief report on the basis of Reuven's rather disjointed account of the emergency. They chastised Mimi for pouring water on an oil fire, and told her to use baking soda the next time. After she promised to buy a package of baking soda and leave it in easy reach of the stove, they were mollified and left.

The Lerners answered four phone calls from concerned neighbors and followed the instructions they had been given for clearing out the smoke. Eventually, they got the children back to sleep and Mimi pulled some frozen pizza out of the freezer for their supper.

"I'm terribly sorry," Reuven apologized. "Your whole meal was ruined because of me."

"Maybe you were destined to eat pizza today, as you had originally planned, and I got into trouble for interfering," suggested Mimi jokingly.

"No, I mean it. I feel awful about what happened," Reuven insisted.

"Take it easy," said his brother-in-law. "There was no permanent damage at all, and I like pizza every once in a while as a change."

"That dishrag is gone."

"It was already slightly torn. I won't miss it at all," insisted Mimi.

After sending Reuven off to catch his ride to Lakewood, they climbed wearily up the stairs.

"Why was Reuven so apologetic?" asked Benny. "You would think he was a firebug who had set everything on fire on purpose."

"I suppose he feels that I wouldn't have burned everything if we hadn't been talking."

Benny glanced at her. "Personal?"

"Personal," agreed Mimi.

Mimi's mother and father were driving home from the wedding they had attended in Queens. Mendel Adler gripped the wheel tightly with both hands. "Let's go back to what we were saying when we were driving out. Mimi and Benny are grown up. If this is what they think is best for them, we don't want to interfere."

"Of course, we don't want to interfere," Mrs. Adler agreed. "But it's so dangerous over there. I was sure they had dropped the whole idea because of what happened to Benny's cousin, and then, boom, Benny gets a job and they're going to hop onto the next plane."

"Three months is not quite 'the next plane,'" pointed out Mr. Adler.

"The nearest thing."

Their car slowed, and other motorists honked as they maneuvered past them.

"What's wrong with the car, Papa?" asked Mrs. Adler, as the noise penetrated her consciousness.

"I'm not sure." He was scanning the gauges and dials of the control panel, looking for a red light. Only at the end did he think to check the most obvious thing. "Oh, no, we are running out of gas!"

"Quick, Papa, take this exit. Maybe there's a gas station at the bottom of the ramp. There often is."

The car made it to the bottom of the ramp, more because of its momentum and the downward slope than because of the motor. There was no gas station at the bottom, but they managed to continue on straight for another block or so, scanning the sidewalks on either side for a phone booth.

"Why can't the city require the phone company to put in more public phones," grumbled Mr. Adler.

"It looks like a rough part of town," said Mrs. Adler uneasily. "Maybe there's a problem with vandals."

As the motor gave its last gasp, Mr. Adler swerved over to the curbside in front of a fire hydrant. If a policeman were to come along right now, he would be so happy to see him that he would help him write out the ticket. He dropped his hands from the wheel and they lay useless in his lap.

"What will we do, Papa?" murmured Mrs. Adler.

"It's my fault for not getting gas. I knew we were low and meant to buy some on the way to Queens, but this news about Mimi knocked it out of my head."

Mr. Adler peered dubiously at the windows of the neighboring tenements. Some had boarded up windows, and others had broken panes. "I suppose I could go out and try to find someone who would let me use their phone."

"Don't even think of it!" squealed Mrs. Adler. "They'll probably tie you up and take your wallet and shoes."

"Could be," agreed Mr. Adler. "Well, let's say that you lock yourself in the car and I walk until I get to a major street, with stores and taxis and phone booths. There I can get someone to drive me back with gas."

"Let's go together," said Mrs. Adler. "Staying here alone would be too much for my nerves, and I hope no one will start up with two people walking together." After considering the various alternatives, Mr. Adler agreed. They got out, locked the car, and set off down the street in what seemed the most promising direction. Mrs. Adler had her small evening bag, on its long strap, and she put the strap over her head so that it would be held more securely.

Broken glass crunched under their feet. Some of the houses had lighted windows, but most seemed to be deserted. As they approached a dark alleyway, a large rat emerged and scurried off ahead of them, hugging the wall of the next building.

When they were about three paces from the next alleyway, they heard a rustle from that direction. They moved slightly away from the wall in case another rat wanted to claim its right of passage.

Mr. Adler saw a head poke out of the alleyway. A moment later, a man burst forth, running in their direction. The attacker snagged the strap of Mrs. Adler's purse as he passed. She fell backwards, clutching at her neck, and her head hit the sidewalk. The purse-snatcher got away with his loot.

Mr. Adler bent over his wife. She was still breathing, but did not respond to her name. This was no time for niceties about the neighbors. He ran to the nearest building with lighted windows, found an apartment with a crack of light under the door, and began pounding on it.

"My wife! She is injured! I have to call an ambulance!" he shouted.

A Hispanic woman in a shawl opened the door. In the background were two teenage boys reading comic books.

"Telephone! Quick! My wife is hurt outside!"

The mother, who did not understand English very well, did not respond right away, but one of the boys jumped up and pointed to the phone. Mr. Adler dialed 911 with trembling hands. As he began reporting the mugging, the officer on duty asked, "Where are you? What is the address?"

Mr. Adler realized that he didn't have any idea. He turned to the boy, who took the phone from his hand and gave the dispatcher instructions for getting there. In the meantime, the other boy had explained to his mother in Spanish what was going on. She wet the end of her shawl and vanished through the front door of the apartment. When they finished calling the ambulance and the police, Mr. Adler and the first boy followed her. They found her bent over Mrs. Adler, mopping her face and hands with the wet shawl.

Mr. Adler bent down again, once more checking that his wife's heart was beating and that she was breathing. The Hispanic family stayed with him during the interminable wait for the ambulance. Finally, after twenty minutes, it arrived. The back doors sprang open and two medics jumped out, pulling after them a stretcher with its wheels retracted. One bent over Mrs. Adler and checked her vital signs, while the other positioned the stretcher so that she could be moved onto it with a minimum of dislocation.

After Mr. Adler described the mugging, they checked the bones in her neck to see if anything seemed to be broken. They slipped something under her head and neck to support it as they lifted her onto the stretcher. One of the medics told Mr. Adler to climb into the back of the ambulance, while he himself went around to sit next to the driver. Mr. Adler waved a quick goodbye and called "Thank-you" to the family that had helped them.

The driver turned on the siren, and the ambulance screeched off through the quiet streets.

When Mrs. Adler awoke, she could not at first figure out where she was or what was happening. She heard her daughter Malka's voice pouring out apologies in a very uncharacteristic manner. When she tried to turn in that direction, she discovered that she could not move her neck. On her other side she heard Mimi murmuring *Tehillim* and sniffling. She felt a terrible languor; almost any action seemed to require too much effort, but some undefined worry was nagging at her and would not let her drift off into unconsciousness again. She made the effort and opened her eyes.

"Mama! *Baruch Hashem!* You woke up!" That was Mimi, over on her left.

"Mama! Oh, Mama, I was so worried!" That was Malka, on her right.

Finally her own worry took form. Papa! Where was Papa? Had whatever happened to her happened to him as well? She kept her eyes fixed on the ceiling, hoping that someone would explain where she was and what was going on, but no one seemed to think of that.

"Oh, Mama, as I was sitting there, not knowing if you would wake up, I thought of all the times I could have visited you and didn't find the time. There was always something—the children, or my job, or *simchos*. The reasons all seemed so trivial all of a sudden. I'm going to be better about it, Mama, really I am."

Fine, thought Mrs. Adler, I'm glad you feel that way, but where is Papa?! When would they all figure out that she didn't know why she was here or what had happened? It seemed that she was going to have to make a further effort and try to speak. She moistened her lips, which felt dry and cracked. "Papa?" she got out feebly.

"We made Papa take a rest, Mama." That was Mimi speaking now. "He was exhausted, and the doctor said he was suffering from shock. Yankel drove him to his house and we said that we would call him when you woke up. Leah was here before, but we sent her back to get some rest, too. She'll come in the early morning, when Mimi has to go wake up her children."

"Should we call Papa, though?" asked Malka. "He was so worn out."

"Of course we should," replied Mimi. "Maybe he's lying awake waiting for the call. He's counting on us."

"I'll go call Yankel," said Malka. "He's there on the spot. He can decide." She leaned over and kissed Mrs. Adler. "We're so glad to have you back, Mama." The click of her heels receded down the corridor.

Mrs. Adler made another effort to look at Mimi and winced from pain.

"Don't try to turn your head, Mama," Mimi advised. "The doctors took X-rays and they say that nothing is broken, but your muscles are bruised and strained. You will have to wear a neck brace for a few weeks."

Her neck. What had happened to her neck? She struggled for memories. Mimi had called to say that Benny had gotten a job offer and they were now serious about moving to Eretz Yisrael. Mimi had come over to visit and they had talked about it. Then... then she and Papa had gone to a wedding, and talked about Mimi and Benny on the way. She remembered the wedding; she had been fine then. After the wedding... after the wedding they had driven home, and she had complained to Papa about how dangerous it was in Israel. Had there been a car accident? Was this a whiplash injury? They had driven along, talking about Mimi, and then... Ah! The memories began flooding back. Running out of gas, leaving the freeway, locking the car, the rat, the alleyway, that man!

She was almost sorry now that she had struggled to remember. The memory of the purse-snatcher was not going to go away so quickly. She closed her eyes to escape it, but it didn't help. A picture of the man, his wild face, his unruly hair, was plastered on the inside of her eyelids. She sighed. Mimi squeezed her hand.

Poor Mimi. She must be blaming herself for what happened. Papa surely explained how they happened to run out of gas. She squeezed Mimi's hand back and made the effort to say, "Not your fault. *Bashert*."

"My fault?" Mimi sounded very puzzled. "Why should it be my fault? I was nowhere near!"

Too late, Mrs. Adler realized that her husband had been careful not to tell the story in a way that would make Mimi feel guilty. Indeed, why should she feel guilty? It was, as she had said herself, *bashert*.

For all that they consulted and inquired and decided, in the end the outcome was in Hashem's hands. Mimi might move to Israel and never be in the slightest danger, Mimi might stay here and... Mrs. Adler decided not to complete that thought. How had she gotten mugged in a place she had never been before and never expected to be again?

Mrs. Adler felt a need to communicate her newfound clarity to Mimi, and a conviction that she would fail to get it across. She struggled to speak. "Mimi, it's okay. You can go."

"Go where, Mama? Right now, I don't want to be anywhere except here. Benny is home with the children until it's time for him to go out and *daven*."

"No, not now, later. You can go to Eretz Yisrael. I don't mind. G-tt zoll helfen."

"You mean that, Mama?"

Under normal circumstances Mrs. Adler would have nodded, but now it was impossible. "Yes, I do. You and your family will do what you have to do."

"Why, Mama, I'm so glad you feel that way. It will all be so much easier for me now." Her voice was full of relief. "I've been so torn for months now, between Benny and the rest of the family. As I was saying to Reuven when the fire alarm rang..."

"Fire alarm?"

"Oh, right, you haven't heard about our adventure. We had fire trucks and everything, just because I burned supper."

Mrs. Adler found that the more she spoke, the easier it got. "Tell me."

Mimi told her mother the whole story. They were still laughing over it when Malka returned. "Papa was awake. He wants to take a cab and come back, so, of course, Yankel is driving him right over."

"Papa needs his own bed," said Mrs. Adler.

"You know, Malka, Mama is right. You know how Papa always complains that he doesn't sleep well when he goes away for Shabbos."

"But the doctors don't want him left alone. Because of the shock. They don't know how he will react." Malka sounded worried.

"So someone will stay with him. I have to go home to be there for the children in the morning, but Benny could do it, or Motti."

"As if Yankel would allow that. He's the oldest, it is his job. I will go talk to him again." The click of Malka's heels once again receded in the distance.

It took a while until Mr. Adler arrived, because Yankel had to pack up his things to stay overnight with his father in the Adler home. Mr. Adler took the chair that Mimi had vacated. "I'm so glad to see you awake." Relief filled his voice. He explained how she lost consciousness, and told her about the Spanish-speaking family that helped him summon the ambulance.

When he had finished the story, she said, "Papa, I told Mimi that she can move to Eretz Yisrael."

"Of course, she can. We always said that," returned Mr. Adler.

"We always said that, but now I mean it."

"I'm glad you feel that way now, but I don't think that makes all of this worthwhile." He waved his hand at the hospital room and at his wife's neck brace.

"That horrible purse-snatcher got what he deserved," said Mrs. Adler with satisfaction.

"What do you mean, Mama?"

"There was nothing in the purse but a few quarters."

Chapter 8

Day in Court

Elisha's attacker, Ahmad Zawidat, has been brought to trial. Elisha had asked Chaim Ozer to accompany him on the opening day of the trial. The hospital staff transported him to the court building, but his friend took charge of him at the entrance to the courtroom.

It was not built like an American courtroom. There was no jury box, and the court reporter sat up on the dais, facing the judge's seat on the right. In the United States, there would have been a little box on the judge's left for the witnesses. Instead, there was a lectern in the middle of the room, facing the judge.

The defendant was brought in, handcuffed. He was placed on the defendant's bench, to the judge's left. Two armed policemen brought him in, and one remained standing at his side. Several Arab women in head scarves began weeping quietly when he came in, and Elisha presumed they were family members. The prisoner was stone-faced, displaying no emotion. Elisha studied the face again, hoping that his identification had been correct.

The judge entered, enveloped in black robes, and everyone in the courtroom stood up, except Elisha. When the judge took his seat, they all resumed theirs. The lawyers for the two sides, dressed formally in white shirts or blouses and dark pants or skirts, were seated at two separate tables. A wooden railing separated them from the audience.

The judge banged the gavel. "The State of Israel against Ahmad Zawidat. Counsel for the prosecution, Attorney Gai Har-Paz. Counsel for the defense, Attorney Meir Magen." The judge read the indictment and then asked the prosecutor to present the case against the defendant.

Har-Paz gave a brief statement in which he explained that he intended to bring witnesses to prove two things: First, that the crime of attempted murder had been committed on the night in question, and second, that it had been committed by the defendant.

His first two witnesses were the two *bachurim* who had found Elisha. They were asked to describe the position in which he had been lying and the state of his clothing. The umbrella was entered as evidence, and they each identified it as the umbrella that they had found lying near the body of the victim.

The knife was entered as evidence, and the *bachurim* identified it as appearing to be the knife found in the victim's back. There was a lot of rustling from the audience as people strained to get a glimpse of the weapon. The defense attorney waived cross-examination.

The prosecutor paused for a moment, standing with his knuckles pressed on the table, looking down at his notes. Then he looked at the judge and announced dramatically, "I would like to call Yitzchak Schwartz as a witness."

This struck Elisha as an unnecessary rhetorical flourish. There was no jury to impress, and the judge had a list of all witnesses to be called. Perhaps Har-Paz was playing to the press.

There was a spate of whispering in the audience as people tried to determine who Yitzchak Schwartz was and what his connection to the case might be. It was difficult for Elisha to twist around, but he heard footsteps coming down the aisle. A rather pudgy middle-aged man opened the hinged gate and passed through to take his place at the lectern, facing the judge.

When the defendant saw Mr. Schwartz, his face twisted in the snarl Elisha remembered so vividly. He was no longer the least bit uncertain of his identification. Although his back was beginning to hurt from such an extended period of sitting, he ignored it and leaned forward to hear what the witness would say.

Itzik swore to tell the truth, and the prosecutor looked down at his notes before asking the first question.

"You are a cook at the Palace Hotel?"

"Yes," answered Itzik.

"Do you know the defendant?"

"Yes, he used to work for me in the kitchen, about two years ago."

"Did you work on the night of January 23?"

"Yes."

"What shift?"

"Six in the evening until twelve."

"Did the defendant appear in the kitchen during your shift?"

"Yes."

"When?"

"I really can't be sure. Some time between six-thirty and eight o'clock."

"Why did he come?" asked the lawyer.

"He asked to have his old job back."

"Did you agree to give it to him?"

"No. I told him that he had not been sufficiently dependable."

"He was disappointed?"

"He was furious," declared Itzik. "He said that the main reason he had missed work was because of the curfews, and those weren't his fault. He said that the complaint was just an excuse to discriminate against him because he was an Arab."

The prosecutor brought forward the knife, which was lying on a tray, labeled with a tag and enclosed in a zip-lock bag. "Can you identify this knife as having come from your kitchen?"

Itzik examined it closely. "Can you turn it over?"

The prosecutor lifted the top edge of the bag and managed to turn the knife over.

"Yes," said the witness, "This is from the hotel kitchen. It has the dot of red lacquer that we use to distinguish meat knives."

"Now," asked the prosecutor, "did you chop chives on the night of January 23?"

"Objection!' called out the defense lawyer. "The witness cannot possibly remember such a picayune detail, if indeed it is relevant in any way."

The judge turned to the prosecutor. "Counsel for the prosecution, can you justify this line of questioning?"

"The relevance of the question will become clear shortly, and the witness will be able to justify his ability to answer the question."

"Objection overruled." The judge looked at Itzik. "You may answer the question."

"Yes, I chopped chives on the night of January 23."

"How do you know?" asked the prosecutor.

"One of the fixed items in the winter menu involves chives, and the other members of the kitchen staff do not chop them fine enough to suit me."

The lawyer for the prosecution turned back to his seat, pulled a large transparent plastic bag out of his briefcase, and held it up high. "I have here a cutting board, a knife similar to the knife submitted as evidence and a bunch of chives. Could you demonstrate for the court exactly how you chop chives?"

The opposing lawyer jumped to his feet, his face red with fury; but before he could register his objection, the judge spoke sternly. "Counsel, this is a court of law, not a lesson in cookery!"

Har-Paz did not seem taken aback by the reproof. "Your honor, one of the main pieces of evidence connecting the defendant to this crime is the presence of the fingerprints of this witness on the knife with which the attack was made. I must demonstrate how they got there."

"Counsel," said the judge, "I believe that you are being unnecessarily theatrical, but I will allow you to proceed for the moment."

On the prosecutor's table, before the judge, the lawyers and the audience, Itzik rolled the knife back and forth over the end of the bunch of chives, cutting them exceedingly fine. He held the knife at the top of the blade between his right thumb and forefinger.

Chaim Ozer's attention had been riveted on Itzik the cook as he demonstrated how his fingerprints had gotten on the knife with which Elisha had been attacked. When the prosecutor turned the witness over for cross-examination, Chaim Ozer looked down at his friend's face and saw that it was twisted in pain.

"This is too much for you," Chaim Ozer declared firmly. "We have to get you back on a bed." He reached down and released the brakes of the wheelchair.

"I'm here under subpoena," Elisha reminded him.

"This is a court of law, not a torture chamber. They can call you when they really need you. I will get you settled somewhere and then come back to talk to the lawyers. At the current pace, they may not need you at all today."

Chaim Ozer wheeled the chair backwards down the aisle and out into the hall. He had just turned the chair around and was about to take it over to the desk of the court clerk when a young lawyer burst through the door of the courtroom. "Wait! Where are you going with that witness?"

"I am trying to find him some place to rest. He has been sitting up for too long already. Tell your boss that I will be back soon, and we can discuss the situation at the next recess."

The court clerk knew of one judge who had a couch in his chambers. He managed to reach him at home and obtain permission to use it.

By the time Chaim Ozer had finished taking care of Elisha and returned to the courtroom, the defense was already cross-examining the next witness, another cook from the Palace Hotel.

"Now, Mr. Biton, you have described in graphic detail the imprecations of my client. Tell me, how do you know Arabic so well?" asked Meir Magen, the lawyer for the defense.

"I lived in Morocco until I was ten."

"During the time you lived in Morocco, did you ever hear anyone make a threat that was not then carried out?"

Biton smiled. "Of course."

"Have you yourself ever made a threat that you did not then carry out?"

Biton's smile broadened. "Of course."

Har-Paz rose to his feet. "I object to this line of questioning."

"Your Honor," said Magen, appealing to the judge, "the prosecution has taken great pains to show that my client made certain threats on the night of January 23. I wish to demonstrate that not every threat is carried out, nor is every threat necessarily made with intent to carry it out."

"You have made your point, Counsel. You need not belabor it."

The defense attorney released the witness with a smile of satisfaction.

The next two witnesses for the prosecution were a medic from

Hatzolah and the doctor who had met the ambulance at the emergency room entrance. After the admitting physician described the wounds in detail, the prosecutor asked, "The wounds in question were inflicted by a third party?"

"Of course," replied the doctor.

"And the position of this third party?"

"He must have been standing behind the victim. I would add that he must have been fairly strong."

"In your opinion, based on your expertise in emergency medicine, were the three wounds inflicted with intent to kill?"

The defendant's lawyer popped to his feet. "I object to that question. The wounds did not, in fact, kill the victim, and I do not see how the witness could know the original intent of the blows."

"Objection sustained," agreed the judge. He turned to the prosecutor. "Counsel, could you rephrase that question?"

The prosecutor tried again. "The highest of the three blows. How far was it from penetrating the heart?"

"About three centimeters," answered the doctor.

The lawyer for the defense began his cross-examination. He tried to minimize the seriousness of each individual wound. "Surely the blow at the spinal cord would not have killed the patient?"

"Any one of the three wounds, if left untreated, would have killed the patient, and the three together nearly did," insisted the doctor. "He arrived at the emergency room with barely any pulse and an extremely low blood pressure."

The judge called a recess for lunch, and the lawyers for the prosecution buzzed around Chaim Ozer like a bunch of angry hornets. "What have you done with my witness?" demanded Har-Paz. "He is the key to the whole case."

"That doctor just explained what that knife did to my friend. He can't sit up for long periods. If you won't need him today, let me take him back to the hospital."

Har-Paz hesitated. "I was going to call Micha the forensic expert and Grisha the detective before him…"

The young lawyer looked distressed. "Gai, suppose the doctors won't let him come back tomorrow?"

That decided it for Har-Paz. "All right, I'll call him immediately after the recess. The others can wait."

Five minutes before the end of the lunch break, Chaim Ozer wheeled Elisha back into the courtroom. Once again everyone else stood as the judge entered the room. Har-Paz remained standing as the others resumed their seats. "Your Honor, I wish to call Elisha Sheinfeld as my next witness."

Chaim Ozer moved Elisha into position next to the witness stand and retired behind the railing again. "Why were you on that street the night of January 23?" asked Har-Paz.

"I was returning to my apartment to pick up my books, my wallet and my umbrella."

"Returning from where?"

"From Mattersdorf, where I had eaten a Shabbos meal with the Wahrhaftig family."

"Describe the weather conditions."

"Very stormy. Rain was falling continually, but gusts of wind made it impossible to use the umbrella."

"You were carrying an umbrella?"

"It was lent to me by my hosts."

"Were there other people on the street?"

"Hardly any. As I drew nearer to my apartment, none at all."

"Did you hear anything unusual?"

"I heard quick footsteps behind me. It was not particularly unusual. Anyone out in that weather would have walked quickly. I was also walking quickly."

"Did you ignore the footsteps?"

"Not exactly. They made me slightly nervous, because the area was so deserted. As they approached quite close, I glanced over my shoulder to see who was coming."

"Over which shoulder?"

"Over my right shoulder."

"Can you demonstrate?"

"I am afraid that it would be too painful."

Har-Paz demonstrated in his place. "When I look over my right shoulder, my left shoulder moves forward. Do you think this happened to you on the night of the twenty-third?"

"Objection!" Magen jumped up. "Counsel is leading the witness."

"Objection sustained," said the judge.

"Your Honor, I am trying to establish that the blow that entered between the sixth and seventh ribs was originally aimed at the heart."

"You can bring an expert witness to prove your point. The witness surely does not remember."

Har-Paz, disgruntled, turned back to Elisha. "When you glanced over your shoulder, what did you see?"

"The face of the accused, very close to me."

"As he looks now?"

"Then his face was contorted in anger or in some other strong emotion."

"Are you certain of the identification?"

"Absolutely positive."

Mrs. Sheinfeld looked around her living room. In some ways it was so familiar, in others, it seemed to belong to a stranger. The thick, wall-to-wall carpet, so impractical for a wheelchair, had been removed, and the short-pile replacement had not yet been laid. Her beloved walnut coffee table had been sent to Minna, and the three over-stuffed couches had been sent to her second daughter. Less space-consuming replacements were on order, but they too had not yet arrived.

The trial was over. Ahmad had been convicted of attempted murder and sentenced to a term in prison. The doctors had agreed that her son could manage the trans-Atlantic flight. Elisha was on his way home.

She walked toward the kitchen. They had considered downsizing the enormous dining room table as well, but in the end had just decided to remove all the leaves during the week. On Shabbos, when the table was opened up, it would be hard for Elisha to get past it into the kitchen, but then he would not be making any meals for himself.

Her kitchen pantry was gone. It had been annexed to the downstairs facilities to provide space for a shower. That had been her first priority as soon as she returned from Israel, and that part of the renovation was complete. The back porch was being glassed in, and she would have a new cabinet there for food storage.

The back steps were very wide, which was just as well, because half the width was now taken up by the ramp. Wheelchair access in the front had been much more difficult to arrange. The front door was close to the sidewalk, and the ramp would have been dangerously steep. They had installed French doors in the room that would now be Elisha's bedroom, and a ramp sloped gently along the front of the house.

"Okay, Mom, the baby has been fed and we're ready to go." Her second-youngest son, Motti, came down the stairs with his *bechor* in a snap-in safety bed. Her daughter-in-law followed with a diaper bag and a baby blanket. Mrs. Sheinfeld had asked them to stay for the first week Elisha was home, assuming that Elisha would probably need his brother's help here and there. Once she knew exactly what was needed, they could try to hire someone.

"Let's go, then. Tatti is coming straight from the office." She had asked the rest of the family to hold off visiting for a day. She was serving dinner tomorrow for all the siblings and their families, with an open house after that for the extended family. Today she wanted to be able to concentrate on getting Elisha settled, and let him get over his jet lag.

When they arrived at the airport, Mr. Sheinfeld was already waiting for them in the arrivals' area. The group stood impatiently behind a shiny metal bar, crowded by people holding signs for travelers not known by sight. After fifteen minutes, the younger Sheinfelds tried to convince their parents to go sit down, but there was no seating in sight of the door, and Mrs. Sheinfeld was not willing to give up being among the first to greet her son.

When she had left Eretz Yisrael to return home, she had been certain that she would soon go back to accompany Elisha. But he had found a *yeshivah bachur* to travel with him and had insisted that her presence was unnecessary. Since the renovations had required constant supervision, Mrs. Sheinfeld had allowed herself to be persuaded.

A boy in a black hat came through the automatic door from Customs, his cart piled almost to his eyes with luggage. Mrs. Sheinfeld recognized some of Elisha's suitcases on the cart and realized that this *bachur* must be helping Elisha. Redcaps were hovering nearby with their wagons, waiting for customers, but the young man didn't seem the type to hire one. Instead, he swung around to face the door that had just swung closed behind him.

Motti ducked under the bar and past the *bachur* with all the luggage. He got to the automatic door just as it opened and Elisha came through, propelling himself forward by pushing the circular metal handles that ran around the wheels of the chair.

Motti caught on before I did, thought Mrs. Sheinfeld ruefully. Motti wrung his brother's hand and kissed his cheek. Then he took hold of the chair's handles and propelled it toward his parents. Posts embedded in the floor stopped the wheelchair — as it stopped the luggage carts, but Motti and the other boy simply picked it up and lifted it over the posts, while Elisha held tight to the chair's arms.

Mrs. Sheinfeld could not see her son in the wheelchair without tears coursing down her cheeks. So many other memories of Elisha flashed through her mind. Happier memories of him as a two-year-old, his hair still uncut, chasing a butterfly; as a seven-year-old crossing from one end of the monkey bars to the other and crowing at his accomplishment; as an eleven-year-old, winning a race against his brother. She dashed away the tears and strained for a smile.

After Elisha greeted his mother and father, his sister-in-law handed him his new nephew. "I missed your *bris*, didn't I, big boy?" said Elisha, chucking the newest Sheinfeld under the chin. "You'll have to forgive me. It really wasn't my fault."

Mr. Sheinfeld called over a redcap and they off-loaded the luggage from the cart onto the wagon. Mr. Sheinfeld and Motti went to bring the cars around. "Yanky, who helped me travel, is from Monsey," Elisha explained. "You told me you'd have two cars at the airport, so we arranged that his father would pick him and his bags up from our house in a couple of hours, when he finishes work in the city."

Mrs. Sheinfeld was annoyed that her plan of a quiet homecoming for Elisha was spoiled, but she pushed the feeling aside. This Yanky had done a big favor for Elisha and for her as well, saving her from two exhausting plane flights. It wouldn't hurt her to feed him supper, despite her premonition that with Elisha back home things were not always going to go quite as she had planned them.

When they reached the Sheinfeld home, Elisha wheeled himself around the house, commenting on the renovations and all the effort that had gone into making the ground floor wheelchair accessible. "This is pretty impressive, Mom. You did all this in three months?"

"It's not finished yet, of course. I rushed with the most important things. I'm planning eventually to have some living room furniture." She looked around at the bare room and shrugged. The family would have to sit around the dining room table tomorrow. "What can I give you and Yanky to eat?"

"I'm really not hungry now," said Elisha, "but Yanky might be interested."

Shortly after Yanky's father picked up his son, Motti vanished upstairs to help his wife bathe the baby, a job she was still afraid to tackle alone. "Elisha, as soon as you want help getting settled in bed, just holler. We'll take the baby out and I'll be right down."

Elisha and his parents were left sitting at the table together. "Tatti, Mom, there's something I want you to start thinking about."

The elder Sheinfelds looked at each other. "What?" asked Mr. Sheinfeld.

"*Shidduchim.*"

"*Shidduchim*?!" Mrs. Sheinfeld was astonished.

"*Shidduchim,*" Elisha reaffirmed.

"Isn't it a little early to start thinking about a *shidduch*?" objected Mr. Sheinfeld. "You can't even sit up comfortably for two hours at a stretch."

"I didn't mean that it was time to start. I just want you both to begin thinking in that direction. I'm twenty-two now, almost twenty-three, and we had originally planned that I would begin this summer, when I got back from the Mir."

"A lot has happened since we made those plans," said his father with a sigh.

"I know that a lot has happened, Tatti, but because I've regressed physically doesn't mean that I'm emotionally less mature than I was." Elisha looked and sounded very earnest.

"Of course not," agreed Mrs. Sheinfeld. "We're glad that you mentioned the matter." A *shidduch*? Where would they look? How would they find the right girl?

"Of course, it will be difficult," admitted Elisha. "I know that. The *shadchanim* you used for my brothers and sisters may not be any help at all. You may have to find a new list of contacts. That's why I wanted to give you plenty of time to look around. From what the doctors told me in Israel, it will be at least six months before I'll be able to propel myself in the chair for hours at a stretch. My back has to heal more before I can use my shoulder muscles that much. Also, have you given any thought to my driving?"

Mr. and Mrs. Sheinfeld looked at each other again. "Not yet. You seem to be ahead of us on a lot of things."

"It's just that until I can drive, I'll probably be wasting a lot of Mom's time *shlepping* me to and from therapy sessions."

"I was planning to hire a man to do it," said Mrs. Sheinfeld. "He can help you with getting dressed, too. We'll try to concentrate as much of the traveling as possible into the morning hours, or something like that."

"In the long run, I'd rather be more independent than that."

"Let's take the same six months," suggested Mr. Sheinfeld. "We'll have this helper for six months, and try to get you organized to drive by the end of it. Do you know anything about what's involved?"

"Well, obviously, I need hand controls for accelerating and braking. As for the wheelchair, the social worker in the hospital showed me a couple of options. Here they convert a van with a ramp. In Israel they make a device that stores the chair on the roof."

"We're lucky we're not poor," said Mr. Sheinfeld. "This rehabilitation business costs a bundle."

"Maybe, now that we know, we should include some rehabilitation organizations on our *tzedakah* list," proposed Mrs. Sheinfeld.

"When can we get started with the rehabilitation programs?" asked Elisha.

"Not until after Shabbos," said his mother. "Everyone and his brother is coming over tomorrow to see you, and we also have a big Shabbos planned. I want to go with you to your first appointments with the doctors and hear exactly what they say, in what tone of voice."

"So we'll get started early Sunday morning?"

Mr. Sheinfeld laughed. "You've been living in Israel too long. You can get started early Monday morning."

"Then tomorrow I should try to set up appointments."

"Okay," agreed Mrs. Sheinfeld.

"Now, about a career," continued Elisha.

"Yes?" asked his father a little warily. It was becoming clear to both of Elisha's parents that leaving their son by himself in the hospital for three months had led to a divergence in thinking between the three of them.

"I'm hoping to continue in *chinuch*, just as I always planned."

"Wouldn't computers or accounting be more practical? In either of those professions you wouldn't be at any disadvantage." Mr. Sheinfeld was an accountant, and had rather hoped that one of his sons would join the firm at some stage. So far none of them had shown any interest, but he had thought that this might be an opportunity.

"I would rather work with people," said Elisha. "I'd rather be shaping people. By comparison, pushing numbers around seems much less meaningful."

Less meaningful, perhaps, but it paid better. Mrs. Sheinfeld chased the thought away. They had plenty of money set aside. Elisha had lost a great deal that gave his life meaning; they could afford to let him choose a less lucrative career.

"I can no longer teach young children. I'll have to plan to work with older boys, and for that I'll have to stay in learning for quite a while. As soon as I can sit up for three or four hours at a time, I want to try to set up a learning schedule."

"I'll do everything possible to help, *tzaddik*," said Mr. Sheinfeld. "Maybe we can do some learning together on Sundays. Even now. We'll get something to hold the *Gemara* at an angle that will allow you read without strain."

"I'd like that, Tatti," said Elisha, a little shyly.

Motti came clattering down the stairs. "The baby's bath is finished. Our offspring is sparkling clean, and will soon be reintroduced into society in yet another stunning outfit. Have I missed anything?"

"Missed anything?" said his father, with a yawn and a stretch. "Hardly. We only discussed Elisha's driving, his rehabilitation, his career, and his learning." He left out the *shidduch*, which was a more private matter.

"Wow, sounds like you've been talking a mile a minute. Should I leave? Is there some subject still to be covered?"

"Not really," said Elisha. "I think we've covered everything that's relevant at the moment." He looked down at his hands, which were folded in front of him, and pursed his lips.

Mrs. Sheinfeld's instincts as a mother screamed out that another issue was on Elisha's mind. "You know, Motti, I think that there *is* a little bit more. Could you give us another ten minutes, just to round off the discussion?"

"Sure, fine by me." He took the steps again, two at a time.

Mrs. Sheinfeld turned to Elisha. "What else is there? This issue that's not so relevant at this time?"

"You and Tatti seemed a little startled by some of my ideas. Maybe this is not the moment for anything else."

"Tatti and I were a little startled because we were unprepared, because we haven't had much chance to talk. If there is more coming, we would like a warning."

Her son did not seem enthusiastic about this invitation to talk further. He began slowly. "After a couple of years of rehabilitation, for the learning, maybe for a job…" Elisha paused and took a deep breath, then rushed forward, "I was thinking about moving to Eretz Yisrael."

"No," said Mrs. Sheinfeld, crackling with anger. "No, no, no, no, no! A *shidduch,* yes; driving, okay; learning, of course; a career in *chinuch,* if that is where your heart is. But you are *not* moving to Eretz Yisrael."

Elisha woke up very early the next morning. There was no light coming in through the cracks in the shutters, but a few birds were singing. Dawn could not be far off. He stared up through the darkness at the ceiling. Where had he gone wrong yesterday? Was it that he had spurted out too many new ideas at once? Should he have mentioned the *shidduch* but not the driving? The driving but not the *shidduch*? Should he have put the whole discussion off until he had more of an idea of how his parents had envisioned his future? That was probably the answer. All right, it had been a mistake, but the mistake had been made. Now he would have to live with it.

Elisha stirred uncomfortably. His parents had gotten him a hospital bed, so he could adjust the angle at which he was lying. When the controls had been explained to him, he had been too tired to pay close enough attention. Now he wanted to raise the head of the bed a bit, and he thought it might have something to do with a button or lever over on the left side. He felt along the bed frame until he found a button and pressed it. The bottom of the bed shot upwards, raising his feet above the level of his head. This didn't bother his feet, which he couldn't feel anyway, but it sent a lot of blood to his head.

What should he do? Continue experimenting? Suppose he did and the bed folded up like a sandwich? That wouldn't be very good for his injured back. He would have to put up with the extra blood in his head until a family member woke up and came downstairs. Maybe lying in this position would help him think.

It was clear that not all his plans were equally acceptable to his parents. In particular, it seemed that he would have to give up the idea of living in Eretz Yisrael. Well, *nisht azoi gefehrlich*. Until the attack, he had always assumed that he would spend his entire life in the States. Life probably would be easier with his whole extended family as a safety net.

What else did he have to do so he'd be pulling together with his parents rather than against them? The rehabilitation part was fine. They all agreed that they wanted to get started right away and do the maximum to rebuild his strength and his abilities. As for his desire to be as independent as possible as soon as possible, he would have to tone it down. He'd have to put up with this driver they were going to hire to take him around from place to place, and be thankful for the luxury, glad that he wouldn't be at the mercy of taxi drivers of uncertain temper.

His father, who always got up early because he had a *shiur* before *davening*, came down the stairs and walked over to the door of Elisha's room to look in on him.

"Good morning!"

"Tatti?"

"Yes, *tzaddik*? Can I do something for you?"

"Could you adjust this bed? I was trying to raise the head and I lifted the foot instead."

"All right, let me see." Mr. Sheinfeld pulled over a chair, sat down, and studied the controls. He pressed something that at first started to raise the foot of the bed yet higher, but then managed to reverse it. Then he got the head raised just as Elisha wanted it.

"Thanks, Tatti."

"Need anything else?"

"Not at the moment."

"I heard Motti's alarm going off, so he may be down soon."

"Why did he set it so early?" Elisha asked.

"No, I didn't mean a mechanical alarm clock. I meant my new grandson."

Mr. Sheinfeld went to get his *tallis* and *tefillin*, and Elisha relaxed back into the mattress and began thinking. Take this bed. How had he gotten into trouble? First of all, he had been too tired, and perhaps too upset about the disagreement to listen carefully when the system had been explained. Second, he had been impetuous this morning about using controls he didn't understand. Motti could still afford to be impetuous. He could decide where he wanted to go, and dash off to get there as soon as possible. If there were some error, he would backtrack a little and try again. Elisha would have to foreswear impetuosity. He would have to consider every step, every move beforehand. It wouldn't be easy.

Motti did, indeed, show up soon, and he helped Elisha get dressed and ready for shul. Soon he was in the wheelchair, holding his *tefillin*, and Motti was pushing him down the ramp. Many of the geraniums and sweet peas in his mother's flower garden had survived the ravages of construction. He drew a deep breath of cool, scented air.

"Could you tell the *gabbai* that I have to *bentch gomel* for the plane flight?" requested Elisha as they approached the shul. It was Thursday, so there would be a Torah reading.

"Sure. You already *bentched gomel* for surviving the attack?"

"Yes, in the first hospital, the one where I had the operation. They have a *minyan* on Shabbos, and someone took me down as soon as I was up to it."

"What about a *seudas hodaah*?" asked Motti.

"Nope, haven't had a chance yet," said Elisha, shaking his head.

Motti paused a moment, deep in thought. "You know, we'll have eight men at this dinner Mom is making this evening. If we invite Uncle Meir and one or two of our Lerner cousins, we could turn it into a *seudas hodaah*."

"It's a good plan," Elisha said, "except that I don't feel like springing any new ideas on Mom at the moment, particularly any new ideas that are going to mean extra work for her. Why don't you mention the plan casually, and if she doesn't seem enthusiastic, just drop it?"

"Will do."

The shul had no ramp, so Motti had to bump the wheelchair up three steps. Because it was his parents' shul, everyone knew him; so Elisha was hard pressed to get his *tefillin* on and recite the *Birkas Hashachar*, because people kept coming over to shake his hand and welcome him back.

"We've been *davening* for you, buddy," said one of his father's friends. "We thought of you every day."

It felt good to be *davening* with a *minyan* again, very good. His own prayers, limp as they might be, were lifted up with those of the congregation, and Hashem was waiting for them.

When he reached *Shema Koleinu*, he paused. Hashem was listening. For what did he want to ask? To regain his health and strength, as much as could be expected. For a wife, an *ezer kenegdo*, who would be his partner in building their future. For a livelihood, a *parnassah bekavod*. For children, *zera shel kayama*, who would link his future to that of his people, just as his past was so strongly linked with their past.

On the way back home, he asked Motti to make a slight detour and take him past a small park. "I like looking at the trees and flowers."

"You know, Shaindy's parents have invited us up to their bungalow colony next week. Maybe we could take you as well. It's right near our old camp. It's a long drive, but we could recline the front seat as far as it goes, the way you managed on the plane."

Elisha didn't even have to think twice. "I couldn't do that to Mom. I'm sure she has the next three Shabbosos all planned out. If there is another opportunity later in the summer, you can run it by her."

In fact, Mrs. Sheinfeld took immediately to Motti's suggestion that they turn the family dinner into a *seudas hodaah*. She told him that it was a stroke of genius, and got straight on the phone to the Lerners. The rest of the morning was spent arranging for more food, as well as getting extra tables and benches from a *gemach*.

"It compensates for not having furniture," said his mother happily. "I don't have to worry about moving it. I also won't have to worry about the children spilling juice on the rug, since I don't have a rug."

When the family was gathered together and everyone had had a chance to say a word to Elisha, they washed and sat down to eat.

Elisha, who wasn't sure how long he could sit in the wheelchair, spoke first, on the topic of *Birkas Hashachar* and the many gifts we have from Hashem.

"I am thankful that I can still draw breath. I am thankful for my mind, for my sight, for my hearing, for my hands, for my family." He paused and looked around. "And I am thankful for the gift of thankfulness, which enriches my life in so many ways."

Chapter 9

Least Likely Pioneer

T he date of Mimi and Benny's departure for Israel was fast
approaching.

Mimi pawed frantically through the pile of lists lying
before her on the desk. She was sure she had made a list of medical records that they were supposed to take with them, and she
absolutely could not find it. The pediatrician's secretary was
already putting her through to the doctor herself. Would she have
to apologize and say that she would call back later?

Be calm, Mimi, she told herself. You, yourself, made up that list
in the first place. What was on it? Birth weights, childhood dis-
eases and ... and ... ah, dates of vaccinations. She turned over one
of the pages in order to write this down, and there was the list of
medical records for which she had been searching.

When she had finished making her request of the doctor, she
pushed back her chair, wondering again if she had taken on more
than she could manage. Back when she had been resisting the
whole idea of the move, she had been thinking about living in a
strange environment, far from her family. She hadn't spared a
thought for the difficulties of packing and shopping. She seemed
to be drowning in details, never-ending details. If just packing was
this hard, what else had she forgotten to consider?

Mimi thumbed through the pile of lists again, pulling out the pages of things to buy. She had been writing down items haphazardly as she had thought of them, but it was time to organize the list by type of store, and to begin the actual buying. She made columns for the grocery, the pharmacy, the hardware store, the electrical appliance store, the clothing stores. With certain hesitations, she began transferring items from the old list to the new one.

When she got to twenty packages each of diapers and toilet paper, she stopped. She had written that down because a friend had told her that they were much more expensive in Israel, and were good for stuffing around bulky items in the lift. As she tried to think where she would store twenty packages of diapers until the movers came to take their possessions for the lift, she realized that storage would also be a problem at the other end. Did she want a house filled with packages of diapers and rolls of toilet paper? Wouldn't it be better to pay a bit more and let the grocery store worry about storing them for her? As a compromise, she put down five packages of each, and added the price of paper goods to her list of questions to ask Ella.

Mimi heard Tami babbling to herself in the next room as she awoke from her nap. Since she hadn't quite finished transferring all the items from one list to the other, she clipped both lists together and went to get the children.

She had just picked up Tami and soothed her into a pleasant gurgle when the phone rang. Leaving Shimmy still sleeping in his bed, she and Tami went to her bedroom to answer it.

"Hello, Mimi? This is Sheindy."

"Oh, Sheindy. How are you? I don't think we've spoken since Pesach."

"Could be. I have to admit that this is not merely a social call. I've been roped into organizing the fund-raising bazaar in the fall for P'tach, and I'm lining up people who can help me. I remember that you did some of the decorations last year for the same affair."

"That's right, I did but ... I mean ... you see, we're supposed to be moving to Eretz Yisrael at the end of the summer."

"Mimi, you're joking."

"No, I am perfectly serious. Benny has gotten a job offer that he likes, and he has already given notice at his job here."

"But ... what will you wear there? What will you eat? Visiting

Israelis all go on spending sprees as soon as they get here. And daily life there is so primitive. No dishwasher, no dryer, no car. I find it hard to picture you managing."

"If Israelis and other Americans can manage, then I imagine that I can," said Mimi, a little tartly.

"But how well do they manage? Think of all the Israelis who have moved to the States, or all the Americans who have given up and come back!"

"I'd rather think of all the Americans who have stayed, of whom there are plenty."

"I bet they're mostly out-of-towners who are used to a simpler life style? I had a friend who moved out-of-town, and she told me that sometimes she wore clothing for Shabbos that would barely be acceptable on a weekday in Boro Park. She was almost proud of it."

Mimi thought that said more about Sheindy's friend's social circle than about the general standards of Boro Park. Although Mimi and her own mother did tend to dress up a bit to go out shopping, surely her mother-in-law's weekday attire was distinctly casual. "Maybe it's not such an awful thing to get used to a simpler lifestyle."

"Sure, if you can do it. But can you?"

There it was again. "Mimi Lerner" seemed to be written at the head of everyone's list of "least likely pioneers."

When Benny got home from work, Mimi handed him a sheaf of papers.

"On top of this pile is a list of medical records you should get from your doctor, and also you're supposed to have a reserve pair of glasses."

"Why?" asked Benny.

"Because if your glasses break just after you arrive, that isn't the moment when you want to have to start looking for a good optometrist."

Benny picked up the stack of lists and started thumbing through it. "Why do we need twenty-five packages of diapers and twenty-five packages of toilet paper?" he asked. "Are you counting on us all getting dysentery?"

"If you look more closely," said Mimi calmly, "you'll realize that you're holding two different versions of the same list."

"True," said Benny. "Well, that reduces the number of jars of peanut butter from forty-eight to twenty-four. Why do we need twenty-four jars of peanut butter?"

"They tell me that Israeli peanut butter is not emulsified, and that Americans in Israel are always asking friends to bring them peanut butter from the States."

"They probably make the Israeli stuff by some primitive process like grinding up peanuts. Why all the cans of tuna? I remember that I was given American tuna fish at the Wahrhaftigs' house, so it must be available in the stores. "

"Packed in oil?"

"Oh, it was definitely packed in oil," Benny assured her.

Mimi unstrapped the children from their car seats and set Shimmy on the sidewalk. Her mother-in-law had volunteered to baby-sit while she did some clothes shopping. Mimi found it hard to try things on when she had the two children with her. "Do you know what Savta told me? She's going to let you help her bake cookies for Shabbos. Do you like Savta's cookies?"

"Yes!" nodded Shimmy.

"She'll put Tami in the high chair so that she can watch. You can stand on a chair and help."

"I put in flour. And sugar."

"Right. Whatever Savta tells you to pour in."

"Not salt."

"True. Only Savta puts in the salt." During his last "cooking les-son" at the Lerners' house, Shimmy had enthusiastically poured half a cup of salt into the bowl. Her unflappable mother-in-law had managed to rescue most of the dough without scolding him, but she had made a new rule that salt was out-of-bounds. Mimi sighed. Another thing she would miss in Israel was having two grandmothers as cheerful baby-sitters. She rang the doorbell.

"Ooh, here is one of my favorite helpers," Mrs. Lerner greeted them, picking up Shimmy and giving him a kiss, which he returned. Then she set him down, accepted Tami, and began to lead Shimmy into the house. "Come straight into the kitchen and I'll show you what we're going to do today." She gave Mimi a nod and a smile over her shoulder, apparently feeling that a formal goodbye might make the children decide to cling. Mimi returned to her car.

An hour and a half later she was back, sitting in the kitchen "trying out" one of "Shimmy's" cookies and showing her purchases to her mother-in-law. "I wish I had paid more attention to what kind of clothes Israelis consider practical when I was living there. Ella is always urging me to 'go native' and make do with whatever is available locally, but if I have to meet a lot of strangers, I want to feel comfortable with the way I look."

"That's reasonable," agreed her mother-in-law.

Encouraged by the mild answer, Mimi shared more of her concerns. "I'm constantly having to make decisions with too little information, while bombarded with contradictory advice. My friends here are telling me to buy out half the stores in New York and load up a freighter with the merchandise, while Ella doesn't seem to think that we need to bring much more than ourselves."

"Listen, Mimi, I can almost guarantee you that some things you stocked up on will turn out to be cheaper there, and some things that cost pennies here you will never think of. It doesn't matter."

Mimi took exception to this. "Shouldn't one try to get the best value for one's money?"

"That's like always trying to run one's errands so that one doesn't have to backtrack. The effort to be maximally efficient also has a price in time and energy, and the heaviest price of all is one that is rarely felt. Who are the people who really can plan out their shopping and their errand-running so that there are no mistakes and there is no duplicated effort?"

"I can't tell you. I don't know any such people."

"People who are very conservative and live very much by routine. By the time someone does exactly the same thing fifty or a hundred times, he has probably figured out the best way to do it, and may be very annoyed by the suggestion of even trivial changes. Most of us, as you point out, prefer to be more flexible."

"The mothers among us have to be," said Mimi.

"Exactly. I wasn't accusing you of perfectionism or stodginess, dear. I was only trying to say that the quest for perfection works against the spirit of adventure in ways that we don't always consciously feel."

Mimi thought that one over. "Should I just chuck my lists into the waste-basket?"

"Not at all. I'm sure your lists help keep you sane, because you don't have to hold everything in your head. I just think you should add two more items to the list of things going in your hand luggage, not in the lift." Mrs. Lerner hesitated.

"What items?"

"I'm a little concerned that I may have already gone over my monthly budget of advice, which for modern mothers-in-law is very tight."

"Since we won't be here in September, I'll let you borrow on that. Go ahead."

"What I thought you would need is a sense of humor and a sense of proportion."

The sense of humor Mimi had already known about. The sense of proportion? That was a good way to describe what she felt she had been lacking for the last few weeks. "Thanks. That's good advice. In fact, this is probably the most helpful conversation I've had in the last month or so. Mom, I'm going to miss you terribly." She reached out and squeezed her mother-in-law's hand.

It was not accidental that Mrs. Lerner had praised being adventuresome. What she had always admired in Benny's family was exactly their spirit of adventure, and their willingness to do things for others, even though it would interfere with the smooth flow of their daily lives. Even though Benny's spirit of adventure had now turned their personal life into white water rapids, she still admired it.

Mrs. Lerner laid her other hand on top of Mimi's. "We'll miss you too, dear. We're proud to have you in the family."

Mimi, despite the emotionality of the moment, felt a little glow of satisfaction. She had never been quite sure on that point.

Two days before they were to leave, Benny was ready to drop from exhaustion. Mimi had been well-organized, but a lot of the things that only he could do, like sorting his personal papers, had been left until he had finished off at work three days ago. Then there had been all the complications of selling the car, a project that they had put off so that they would have it available for running errands.

He had just gone for a short nap when the phone rang.

"Benny?" It was his older brother Tzvi.

"Yeah?" answered Benny with a yawn.

"Have you been listening to the news?"

"No, it hasn't interested me at all."

"Well, it is going to interest you now. The Israeli government is restructuring its whole relationship with the Palestinians. I think you should reconsider whether this is the time to move there."

"Tzvi, we gave up the lease on this apartment, I quit my job, and our things are all packed. If we don't get on that plane in two days, we will be out on the street and destitute. For us, it's now or never."

"Couldn't you at least postpone the trip for a few days until the details are released? The family would take you in for that long."

"In all the news you've heard, was there any hint that the PLO might be occupying Mevasseret Tzion in the near future?"

"No."

"Then we're taking off as scheduled."

Benny was helping the car service driver unload the bags from the back of the station wagon. Everyone in both families was planning to come see them off, so all the cars were full. Their own car had been delivered to its new owners yesterday.

"One, two, three, four ..." He heard Mimi counting the suitcases and carry-ons. There had been thirteen pieces, counting Tami's stroller.

"...eleven, twelve! Benny, something is missing. Have you got the things that were on the floor in the back of the station wagon?"

Benny checked again and saw nothing there. "Did you count the stroller?"

"Yes, definitely. I started with that." She began again. "One, two, ..."

"How about your own purse?"

"Ah, that's it. Thank you." Mimi finished her recount just to make sure, while Benny paid the taxi driver and tipped him generously.

"Have a nice vacation!" called the driver as he climbed back into his vehicle.

"Thanks!" said Benny. He still felt uncomfortable admitting to fellow Americans that he was moving away permanently. Somewhere in the direction of the parking lots there was a flagpole with a large American flag flapping vigorously in the wind. The Fourth of July had hit Benny harder than usual this year. He had actually gone out to watch a parade with marching bands, and had gotten a little misty-eyed when they had struck up the "Star-Spangled Banner." He shook off the mood and turned to his family. "I'm going to find a redcap."

"I can come, Abba?" asked Shimmy.

"Sure, Shimmy. Just keep tight hold of my hand. This is a big place."

Benny set off on his search, grumbling to himself about the fact that one of the largest airports in the world was one of the few that did not provide curbside luggage carts. The redcap would get them in, but they would have to shepherd all thirteen items down the long line to the security check without the benefit of wheels.

The first members of their family arrived when they were halfway down the security line. It was Mimi's oldest sister, Malka, with her husband, Mendel, and four of their seven children. "My, what a lot of luggage!" she commented.

"Benny, Shimmy and I each get two carry-ons," said Mimi, "and we brought as much as we could. We're supposed to live out of this for two or three months."

"What are you going to eat off and cook with? You can't have two sets of dishes and pots in there."

"Ella has promised me the pots and dishes she used before their lift arrived with their wedding presents. She and Chaim Ozer are coming out to the immigrants' hostel to bring them to us."

"You know what you should do right now? You should count all the bags, and then count them again every time you move from one place to another."

"I counted them before I left the house, Malka, and I have counted them twice since then."

Tzvi, one of Benny's brothers, arrived next, with his wife, Channah, and three of their six children. "Well, old boy," he said, clapping Benny on the back, "I see that you're going through with it. I didn't think you would."

"Benny," interrupted Mimi urgently, "Where is Shimmy?"

Benny looked down, then to the right and the left. "Shimmy!" he called. "Shimmy, where are you?" There was no answer.

"He was standing right between the two of you when I arrived,"

Malka piped up. "Which of you was supposed to be watching him?"

"I was," said Benny grimly, though he could hardly see how that was relevant to the current emergency. He rotated slowly, scanning the huge hall with his eyes. Shimmy was so short that even a tall pile of luggage would hide him from view.

"Kids," said Tzvi, addressing all Shimmy's cousins, "Fan out and look for him."

"If you see a stranger holding him, scream for the police," added Malka.

"Channah and I will go to the right. Mendel, you and Malka go to the left. Benny, you stay here and calm Mimi."

"Mimi will be much calmer if her husband is also looking for her son," Benny said. "I'm going to the information desk to have them announce a missing child, and then to airport security." He set off briskly for the information desk, his eyes darting around constantly in search of Shimmy. He caught sight of Malka's oldest daughter, Sarah, walking purposefully toward the security line, and there, clutching her hand, was his son.

Changing direction, he intercepted them. He picked up Shimmy and gave him a hug, then turned around and waved to Mimi. "Where did you find him? Was he crying?"

"I didn't have to find him anywhere. He wasn't lost."

"Well, where was he?"

"Just after we got here, I took him to the souvenir stand to buy him a present. I wanted him to pick it out."

"No real harm done, but next time you take Shimmy somewhere you should tell us. We were very worried." Not that there was likely to be a "next time" for quite a while.

"See, Abba?" Shimmy held up his gift, a key chain with a plastic tag shaped like the American flag. "I can have a key?"

"Don't know," said Benny doubtfully. He pulled his own nearly empty key chain out of his pocket. He had given the office keys to his boss, the car keys to the buyer, and the apartment keys to his landlord. There were four luggage keys that he needed, and one more whose provenance he hadn't been able to remember, and which he had therefore been afraid to throw away. He surely wouldn't need it any more, whatever it was. He pulled it off his own key chain and attached it to Shimmy's.

Shimmy held up the dangling key and admired it with shining eyes. "Thanks, Abba!" He turned to show it to Mimi.

By this time both sets of parents had arrived, and the travelers behind the Lerners were getting annoyed at the big bulge in the middle of the line. After Benny had intercepted a few poisonous looks and guessed what they meant, he whispered to his wife, "Mimi, take the two children and all the family off to the side there." He pointed to a row of empty chairs. "When you see that I'm up to the security check, come join me with the children."

"All right, just let me count the bags again before I go. One, two, …"

Mimi and Mrs. Adler sat side by side, with the rest of the family members speaking over their heads. Mimi had her arm around her mother's shoulders, and Mrs. Adler was holding one of Mimi's hands between hers.

"You *will* try to write, won't you?"

"Yes, of course, Mama."

"And you'll send us pictures of the *eineklach*."

"That may be a little hard, Mama. I accidentally packed the camera among our things in the lift. Maybe Ella will have a camera."

"Maybe for special occasions you will call. Or we can call you," suggested Mrs. Adler.

"All that's going to be hard until we have our own apartment and our own phone, but I hope that will be very soon. And you will come visit us, won't you?"

Mrs. Adler, with a slight sob, searched in her purse for a handkerchief.

Two hours later, all the tearful farewells behind them, they were arranging themselves and their bundles on the plane. Mimi was counting the bags, subtracting six for the suitcases that had been checked. "You know," said Benny, "it can't have escaped your attention that some members of our family treat us as if we have not yet reached adulthood."

"Not our parents."

"No, not our parents, but you know what I mean, and I wonder if we're not partly to blame."

"Why?"

"Because we're still using our childhood nicknames. Tzvi used to be Tzviki, but no one calls him that anymore."

"No one says Malky or Leiki either," admitted Mimi.

"Right now we have a wonderful chance to change what people call us. You know, *ba'alei teshuvah* often start using their Hebrew names when they become *frum*. Well, our Hebrew and English names are more or less the same, but we could start calling ourselves Binyamin and Miriam."

"It won't be easy to remember."

"No, it won't, but I really think people will treat us with more dignity. My father tells me that Kennedy used to be called "Jack" in newspaper headlines, but once he became president-elect he asked the newsmen to use "JFK" instead. Tatti said it was like magic. Everyone immediately began taking him more seriously."

"I'll try," promised Mimi.

After fourteen hours of fighting unusual head winds, their plane landed at Ben-Gurion Airport. It was the first time either of the children had flown, and they had been pretty squirmy. Mimi counted the luggage. "Ben— uh, Binyamin, we're missing a bag."

"The stewardess has to bring us Tami's stroller."

The wait for the stroller, and the fact that they didn't want to be separated, meant that they were almost the last to deplane. Mimi went first with Tami, and Benny followed, carrying Shimmy. As Benny set the boy down, he bent a little farther and pressed his hand to the tarmac. Then he raised his fingers unobtrusively to his lips and kissed them. That was the best he could do.

After counting the bags three more times, with a long immigration procedure in the middle, they were finally in line for a taxi to Yerushalayim. When their turn came, the dispatcher handed them a slip of paper with a price and indicated which taxi to take. The driver quickly began stowing the suitcases in the trunk, interfering with Mimi's third attempt to count them. "A lot of luggage here," he commented, without looking up.

"We're going to the immigrants' hostel in Mevasseret. We just made *aliyah*," explained Benny proudly.

The taxi driver straightened up and stared at him. "Two-thirds of the population of the world wants to move to America, and you came here from America?!"

"Yes," said Benny, feeling put down.

"You work?"

"I'm a computer programmer."

"Do you realize that you can make $60,000 a year in America? Who knows? If you are really good maybe you can work your way up to $100,000 a year."

"But in Eretz Yisrael there is more *kedushah*. That's what we came for. We know that we'll have to make do with less financially."

"But $60,000 a year is $5,000 a month!" He shrugged and climbed into the driver's seat, muttering under his breath, "Some people just don't catch on."

As they entered She'ar HaGai, Benny began pointing out the sights to Shimmy. Shoresh, Beit Meir, Telz-Stone, and finally the Castel interchange where the taxi sped up the ramp and crossed the bridge.

"And here is Mevasseret Tzion!" said Benny proudly, as if he had built the town himself.

"Long name," said Shimmy, with a note of disapproval.

"I know it's from the *Tanach*, and I know it has something to do with good news," said Mimi.

"It's from *Yeshayahu* and it's usually translated as 'glad tidings of Zion,'" Benny explained. "It's one of the last big towns before Yerushalayim proper."

The taxi driver helped Benny carry all the luggage into a small building that served as the office of the immigrants' hostel. Mimi counted the bags again while Benny paid the driver. "Have an easy absorption!" Benny hadn't been embarrassed to tell the Israeli taxi driver that he was coming to settle, though in fact the driver had reacted as if he were slightly unbalanced to want to leave the *goldene medinah*.

"...eleven, twelve, thirteen," finished Mimi. She looked up at Benny. "I think that from now on, the way other people count imaginary sheep to fall asleep, I will count imaginary pieces of luggage."

Benny walked up to the desk to check in. "Excuse me," he said in Hebrew, "I believe we have an apartment reserved here. Ben—I mean, Binyamin and Miriam Lerner."

The man looked down his list. "Dunno. Don't see anything here." He called into the inner office. "Hey, Dudi, you have anything for 'Lerner'?"

Benny and Mimi looked at each other nervously. What would

they do if there had been a mix-up and there was no room for them? Go to a hotel? Crash with the Wahrhaftigs?

"Rafi, it's okay. I've got it here. Lerner, starting today. Two kids, right?"

"Right."

"They've got one of the apartments with the yard in back. Number seventeen."

Rafi took the key to number seventeen out of the cabinet behind him and handed it to Benny. Then he looked over at Mimi, holding the two children, as she stood surrounded by their luggage. He called to a tall young man with short-cropped blond hair walking past the desk. "Hey, Yevgenie. Come do a *mitzvah*. Help Bibi and Miri here get all this luggage over to number seventeen."

Benny and Mimi looked at each other and burst into laughter with an edge of hysteria in it.

Ella looked out the window of the Mevasseret Tzion bus, which was just passing through the valley at Motza. A welcome breath of cool air struck her face. It reminded her of the first few months of her marriage, when she had taken this ride every afternoon on her way home from work. She and her husband had decided not to waste time and money on renting, but to remain patiently in the low-rent immigrants' hostel until they could move into an apartment of their own. She thought now that that might have been a mistake. Although she was not dissatisfied with their apartment, she might have done better if they had been living in the community where they were planning to buy. She would advise Mimi to rent for a year.

The bus went into low gear and began grinding up the long slope to Mevasseret. Ella glanced at Chaim Ozer to see if he was available for conversation or absorbed in something else. He turned to her and asked with a smile, "Brings back memories?"

Ella smiled in return, "It sure does." She dropped her gaze and then looked out the window again, a little embarrassed by the direction of those memories. She had been so proud of her husband! She was newly married to Chaim Ozer Wahrhaftig, who had been known as a prodigy since he was three. As she had ridden home every afternoon, she had been filled with good resolves for how she would protect him from the mundane distractions of day-to-day life and allow him to devote every possible moment to Torah study.

Not that she was even a bit less proud of him now. His reputation as an *ilui* had stood up to the stiffer competition in Israel. He was everything she thought a Torah scholar should be. It was just... She was no longer a new bride. She had other responsibilities as well, to their children, to her school. Did she still protect him as much as she ought? It had seemed to her unnecessary for him to accompany her on this trip to welcome the Lerners, but he had insisted that it was important for him to come.

When the bus stopped near the hostel, Chaim Ozer unloaded the boxes of dishes and pots from underneath the vehicle. He took the food she had brought and one of the boxes, while Ella hefted the other box. They stopped at the desk to get the unit number.

"Lerner? Bibi and Miri, right? They arrived an hour ago with two kids and a thousand pieces of luggage. You'll find them in seventeen, out that way." He pointed to one of the doors.

Ella and Chaim Ozer looked at each other when they were out of the manager's sight. "Bibi and Miri?" she asked in wonder.

"It does sound odd," agreed Chaim Ozer. "I suggest a policy of waiting and watching. We'll see what they call each other."

"Of course, they may call each other 'Abba' and 'Ima' the way we do."

They heard voices from inside number seventeen as they knocked on the door. Benny opened it.

"Welcome to Eretz Yisrael," said Chaim Ozer, shaking his friend's hand.

Ella and Mimi embraced. They brought in all the dishes, and Ella explained the marking system, what was for milk, what for meat, and what was pareve. "I also brought you tuna salad and *borekes,* so that you can have supper without having to heat anything up. Oh, and this." Ceremoniously, she held out a package of rolls and some salt. "It's supposed to be the first thing you bring into your new home, but at least we got it for you now."

The conversation went on for a few minutes, with no one calling either of the Lerners by name. Then Mimi took a deep breath and said, "We've decided to call ourselves Binyamin and Miriam here in Eretz Yisrael."

Benny looked apologetic. "Did ... did we mean to impose it on all our old friends?"

"Wasn't that the main point?" asked Mimi.

It wasn't clear to Ella quite what the main point was, but she was too curious about something else to care. "If you're going to go by Binyamin and Miriam, why did the manager call you 'Bibi' and 'Miri'?"

Mimi giggled, "Believe me, that was entirely his idea."

"'Miri' is not so bad, but 'Bibi'?" complained Benny.

"Lucky thing your name isn't David. He would have called you 'Dudu,'" Ella pointed out.

"You have a fine name, Binyamin," Chaim Ozer said, "and you shouldn't let one incident discourage you from using it if you want to."

Ella realized that he would have liked to address Mimi by her full name too, but of course he wouldn't call another man's wife by her first name. She did it for him. "You, too, Miriam. You're named after a prophetess."

"I'm actually named after a great-grandmother, but I'm not ashamed of my name. I welcome the idea of using it." Mimi seemed to relax a bit.

"I'm not so sure it was a good idea," said Benny. "If nicknames are endemic in Israel, I think I'd rather stick to the one my parents gave me."

Realizing that their hosts were probably exhausted, the Wahrhaftigs did not stay long. As they stood waiting for the bus back to Yerushalayim, they reminisced about their own months in the hostel.

"Remember the ants, and how you refused to kill any of them?" asked Chaim Ozer.

They had always trooped from the living room into the kitchen in a long line, and Ella would put a blockade of water across the door to cut them off. "Then we found the nest, and I had you take the queen out to the garden so that she could start a new nest if she wanted." By now Ella regarded herself as being in full-scale war against the insect kingdom, and had no compunctions about spraying ants that invaded her kitchen.

"One thing troubles me when I think back to what we did then," said Chaim Ozer.

Ella tensed a little. "What do you mean?" She didn't remember him ever expressing dissatisfaction with their first year of marriage.

"I keep thinking, 'But where were the children?' and I have to remind myself that they didn't exist yet."

Ella relaxed again.

While Miriam was organizing the kitchen, Binyamin set out to look for a shul where he could *daven Minchah* and *Maariv*. Chaim Ozer had told him that there had been a *minyan* in the hostel when they had lived here, but, of course, that had been years back. He went to the office to inquire, but it was closed. He drifted along the lanes that separated the various buildings in the hostel complex, keeping his eyes out for someone wearing a yarmulke. The first man he saw who was identifiably religious appeared to be an immigrant from Ethopia. Binyamin walked over to him and asked in Hebrew, "Is there a *beit knesset* in the hostel?"

The man nodded and pointed, "Over there."

"Is there a *minyan* for *Minchah-Maariv*?"

Another nod. "At seven. See you there?"

It was Binyamin's turn to nod.

Supper was a brief affair of tuna sandwiches and *borekes*. When Binyamin found the shul, a *minyan* hadn't gathered yet. The Ethopian immigrant introduced himself as Asaf Almio, and acquainted Binyamin with some of the other *mispallelim*.

In the evening, after Miriam had put the children to sleep and fallen into an exhausted slumber herself, Binyamin let himself quietly out the back door. He looked around the yard and then upward. Over his head were many more stars than he had ever seen in New York. *Hashem Yisbarach* had promised Avraham that the Jews would be as plentiful as the stars, but it hadn't seemed like such an impressive promise in Brooklyn.

The back fence overlooked the road from the bridge. Binyamin thought he could smell the pine trees planted along the main highway. He turned back toward the house and paced off four *amos,* about the height of a man. For two thousand years his ancestors had dreamed of doing that, of walking four *amos* in Eretz Yisrael, and he was the first one in his family, since the beginning of the *galus,* to actually come here to settle. He turned again in the direction of Yerushalayim.

Binyamin looked around furtively, to make sure that no one was watching. Then he dropped to his knees, bent over, and kissed the earth.

Chapter 10

Language Barrier

When Miriam first woke up, it took her a while to remember where she was. In Eretz Yisrael. This was her first morning in the immigrants' hostel. She looked over at her husband's bed, but it was empty. He must have gone out to *daven*. There was no particular need to wake up the children, whose circadian clocks would be telling them that it was midnight. They could breakfast off the bread Ella had brought yesterday.

Binyamin was home by the time she finished getting dressed. He looked around for a place to put his *tallis* and *tefillin*, but since there were no bookshelves in the room, he put them back in the suitcase for the moment.

"How was the *minyan*?" she asked.

"I'm a little out of breath from trying to keep up," admitted Binyamin, "but they were friendly enough. There's something that worries me. Starting this Rosh Hashanah the Hebrew year will be divisible by seven and therefore ought to be a sabbatical year. I couldn't find any information posted at the shul about *shemittah*. I don't know what we should be doing to get ready."

"Why didn't you ask some of the other people in shul?"

"I don't want to look like a 'greener.' I'll figure it out. There must be someone giving a class about it."

"Maybe you could call Chaim Ozer?" suggested Miriam. "He already knows that you're a 'greener,' as you put it."

"That's an idea. He'll be gone now. I'll try to remember to call him at 1:45." He programmed this into his watch alarm. "Don't forget that you're supposed to call your mother at three. I may not be here to remind you."

"Can you stay with the children while I go to the grocery store after breakfast?" Miriam asked.

"If I want something more for lunch than dry bread, I guess I had better. When are you planning to wake them up?"

"I thought around ten, if they haven't gotten up by themselves before that."

"Do you need my help with the unpacking, or can I go in to work later in the day? I'd like to get through the red tape, so that I can start drawing a salary as soon a possible."

Miriam was disappointed. She had looked forward to having him at home with her for a while, but she had to admit that there wouldn't be much for him to do in the apartment. "Sure, go ahead. If there is anything I need help with, I can leave it for the evening."

After breakfast, Binyamin succumbed to jet lag and lay down for a nap. Miriam wasn't even tired. She was too nervous about her first adventure with grocery shopping for the family in Hebrew. She succeeded in finding the grocery store, which was part of the hostel complex. The store was self-service, but no shopping carts or baskets were provided. One was just supposed to pick a corner of the counter and pile up groceries as they were selected.

Ella had provided her with a list of the various *hechsherim* on which she could rely, and she wandered about the store picking up packages and searching for the *hechsher*. Many of the packages had two or three *hechsherim*, and sometimes the one she wanted was hidden under a flap.

When she got to the dairy department, she paused in confusion. The milk was all in bags. She knew from her year in seminary that one was supposed to prop the bag up in a plastic container and slice off the corner, but she didn't remember seeing such a container in the box of milk dishes that Ella had brought, and she had no idea where she was supposed to buy one. Then, in the back, she noticed a couple of quarts of milk in the kind of cartons she was used to. They were probably more expensive but she didn't care. She simply checked to see that they were fresh and had the proper stamp, and then added them to her pile.

She got through the checkout fairly easily. Rather than trying to remember what each item was called in Hebrew, she just held it up for the owner to inspect. Having run a store in an immigrants' hostel for years, he was used to that.

Miriam had been thinking of stocking her kitchen, forgetting that she no longer had a car in which to bring everything home. She found herself surrounded by six bags of groceries and no means of transportation. She picked out the bag with the milk, the bag with the corn flakes, and one bag with freezer items. She handed the other three bags to the owner of the store and said, "*Lishmor, bevakashah.*"

When she got home, Binyamin was sound asleep, but Shimmy was waking up. After helping him wash and get dressed, she took out the corn flakes and the milk and began rummaging in the box of milk dishes for a cereal bowl. The first item she found was a plastic container for milk, apparently brand-new. Count on Ella to think of everything.

She poured the cereal into the bowl, splashed on some milk, and set to work putting away the groceries in the refrigerator. "Shimmy," she called to him, "come have breakfast."

Behind her, she heard the scraping of a chair and the crunching of a spoonful of cereal. "Yuck!" objected Shimmy.

She'd been afraid of this. "When we move to a new place, everything tastes slightly different," she said brightly. "You just have to get used to it."

"The milk is yucky," said Shimmy stubbornly.

"All right, then you don't have to eat the cereal," she said. She had gotten through four years without turning Shimmy into a problem-eater, and she wasn't going to start now. She picked up his bowl of cereal to throw it away. If he changed his mind later, she would start over with a new bowlful. As she tipped the bowl over the garbage, she noticed that the milk didn't pour; it dripped in gobs. He was right; it was spoiled. She would take it back and complain; it was supposed to be good for another two weeks. She picked up the carton to check the date again, and this time she bothered, for the first time, to read the name of the product. It wasn't milk at all; it was buttermilk!

Miriam sighed. That was what it was like, living in a country where one was a functional illiterate. "Come, Shimmy," she called. "You were right about the milk. I'll give you a bag of crackers for now and we'll go to the store to get some good milk." This time she remembered to take Tami's stroller so that she could bring the groceries back in it. She would just have to expect that the first time she did anything here in Eretz Yisrael, she would make mistakes. That's what her mother-in-law had claimed; the only way not to make mistakes is never to do anything new.

Benny knocked on the door of Mitch's office. In his attaché case he had the precious letter in which the firm had offered him a job, "pending security clearance."

"Come in!"

"It's me, Binyamin Lerner. My family and I arrived yesterday."

"Glad to see you, and welcome to Eretz Yisrael," Mitch reached out and shook Binyamin's hand. "I presume you're here about your job, but I can't help you much. I can't so much as offer you a chair to sit on until Livneh is satisfied that you have taken care of all the formalities."

"What are these formalities?" asked Binyamin apprehensively.

"He will have to tell you. I have blessedly forgotten whatever it was that I had to go through when I was hired. I'll just give you two rules for dealing with Israeli bureaucracy. The first is that you should never plan to do more than one thing in a day. If you finish in time to do something else, consider it wonderful; but if you plan three errands in a day you'll simply frustrate yourself."

"And what is the second rule?"

"You have to have the right approach. If you come in demanding your Knesset-granted rights, you may run into a lot of inaction or even outright obstructionism. You need to project the attitude, 'You are great and powerful, I am poor and weak. Help me!' Then they will do anything for you."

A man Benny recognized walked in through the main door of the programming section and turned toward one of the side rooms. Mitch raised his voice, "Rami, can you come in here for a second? You remember Binyamin Lerner? He's coming to work for us whenever he can get things straightened out with Livneh. I'll probably be asking you to break him in to our routine."

"What sort of things do you mean?" Rami asked, not sounding enthusiastic.

"The proper form for a password, department policy about standardization of names of variables in joint projects, adequate documentation of modules in a program, that sort of thing. If I have to, I'll make you a list when the time comes, but it shouldn't be necessary. Just put yourself in his place and imagine what you would need to know."

"Okay with me, as long as you don't expect me to do five other things at the same time." Rather belatedly, he extended his hand to Binyamin, after which Rami continued on his way.

"Okay," said Mitch. "Off to deal with the bureaucracy."

Binyamin retraced his way through the corridors to Livneh's office. This time he had left his hat and jacket at home, guessing that he would probably have to deal with Livneh. He was kept waiting for half an hour, during which time he got through much of the daily *daf*.

Livneh greeted him by stretching out his hand and saying, "*Teudat oleh.*" He was asking for proof that the Lerners were registered as immigrants.

Binyamin handed over the form that the immigration official had filled out at the airport.

"No, not that," said Livneh impatiently. "The booklet from the absorption ministry, with your picture in it."

Benny wondered if his identity were being questioned. "This form has my passport number on it, and I can show you the picture in my passport," suggested Binyamin.

Livneh looked at him as if he were slightly retarded. "I don't need to see a picture of you, I see you in front of me. I need to know that you have been to the absorption ministry."

"Well, I haven't," admitted Binyamin. "We only arrived yesterday."

"So go, and come back when you have your *teudat oleh.*"

Binyamin started to stand up, then realized that if he were not careful, this scene could be repeated several times over. "After I bring in my *teudat oleh,* is there anything else you will need?"

"The number of your bank account."

"Why?" Were they going to poke around in that to see if he were laundering money for some terrorist organization?

"So that we can pay you, of course."

"I can't just get a check?" asked Binyamin.

"No, all salaries are direct deposit."

"I don't have a bank account yet."

"So open one."

Binyamin took out a small notebook and wrote down both items. "Anything else?"

"Your identity card."

"Where do I get that?"

"At the Interior Ministry."

"And then?"

"The form from the Sick Fund, saying that you have registered."

"I get that from the Sick Fund?"

"Yes, but you probably have to get your *teudat oleh* first."

"Why?"

"Because the government pays the first six months for new immigrants."

"Anything else?"

"You have to have registered with the National Insurance. Actually, I think that has to be done before you can apply to the Sick Fund."

Binyamin sighed. This list was getting very long, and beginning to show signs of gridlock. What would happen if one of them needed something from a doctor before they had the *teudat oleh* or the National Insurance? "Is that all?"

"Yes, it is."

Binyamin cleared his throat, hating to remind the other man of this, but afraid of being stuck later if he didn't say anything. "Uh, the letter said something about a security clearance."

"Oh, that," said Livneh with a dismissive wave of his hand. "We won't even start with that until you have your file in order."

"But maybe you will need documents that I could be getting ready in the meantime."

"Nothing except names, addresses, phone and fax numbers for every past employer and for every organization you ever belonged to, as well as the dates, destination and purpose of every trip you ever made outside the United States."

"That's all?" asked Benny, trying to keep the sarcasm out of his voice. He jotted everything down on his list. His parents would have to get some of those numbers for him. He presumed that this was just for show. They weren't actually going to call everyone he ever worked for to see if he might be a Syrian spy.

"That's all."

Binyamin said goodbye and was almost out the door when it occurred to him to ask, "Will you need a passport photo for my file?"

"Of course," said Livneh with scorn. "How else will we issue you your security badge?"

"One or two?"

"Two."

"Color or black and white?"

"Color."

"Goodbye. Thank you for all the information," said Binyamin quietly. Inwardly he was fuming. He could have gone back and forth from Yerushalayim to Tel Aviv five times before finding out all that he was required to bring. For that matter, couldn't they have listed it in the letter? The least they could have done was to advise him to take a short course in dentistry; that might have helped him in extracting the necessary information from Livneh.

The bus from Tel Aviv actually had a stop at Castel, which would have been convenient for getting home, but he decided to continue on into town and open an account at the bank. Since he didn't yet know where they would be living, he would choose a bank near the central bus station, and change branches later. He found a bank, but it was locked. Looking at the sign, he saw that the bank was closed on Monday and Wednesday afternoons.

He walked back to the bus station, inwardly grumbling at himself for not inquiring about bank hours. There was a forty-minute wait for the next bus. At least he could finish today's *daf* and get a head start on tomorrow's. Then he would have time for the children in the evening, when it would probably be hard to get them to sleep.

By the time Binyamin got home, it was already 6:30. He was hoping that Miriam would ask him about his day, so that he could pour out his frustrations with Livneh, but instead she said, "Oh, before I forget, our landlord left a message with our parents. The new tenants have moved in, and they say that there is a padlocked cupboard in the shed. He asks that you either mail him the key or agree to pay for a locksmith to open it."

A padlock. He had removed the roof from the shed to use it as a *sukkah*, and had bought the padlock to lock the shed during Sukkos so that Miriam's silver candlesticks wouldn't be stolen when she lit her candles there. After Sukkos he had put all the decorations in one of the cabinets and closed it with the padlock. And the key? He had put the key on his key chain and forgotten about it. That must be the key he had given to Shimmy.

"Where is Shimmy?"

"Out in back. He's been making friends with the son of the Ethiopian family on our right."

"Do they speak English or Amharic?"

"They speak four-year-old-ese."

Binyamin went out through the back door, where he saw Shimmy chattering through the chain-link fence with a boy about the same height. The neighbor's child, when he saw Binyamin, retreated into his own house.

"Shimmy!" Binyamin greeted him. "How was your day?'

"Nice. I have a friend."

"Good for you. Ima and I haven't gotten to that yet."

"Ima has," said Shimmy. "She made two friends."

"Glad to hear it," said Binyamin, rather surprised. Miriam wasn't usually one for making friends quickly. It had taken her quite a while to make acquaintances in Lakewood, and most of them were women she had known at least casually from her school days. "Shimmy, do you remember that key chain that Sarah bought you in the airport?"

"Yes," said Shimmy, nodding.

"Do you know where it is?"

"Yes," said Shimmy, but made no move to get it.

"Could you bring it to me?"

"No."

"Why not?" asked Binyamin, surprised.

"'Cause my friend and I swapped." He pulled out a key chain with a *magen David* on it, and a number of keys.

What could he do now? "Would he swap back?"

"Not nice," said Shimmy petulantly. "We swapped forever and ever."

Binyamin didn't want to ruin Shimmy's first effort to make new friends in Eretz Yisrael, but he also didn't want to pay New York scalper's prices for a locksmith. He went back into the kitchen. "Miriam, do you know what languages the neighbors speak?"

"Who, the Zagbadis?" asked Miriam. "Only Amharic."

At shul later that evening Binyamin found one of the Ethiopian immigrants, Asaf Almio, who agreed to act as translator. He explained to the Zagbadis that the Lerners needed back only the key that had been on Shimmy's chain. Dani produced the beloved key chain with its gaudy American flag from the depths of his pocket. Only one little problem remained. He had added nine other keys to the ring!

It was already 9:30 by the time the key crisis was finally resolved. Miriam finished cleaning up from dinner, while Binyamin went out to call Chaim Ozer for advice about *shemittah*. He reappeared shortly and announced, "Ella asks if we'd like to come for Shabbos."

Packing again. Plunking the children down in yet another new, strange place. "I don't think it's a good idea, Binyamin. We've been moving around too much. I think we should just stay put for a while, and let the children regain their equilibrium. One of my new friends here invited us for the morning meal, and I'll manage to put something together for the evening."

"She also asks about Rosh Hashanah and Yom Kippur. I would like that, Mimi." There was a slight tone of pleading in his voice. The mistake in her name was another sign that this mattered to him. "The *minyan* here in the hostel is a mixture of customs from all over the world. For Rosh Hashanah everyone adds different *piyutim*. I'm afraid that I'll end up feeling that I didn't *daven*."

Miriam thought that one over. He had a good claim. And frankly, cooking for two days of the holiday and Shabbos immediately after wouldn't be easy with the few pots and containers that she had. "I think you're probably right about Rosh Hashanah, but I doubt that we want to go for Yom Kippur. I remember Ella telling me that she lives on the third floor, and it would be hard to manage going up and down with the children on a fast. Send her my thanks for the invitations."

Early the next morning, Binyamin set out to storm the Israeli bureaucracy. He arrived home at two, exhausted. All he had accomplished was to buy six geranium plants for Miriam and four books on *shemittah* that Chaim Ozer had recommended. "The *sefarim* saved my sanity," he told her. "From now on you don't let me set off to any government office unless I am equipped with a *sefer*."

They only planted four of the geraniums in their own backyard. The other two were set out in the Zagbadis' yard. Once again Binyamin brought over his Amharic-speaking acquaintance, Asaf, to explain how they were to be watered. Asaf had questions of his own about the sabbatical year, and Binyamin promised to try to answer them in a few days, when he had progressed further with his own research. He had gotten far enough to discover that anything they wanted to plant had to have taken root by Rosh Hashanah, and thus he had rushed out to buy the geraniums.

Since government offices are closed on Friday, Binyamin used the morning to buy things they were missing. When he went to purchase the electric food warmer for Shabbos, he took the two little boys to the hardware store and bought three key blanks for Dani to replace the three keys with English writing that he had mailed to his landlord in Boro Park.

Miriam dressed Shimmy and Tami and went over to her new friend Sandra, who had arrived seven months before from Johannesburg with her husband and young children. She would wait there for the men to arrive home from shul.

"We just signed a contract for an apartment that will be ready in a few months!" Sandra announced. "We are very excited about it. A nice apartment in an area we think we will like. Of course, the whole deal is very complicated, and now we discover that we need all sorts of sums of money for various taxes and fees. *Nisht oif Shabbos geredt*. How are you settling in?"

Miriam told her the story of the extra keys on the key chain and their attempt to explain their problem to the Zagbadis.

"How is your Hebrew?" Sandra asked her.

"Not so strong. Of course, I can understand what I read in the *davening*, but I have trouble getting out a full sentence in spoken Hebrew, particularly if it happens to contain a verb that has to be conjugated."

"Your husband's Hebrew is better?"

"Much. More or less grammatical."

"I think you should take the *ulpan*," Sandra urged her. "It's right here, it's inexpensive and you need it. The *ulpan* works on the immersion method. You are hearing spoken Hebrew all the time, and they even manage to get you to speak some of it. It will be so much easier doing everything if you can explain your problems. Suppose a pipe springs a leak. Do you want to wait for your husband to come home before you call a plumber? The whole place could be flooded by then, and maybe the plumber doesn't like to work the night shift."

"Did you take the *ulpan*?"

"Yes, I did."

"What did you do with your children?"

"There was an Argentinian immigrant who did baby-sitting, and she took them."

"Does she still do it?"

"No, she left last month."

Miriam thought that was just as well. Shimmy was already trying to cope with English, Hebrew and Amharic. Did he need to add Spanish as well? "Is there no English-speaking baby-sitter?"

Sandra looked thoughtfully at Shimmy, who was playing with her three-year-old. "You know, Shimmy is old enough to start kindergarten, and I would be willing to take Tami."

"I would only consider it if you would let me pay."

"We'll work it out after Shabbos, but I think we can come to an agreement."

Sunday morning all four of them traveled to Yerushalayim to the Interior Ministry to apply for their identity cards. This allowed Miriam to postpone for another day the decision about whether or not to take the *ulpan*. Binyamin had learned enough about procedures on Thursday that he went upstairs to the waiting room and took a number before taking the whole family to a photographer for passport photos. Miriam went first.

"Can I be next?" asked Shimmy.

Miriam looked at Binyamin. She remembered her mother's tearful request for pictures.

"We don't need them for the identity cards," he said.

"My mother needs them for her wallet," said Miriam, "and I bet your mother does too."

"Okay," Binyamin agreed. "They aren't very expensive."

Shimmy was very impressed to see himself multiplied by four, and protested when the photographer cut the photograph into four separate pictures. Binyamin had a second set taken of himself, so that he would have enough for the *teudat oleh*, for work, and for who knows what else.

They both filled in long forms. When Miriam wasn't sure what was being asked, she glanced at what Binyamin had answered on his form and guessed at the question. When their turn came, they all went up together to sit in front of the Interior Ministry clerk. She kept firing questions at Binyamin, which he fielded neatly. If Miriam had been expected to supply the answers to this verbal barrage, she would have been pummeled to a pulp.

After they finished with all the forms and had their new identity cards in hand, they crossed Jaffa Road, the main shopping street for the secular population, and walked four blocks north to Malchei Yisrael Street, the main shopping street for the religious community. Merchandise spilled out onto the narrow sidewalk, and the customers spilled out onto the narrow street, the site of a permanent traffic jam. The Lerners bought some children's books, and had lunch in a pizza place. As they were looking around for the stop of the bus that would take them back to Mevasseret, up pulled a number one.

"Binyamin," said Miriam urgently. "We have been here for a week and we haven't been to the Kosel. Neither of the children has ever seen it. Why don't we just hop on?"

"The temptations of living in Yerushalayim," said Binyamin with a laugh. And hop on they did.

The trip to the Interior Ministry actually made up Miriam's mind for her. At her current level of Hebrew comprehension, she was too dependent on Binyamin. As long as he hadn't started work it didn't so much matter, but once he was gone all day she couldn't afford to be so helpless.

The very next morning she left Tami with Sandra and set out to register Shimmy in *gan*. She succeeded in finding the kindergarten complex from the manager's instructions. She was pretty solid on the words for "right," "left" and "straight ahead." The building was a single story and had several different entrances, each with its own separate yard for the children to play in. Not knowing which was the right one, she hovered outside until she saw a mother bring a boy about Shimmy's height, wearing a yarmulke. The children were sitting on chairs around low tables, playing with Lego and similar construction toys. Shimmy was used to following her around and playing on the floor at her feet. How would he take to sitting on a chair?

"I … uh … want … my boy … uh … to go … uh … to *gan*," Miriam got out in Hebrew.

"*Aht rotzah lirshom oto legan?*" asked the teacher.

Good heavens, what did *"lirshom"* mean? She couldn't think of any place in the *siddur* where the word occurred. Taking the option always available to uncomprehending foreigners, she smiled and said, "Yes," hoping that she hadn't agreed to have Shimmy sold into slavery or some such destiny.

"Identity card?" requested the teacher.

Oh, dear. They had actually gotten them yesterday, but Binyamin had taken hers with him to the Absorption Ministry today. "Tomorrow?" suggested Miriam.

"Okay. Bring him at ten, for one hour."

One hour. Not so bad. He could probably sit still for one hour.

On Wednesday, the nursery school teacher had Shimmy stay for two hours. Miriam took the opportunity to go back to the hostel and sign up for the *ulpan*. She arrived during the midmorning break. After speaking to her briefly in Hebrew and asking her to read a paragraph from the newspaper, the *ulpan* teacher decided to place her in the second level. Miriam was relieved to hear that she was not at the "Abba comes. Abba comes home," stage.

Thursday was Shimmy's first full day of *gan,* and Miriam's first day of *ulpan.* She arrived late, after having dropped off Tami at Sandra's and Shimmy at *gan*. She slid into a chair in the back of the classroom, hoping no one had noticed her arriving in a huff.

"Ah, class, we have a new member today. This is Miriam Lerner. Miriam, stand up and tell everyone where you grew up and went to school, where you used to live, what you are doing now, and what your plans are for the future."

Miriam did not think that she had ever in her life been faced with such a sweeping demand for information, and she was supposed to ad-lib this all in Hebrew! She could refuse, of course, but that would surely get her off to a bad start with the teacher.

"I grew up in New York. Also I went to school there. One year I studied in Yerushalayim. … uh … made a *chatunah* and lived in New Jersey. Now I am raising two children and learning Hebrew. We want to … uh … take an apartment."

"How will you make a living?"

Good heavens. What kind of personal questions was this lady allowed to ask as part of coaxing her to speak? "My husband will work."

"And you?

"I will raise the children." This last response got some raised eyebrows from the other immigrants.

"All right," said the teacher. "You are pretty solid on the present tense, the past tense is a little weak, and you need a lot of work on the future."

All that angst, just to let the teacher know whether or not Miriam could conjugate a verb!

By the end of the class on Friday, Miriam felt that she was beginning to get used to it. She had never again been put on display as badly as in her first moments, and she was beginning to pick up new words. So was Shimmy. He had come home yesterday with a few rudimentary phrases about blowing the shofar, and a very clear, "That's mine!" which he tried out on his friend Dani.

Miriam glanced at her watch. The class actually ran until one, but she had excused herself early in order to be at Shimmy's *gan* before his 12:30 dismissal. She wanted to be there for him the moment he came out.

She got to the *gan,* but didn't see any of the other mothers who had waited with her yesterday. Could it be that she was late and they had already taken their children? If so, the kindergarten teacher should be standing in the open door waiting for her to collect Shimmy. She crept up to the door and listened. Not a sound. She rattled the handle. It was locked. Where was her son?

Miriam walked around the building, trying to find someone who could tell her where everyone had gone. The door of the next kindergarten class was also locked. She rounded the corner of the building and found a man who looked as if he might be the custodian. He was locking the gate leading into one of the yards.

"Excuse me," she asked, "where are all the children?" She wanted to hear that they had gone on a field trip and would be back shortly.

"Gone home," said the man.

"But I have been here since 12:30. *Gan* ends at 12:30."

"Today is *erev Shabbat*," said the man curtly.

"So what if it is *erev Shabbat*?"

The man looked at Miriam as if she were slightly retarded. "*Gan* ends at twelve on *erev Shabbat*." He said it as if it were a law handed down to Moshe on Har Sinai, which any Jew should know.

Maybe the teacher had asked Shimmy to show her the way to his house. She knew that he lived in the immigrants' hostel, and once she got him there, he would know the way to their apartment. He could be waiting there now. She hurried home. No sign of either Shimmy or her husband. She went to Sandra's to pick up Tami. Could Binyamin have taken him along to *Minchah*?

As she arrived back at the house, she saw her husband approaching from the direction of the shul, alone. "Oh, Binyamin!" she exclaimed in panic, "Shimmy is missing!"

After they had checked at the desk and ascertained that no one had inquired for them there, Binyamin said, "Probably the *ganenet* took him home."

"We're not going to leave him there for Shabbos!"

"Of course not! What is her name?"

"Elisheva."

"You don't know her family name?"

"No, she never mentioned it."

"I wonder how she thinks we're supposed to find her. The other mothers who come to get their children, do they come in cars or do they walk?"

"Most of them walk."

Binyamin and Miriam combed the neighborhood near the *gan*, looking for four-year-old boys wearing yarmulkes. When they found one, they would ask him, "Are you in Elisheva's *gan*?" After an hour of this, they finally found another mother whose son was in Elisheva's kindergarten class. She also did not know Elisheva's family name, but she did know that Elisheva lived within walking distance of the *gan*. "A few streets over, in that direction," she said, pointing.

It was three o'clock in the afternoon by the time they finally located Elisheva's house. Tami was wilting from being pushed around in the stroller in the hot sun, and Miriam didn't feel very lively herself. They rang the doorbell, hoping that there had been no mistake. Elisheva herself opened the door. "Well, well, you finally remembered to come!" she expostulated. "You know, I also have to make Shabbos."

This was more than Binyamin could take. "Excuse me," he said, "did you tell my wife that *gan* ends early on Fridays? Did you leave a note on the door of the *gan* giving your address and telling her that you had taken Shimmy home with you?"

"Everyone knows where I live," she said angrily.

"Well, obviously not, if it took us two hours of pushing our baby around in the hot sun in order to find you!"

Shimmy came running from inside the house. He squeezed past Elisheva and buried his face in Miriam's skirt, bursting into tears. She picked him up and hugged him tight, shedding a tear or two herself, both from relief and from frustration

Elisheva's demeanor changed and she became much more sympathetic. "He didn't cry at all until this moment. He was just fine. A little hero."

Miriam took advantage of this moment of calm to hold out Tami's bottle and said, "Thank you for taking care of him. Please, Elisheva, could you fill this with water?"

"Sure!" said Elisheva. She chucked Tami under the chin and said, "Cute." She brought back the bottle filled with cold water, together with cups of water for Shimmy and his parents. They all wished each other a good Shabbos and departed with no further recriminations on either side.

"I guess it's not just government offices," said Binyamin.

"What?" asked Miriam.

"Where you need to assume the 'I am weak and helpless' position in order to get good treatment."

"Still, even if it did antagonize her, I'm glad you stood up for me. I would never have defended myself, but I would have been seething inside at the injustice."

When they got home, Miriam fed the children, bathed them, and put them down for a nap. Then she looked at a clock. It was 4:30 already, she hadn't started her preparations for Shabbos, and she was supposed to light candles in an hour and a half. Fortunately, they were once again invited out for the morning meal. She filled the two largest pots she had with water, set them to boil on the two-burner stove, and began peeling potatoes and vegetables. Within fifteen minutes she had the chicken cooking in the soup pot, and potatoes boiling in a second one.

"Go lie down," said Binyamin, who had been straightening up the apartment. "I'll watch the soup and set the table."

Miriam sank down on her bed without protest. The idea that she could actually prepare an entire Shabbos meal in a quarter of an hour was new to her, but at the moment it was welcome information.

Chapter 11

Culture Shock

W hen Shabbos was over, Binyamin said, "You know, with all the excitement chasing after Shimmy, I never showed you what I bought Friday morning." He pulled a plastic shopping bag off one of the shelves in the closet. Taking out a folded piece of cloth, he opened it out into a large square, which he could barely hold off the floor. It was white satin, with a white fringe around the edges and a Star of David embroidered in white in the center..

"What is it?" asked Miriam.

"It's a cover for the table in the shul, and this," he said, pulling out another bundle of folded cloth, also entirely white, "is a curtain for the *aron kodesh*. The shul doesn't have special ones for the *Yamim Noraim*, so I decided that we would donate them. And this," he continued, pulling out an electronic gadget from the bottom of the bag, "is a monitor for the children's room so that you will be able to go to *Selichos* tonight."

Miriam had been so caught up in starting *ulpan* and her baby-sitting arrangements that she had hardly noticed the approach of the *Yamim Tovim*. Rosh Hashanah came out on Wednesday night this year, so there were only four days of *Selichos*, starting tonight. It took them a while to find someone within range of the monitor who was planning to be up until midnight, but eventually it was all arranged. When Miriam got to the shul and looked over the *mechitzah*, she saw Binyamin hanging up the new white curtain in front of the *aron kodesh*, while someone else was folding up the red velvet covering on the table where the Torah was to be read and spreading out the new white one that Binyamin had bought. Stacks of *Selichos* booklets were distributed to the men and women's sections. The men who had been setting everything up, Binyamin included, gathered at the table for some sort of consultation.

Sandra joined her at the *mechitzah*. "It looks very nice," she said. "Now I feel that Rosh Hashanah is almost here." The women's section was filling quickly. Many women, who, like Miriam, hardly ever went to shul, would come for the first night of *Selichos*.

The men's section was also filling up. The huddle at the table broke up, and everyone took a place except Binyamin. He reached inside the table and pulled out a *talis*, which he began to put on. There was no official *chazzan*, and the various religious immigrants took turns leading the services. Miriam was very pleased. Binyamin *davened* beautifully, and it was rare that she got to hear him. He began with the first line of the canonical *"Ashrei...,"* and everyone began reciting it by heart as they found their places in the unfamiliar books. The rest of the *teffilos*, which they said once a year instead of three times a day, they would have to read.

Miriam and Binyamin were both in a quiet mood as they walked back to the apartment after *Selichos*, very conscious of just how pivotal the coming year would be in fixing the entire direction of their lives. When they were nearly at the door, Binyamin said, "This evening they decided who would *daven* each of the *teffilos* during the *Yamim Noraim*. They wanted me to lead *Shacharis* on Rosh Hashanah, but I told them that we were going away. I did agree to take *Shacharis* on Yom Kippur."

Having stayed up for *Selichos* and gone to sleep late, Miriam did not wake up the next morning until a quarter of eight. She threw on her clothes haphazardly and woke up the two children more brusquely than usual. Not until she had gotten Tami's bag packed for her morning at Sandra's house did she realize that Shimmy was not his usual cheerful self. She had gotten him into his underwear and laid out his shirt, pants and sandals. When she popped back in to help buckle his shoes as usual, she found that he hadn't even started getting dressed.

"What's wrong, Shimmy?" she asked, as she pulled the shirt smoothly over his head and began bunching up the right sleeve to slip his arm through the hole. "You usually get dressed so nicely all by yourself."

"I don't want to go to *gan*," muttered Shimmy, who remained limp as a rag doll while Miriam dressed him."

"But you're learning all about Rosh Hashanah. That's very important. It's almost like learning Torah."

"You can teach me."

He was dressed, and she was buckling his shoes. "But all the children go to *gan*."

"I want to stay home."

Since the conversation didn't seem to be getting anywhere, she led him silently into the kitchen and started to pour him a bowl of cereal.

"Not hungry," pouted Shimmy.

Miriam quietly slipped a few extra crackers into his lunch bag. She herself had not had time to eat anything and had been hoping to eat while he did, but they were so late that she decided just to get going. Binyamin had not arrived; she didn't quite know why.

She delivered Tami to Sandra's and began the walk to *gan*, with Shimmy trudging unhappily beside her. She was holding his hand, but he was not applying any counter-pressure. If she dropped it, his hand would fall to his side and he would presumably stop walking. She didn't try the experiment, fearing that it would be hard to get him to move again.

"Shimmy, last week you liked going to *gan*. Is this because I was late picking you up on Friday?"

Shimmy didn't answer.

"I explained that it was a mistake and that now I know all the dismissal times. I'll be there with all the other mothers today, *b'ezras Hashem*."

"Uhn," grunted Shimmy. The sound expressed disbelief.

All right, so that was part of it. It was a pretty traumatic experience for a child who had rarely been separated from his mother. "Is there anything else, Shimmy? Are you having trouble with any of the other children in *gan*?"

Silence.

"Are you worried about not speaking Hebrew? Everyone tells me that you'll learn very quickly."

Silence.

When they got to the door of the *gan,* Shimmy drew back. Miriam more or less dragged him into the room. She said with forced brightness, "*Shalom,* Elisheva."

"*Shalom,* Shimmy," said Elisheva.

Shimmy took one look at her, burst into tears and clutched at Miriam's skirt.

Miriam pulled a tissue out of her purse, stooped down to Shimmy's height, and wiped his cheeks. She stroked his hair and said softly. "There's nothing to be afraid of, Shimmy. Elisheva isn't angry with you, and she isn't angry with me either. I'll be back right on time to pick you up."

Shimmy cried even more forcefully.

Elisheva leaned forward and took one of Shimmy's hands. In heavily accented English she said, "Today we are being *madbik* the shofar." She looked at Miriam over Shimmy's head and said in Hebrew "He won't cry for more than five minutes. I have lots of experience. It would be best for you to go right now."

When she was halfway down the path, Miriam allowed herself to look back, but Shimmy was no longer looking after her. Elisheva was propelling him toward one of the tables.

By the time Miriam reached the *ulpan,* it was already nine o'clock. She was a full hour late. She slid into her place, hoping that her arrival would not be noticed. It was a vain hope.

"Miriam! There is absolutely no point in signing up for an *ulpan* if you're not going to take it seriously," said Ronit sternly.

"My little boy didn't want to go to *gan,*" mumbled Miriam.

"Who decides things, you or him?"

Miriam did not answer. She had already said too much. The other students in the *ulpan* were turning around to look at the lady who allowed her child to push her around.

"If it were just once, I might ignore it," the teacher continued, "but you always come late and you always leave early. Besides that, since you entered the class, you haven't done a stitch of home-work!"

"Homework? What homework?" asked Miriam, astounded. She

had thought the *ulpan* was entirely oral.

"Every day at the end of class I give an assignment, and the first thing I do each morning is collect it."

"I was never there at the beginning or the end, so I never knew!"

"You must have gone to school for at least a few years. Didn't they teach you to make up what you miss?"

Miriam blanched. Everyone was looking at her. The teacher had implied that she was uneducated, and had said straight out that she was irresponsible. Miriam rose to her feet, turned, and walked out of the room, trying to maintain at least a semblance of dignity as she retreated. She continued to move with a sort of frozen precision until she was quite far from the classroom. She sank down on a bench, torn between two conflicting impulses.

Should she go reclaim Tami from Sandra and rescue Shimmy from *gan*? If she did that, she would have to act normally before the children. Should she go home and collapse in tears on the bed? What excuse would she have for leaving Shimmy where he was miserable? Since she was quitting the *ulpan*, there would be no point in having him continue in *gan*. Unable to decide, she continued sitting where she was, staring down at the red earth at her feet.

Binyamin, she realized, would not be happy about pulling Shimmy out of *gan* the first moment he showed some resistance. Soon he would be of age to go to school, and an experience like this would make it harder for him to adjust. That's really what Elisheva had been telling her this morning when she told her to leave quickly. If she went and got him now, she would be teaching him to be a quitter.

Quitter. Quitter, quitter, quitter. The word seemed to reverberate in her mind, with eerie echoes. She listened as it nearly faded out and then gathered strength again: quitter, Quitter, QUITTER.

Was she being a quitter, dropping out the moment the going got rough?

Miriam settled back onto the bench. She wouldn't take Shimmy out of *gan* without talking it over with her husband, and as long as her son still had to cope, she wasn't comfortable with the idea of just collapsing herself.

How she wished she were back in Boro Park, where she knew just what was required of her in every situation, where there were no hidden bits of information waiting to trip her up at every turn.

How nice it would be if she were once again Mama's Mimi, with the few little obstacles in her way generously taken care of by a loving family.

Why were the people here so quick to condemn her for lacking information she didn't know that she had to know? Why hadn't Elisheva given any thought to the question of how Miriam was supposed to find Shimmy if Elisheva took him home? Why had Ronit been so harsh with her?

Miriam, unaccustomed to taking such a critical view of other people's actions, groped toward a fairer assessment. It was cultural myopia to assume that what was common knowledge in Israel would be known to her as well; but perhaps she had also been guilty of cultural myopia in framing her questions. That's what culture shock was about, finding out just how differently a divergent culture sees things.

Miriam felt a little better now that she had a name for what she and Shimmy were going through. They were suffering from culture shock, like the shock of jumping into a cold pool. She'd always heard that the *ulpan* used the immersion method for teaching languages. The immigrant's hostel seemed to use the immersion method for teaching Israeli culture. There were, she knew, social workers at the hostel for people who had trouble making the transition, but then everything took much longer. Miriam, when going swimming, had always preferred jumping straight in to climbing down the ladder inch by shivering inch.

Miriam realized that she was psyching herself up for another try at the *ulpan*. Just not today. After the humiliation that morning, she could not face them again today. She needed to speak to Ronit privately and explain her situation, but it was hard to see when. She surely wasn't going to be late to pick up Shimmy after what had happened on Friday. Maybe she could get Ronit's phone number somehow, although she hated trying to speak Hebrew over the telephone.

Miriam glanced at her watch. Where had all that time gone? The *ulpan* had a fifteen-minute break at ten, and it was already half over. Miriam pulled out a note pad and wrote a short note to Ronit asking her to please leave her phone number and, if possible, a copy of today's assignment, in box 17 at the desk.

Ronit had, as usual, vanished promptly at the beginning of the break to go have a cup of coffee. That made it easier for Miriam to march into the room and lay the note conspicuously in the center of her desk. She walked in with the same frozen carriage with which she had left an hour before, and carefully avoided meeting the eyes of any of the other students. She had almost made good her retreat, when she collided with the teacher at the door.

"Oh, good, you came back," said Ronit with a smile. "Sit down and relax. We'll work it all out later." If she had noticed that Miriam was leaving the classroom, she must have assumed that she was looking for the teacher. Miriam did what seemed most graceful under the circumstances and sank into her former seat in the back. She was not called on. At 12:20, she got up and walked out.

Shimmy ran to her as soon as the door was opened and buried his head in her skirt. Elisheva said in Hebrew, "Just as I told you, he didn't cry for more than twenty minutes." Hand in hand, she and Shimmy walked off to get Tami.

Once the children were down for their afternoon naps, Miriam checked the mail and found that Ronit had left both the phone number and the assignment. She sat down quickly to do the homework, which took her over an hour.

Binyamin returned from town at five, and by then Shimmy was playing with Dani in the backyard. Miriam told him all her frustrations, not even leaving out her wish to take Shimmy home from *gan*.

"I'm glad you went back," said Binyamin approvingly. "That was brave of you."

"But what am I going to do now? Today Ronit did me a special favor and wrote out the assignment, but can I really ask her to do that every day?"

"You'll have to get to know one of the other students from whom you can get the work."

"I doubt anyone there wants to know me, after the poor impression I made during the first three days. And I don't think it's going to be any easier to get Shimmy to *gan* on time tomorrow."

Binyamin considered the problem. "You know what? I'll take Shimmy to *gan* and pick him up for a few days, so that you can be a normal member of the class. I've finished filing all the applications for the documents we need. Now it's just a matter of waiting for them to arrive."

The next morning Shimmy woke up groaning and complaining that his stomach hurt. Miriam was just as happy to allow Binyamin to decide whether he was really sick. She got Tami and her diaper bag ready for Sandra, and slid into her place in the *ulpan* at one minute to eight. She handed in her homework with the others when Ronit collected it.

Shimmy said nothing about his stomach as he ate a very substantial lunch, chattering about the *Shanah Tovah* cards they were making in *gan,* and about the interesting bugs he and his father had seen on the way back. Miriam, who disliked all insects, shuddered, but she let him talk on. The "I don't want to go to *gan*" crisis seemed to be over for the moment.

Over Rosh Hashanah, Miriam and Ella had their first long talk since the Lerners had arrived in Israel. Miriam told the story of coming late to pick up Shimmy, but left out her own troubles with the *ulpan*.

"Did you realize that there would be no *gan* on the day before Rosh Hashanah?"

"Binyamin thought to ask. Also, it was pretty obvious when they brought home their *Shanah Tovah* cards on Tuesday."

"I'm sorry I didn't think to warn you about that business of *gan* closing at twelve o'clock," said Ella, as if she had been made personally responsible for protecting the Lerners from culture shock and had somehow fallen down on her job. "Let's see, has anyone told you about head lice?"

"About what?!"

"Well, that's not really a subject to discuss on Yom Tov. Remind me after Shabbos to tell you about that, and about the car."

"We don't have a car yet," said Miriam.

"I mean, why you shouldn't get one."

Miriam could think of many reasons why they should, but had to agree that this was not an appropriate subject for Rosh Hashanah.

Binyamin found the *tefillos* very inspiring, and felt that they had made the correct decision when they had originally decided to come. Miriam, who only came to shul on the first day with the other mothers and babies for the blowing of the shofar, was considerably less impressed.

For the second day, when her children were already used to their new surroundings, she and Ella traded. First Ella went to *daven* with a *minyan* that started before sunrise, and then Miriam took Ella's seat for the *tefillos* in the Lakewood *minyan*. This time she did get some feeling of the *Yom Hadin*, particularly when she reminded herself what a crucial year this was in their lives.

Shabbos, after two days of Yom Tov, threatened to be something of a letdown, but Ella managed to keep back enough treats and new ideas for pastimes so the children did not get overly whiny. Yet it was something of a relief when they finally sorted out their things and set off for their own home and their own beds.

Only as the bus was climbing the hill toward Mevasseret Tzion did Miriam remember that she hadn't spoken with Ella about the subjects of head lice and a car. She was happy not to have discussed the necessity of owning a car, but she was afraid that head lice were a part of her initiation into Israeli life that she would not be allowed to forgo.

Miriam was sitting out in the back yard finishing her *ulpan* homework and watching the children play. She would never have thought that they could find so much to do in a yard without grass or a swing set. Shimmy had built a highway and was pushing a toy truck along it. Tami was pulling at one of the isolated tufts of grass. As Miriam watched, Shimmy reached up and scratched his head.

Oh, no! Not that! Maybe it was just sand.

Shimmy dropped the truck and scratched with both hands.

A few minutes later, Miriam was standing at the pay phone dialing Ella's number. "Listen, Ella, you never did get a chance to tell me about the head lice."

"Why? You think one of the children has it?"

"I'm worried about Shimmy. He's scratching his head a lot."

"Well, look through the hair in back of his ears to see if you see any eggs: tiny white ovals stuck to the hair follicles, not lying loose like dandruff. If you're lucky, you might even see one of the adults walking around, but that's harder."

Lucky! Ella calls that lucky. "Yuck! What happens if I accidentally touch one of them?"

"Absolutely nothing." Ella seemed amused. "If that's what he's got, you're going to touch an awful lot of them before this is over."

Miriam shuddered. "Suppose he has it? What do I have to do?"

"Go to the drug store and buy some lice shampoo and a lice comb. Follow the instructions on the package. It's not considered good manners to send him back to *gan* until his head is clean. Also, you should change his sheets and pillowcases. If he has any friends who might catch it from him, you should warn their mothers."

That last was the hardest. How could she admit to anyone else that her son was—infested.

Miriam pushed Tami's stroller into the drugstore, with Shimmy holding on to the handle at one side. She sidled up to the counter, first throwing a quick glance around to make sure no one she knew was there. "Do you have any"—here she dropped her voice so that it was barely audible—"lice shampoo?"

"Lice shampoo?" boomed the clerk. "Oh, sure, plenty. Which kind would you like?" He extracted two packages from under the counter and held them up for her inspection. One showed two smiling blond children with flowing hair. The other had a large picture of a louse.

"I'll take that one," said Miriam, pointing to the one with the children. "In fact, I'll take two." She also purchased two lice combs. "Uh, could you put it all in a paper bag?" she requested, as the clerk was about to drop all her purchases into an all-too-transparent plastic bag.

"How will you carry it?" he asked reasonably. Then, deciding to humor this skittish American, he put the items first in a paper bag and then into a plastic one with handles, which Miriam hung onto the stroller.

Binyamin was still getting Shimmy off to *gan* every morning, but it was Miriam who took Tami to her baby-sitter. Should she tell Sandra? Since Tami had been clean, perhaps she could spare herself that additional humiliation. When she walked into her friend's house after hearing a cheery "Come in," she found Sandra poring over some kind of pamphlet. The picture on the cover seemed suspiciously familiar.

"Sandra, what's that?"

"This is a pamphlet describing the life cycle of the head louse. I picked it up at the clinic. If you want, you can borrow it from me when I am finished."

"No, thank you!" said Miriam. "Bugs give me the willies. I don't know how you can bear to read about them."

"Know the enemy, that's my philosophy."

Chapter 12

New Immigrant

"Shloimi, your slippers are next to the door of your room. Leah'le, come, sweetheart, tie your bow." This year the two older Wahrhaftig children were being allowed to go to *Kol Nidrei*, since they knew how to read the *tefillos*. The two younger ones would stay with a neighbor.

Ella washed her hands. "All the *kinderlach* to the living room. It's time for Abba to bless you." She went to rescue the baby from the crib. Actually, Esti wasn't such a baby anymore. She was more than a year old.

The children stood in a line, and Ella did some deft tucking in of shirttails and straightening of bows. Chaim Ozer had already put on his *kittel* and his cloth shoes. He placed his hands on Leah's head, closed his eyes, and began to *daven*. When he finished, he sent her to Ella, who added a blessing of her own. After both parents had blessed all the children, and Ella had lit her candles, they gathered their *machzorim* and *sifrei Tehillim* and walked out the door. On Shabbos and Yom Tov they didn't lock the door behind them, but simply closed it. They didn't expect anyone untrustworthy to be in the area.

Ella left Shaya and Esti with a neighbor and the Wahrhaftig family set off down the front steps. They would be *davening* at the Lakewood *kollel*, just as they had on Rosh Hashanah. Thinking of Rosh Hashanah reminded Ella of the Lerners. She hoped everything would go well for them, and that they settled in successfully. She had tried to call them for the traditional request for forgiveness, but the desk clerk at the hostel claimed to have no way to leave a message.

The streets were almost empty of vehicles. The buses had stopped a while back, and all they saw occasionally was a private car tearing past at breakneck speed, trying to get its passengers to shul in time for *Kol Nidrei*. There were some groups of young girls out jumping rope as they baby-sat younger siblings, but most of the people around were family groups on their way to shul.

"Think how much has changed since last Yom Kippur!" exclaimed Ella. "Then Elisha was perfectly healthy, and no one had an inkling that the Lerners might move here."

"Just keep that in mind as you *daven*, and you too, children," said Chaim Ozer. "Anything could change. Who knows where we will be in a year?"

"Won't we be right here?" asked Leah.

"*Im yirtzeh Hashem*," answered her father.

Elisha heard what sounded like Joe's knock on the outside door to his room, but that was strange, because he had given Joe off this afternoon and all of Yom Kippur. Motti and his wife had come to stay, so that Motti could help Elisha in and out of bed.

"Come in!" Elisha called, pressing the buzzer that released the lock. His enormous attendant, who could move him from bed to chair without feeling any strain, poked his head in.

"Hi, 'Lisha. Ah was goin' by and thought as ya might want a nap 'bout now."

"Thanks, Joe. I am tired but we're about to have a big meal."

"Can't ya eat later?"

"No, Joe. After this meal I can't eat or drink for twenty-five hours."

"Not even water?"

"Not even water."

"Wow, that's something! So whatya gonna do all day?"

"Pray, Joe. Pray really hard."

Motti and Elisha set out for shul a bit before their parents, with Motti pushing the wheelchair. Elisha sighed and Motti leaned forward a bit to hear what he had to say. "What weighs on my mind is wondering if there is some message in this," Elisha tapped the arm of the chair, "that I haven't gotten. Is there something special I should be thinking about when I get to 'the sin we have committed with legs running to do evil?' Too much jaywalking? Too many trips to the coffee machine when I was supposed to be learning? Something else that I did that I don't even realize was wrong?"

"You can wonder about that. I'll go on thinking that it was a *kapporah* for all of us and try to set my own house in order. When we got that call that you were injured and might not make it through the night, I was a fountain of regrets and good resolutions. I'm sure that, as the shock ebbed, I didn't manage to carry out even half of them. That's what's weighing on my mind right now."

"Last year I was in Yerushalayim, walking to shul."

"I was thinking the same thing, but I didn't want to say it," admitted Motti.

"I was full of plans about coming back to New York in the summer and getting started in *shidduchim*. I was even thinking that I might be engaged within a year. It just shows, Motti, how much we have to *daven* for things we just don't normally think to put into our *tefillos*."

"Not just for ourselves. For all of *Klal Yisrael*," added Motti.

The early morning light filtered through the half-closed blinds. "Come, Shimmy, take Abba's hand." Binyamin, dressed in his white *kittel* and his black-striped *tallis*, was waiting at the door. Shimmy came forward slowly, somewhat overawed by his father's Yom Kippur attire. Miriam picked up Tami, the diaper bag and her white Yom Kippur *machzor*. Miriam and Sandra were taking turns baby-sitting for the children during the *davening*, and Miriam had elected to be in shul for *Shacharis*, while Binyamin would be leading the *tefillah*.

They left the two children with Miriam's friend and turned toward the shul, which was actually just another long prefabricated building similar to all the offices in the hostel complex. Although they had been fasting for fourteen hours already, neither of them felt it yet. "Are you nervous?" Miriam asked him.

"I don't know if 'nervous' is quite the word. I feel a sense of responsibility pressing down on me. You know how hard it is to keep your mind from wandering during the *davening*, and here I am supposed to be representing everybody else on the most important day of the year."

"I'm sure you will mean every word," said Miriam with confidence.

"It's also...you know, that Eretz Yisrael is described as the King's palace, and Yom Kippur is one day of the year when He allows us to come closest to Him. The two together...it is kind of overwhelming."

"I will try to hold on to that thought as I *daven*," said Miriam with a nod.

They parted at the door to the women's section. Binyamin went into the men's section, sat down, and opened his *machzor*. Someone else would be leading the service for the *Pesukei Dezimra*. Thoughts about how crucial this coming year would be for them and for the other immigrants tugged at his consciousness, and he struggled to keep his mind on the words he was reading.

"Nishmas kol chai..." The soul of every living being will bless Your name...My soul will bless the L-rd. ... *"Hagibor la'netzach v'hanora b'norasecha ..."*

When his turn came to be *shaliach tzibbur*, Binyamin stepped up to the podium and began the wordless tune that introduces the *Yamim Noraim* service in Ashkenazic communities. Behind him, in a rising swell, the congregation hummed along. When they finally reached the crescendo, he alone called out, *"HaMelech!"* Binyamin felt at that moment as if he had stepped into the very throne room, bearing his people's petition.

Binyamin finally had all the necessary documents and could return to Livneh. As he was riding in the bus toward Tel-Aviv, he wondered if they would have him start work before Sukkos. Anxious as he was to start earning a salary, he almost hoped that the security clearance would take a full week, and then he would suggest that there was no point in starting until after Sukkos. In Israel, unlike America, he would not have to use up precious vacation days on the major Jewish holidays, but he would have to use them for the intermediate days of the festivals. Why should he start with a negative vacation balance?

After a brief wait, he was ushered into Livneh's office. He counted out the documents on the table, uneasily hoping that the personnel officer would not come up with some new idea for what he should have brought, perhaps labor union membership. However, it seemed that he had actually assembled the full list of necessary forms.

"Fine," said Livneh, "we'll start processing your application now, and I'll ask the government to get started on your security clearance. "

"When do you think I can begin working?"

"That will depend on the government. Why don't you call me, let's see," he began thumbing through his desk calendar, "in four weeks."

"In four weeks! What's going to take so long? I've only belonged to the most innocuous of organizations."

"You're not the only job applicant to a firm with defense contracts," said Livneh coldly, obviously meaning to put Binyamin in his place. "Besides, nothing ever gets done in Israel over the holidays."

"I thought that in most places of business the intermediate days of the festivals are ordinary work days, or at least half days."

"Some people come in, but nothing gets done anyway. I can guarantee you that even if we send it in tomorrow, no one will look at this list until after Simchat Torah." He held up Binyamin's neatly printed list of organizations, employers, and phone numbers.

"But you will send it in now, just to get it in line?" asked Binyamin urgently. "I have a wife and two children, and no income at the moment."

"Sure, why not? But I tell you that it won't make a difference."

Binyamin wandered disconsolately down to Mitch's office, and reported his conversation with Livneh.

"I expected something of the sort," said Mitch. "Eretz Yisrael is one of the things attained through suffering. Be glad it's only the red tape of the security clearances and not the malaria that the first pioneers caught."

"So don't assign me to any projects until this clearance comes through."

"I don't intend to. In the meantime, don't mope. Be frugal and enjoy having some time with your family. Once you're commuting to Tel Aviv, it will be a very precious commodity."

"I'll try," said Binyamin, managing a smile.

"Oh, and one more thing. Call Livneh tomorrow afternoon to make sure he sent that list."

"Miriam," Binyamin took a breath, "if you don't object, I'd like to give a *shiur* twice a week in the evenings."

"Why should I object? I think that would be wonderful."

"Well, I'm hoping to start work soon, and then this *shiur* and the preparation will cut into the time I have to help you get settled. Anyway, pending your agreement, I arranged that it would be on Mondays and Wednesdays. That way I can prepare on Sundays and Tuesdays and I'll still have Thursdays free to help out."

Miriam thought that for a *Daf Yomi* wife a little *shiur* twice a week seemed trivial, but she understood why he thought she needed more help here than in New York. What would she have done on Friday without him? "What's the subject of the *shiur*?" she asked.

"The sabbatical year."

"*Shemittah*? But I thought you didn't know anything about it."

"Well, after a week and a half of spending most of my time waiting in government offices and reading up on the subject, I know more than I did, and more than most of the other new immigrants. But you're right, it will still be a struggle. That's why I left a lot of time for preparation."

"I'm sure you'll give a terrific *shiur*." Miriam was glad that other people would have a chance to appreciate her husband.

There was nothing for Binyamin to do about his job except wait. Before Yom Kippur, he had tried to make a spiritual accounting of the year. What had he done right? What had he done wrong? The big things, the decision to move to Israel and the question of whether he had put too much pressure on Miriam, these he easily remembered. But there were so many small things that had bothered him at the time that now he didn't remember at all. He wanted to do something so that he wouldn't be in the same situation next year.

Several times while he was still learning in Lakewood he had tried to keep a notebook in which, at the end of each day, he'd write down what he had done right and what he had done wrong. Unfortunately, after a month or two, he had become lax about writing things down, and eventually the project lapsed.

Binyamin had an idea. He went into the house to get his laptop computer and brought it out. It had a very small hard drive by current standards, so he couldn't keep any modern software on it, but it had some minimal programming capacity. He set to work blocking out his program. It felt good to be programming again, even in a language as dinky as BASIC. After a while, Miriam came out and stood looking over his shoulder.

"What are you doing?" she asked.

"Setting up my computer to act as a watch dog. I want it to compile a list of my good and bad deeds to print out for me before Yom Kippur next year. I'll call you when I have something working and I'll give you a demonstration."

"Why do you need the good deeds?"

"To see what I used to be better at. Also, I thought that the idea of being asked if I had done anything nice for anyone lately might make me look around for good things to do."

It was another hour before he had something he was willing to show her. "Here," he said as he booted up. A date appeared on the screen and then the question, "Good deeds?"

Binyamin typed in, "Watered geranium," and double-spaced.

"Sins?" asked the computer.

"Forgot to write to parents," confessed Binyamin, "Forgot to make bed." He double-spaced again.

"OK." said the computer.

"Isn't that kind of ... too easy?" asked Miriam. "Instant absolution of sins."

"That's just a technicality. This programming language always says 'OK' when it finishes a task, but if it bothers you I can fix it."

He called her back fifteen minutes later for a new demonstration. This time, after he had confessed his sins, the computer wrote, "Repent now if you want it to be OK."

Binyamin set to work building the *sukkah*. One of the neighboring families had gotten their lift from Argentina a few days before. They were so ecstatic about finally getting a supply of yerba maté to drink that they agreed to give him the plywood walls of the lift without a second thought. Binyamin bought some two-by-fours and spent several hours cutting and sawing. By nightfall he was ready to assemble his project.

Binyamin let Shimmy stay up an extra half-hour to hand him the nails as he needed them. As he hammered at the plywood, he began thinking about when they should order their own lift. It would take six weeks to arrive. To store the contents in their tiny apartment in the hostel would be terribly uncomfortable, but they would want all those things as soon as they moved into a real apartment.

"Abba?"

"Yes, Shimmy?" Binyamin regretted having ignored his son while mulling thoughts about the lift.

"The teacher says we're going to eat in the *sukkah*."

"Yes, that's right. For seven days."

Shimmy looked down at the ant holes in the ground. "Won't we get ants in our food?"

"We'll bring out the table and chairs. We'll have to squeeze a bit, but we'll manage."

"If the table is out here, how will we eat breakfast?"

"We'll eat breakfast in the *sukkah*, too." Binyamin turned as he perched on a borrowed ladder and called into the house, "Miriam, could you please come hold two walls while I nail on the third?"

"Sure, be right there." She came out, drying her hands on a towel. "Are you being a big help?" she asked Shimmy.

He nodded.

"There isn't going to be much room for a bed," she commented to Binyamin.

"We'll have to take out the table at night."

Shimmy opened his eyes wide. "Are we going to sleep in the *sukkah*, too?"

"I am," said his father. "You're still too young. Maybe next year."

Shimmy, seeing that this *sukkah*-building business was a big man's thing, looked around for some way to be more helpful. Miriam had taken up her position at the outside corner between the first and second walls. "Can I hold a wall like Ima?"

"Don't think you're tall enough. I'm afraid it might fall on you and squash you like a pancake." Binyamin got down and moved the ladder to the open part of the U shape with one hand while supporting the wall with the other. "All right, Miriam, here's the hard part. I have to try to nail this two-by-four across the opening without letting go of the third wall. Once that's done, it will be stable and you can go back to the house."

"And put Shimmy to bed," said Miriam significantly.

Shimmy ducked behind the third wall. Perhaps if he were not in sight, his mother would become engrossed in talking to his father and forget that it was way past his bedtime.

Binyamin nailed one end of the beam to the top of the third wall. He used that beam to hold up the wall as he pushed the ladder to the other side of the opening with his foot. He was climbing backward up the rungs, holding the beam awkwardly high in the air, when the foot of the ladder sank into an ant hole and threw him off balance. The beam dropped and the third wall began falling outward, wrenching itself loose at the corner. "Shimmy!" shouted Binyamin as he fell. "Watch out!"

Miriam let go of her corner and ran to catch the falling wall. "Shimmy! Binyamin! What's happening?" The other two walls also fell outward. The *sukkah* walls lay flat on the ground. Binyamin was on his back, tangled up in the ladder, and Shimmy and Miriam, unscathed, stood looking at each other across the ruins.

Binyamin picked himself up, dusting the streaks of red earth off his dark pants. "Well, so much for that attempt to build the *sukkah*. Let's call it quits for the night."

Shimmy burst into tears. "How will we eat? Where will you sleep?"

Binyamin picked him up and rubbed his cheek against Shimmy's curls as he carried him into the house. "Don't worry, *tzaddik*. You just go to *gan* tomorrow and make us a nice decoration to hang up in our *sukkah*, and I'll worry about building it. I guarantee you that within three days it will be ready, just when we need it."

"And I hope that the next one will stay built," muttered Miriam uneasily.

The next morning after taking Shimmy to *gan*, Binyamin got Asaf and another immigrant named Carlos to come help him put up the *sukkah*. With each of the back two corners being firmly held, it was a matter of minutes to nail a beam across the fourth side and attach the two partial walls. Then they held the end of the cross-beams, which would support the *s'chach*. He shook hands with his two friends in thanks and walked out to the bus stop. He still had to get more *s'chach*, as well as his *lulav* and *esrog*.

If Binyamin had thought that the streets of Geula were crowded the last time he was there, he had to admit it was nothing compared to the crush that prevailed three days before Sukkos. Whole storefronts had opened up selling nothing but *arbaa minim*, and on other streets new tables for *lulavim* and *esrogim* had been squeezed in between existing displays. Bookstores were advertising new books, music stores were advertising new tapes and CDs, and *sukkah* decorations were strung overhead everywhere. Binyamin bought a few gaudy ones and several colorful posters.

The next thing Binyamin bought was a thick *sefer* on how to choose the *arbaa minim*. Then he joined the connoisseurs browsing the tables. Nothing as simple here as just choosing a pre-matched set. He was expected to buy each of the four species separately, from a different dealer. Most of the merchandise was so fresh that it looked as if it had been picked yesterday, and perhaps it had.

When he finally made his selection, paying by check and reserving the right to cancel the deal if the merchandise was not approved by a rabbi, he stood in a long line to get his *arbaa minim* checked. He had to go back to change the *lulav* and then wait in line again for the rabbi. By now he was hungry and worn out, but he didn't want to take his *lulav* and *esrog* into one of the crowded falafel shops where they might be damaged, so he resigned himself to waiting for lunch until he got home, and moved on to the *s'chach* market. His favorite choice would have been the long palm fronds, and his second would have been canes, but he couldn't figure out how to get either back to the hostel, so he settled for a mat he could roll up and fit into the compartment under the bus.

It was very awkward standing in line for the bus holding seven packages and a tall mat. When a beggar approached jiggling coins in a plastic cup, he was sorely tempted just to let other people give, but finally shifted all his bundles to one hand while digging into his pocket for a donation. This happened three separate times, so it was a relief when the bus finally pulled up. He stowed the mat in the baggage compartment under the bus and sank into his seat exhausted.

When Binyamin got home, Shimmy took him out to the back to show him that he had already hung up one decoration. Binyamin spread the *s'chach* over the beams, and they admired their creation. It looked perfectly solid. As they walked together toward the house, Binyamin glanced back, remembering last night's disaster. He hoped that their attempt to build a home in Eretz Yisrael would not fall as flat as had his first *sukkah*.

Since Binyamin had finally gotten them registered in a medical plan, he celebrated by going to the doctor the day before Sukkos about a rash that had been bothering him since they arrived. He got home in time for lunch.

"How was it?" asked Miriam.

"Very educational," said Binyamin. "I discovered that Israelis come in three flavors."

"Yes?"

"Line jumpers, line guarders and spectators. I was a spectator this time, but next time I might sign up with the line guarders."

"What does that involve?" asked Miriam, amused.

"Well, when anyone arrives, he's supposed to ask, 'Who is last?' Since I didn't know that, I was under immediate suspicion as a potential line jumper. When I strolled over to the door to look at the list of patients on the bulletin board, someone said to me, 'Excuse me, Mister, it is far from being your turn.' When I apologized, and denied any intention of cutting in before my time, they let me off.

"Up waltzed some fellow who asked, 'Who is next?' One of the self-appointed line guarders said coldly, 'I am.'

"The first fellow responded, 'Could you let me in for a few minutes? I just want to get a prescription.'

"The other guy replied, 'Yeah, I've heard that one before, from people who stayed inside for twenty minutes and got themselves examined from head to toe. You can go in with me, and ask for your prescription. I warn you, if you want him to do three different things, you can just wait your turn like the rest of us.' Actually, he was in and out in a snap."

"Waiting in line seems to have made more of an impression on you than the actual visit to the doctor," commented Miriam.

"Not too surprising. All that the doctor had to say was, 'You got that rash because it was summer. When winter comes it will go away.'

"'But it bothers me now!' I protested. 'Isn't there something you can do?'

"'Sure,' the doctor said. 'I'll write you a prescription for a salve, which you can rub on the itchy places twice a day. But it won't clear up until the winter.'"

Sandra had "helped" Tami make a decoration for the *sukkah* walls, and Miriam hung it up in a conspicuous place. Shimmy's contributions included a *"Baruch Haba"* sign and a picture of Yerushalayim. Binyamin hung up the posters and decorations he had bought in Geula.

Miriam wanted to invite Sandra's family for the first night of Sukkos, since they were using the communal *sukkah;* but there was simply no way that another four people could sit down to a meal in the Lerner's tiny *sukkah.* She compromised by having Binyamin's friend Asaf in the evening and inviting Sandra and her husband Cyril for *Kiddush* on Sukkos morning.

She set out the food on the table and each adult sat on one of the four chairs with a child in his or her lap. The children thought that it was great fun, but Miriam was glad that she didn't have to eat anything more demanding than a slice of cake that way.

"*Lechaim,*" said Cyril, raising his paper cup full of wine. "By this time next year may we all be in our own homes with our own *sukkah.*"

"*Lechaim,*" they all echoed.

"Better yet," proposed Binyamin, "let's have the *Beis Hamikdash* rebuilt, and we can all go to Yerushalayim for the *chag.*"

"*Amein,*" seconded Cyril.

Miriam's first attack of pain came during the evening meal on the second night of *chol hamo'ed.* She attributed the first twinges to the cold. Nights in the hills around Yerushalayim were chilly, and they were eating outdoors. All their own winter clothing was in the lift, but she had borrowed two sweaters from Sandra and was wearing both.

After they had eaten the main course and Miriam was stacking the plates so that she could carry as much as possible into the house in one trip, she felt a stab of pain in her chest so severe that it made her gasp. She stopped in the middle of what she was doing, afraid to move.

"What's wrong?" asked Binyamin with concern.

"Pain," murmured Miriam. "In my chest."

"Can you sit down without making it worse?"

Still holding her arms in the same awkward position in which she had frozen, she flexed her knees and managed to lower herself into her chair. Then she concentrated on trying to move her arms into a more natural stance. She still felt as if a deep breath or a sudden movement would cause another shooting pain, but at least she was now reasonably comfortable. After some rest and further efforts to relax, they finally managed to transfer her to her own bed, where she snuggled down under the covers.

"Should I call an ambulance?" wondered Binyamin aloud.

"I don't think so. Now that I'm beginning to warm up, the pain is melting away. I'm pretty sure that everything will be fine."

"If the pain doesn't come back, I'm willing to let it ride until the morning, but then you'll have to go see a doctor."

"Why, so that he can treat my pain the way he treated your skin rash?"

"He can hardly tell you that you have a pain because it is summer and that it will go away when winter comes. Besides, he was perfectly willing to prescribe creams; he just said it wouldn't do any good."

"Well, he can tell me that I have a pain because it's winter and that it will go away when summer comes."

"Do you want me to go with you to translate?"

He was, of course, perfectly right in thinking that it was the idea of tackling the Sick Fund bureaucracy in Hebrew that daunted her, but it hurt anyway. "No, you stay here and take care of the children. I'll manage this one on my own."

Binyamin called up in the morning and made an appointment for her, but of course it was not quite as simple as just waiting politely for her turn. First she had to stop at the main desk so that they could open a file for her, since this was her first visit to the doctor. Then she was sent to wait outside room 103.

"What's your number?" asked one of the other women on line.

"I have no idea," admitted Miriam. "How would I find out?"

"Check the list."

Sure enough, there was a list posted next to the door. She was number fourteen, due to go in at 10:20. It was now 10:25. "I'm fourteen."

"Number ten is in there now, so you have a while to wait."

A rather disheveled woman rounded the corner and came puffing up to the door and peered at the list. "I'm number eight," she announced.

"You missed your turn," someone told her, with a slight hint of satisfaction. "You were supposed to be here at 9:20."

"These times are never exact," said the newcomer, still standing next to the door.

Another man stood up and came to stand next to her. "Numbers nine and ten already went in. You know the rules. If you miss your turn, you have to wait for two more people to take their turn. I'm next and you will be after that woman." He pointed to someone seated next to Miriam. Defeated, the latecomer went and sat down.

When Miriam's turn finally arrived at 11:05, she went in and took a seat across the desk from the doctor. "I've been having chest pains," she said.

"Are you a new immigrant?" asked the doctor.

"Yes," said Miriam, wondering why that would be relevant.

"Then that is why you're having chest pains," said the doctor.

"What should I do about it?" asked Miriam.

"Nothing," said the doctor.

Miriam, realizing that she had been dismissed, got up and walked out. When she got home, she told Binyamin, "He says it comes from being a new immigrant."

"It seems odd to me that he didn't do more tests."

"Yes," said Miriam, "I had rather expected that he would listen to my heart with a stethoscope."

"What?!" exclaimed Binyamin. "I was talking about an electrocardiogram. You seriously mean to tell me that he didn't even use a stethoscope?"

"Why should he?" asked Miriam with a hopeless shrug of her shoulders. "He knew why my chest hurt. I'm a new immigrant."

Binyamin approached the door of Livneh's office. It was a week past Sukkos, and he hoped that by now the government would have come through with his security clearance. Who knows, he fantasized, perhaps he would even be able to begin work today.

"Has it come through?" Binyamin asked, as soon as he was shown into the older man's office.

"What?"

"The security clearance."

"No."

That answer he could have gotten on the phone. There was a reason he had chosen to come in person.

"Did you ask them why not?"

Livneh shrugged. "I presume that they just haven't gotten around to it yet. Backlog from the *chagim*."

"Have you checked to make sure that the list arrived?"

"What's the matter? You think that the mail in Israel isn't reliable?"

"You know," said Binyamin, "I am totally reliant on you. My cash is running low, and soon I won't know how to feed my family. Would it be so difficult for you to make one phone call?"

"Oh, all right," agreed Livneh grudgingly. He lifted the receiver and dialed a number. "Hello, Shmulik, Dudu here. ... Oh, we're fine. How's Dafna? ... No, this is actually a business call. Listen, some time back we sent you material on some fellow named," he peered at Binyamin's file, "Lerner, Binyamin Lerner. You must have gotten it already. I sent it out before Sukkot. Look harder. ... See, I told you so. That means you haven't gotten anywhere on it yet? ... Look, maybe you could fax it to the States. ... Thanks. Send my best to Dafna and the kids." He replaced the receiver, and looked up at Binyamin. "They're working on it."

Does he really think I don't understand Hebrew? Binyamin asked himself. All he said out loud was, "Thanks, I'll check again in a week."

He was so discouraged that he skipped his usual visit to Mitch for commiseration. Instead, he went straight back to Yerushalayim. He didn't get off at Castel, but went on into town and took a bus to Mattersdorf. He would arrive at Chaim Ozer's *kollel* in time to *daven Minchah* with them at the end of the morning session. Today was Rosh Chodesh Cheshvan, the first day of the new *zeman*.

Chaim Ozer, of course, invited him for lunch, and he poured out his woes as they walked to his friend's apartment. Chaim Ozer thought the whole thing through for a few moments. Then he said,

"It might not hurt to contact one or two of these software firms in Bnai Brak, and let this Mitch know that you did so. Despite his casual attitude about bureaucratic delay, he must really want you or he would never have persuaded Livneh to hire you in the first place."

It sounded like good advice, and Binyamin was inclined to take it, if Miriam would agree.

Chaim Ozer, who had turned silent and thoughtful, now spoke again. "Until you get your job settled, why don't you come learn in my *kollel*? We're an odd number this term, so I think I can find you a learning partner."

"This would be without a stipend, I presume?" asked Binyamin.

"You usually learn without a stipend, don't you?"

"What are you learning?"

"The *Mishnah* and *Talmud Yerushalmi* pertaining to *shemittah*."

"You're on," agreed Binyamin. That should provide just the sort of theoretical background he was missing for the class he taught twice a week at the hostel.

Life settled into a routine. Every morning after breakfast Binyamin took Shimmy to *gan* and caught the bus into town. The learning partner Chaim Ozer had found him was sharp, if slightly erratic in attendance. Once a week Binyamin took the day off and went to Tel Aviv to nudge Livneh. After that, he went to Bnai Brak for interviews. They had ordered their lift, which was somewhere on the Atlantic Ocean or the Mediterranean Sea.

One day a security agent arrived to interview Miriam.

"Have you ever belonged to any communist organizations? Pacifist causes?"

"No."

"Sympathizers for the Palestine Liberation Organization?"

"Surely not."

"How many years of education do you have?"

"Fourteen."

"Employment history?"

"I did secretarial work for two years after I finished school. Now I am raising my children."

"Do you belong to any political party? Consumer rights organizations? Lobbies? Feminist causes?"

"No."

The agent looked down at his tally sheet in disgust. "How in the world am I supposed to make up an ideological profile for you if you're such a namby-pamby about joining things?"

"I did belong to a group called Ahavas Chesed, which raises money for needy families," ventured Miriam.

"Well, that's something, at least. I'll put you down as a do-good-er." He made a notation on the pad, happy to have found a label for Miriam. His glance swept the apartment. "How much longer will you be staying here?"

"Believe me, I wish I knew!"

On Rosh Chodesh Kislev, Binyamin traveled to Tel Aviv again. This time he didn't bother with Livneh. He went straight to Mitch.

"I have another job offer," he announced. "Should I take it?"

"Of course not," said Mitch. "How long have you been here?"

"Two and a half months," said Binyamin bitterly.

"That really is ridiculous. Come with me. We're going to settle this today."

Binyamin trailed along behind Mitch as he stalked into the personnel office. "Livneh, what is this nonsense of spending nearly three months on red tape? I am going to America in January, and I need Lerner broken in and ready to cover for me. Do those klutzes over there in security really think he is a Syrian spy?"

"Russian, actually. He belonged to some organization that taught him Russian and sent him to Kiev for two straight summers. Then the organization went underground."

"I never heard such *narishkeit* in my life." He turned to Binyamin, "What were you doing in Kiev?"

"Teaching *Yiddishkeit* to Jewish teenagers."

"Thought so." Mitch turned to Livneh. "Call this pal of yours in security, Shmulik. I want to talk to him myself." As Livneh dialed, he turned back to Binyamin. "The current Rav in Kiev is an American, a *Karliner chassid*. Would he know you? Do you have his phone number?"

Binyamin nodded yes on both counts.

Mitch spoke firmly to Livneh's contact in security, gave him the phone number of the rabbi in Kiev, and said that he expected an answer by the end of the day. "In the meantime, I'm going to see about getting Lerner a work station, and you can order the security badge."

"I'll need two color pictures, 3 centimeters by 5."

Binyamin pointed wordlessly to the two pictures, which were clipped to the back of his folder. "Okay," said Livneh, "I'll order the badge."

"I'm sorry about the long delay," apologized Mitch after they left the office, "but I couldn't have pulled that kind of railroading until they had actually botched the job in a way that was obvious. If I had tried that two months ago, Livneh would have been so balky that you would have suffered from him for twenty years. At the moment he's annoyed at me, not at you, and he has good reason to want to forget the whole incident."

Chapter 13

Chanukah Present

On his way home, Binyamin bought two of the largest secular newspapers, ripped out the classified ads and dropped the rest of the paper into the trash. Over dinner they talked about where they would like to live. He fingered one of the *sefarim* he had bought on *shemittah*. "I'm going to miss teaching the *shiur*," he said with a sigh.

"Why should you?" asked Miriam. "Why don't you go on giving it?"

"But we won't be living anywhere near here!"

"You'll be driving past every day. Once you have a car, it won't be such a big deal to stop here on your way, give the *shiur*, and then continue on home. It's only twice a week."

Binyamin felt himself cheering up at the suggestion. The teaching had come to mean a lot to him in the last couple of months, and he knew that most of the men in the *shiur* would not be learning nearly as much if they didn't have this opportunity. Where they were moving, any kind of a class he could give would be superfluous. If Miriam was willing, shouldn't he agree? "I think you're on!"

That evening, he and Miriam pored over the Apartments for

Rent-Yerushalayim section.

"Here are two rooms in Katamon," said Miriam.

"I think two rooms means a living room and a bedroom. Even if we're trying to be frugal, I don't think we should push it that far. Here is an ad for three rooms in Talpiot."

"I suppose we could look into it," said Miriam dubiously.

"I'll make a list of everything that seems even vaguely possible," suggested Binyamin, "and then we can call up the two that seem most likely. I doubt we can see more than two apartments in a day."

"Isn't it sort of odd that there don't seem to be any apartments for rent in the religious neighborhoods?" asked Miriam.

"I understand that there's a housing crunch at the moment. Maybe the apartments in the religious sections are snapped up as soon as people hear that they're available."

"No, I think there's something more seriously wrong. None of these apartments is anywhere we would want to live." She took a deep breath and let it out. "I think you had better call Ella for advice."

"Why don't you do it?" suggested Binyamin. "I'll stay here with the children."

Ella was delighted to hear that Binyamin was finally going to be allowed to work.

"So now," continued Miriam, "we're looking for an apartment to rent. Binyamin brought home the classified ads, and there doesn't seem to be anything appropriate in Yerushalayim."

"That can't be," said Ella. "Wait, let me get the paper... Here, three rooms in Unsdorf, three and a half in Ramot, three in Har Nof. What's wrong with those?"

"I don't have any of those listed here," said Miriam, struggling with the fine print of the Hebrew ads.

"Well, I happen to be looking in *Hamodia*, but I would imagine that the other papers would have the same sort of thing. Also, the local papers with free classified ads have a lot of apartments listed."

Miriam was embarrassed to admit to Ella just how egregious a mistake they had made. "Okay, I see. Thanks." She went back to Binyamin, gathered up the classified ads, and ceremoniously dropped them in the wastebasket.

"What does that mean?" he asked.

"That means that apartments in the religious areas are advertised in the religious dailies, not in the secular newspapers."

In order to get to Tel Aviv on time, Binyamin had to go to a different shul in the morning, and straight from there to work, without coming home for breakfast. Miriam fixed him his lunch, as well as a breakfast, the night before and left it out on the table. She asked him to wake her up as he went out, since she would have to take Shimmy to *gan*. She would just have to come late to *ulpan*, but she wasn't afraid of the *ulpan* teacher any more. As for the afternoon, she was planning a surprise for Binyamin. She would go into Mattersdorf with the children and do the preliminary screening of apartments herself, or rather, with Ella's help.

By 3:30, Miriam and Ella were settled at Ella's kitchen table going over the listing of apartments for rent. Tami was asleep in one of the bedrooms, and a neighbor's daughter had taken Shimmy and Ella's children to the park.

"Now, the first thing to do," said Ella with authority, "is to make a list with nothing more than area, number of rooms, and rent. That will give you a general picture of the market and the variation between neighborhoods. We will put down even the apartments that are too big or too small, since we're mostly doing this for comparison."

"A lot of these ads don't list the rent," Miriam pointed out.

"I know," said Ella. "That's why we're doing this, so that we won't have to waste a lot of time with phone calls about apartments that are much too expensive. If the apartment is a real bargain for its size and area, they'll probably let us know in print."

After they had finished the first list, Ella had them make a second list of the most promising-looking apartments, with details and phone numbers. When that was finally finished, she glanced at her watch. "It's 3:50. I'd rather not call these people until the end of the two-to-four rest period. Why don't we break for coffee?"

"That would be nice," said Miriam, whose head was pounding from poring over the fine print of the newspaper. "While the water is heating, do you think I could call Binyamin? He gave me his boss's phone number. I forgot to leave him a note telling him where I was going."

"Why not invite him to come straight here and have dinner with us? Then if one of these apartments is something you should jump at, I can watch the children while you two go look at it."

"I don't know," said Miriam dubiously. "He's probably very tired, after getting up early and going through all the tension of the first day at a new job." She herself was very tired already, and her day had been less strenuous than his.

"It won't hurt to ask," insisted Ella.

Binyamin thought Ella's suggestion was wonderful. "Tomorrow I'll be teaching my *shiur*, so I won't be able to get out to look at anything. Why don't you try to set up appointments for us to see one or two of these places this evening?"

Miriam hung up with a vague feeling of dissatisfaction. It took her a while to pinpoint the source of her unhappiness. Her own initiative in bringing the two children to Mattersdorf had been eclipsed by this new plan. Binyamin probably thought that that had been Ella's idea as well.

"Why don't we call this one first?" proposed Ella. "Two and a half rooms in Rommema." She held up the classified section on which she had circled one of the listings.

"Won't that be rather cramped?" asked Miriam dubiously.

"It's in an older neighborhood, and often the rooms are bigger there. The point to Rommema is that it's close to the Central Bus Station."

This didn't seem like much of a recommendation to Miriam, who had never considered the Central Bus Station to be one of the tourist attractions of Yerushalayim. "Why would we want to live there?"

"So that it will be easier for your husband to get to work in the morning. Almost all the traffic to Tel Aviv funnels out through that one three-lane highway down the Yerushalayim corridor, and it can get badly tied up. At least if you live within walking distance of the bus station, he can avoid adding on time for one or two bus rides in rush hour traffic inside Yerushalayim."

"Oh, we're planning to get a car," said Miriam blithely.

"Get a car!" exclaimed Ella. "Don't do that!"

"Why shouldn't we buy a car?" insisted Miriam.

"Because the expenses will simply eat up all your spare income. There's registration, insurance, repairs, gasoline, and financing.

Even in America, *Consumer Reports* did a study showing that it would be cheaper to take taxis than to maintain a private car. "

"Traveling to Tel Aviv every day by public transportation will also cost money," Miriam pointed out.

"Not as much as owning a car," Ella insisted.

"He could carpool with someone."

"Is he really likely to find someone from near where he lives going to the same industrial park south of Tel Aviv?"

"But Ella, if he has to commute by bus, it will take so much time that he will either have no time left over for learning or no time for us."

"You could decide to live near Tel Aviv."

"We didn't come to Eretz Yisrael to live in Tel Aviv. We came to Eretz Yisrael to live in Yerushalayim."

"You have to make some sacrifices to live in Eretz Yisrael."

"But if those sacrifices are going to be my husband's learning or his family time, maybe we would be better off going back to America!" Miriam was getting quite upset.

Ella placed her hand on Miriam's. "I think for the moment we should be concentrating on the apartment. You're not planning to buy this car tomorrow, are you?"

"No," said Miriam with a sullen undertone in her voice.

"Then there's still time to talk about it. Maybe over supper."

Miriam realized that she didn't want Ella discussing this question with Binyamin, but she had a hopeless feeling that there was no way she would prevent it. They tackled the list of phone numbers, Ella making the calls and Miriam recording the results. Some of the apartments had been taken since the ad was placed, and some seemed overpriced, but after seven calls, they found something that seemed reasonable.

"Could my friends come over at eight o'clock to look at it?" Ella asked.

Miriam had a sudden inspiration. "Make that 7:30," she instructed Ella in a stage whisper.

Ella put her hand over the receiver. "Are you sure? That won't leave your husband much time to eat."

"I'm sure," said Miriam. "Otherwise, we'll miss the 9:30 bus to Mevasseret and will have to wait until 10:30."

Ella nodded and then spoke to the owner. "Actually, 7:30 would be better. Will you tell the current tenants to expect them?"

That arrangement made, they continued the phone calls until they had exhausted the list, reducing it to a total of four possibilities. One of the other apartments was near the first one they were going to see, and they arranged to see that one at 8:10. "What about the 9:30 bus?" asked Ella when Miriam proposed this addition to the schedule.

"We can get to the bus station by taxi," said Miriam.

The baby-sitter brought the children home from their trip to the park, and Miriam helped Ella get them fed and ready for bed. She wanted to be able to step out the door the moment Binyamin arrived. When the bell rang, she was standing right there with her coat on, and was a little disappointed to discover that it was only two *yeshivah bachurim* collecting *tzedakah*. However, as she handed them a donation, Binyamin came into sight on the stairs.

"I'm all ready," she called. "Our first appointment is at 7:30."

"Good," said Binyamin. "Uh, is there time for me to snatch something to eat?"

"I'm afraid not," said Miriam, with unusual firmness in her tone. "We'll try to pick up something for you on the way."

"Maybe there's a falafel stand near this apartment," said Binyamin hopefully.

There wasn't. No pizza, either. "We could buy you a candy bar at that kiosk there," suggested Miriam, who was beginning to feel quite guilty about Binyamin's hunger pangs.

"I don't want candy, I want food," said Binyamin.

"I could cook you something when we get home."

"Start cooking at 10:30 at night? Let's not be ridiculous. I'll eat a half jar of peanut butter or something. I'm beginning to get used to Israeli stuff."

The first apartment did not appeal to either of them, but the second, in Givat Shaul, seemed like a definite possibility. There were two and a half bedrooms, so that they could have guests. The standard Israeli floor tiles were worn and the marble countertop in the kitchen was pockmarked from corrosive cleaning agents, but they didn't expect much from a rented apartment, and the front balcony had a nice view of the street. Binyamin called the owner and entered into preliminary negotiations. At nine o'clock, Miriam called Ella to alert her that they were coming to pick up the children and would have to leave straightaway.

"Did your husband get anything to eat?" asked Ella.

"I'm afraid not," admitted Miriam with another stab of guilt, "but we really have to catch that 9:30 bus."

"I understand," said Ella.

With the taxi waiting downstairs, Binyamin and Miriam dashed upstairs to the Wahrhaftigs' apartment to pick up their sleeping children. "Thanks for everything, Ella," said Miriam breathlessly. "We couldn't have done this without you."

Ella handed her two bags. "One is the children's clothes," she said. "The other one is for you."

They managed to catch the bus they wanted, and when they were seated and the children were asleep again, Miriam opened the second bag as instructed. "Wow! Look what Ella sent along! Salmon steak, two pieces of *kugel,* salad in a plastic container, and a piece of cake."

"Don't you want some, too?"

"I'm not hungry."

Once Binyamin had eaten, he seemed to relax. She thought he was drifting off to sleep like the children when he startled her by asking, "Whose idea was this trip to Mattersdorf?"

"Mine," admitted Miriam, doubting that he considered it an unqualified success.

"It was a terrific idea. I'm proud of you for taking that kind of an initiative."

Although they saw two more apartments in the next few days, they eventually rented the one in Givat Shaul. It had basic furniture and the major appliances, so they wouldn't have to make those purchases right now, in the midst of a hectic week. Binyamin had insisted that the apartment needed painting, and, in the end, the landlord capitulated.

"This seems to be going too smoothly," said Binyamin. "Could it really be true that we found an apartment within a week?"

"We didn't find an apartment, we chose one," said Miriam. "We are only renting, and it's only for a year, so we just took the most reasonable among the apartments on the market. Success was almost guaranteed."

"You mean to say that if we had had a lot of preconditions, we might not have found anything to suit?" asked Binyamin thoughtfully.

"Exactly."

"Shouldn't you factor in *siyatta diShmaya*?"

"Of course. That's why I said 'almost.'"

The lift was scheduled to arrive two days before Chanukah, and Binyamin hoped that the painters would be done by then. They began winding up their life in Mevasseret. The six suitcases with which they had arrived had inexplicably grown to include an additional eleven boxes. "Where in the world did we get all this stuff?" asked Binyamin, puzzled.

"Well," said Miriam, beginning to tick things off on her fingers, "there are about six boxes of things we borrowed from Ella, which I am not ready to return until we unpack our own lift. Then, there are containers of food, *sefarim* that you bought, papers from my *ulpan* and Shimmy's *gan*, the two heaters we bought after the first rain..."

Binyamin held up his hands in surrender. "Okay, I get the idea."

When the lift was due, Binyamin took a day off from work to wait for it. The painters were not finished—at least, not to Binyamin's satisfaction—and he spent the morning trying to get them to clean paint spills off the floor, windows and doors. Why they couldn't have used drop cloths was completely beyond his understanding. They finally left at noon. At 2:30, Miriam arrived, having left the children with Sandra. When she walked in and found that their things had not arrived, her face fell. There were lots of items in those boxes for which she was waiting impatiently.

"Now that you're here," Binyamin said, "I can go get us something to eat and call the movers to see why they're delayed."

"Don't get anything for me," said Miriam. "After that long bus ride I'm not hungry."

He returned with a falafel and the unsatisfactory information that the lift was on its way, but the secretary didn't know when it would arrive. They sat and talked as they hadn't had a chance to do since Binyamin had started work. They spoke about Miriam's progress in Hebrew, about Binyamin's new job, about what teaching the *shiur* meant to him, about Shimmy's frustrations in *gan*.

There was a rap on the door, and then it was pushed open by a man holding a stack of five 24-roll packages of toilet paper.

"Where do these go?" he asked gruffly.

"In the bathroom," said Binyamin, startled, pointing in that direction.

The next hour was torturous, as they tried to decipher the marks they had made on each box fast enough to satisfy the impatient movers, who would have preferred simply to dump everything in the center of the living room. By the time the entire contents of the lift were in the apartment, the house was heaped with teetering piles, while Binyamin and Miriam were limp and frazzled.

"What in the world do we do now?" asked Miriam, looking around in despair.

"Go home and put the children to bed," said Binyamin decisively. "We'll worry about all this tomorrow."

The senior member of the moving team came up to Binyamin, held out his hand, and said, "Tip!"

No one had said a word to Binyamin about tipping the movers. "Just a second," he mumbled. "I have to make an emergency phone call." He frantically dialed the Wahrhaftigs' number and asked Ella in Yiddish how much he was supposed to give. Since the mover had told him that he was from Morocco, Binyamin presumed that it was safe to speak in Yiddish.

"Let's see, for the contents of a lift? Two workers? Probably fifty shekel apiece. You can give it to the one in charge and he'll divide it."

Binyamin turned to Miriam and asked, still in Yiddish, "Have any money?" Miriam pulled her wallet out of her purse and extracted a fifty-shekel note. Binyamin added one from his own wallet and placed both bank notes in the outstretched palm. "For both of you."

"*Zol zein mit hatzlachah,*" said the mover as he pocketed the money. Just their luck to draw a Yiddish-speaking Moroccan.

Binyamin left work early and arrived in time to help carry out the last two boxes to the small van. Binyamin and Shimmy got into the back with their boxes, while Miriam, holding Tami, climbed into the cab of the truck. The Zagbadis turned out to wish them goodbye, and Dani gave Shimmy three keys as a going-away present.

When they reached their new apartment, Binyamin and the

driver unloaded the boxes and suitcases onto the sidewalk. Then the man held out his hand for his payment.

"Aren't you going to carry it upstairs?" asked Binyamin.

"The price I quoted was for hauling the goods to this address. If you want me to *shlep* them upstairs, that's extra."

"How much extra?" asked Binyamin.

"Which floor do you live on?"

"Second."

The man looked the pile over. "A hundred and fifty shekels."

"That's almost as much as you charged for the moving," said Binyamin, outraged. "I'll carry it upstairs by myself, thank you." And so, with Miriam and the children sitting downstairs to guard their property, he did.

It was 4:15 by the time they were finally all in the apartment. Binyamin began systematically putting each box from the lift on the floor, opening it, and rummaging through, with Miriam and the children trailing behind. It was like a treasure hunt.

Miriam took a break. She emerged a few minutes later with shining eyes, to find Binyamin standing disconsolately in the middle of the living room, surrounded by boxes.

"It's all right," Shimmy was saying, holding up the gilded menorah he had made in *gan*, "you can use mine."

"It looks like I'll have to," said Binyamin sadly.

"What's wrong, dear?" Miriam asked. She couldn't deliver her news when he was looking so miserable.

"It's time to light already, and I can't find our Chanukah menorah." It was a silver one that her parents had bought him during their engagement, and he was very fond of it.

"When I was packing, I wrapped it in my white angora sweater so that it wouldn't be damaged. I saw it just a second ago." She pivoted slowly, surveying the boxes, and then pointed. "Try that one over there."

Binyamin dived into the indicated box and emerged triumphantly with a sweater-wrapped box swathed in plastic. "Got it!" He began removing the tape from the bag.

"Listen, Binyamin, that day last winter when we went to my parents to tell them that we were thinking of moving to Eretz Yisrael, do you remember what my mother had hoped we were coming to tell them?"

Binyamin looked up with dawning comprehension. "You mean ... ?" He broke into a grin.

Miriam nodded with a smile as broad as his. "Can I splurge on a telephone call to my mother to give her the good news?"

Binyamin glanced at his watch. "I think you had better help Shimmy set up his menorah and light it while I take care of mine. Then, in honor of our aspiring new family member, you can call your mother and talk for just as long as you like."

After Binyamin and Shimmy lit their *menoros*, the entire family stood together on the front porch, watching the lights of the flames appearing in window after window up and down the Yerushalayim street.

Chapter 14

Independent Living

Elisha looked at the calendar with satisfaction. The six months he had scheduled for his preliminary rehabilitation were over, and he was ahead of where he had hoped to be. His back had healed. He could sit up for a full day.

"Want anything for breakfast, Joe?" he asked his attendant. It was a ritual question and got a ritual answer.

"Nah, 'Lisha. Ah had a coffee an' a donut while you was a-prayin'." Joe wasn't comfortable eating in Mrs. Sheinfeld's kitchen, which seemed to him to have a number of booby traps. There was that two-sinks business, and then he was never quite sure where to put anything down. Elisha puttered about from refrigerator to table, getting himself a breakfast of milk and cereal. His mother had reorganized the cabinets so that the things he needed most frequently were on low shelves where he could reach them easily, and she was just as happy to have him manage feeding himself without help from Joe, who hadn't taken to the kosher kitchen concept.

"Want to hear the schedule for the day?"

"Sho' do."

"Well, after you drive me to yeshivah, you need to have the car back here for my mother by 9:30. She has some shopping to do, but will be able to give you the car again by 12:30. You can have the morning off. Today is one of the days for my bike session, and I'm supposed to be there as usual by 1:30. After that, a doctor's appointment in Queens, and back here by 4:00 for my *chavrusa*."

When Joe first started working for him, Elisha used to translate everything. He would say "study partner" instead of *chavrusa* and "synagogue" instead of shul. However, most of the concepts he had to translate were unfamiliar to Joe even in English. Once Joe figured out what was meant, he was just as happy using the Hebrew or Yiddish term, as long as he wasn't expected to pronounce a "*ches*."

"Whatcha gonna do at five, when yo' friend goes away? Take a nap?"

"I was hoping to skip it today."

"Don' know if that's so smart, 'Lisha," Joe warned him. "That bike thing allus knocks ya fo' a loop." This was a rather controversial therapy, meant to keep his leg muscles from atrophying and improve his circulation. Although his parents were dubious about anything experimental, Elisha had volunteered to participate in the clinical trials three times a week, and he thought it helped. However, as Joe pointed out, the sessions did always wear him out.

Elisha sighed. "All right, we'll schedule a nap, but only for an hour. After that I want to practice with the lift." This piece of equipment was meant to allow him to move himself from the bed to the chair and back. He couldn't manage it well yet. He was neither deft enough nor strong enough. Joe, of course, didn't bother with it. He just picked Elisha up and put him where he wanted him.

"Ya wants to put me out o' a job?"

"I want to get married, Joe. It's going to be hard enough finding a girl who can put up with me. It will be harder to find one who will put up with both of us."

Mrs. Sheinfeld glanced at her watch. In another fifteen minutes she was supposed to have the car back for Joe. Her forehead puckered. She had noticed that Elisha seemed restless lately. It was probably time for them to have a talk. She had not forgotten his ideas about driving and looking for a *shidduch*. She had made the preliminary phone calls back in the summer. As she had suspected, the *shadchanim* whom she had used when looking for spouses for her other children could not help.

She pulled the car into the reserved parking space in front of the house. She had gotten that arranged, along with the "Disabled" sticker for the car, before Elisha came home, and it was very convenient. It would have been unpleasant to have to wheel him several blocks to wherever the car was parked every time he wanted to go someplace.

Joe was sitting on the low wall waiting for her to return. He waved and called out, "Glad to see ya, Mrs. Sheinfel'"

"Hi, Joe," she waved back. She wondered what Joe did with himself during these two-to-three-hour gaps when Elisha didn't need him. Maybe he just went home. When he took the job, she had paid his moving expenses so that he could live nearby. She had wanted him within walking distance so that he could easily come at 6:30 to get Elisha out to *minyan*, and again in the evening to help him get into bed. It would have been hard on Joe if he hadn't lived close by.

After she pressed the button to open the trunk, Joe took out the grocery bags. She gathered a shopping bag of white shirts she had bought for Elisha, another one of outfits she had gotten for her grandchildren, and then slid out of the car. She handed Joe the car keys and a tip for helping her with the groceries.

After Joe left to pick up Elisha and she had put away the groceries, she sat down at her desk. She opened a file drawer and pulled out a folder with an "S" written on the tab. She opened the folder and pulled out a list with an "S" in the upper left-hand corner. The "S" on the folder was for "*shidduchim*." She hadn't labeled it clearly because she hadn't wanted any mischievous younger children taking an interest in their older siblings' marital prospects. That was no longer a consideration, but she was still using the same folder. This time the "S" stood for "special." It was a short list, with only three names and phone numbers.

Should she start or not? Once she had her talk with Elisha and he knew that she was contacting *shadchanim*, it would also be pretty obvious if she didn't come up with any prospects. From that point of view, it would be better to get started before he knew that she was working on it.

Mrs. Sheinfeld reached for the phone, but didn't pick up the receiver. This leaden feeling was in stark contrast to the energy with which she had set out to marry off her other children. Then, she had known that she had good "merchandise" and had expected her children to be appreciated. If someone turned them down, it was more a sign that the other side had poor judgment than a reason to feel insulted. But was Elisha one bit less clever, less *frum*, less precious in the eyes of Hashem? Of course not! So why did externals have to play such a huge role in this process?

Mrs. Sheinfeld pulled the phone closer. She lifted the receiver and dialed the first *shadchan* on her list.

During the week, the family ate at the end of the long dining room table nearest the door to the kitchen. Mr. Sheinfeld sat "in state" at the other end, Mrs. Sheinfeld on the side nearest the kitchen, and Elisha on the living room side. After the soup, Elisha looked at his parents and said, "I spoke to the doctor today about my rehabilitation program. He thinks I can drop the physical therapist and join an exercise group for paraplegics."

"I'm impressed," said his father sincerely. "I'm sure that it is because you have been so disciplined about doing your exercises." To save time and trouble, his parents had installed an exercise unit on one wall of the room. They had also installed a sink and basin, after having watched him cross the living room with a *nagel-vasser* basin balanced on his knees to refill the cup.

"Do they have programs like that?" Mrs. Sheinfeld asked.

Elisha nodded. "I found one at a men's gym. Partly aerobics, partly to strengthen individual muscles. The group meets twice a week, and I'll schedule the bicycle therapy for the other three days. If it's okay with you, I was planning to start tomorrow."

"Of course," said his father. "Why should we object?"

Mrs. Sheinfeld went into the kitchen and brought out the next course. The aroma of barbecued chicken filled the room, and there was a brief pause in the conversation as they each took one succulent piece.

"I've been working hard to be able to hold my weight with my arms. I think I'm ready to swing myself in and out of a car seat, if the car has a properly placed bar over the door."

"Is that really safe?" asked Mrs. Sheinfeld. "Can you put that much weight on a small bar?"

Mr. Sheinfeld's answer was more to the point. "I understand that you think that you're ready to start learning to use hand controls?"

"Once the car is converted, yes."

"And have you looked into this?" asked Mr. Sheinfeld.

Elisha nodded. "I'm interested in the crane that stores the chair on top of the car."

"All right, get me an estimate, or better, two estimates, and find out how long the car will be out of commission. If it sounds reasonable, we'll put in an order."

Elisha relaxed into his chair, pleased that that had gone so smoothly. As he had learned to his dismay on his first night home, it wasn't a good idea to tackle a number of separate issues in one conversation.

"Is that all?" asked his mother, beginning to stack the dinner plates, now that they had finished eating.

"What more do you want?" asked Elisha, caught off guard.

"I thought that we were going to begin looking for a wife for you after you had been home for half a year."

"Well, yes, that would be a good idea," Elisha got out somehow.

"I have the names of some *shadchunim* who deal with special *shidduchim*. However, before I call anyone up and say that I have a son who is looking for a *shidduch*, I'd like to know if there's anything in particular that you would like me to dismiss out of hand."

Elisha stared at her, still off balance. "What do you mean?"

"I spoke to some of these people. A lot of different problems come under the heading of 'special,' and some of them might be too much for you to deal with."

Elisha groped around. "She has to be *frum*. And planning to stay that way."

Mrs. Sheinfeld nodded.

"Other than that, I don't know. Shouldn't we just deal with each case as it comes?"

"All right, we can leave it that way, but then you have to promise not to be offended if I inquire about a deaf convert from Timbuktu."

Elisha winced. "I'll try."

"That was meant to be an extreme example, wasn't it?" asked Mr. Sheinfeld. "You don't really expect to have to pile up quite so many difficulties at once?"

"No, not really, but the job will be harder if, along with trying to weigh whether a certain suggestion is appropriate, I also have to agonize about whether I can even mention the idea." She picked up the stacks of plates and took them to the kitchen.

Elisha and his father looked at each other. "You know," said Mr. Sheinfeld, "if you think you're not yet ready for all the emotional buffeting this *shidduch* process is likely to bring you, Mom can wait."

"No, no, I'm glad. I'm glad she takes it so seriously, and I'm glad she brought it up herself. I'm sure that there are a lot of girls out there who are being undervalued because of some problem that doesn't reflect negatively on their *neshamah*. I will brace myself, and try to see clearly what's important and what's not."

Mrs. Sheinfeld returned with a tray on which she had placed three small bowls of compote. She didn't usually serve dessert during the week, but this dinner had taken on a more formal cast, marking the change from one phase of Elisha's life to another.

"Mom," said Elisha, "I want to thank you for your initiative. I know we're starting a period that won't be easy for either of us, and I feel much better because you're assuming this burden willingly."

"Let's not call it a burden. Let's call it a challenge," suggested Mrs. Sheinfeld.

After dinner, Mr. Sheinfeld and Elisha went out to *Maariv*. On the flat stretches, Elisha propelled himself. His father helped with the curbs and steps. They still kept up their *chavrusa* every evening, learning together for half an hour after the *minyan* in the *beis medrash*. They had, in fact, become much closer because of it.

Tonight, after they closed their *Gemaras* at the end of the session, Mr. Sheinfeld said, "I've been reading your magazines."

"Which, *Paraplegia News*?"

Mr. Sheinfeld nodded. "I see that they're working very hard researching how to regenerate the spinal cord."

"Indeed they are. I don't see it producing any results in the next five years, but, who knows? Maybe I'll be able to dance at my son's wedding." Elisha lifted his hands, palms up.

"I also read that the unemployment rate among the disabled is seventy percent."

"I saw that too," admitted Elisha soberly.

"As long as we're making important decisions today and you're moving toward independent living, maybe you should reconsider the idea of training as an accountant? You were the best of all our children in math. I don't think you would find the material beyond you. If you want to have a wife and children, you have to think about how to support them. Your wife may also have difficulty finding a job."

"All I can promise, Tatti, is that I'll try to be honest. Honest enough to recognize if my own ideas for a *parnassah* are not working out. Then I'll consider yours."

At breakfast Elisha said to his mother, "What are we going to do about the fact that most Jewish homes are not wheelchair accessible? I do *not* want to go with Joe to meet the parents of the girl."

"I suppose we could try to think of some other sort of meeting place," said Mrs. Sheinfeld, "but it's customary to have the boy go to the girl's house the first time, and you're right that you could not get into most houses. You couldn't even ring the bell."

"Imagine me sitting outside in the rain," suggested Elisha, "while indoors everyone is tapping their feet wondering why I haven't shown up."

Mr. Sheinfeld looked up from his morning paper. "I think the first time your mother and I should go with you. Lots of families routinely do so, and it will help us get you past any obstacles."

"That's a good idea," agreed Elisha. "I'll be happy to have you and Mom meet the girl. We may have some tough decisions ahead of us, and I think you'll be able to give me better advice if you know more about what we've discussed."

Mrs. Sheinfeld nodded. "For later meetings, we could use Bella's place. Since she lives in an apartment and the building has an elevator, there would be no problem with steps."

Elisha had worked hard to arrange a *chavrusa*. When he had decided near the end of Elul that he was up to sitting and learning a full morning *seder*, he had collected phone numbers of many old friends from yeshivah and had called them one by one. Most of them had heard what had happened to him and were delighted to hear him "sounding so normal," as more than one had said. He had found out who was already married, whether they were still learning, and where they would be the next *zeman*. He also asked to be informed if they heard of anyone in the Brooklyn area looking for a *chavrusa*.

On the fifteenth call he found what he was looking for. Yerachmiel Gold, a *bachur* who had been his *chavrusa* in Lakewood a few years ago, said that his *chavrusa* was leaving. He was in a *kollel* in Flatbush, and if the *Rosh Kollel* agreed he would be happy to learn with Elisha.

The *Rosh Kollel* turned out to be an old yeshivah friend of Mr. Sheinfeld's, who leaned on him to accept Elisha for the morning *seder*, promising to review the material with him in the evening. The *Rosh Kollel* resisted for a while, since his policy was to accept only married men who would learn both *sedarim*, but then he called up on *motzaei Yom Kippur* and told Mr. Sheinfeld that he had decided to give it a try.

Because it had been hard to arrange a *chavrusa*, Elisha was anxious to keep the arrangement going; so he was very careful to be punctual and not to let the all-too-frequent medical appointments interfere with his morning hours. Now that he was hoping eventually to teach *Gemara*, he also spent time writing notes on what they learned. That's what he worked on if Yerachmiel was not as punctual as he was. He was typing the summaries on a portable computer when Yerachmiel puffed in.

"Sorry," he apologized. "Wife's birthday."

"I'll remember that one," said Elisha. "I hope I'll get to use it some day."

Joe drove the car up to the entrance of the gym. The building had a ramp and Elisha elected to try it alone. Ramps, particularly steep ones, were still a challenge. He had to push hard enough that the chair wouldn't start rolling backward while he was trying to get a new grip on the handle that circled the wheel.

There were several other paraplegics already waiting. Someone pointed him toward the locker room, where Joe helped him put on his sweatshirt. When he came out, he found that the other participants had already lined up in front of the instructor, a muscular older man with a crew cut.

"I see we have a newcomer today. I am Ted O'Brian. And you?"

"Elisha Sheinfeld."

"Glad to meet you. Have you taken care of the formalities involving payment?"

Elisha nodded virtuously.

"All right, everyone. Let's get those muscles moving. A large loop!"

Elisha rolled himself out onto the smooth floor behind two of the others. They began circling the floor. Elisha enjoyed the challenge of keeping up with the others. In fact, he was just gaining on the man in front of him when Ted called out, "Reverse direction!" Now, all of a sudden, he was at the head of the pack, with the others hard on his heels. "Figure eight," called Ted. "Faster!"

After twenty minutes, Ted told them to slow their pace and cool down. Then he called them all over and lined them up for the next set of exercises, which were designed to work out all the arm muscles. Ted led his pupils through several series of stretch and hold exercises. Elisha was pretty sure that he was using some muscles that hadn't gotten much of a workout for a full year. Several times he just gave up and dropped his arms. "Don't give up. You can do better than that!" Ted barked.

Elisha was worn out by the session's end, and was relieved when the attendants were called to help get everyone stretched out on mats. Joe was a particular asset, because he was very strong.

After another series of stretching exercises, Ted asked everyone to try to turn over and had the attendants help those who couldn't manage.

"Now just imagine that you've fallen," Ted suggested. "There is a telephone six feet away, but you have to drag yourself those six feet. No self-pity—just a long hard pull. Forearms on the ground for maximum traction, hands together, right elbow forward, left forward, pull."

Elisha pulled up his sleeves and began inching forward. It was horribly difficult to drag the dead weight of his legs, and he felt the self-pity Ted had scorned welling up from somewhere inside him. Did their instructor really know how hard this was? A sound between a sigh and a sob escaped him.

"Next two feet with heads down. Someone is shooting at you, and if you lift your head that will be the end of you!" This was such a strange scenario for a group of paraplegics in Brooklyn that

Elisha forgot his frustration and looked at the fellow next to him in astonishment.

The other man leaned in his direction and whispered, "I hear that he used to be a drill sergeant in the Marines. He often says that people have no idea what they can do if only they'd push themselves."

"It sounds like a very appropriate job for him," muttered Elisha with unwonted bitterness. "Why did he give it up?" He looked up at the instructor, who was goading one of the men who had collapsed. He could just imagine him as an instructor in an army camp.

"Notice that he has a slight limp? He lost one of his legs in a battle. The right one is artificial."

Elisha's bitterness vanished.

Chapter 15

Soaked and Salted

Ella was balancing the checkbook. Math had never been one of her favorite subjects. She had done whatever was necessary to keep up her grades, but she hadn't enjoyed it then, and she still didn't. She sat with her statement, thumbing through her checkbook stubs and marking off all the checks that had been deposited. Then she went through the stubs again, making a list of all the checks that were still outstanding and the amount of each. Finally, she worked out the correct balance and wrote it into her checkbook.

What came after balancing the checkbook was even worse. She had to work out the budget for the month. After she had subtracted the cost of utilities, fixed expenses, dental bills, mortgage, and food, there would be pitifully little left for discretionary spending. She desperately needed a new pair of shoes; the old ones had been mended so often that they weren't really presentable enough to teach in. Nonetheless, as she worked her way through the columns of figures, it looked as if once again the shoes would be the casualty of more urgent matters.

She put down her pen and stretched. At least the chore was almost finished, even if the results were not particularly satisfactory. The ringing phone was a welcome diversion. *"Allo?"* she said, expecting an Israeli.

"Hello, Ella? This is Miriam."

"Oh, hi! How are you coming along with your unpacking?"

"It's an absolutely endless job. However, I have managed to get our clothes into the closets and my kitchen put together. That's what I am calling about. Binyamin and I would like to celebrate moving into our own apartment by having guests for Shabbos. I'm calling for suggestions about how to find some. I know you always manage to get guests."

"Hmm. Well, for us it works by a one-brings-another system, and inviting people back. Also, we're on a lot of lists of hospitality committees. I think the best thing for you to do to get started is to call up some yeshivos and seminaries and let them know that you're available. Right now I'm in the middle of something that requires concentration, but when I finish I can try to look up a few phone numbers. The people will all speak English, so you can make the calls yourself."

"I'm sorry I interrupted you at a bad time."

"I don't mind," said Ella. "I needed a break. I'm doing the budget," she added, as if that explained everything.

Miriam seemed to think that it did. "Oh, poor thing," she commiserated.

The next call, from Trudy, came as she was just finishing her calculations. "Rebbetzin Wahrhaftig, is there any possibility that we could come for Shabbos?"

"Sorry, we're booked solid this week and the next. How about the one after?"

"No, thank you very much. It's more urgent than that. I'll try someone else."

"Wait! I have an idea. Let me check it out. Get back to me in ten minutes." Ella pressed the button to close the connection and then dialed the Lerners' number. It certainly was convenient that they could now be reached directly by phone. "Would you have room for a couple with a small baby?" she asked Miriam.

"Yes, we could manage that, though I'm not quite sure where we would put the baby."

"If you can't borrow a folding playpen from a neighbor, you can pull out a drawer and line it with a quilt. That usually works when they're really little. Incidentally, you know this couple."

"Really, who?"

"You remember Trudy and Michael Millman? Your mother-in-law made *sheva berachos* for them last winter. They're living in Bnai Brak now and they had a baby about a month ago. A girl."

"*Mazal tov.* Binyamin will be very pleased to hear the news."

Ella finished making the arrangements, put away her financial records, and got out her notebooks to prepare one more lesson for tomorrow. She glanced at her watch. She probably ought to put in another load of laundry. Something that would be quick to hang out—perhaps sheets.

Ella put her pen down and went out to the laundry porch. She was behind on the laundry this week. She usually tried to do all the housework while the children were awake, but often it didn't work out. Sometimes she just didn't have enough time for everything. The budget for time was as tight as the budget for money, but less aggravating, because she kept track of it all in her head. It helped that every day she got a brand-new allotment of twenty-four hours. If she were given all her hours at the beginning of the month and had to make them stretch until the end, it would be more difficult. She sorted out a load of sheets, bundled them into the washing machine, and was back at her desk in ten minutes.

"*Gut Shabbos! Mazal tov!*" Binyamin ushered the Millmans into their new apartment. Trudy was pushing a baby carriage and Michael was carrying a suitcase.

Trudy looked around with appreciation. "You seem pretty organized for people who moved a week and a half ago. I've moved twice already, and each time it has taken me a couple of months to dig out from under the piles."

"This apartment doesn't have much furniture, but it does have two built-in closets, so at least we've been able to store what we managed to unpack. We won't discuss the neat stack of sixteen cartons in the corner of the room where you'll be sleeping." He ushered them into the bedroom. The pile of cartons was completely swathed in a couple of attractive old bedspreads.

Trudy glanced at her watch and turned to her husband. "I think you had better get a move on. I'll manage fine here."

Michael nodded and turned to Binyamin. "If you'll excuse me, I'm supposed to go speak to one of my Rabbanim this afternoon. I should be back in time for Shabbos."

"Shouldn't you have something to drink before you go? I could make you a quick cup of coffee?"

"No, really, I'm fine. I'll just have a glass of water from the tap."

Trudy did accept the cup of coffee, and then went back to the bedroom to feed the baby. Binyamin was helping Miriam, who had not yet finished the cooking. Everything was taking longer than usual, because she frequently had to interrupt to search for this utensil or that pot. "There!" she exclaimed, plopping into a chair. "We're all done, except for cleaning up this horrible mess." She glanced at the cluttered counters with distaste. Both sinks were full of pots, meat pots in the *fleishig* sink and *pareve* bowls and pans in the *milchig* sink.

"Why don't you go lie down for half an hour while I try to make a dent in this. You need more rest than usual now."

Miriam nodded and stumbled off in the direction of the bedroom. Binyamin bustled around putting salads in the refrigerator and dishes into the sinks until she was out of sight, and then sat down for a few minutes of rest himself. He had only gotten home from work an hour ago. The trip was always very exhausting. After five minutes, he heaved himself to his feet and got back to work on the kitchen.

Having guests had been his idea, and he had to be ready to take the consequences. The chicken soup smelled good, almost too good, and he opened the lid to see if it had enough water. He was used to the fact that the *cholent* always smelled best just as it was about to burn, and he wasn't sure there wasn't some such rule for chicken soup as well, but it seemed okay. The *kneidlach* and carrots were bobbing around in the broth.

Binyamin lifted the lid on the next pot, which contained meatballs in tomato sauce. He got a spoon and tasted the sauce. It was scrumptious. Lunch, a sandwich and a piece of fruit eaten hastily at his desk, seemed very far in the past. Binyamin speared one of the meatballs with a fork and ate it, promising himself that if they were short at the meal, he would be the one to cut back. He also tested the *cholent*, which was quite good. He opened the oven a crack, but that contained a *kugel* and a closed dish of chicken, neither of which seemed very accessible. Finally, his inspection completed, he took a sponge and began washing the dishes.

Not until the middle of the meal, after all the children had been put to bed, did Binyamin and Miriam finally find out what had brought the Millmans to Yerushalayim.

"We were doing so-so, as long as I could bring in some income," Trudy explained. "I was writing thank-you letters in English for a couple of yeshivos, and also making artistic plaques for decorating children's rooms, for which I was getting orders through friends. Michael was really enjoying the learning in Bnai Brak, and we didn't mind living in absolute simplicity.

"However, ever since Yehudis was born, I haven't been able to work, and of course, I had no social benefits or anything to pay me maternity leave. The rent in Bnai Brak is very high, so we're thinking of moving to Kiryat Sefer, or Tzefat, or some place else where it's cheaper to live. It would also help if Michael had a position in which he could earn some extra money tutoring or teaching within the yeshivah. He wants to consult with the Rabbanim from his old yeshivah here in Yerushalayim, to see if they know of any such possibilities."

"Sounds pretty grim," commented Binyamin. "How in the world do all the native-born *kollelniks* manage?"

"Well," said Michael, "most of them own their own apartment, most of the wives do have jobs which give them maternity leave, and often the parents help out."

"Whereas our parents," said Trudy, "made a pact at the wedding that they would do nothing at all to help us settle in Eretz Yisrael. There have also been broad hints that if we were to move back to the States, the parental heavens would open up, and we would find ourselves much more comfortable."

"Not that I think we would need it," Michael added. "If we were to move back to the States, I would presumably get a job, and then we could manage on our own."

Something about this bothered Binyamin. "Why do you have to move back to the States in order to get a job? Why not just get a job here instead of having to move back?"

Michael looked uncomfortable. "You know, present company excepted, I hardly have any role models here. Almost everyone I know is in *kollel*. Also, going out to work in Israel has to be done cold turkey. We're not allowed to get any vocational training or take any part-time jobs as long as we're drawing a *kollel* stipend and getting a deferment from the draft."

Binyamin grinned. "It's amazing how much the secular government in Eretz Yisrael has been able to do through the years to increase the total amount of Torah learning world-wide just by making the rule that *kollelniks* can't work or train for a job. I'm sure they do it in the hope of encouraging us to give up learning, but it seems to have the opposite effect."

"It surely does," agreed Michael. "If we decide to go to work, we're expected to face a hostile job market with no skills and no immediate way to support our families. And even if we find a job, we may have to leave it for at least two months to do our basic training in the army. Add to that all the positive sides to devoting oneself to learning, and it's not surprising that people put off leaving *kollel* as long as they possibly can."

Binyamin was fascinated. "In America, where the transition from learning to working is smoother, people do make it earlier. One of the things that helped us to hold on was thinking about the Israeli model. If an Israeli *kollelnik* can hang on for twenty years, I told myself, surely I can manage at least four." Binyamin paused. "I'll tell you why it bothers me to hear that you feel you have to go back to the States in order to work. It's because you were the one who convinced us to come here in the first place."

Trudy and Michael exchanged wondering glances. "I don't remember that we ever discussed the matter at all!" asserted Michael.

"No," agreed Binyamin, "we didn't discuss it. A year ago, you considered it so self-understood that it didn't require discussion. That's why I ask myself what has happened in the intervening time."

Michael stared off into space. For a few seconds there was no sound in the room except the drumming of his fingertips on the table. He sighed audibly. "It's been a tough year. Wonderful in many ways," he paused to smile at his wife, "but still tough."

The men had gone out to shul after *seudas shlishis*. Miriam and Trudy sat in the twilight on the porch, waiting for it to get dark enough that they could wash the dishes. Trudy had been pumping her for information about ear infections in babies, the last in a list of subjects on which Trudy had asked her advice during Shabbos.

Except for her husband, her younger brother Reuven back in New York and her own children, Miriam could not really think of anyone else who turned to her for information and suggestions.

"Perhaps you would like to come to us for the Pesach *seder*?" she asked on impulse. "Binyamin and I are used to having enormous *sedarim* with our families, and the idea of having just the four of us at the *seder* table makes me feel homesick."

"I'll have to check with Michael," said Trudy.

"And I'll have to check with Binyamin," admitted Miriam.

"Aren't you scared to try to make the *seder* by yourself?" asked Trudy. "There are so many things to remember!"

"I'm the youngest girl in my family," said Miriam, "and for many years I had the sole responsibility of setting up the *seder* table. My mother concentrated on the cooking, which she did very well. My mother is a terrific cook."

"You seemed to have learned a lot from her," said Trudy. "Everything was delicious. I hope you appreciate what you gained by serving an apprenticeship as a housewife. I have to learn far too many things from scratch. The process is time-consuming, and the results barely reflect the energy I invest."

"I do appreciate it. It was very easy, learning with my mother right there to set things straight when something went wrong. You know, Trudy, there are times when I'm so homesick for my mother and father and the rest of them that I can barely hold back the tears." Only as she admitted this to Trudy did she realize just how true it was.

"Why shouldn't you have a good cry over it? Missing your mother seems like a perfectly good reason for crying!"

"I wouldn't want Binyamin to think that I was unhappy," said Miriam with a shake of her head.

"But if he doesn't know when you're feeling down, how can he cheer you up?"

The men arrived at that point, and with them came the flurry of *Havdalah*, packing and departure. Only when the Millmans had gone did Miriam find time to wonder why she had been so open with Trudy, almost more open than she was with herself. Perhaps she sensed that Trudy respected her more than she respected herself.

Now that Binyamin was working again, the full burden of caring for the house and children was back on Miriam. At least she only had to get Shimmy out in the morning, not Tami as well. At Ella's suggestion, she had found a neighbor who was willing to watch Tami for the half hour it took her to walk Shimmy to *gan* and return home. When she went to pick him up, she took Tami along in the stroller to get some fresh air and sun. She usually did her food shopping then, as well.

The hardest part about the shopping was figuring out what kind of store carried each item. Take fish, for example, which turned out to be sold in the chicken store. Apparently, when the owner of the chicken store married off his daughter, he set up his son-in-law in the fish business in a corner of his own shop. Miriam came in with Tami at a time when the son-in-law was out. The door to the store was open, but there was no one in sight. From the back of the store came unidentifiable noises.

"Hello?" called Miriam. "Can I buy frozen fish?"

"Take it from the freezer and weigh it on the scale," came a voice from the back of the shop.

Miriam, leaving Tami in the stroller, lifted up the hinged part of the counter and started opening and closing doors of the freezer, until she found the frozen sole. She pried loose eight fillets, put them in one of the plastic bags hanging behind the counter, and weighed them on the scale. She blew on her frozen fingers to try to restore circulation, and then went back to Tami.

"It weighs one kilo, 354 grams," she called out to the mysterious being in the rear.

"Just a second. I'm in the middle of salting the chickens." He appeared soon, brushing the coarse salt off his hands. "What kind of fish?"

"Sole," said Miriam.

He punched the price and the weight into an adding machine with buttons covered by plastic and said, "Twenty-seven shekels and fifty-five *agurot*."

Miriam pulled out a fifty-shekel note and tried to hand it to him.

"No, no. Don't give it to me. Put it over there," he jerked his thumb in the direction of the fish department, "and take change." He vanished again to finish his work on the chickens.

Miriam once again abandoned Tami, passed through to the

other side of the counter, and looked for the money. There was a lot of change in a large open bowl. She dropped in the fifty-shekel note and counted out for herself twenty-two shekels and forty-five agurot. As she and Tami left the store, she paused and looked back. The bowl of money was sitting there in plain sight, with her fifty-shekel note on top, weighted down by a few stray coins. She wondered just how long a store run on such self-service principles would last in a different setting.

When Miriam arrived at the *gan*, she stopped to speak to the kindergarten teacher about Shimmy's problems with Hebrew. "There is so much going on that he doesn't understand. Yesterday all the children were asking him what he was looking for, and he says that he wasn't looking for anything at all."

"I think they were asking him what he was dressing up as for Purim. It's the same root, but a different form of the word."

"You see what I mean. All sorts of subtle differences throw him. He gets frustrated when he can't understand what people are saying," Miriam explained. "I tried to tell him that soon he will be speaking Hebrew just like everyone else.

She didn't tell the teacher what Shimmy's answer had been: "I'm sure I'll be able to speak Hebrew just like everyone else," he said, still mournful, "but what good will it do me if I can't understand a word that I am saying?"

"I agree that he's on his left foot socially," said the teacher, "and the language is surely part of the trouble, but it's not everything. Why don't we try to adjust some of the other things?"

"Like what?"

"Well, he isn't dressed like the other children. None of the other children wear corduroy pants, and they all have pullover sweaters for weekday wear. Also, he never gets to wear a badge for being diligent."

All those lovely, warm corduroy pants she had stocked up on for the Yerushalayim winter! Maybe she would compromise, sometimes yes and sometimes no. "What would he have to do to get a badge?"

"I give a badge to every child who brings a note from his parents on Sunday saying that on Shabbos he told them what he had learned all week."

When in the world would people think to tell her in time what she needed to know!

Now that Miriam had a phone, Ella usually called her about twice a week "to keep in touch."

"Hello, Mimi? This is Ella."

"Miriam," came the correction.

"What's new?"

After Miriam described her encounter with the chicken man, Ella said thoughtfully, "You know, now that you're settled so nicely, if you have a store right nearby that sells fresh chickens, maybe you should try *kashering* your own chickens. It's very educational for the children."

It might be more educational, but it was also a lot more trouble. Mama *kashered* her own chickens, and occasionally Miriam would help her out before Yom Tov, taking the order from the butcher and *kashering* them in her own home. "Perhaps."

"Listen Mimi, why don't you just try it once? I think you'll decide on your own that it's worthwhile."

"Perhaps."

Ella forged ahead. "How was your Shabbos with the Millmans?"

"Oh, we really enjoyed it. It was a bit exhausting, but very interesting. You know, we were sort of isolated in a little bubble all the time we were in the immigrants' hostel. Now, we're beginning to feel as if we're rejoining the real world."

"Did you manage to get your kitchen and guest room put together in time?"

"Oh, yes, without any trouble. Now that I'm no longer in *ulpan,* I seem to have a lot of extra time, though very soon that will all go into cleaning for Pesach. We invited the Millmans to come to us for Pesach, and they accepted. Binyamin is excited about leading the *seder* for the first time."

"Oh, dear," Ella sounded distressed. "I had been sort of assuming that you would come to us. I guess I was too casual about getting my invitation out."

"I'm afraid I can't invite all of you to come to us. That would be definitely beyond me at this stage."

"Oh, no, of course not. I hope it goes well. I'm just going to have to think. If both you and the Millmans are scheduled, who are we going to have for the *seder*?"

Miriam finally succumbed to Ella's urging and bought some chickens to *kasher* at home. When she brought the poultry home and opened the package, her eyes widened. She made an emergency call to Ella. "I just got my chickens from the butcher, and they look very different from what my mother gets. They aren't cut as much, and there are extra pieces." Miriam poked at an offending chicken foot. "What should I do?"

"I can't help you much by phone. I don't know what you're used to, and I don't now how this butcher cut them. There are all sorts of styles in Eretz Yisrael, too. Is there some woman in your building who *kashers* her own chickens?"

"How in the world should I know? She's not likely to hang out a sign saying, 'Only home-*kashered* chickens used here.'"

"Maybe the woman who watches Tami in the morning knows. You know, chicken-*kashering* types often wander around the building looking for someone who can lend them an extra bag of coarse salt. It happens to me more than I like to admit."

"I can ask her," said Miriam. It might be just her luck that if there was a "chicken-*kashering* type" in the building, she was so well organized that she never ran out of salt.

Miriam was exhausted. It turned out that her neighbor, Hinda, was an experienced chicken-*kasherer*, and was all too eager to help. In the end, Miriam and the children missed their usual trip to the park. Binyamin would be home from work soon, and she had not yet given a thought to what she should serve him for supper. She was still cutting up the chicken for storage in the freezer, casting an occasional nervous glance at the pot boiling on the stove.

At the very beginning, when her neighbor, Hinda, had been making all sorts of cuts in the chicken and throwing things away, Miriam had pointed to the chicken feet and said, "Don't those get chucked out, too?"

"Those? Not at all. They make wonderful soup."

Miriam had been under the impression that most of the chickens sold in Eretz Yisrael were wire-raised, but those chicken feet certainly looked as if they had been all over the barnyard. "I don't think I want those in my soup," admitted Miriam honestly.

"Oh, well, you peel off the skin first."

"It doesn't look as if it would peel very easily."

"After they've been *kashered*, you parboil them for fifteen minutes, and it comes right off."

Miriam had given up, accepting the chicken feet as a penance. She had soaked and salted them together with the rest of the chicken, and had put them on to boil while she was packing away everything else into the freezer. Hinda, who had been popping in every hour to check how things were going, had left for good. Shimmy was pushing his trucks around on the floor, making motor noises. She could just throw out the feet when no one was looking, but what would she say if Hinda should ask her later how the soup had come out?

Miriam drained off the boiling water, filled the pot again with tap water to cool the chicken feet, picked up one of them, and began to attack the skin with her knife. "Peels right off" indeed! The leg wasn't so bad, except at the joint, but when she got down to the four splayed toes, nothing seemed to work. Sweat was trickling down her backbone, her muscles ached from all the exertion of the day, and her head was throbbing.

There was a sound at the door, and Binyamin walked in, carrying his portable computer and his briefcase. "Hello!" he called out cheerfully.

"Abba, Abba!" shouted Shimmy, abandoning his trucks and wrapping himself around his fathers legs.

"*Shalom, tzaddik,*" said Binyamin heartily, putting down his burdens and tousling his son's hair. He looked up at Miriam, his eyes widened, and he exclaimed, "What is that?!"

"A chicken foot," said Miriam.

"But... what are you doing with it?"

"Skinning it!" her voice rose to a half wail.

"Why?"

"Why? Because my neighbor says that it's wasteful to throw away the feet because they make good soup. But of course no one would want to put anything so disgusting in a soup pot without skinning it first!" She dropped the chicken foot, plopped herself down in a chair with her hands over her face, and began crying. "I never want to see another chicken foot in my life. I want to go back to Brooklyn!"

She heard Binyamin stride over to the kitchen sink and open the door underneath. She looked up. Shimmy was gaping at her, Tami was crawling into the room, and Binyamin was bent over the sink.

"What are you doing?" she asked.

"Collecting all these chicken feet and throwing them in the garbage," said Binyamin. That was indeed what he was doing.

Miriam almost pleaded for mercy for the one she had nearly finished skinning, but on second thought she let that go too.

Binyamin pulled up a chair and sat down beside her, "You probably didn't have a nap this afternoon, right?"

"A nap? A nap?" Again her voice rose on the last syllable.

"Why don't you lie down on the couch and try to relax a little."

"The bathtub is full of salt."

"I'll clean that later."

"There's nothing for supper."

"I'll order pizza."

She did feel better once she was lying down. Binyamin banished Shimmy with instructions that he should take care of Tami. He sat down nearby and waited for her sobs to subside. "Would you rather rest first or talk first?" he asked when her shoulders stopped shaking.

"Talk, I guess."

"Why are you so upset?"

"Because I worked so hard all day. Then you came in and thought what I had been doing was ridiculous. And I agreed with you!"

"Would you like me to rescue those chicken feet and skin them myself?"

"No, no, no! Good riddance."

"Miriam, believe me that I appreciate all your efforts to be a pioneer. You've put up with all sorts of discomfort without complaining, and done many things that were very hard for you. However, it's possible to carry the pioneering spirit too far, and today seems to have been one of those occasions."

Miriam turned her head on the pillow to look at him. Her eyes were beginning to fill up again. One tear broke loose, trickled down her cheek, and ended up as a salty taste on her lips. She reached for a tissue and dabbed her eyes.

"It's a reasonable strategy to try to live like Israelis, but if we carry it too far, we're likely to break, as you almost did today."

Almost?

"Israel is a modern country, and almost every convenience we had in America is available. Even freedom from chicken feet."

Miriam chuckled softly, and this time it did not sound like the advent of hysteria.

"To give our *aliyah* a chance," Binyamin continued, "we have to be willing to behave like Americans on matters that are really important to us."

"Binyamin," asked Miriam, "when are we going to get a car?"

"It's done," announced Binyamin as he walked in. "I had to sign away a hefty chunk of our income for the next year and a half, but after Pesach we should be on wheels."

"Why do we have to wait so long?" Miriam asked.

"We're buying it passport to passport, with reduced taxes, from new immigrants who are giving up and going back to the States. They want to keep it until they're ready to get on the plane. They even tried to persuade me to drive them to the airport, but I reminded them of the existence of taxis."

"Are you happy with it?"

"Yes, I am. It's two years old but looks new. The owner and I took it in to have it checked, and the mechanic agreed that it's in good condition. I'm sorry that we won't have it for the Pesach shopping, but we have learned to manage with taxis."

"Thank you very much, Binyamin."

"I should thank you. I assure you that going to and from Tel Aviv by bus every day has been no pleasure."

The phone rang. "Hello, this is Ella."

"Hello," said Miriam warily. The last time Ella had called she had gotten involved in that business with the chicken feet.

"Listen, I'm calling to ask if you could use some help for Pesach."

She really doesn't think I can do it, thought Miriam. Has she forgotten that I have already made Pesach five times since I got married? "I'll manage somehow," she replied.

"One of the seminaries for American girls is trying to place those few students who aren't going back to spend Pesach with their families. The girl would stay with you for the two weeks before Pesach and for the week of the Yom Tov itself. She doesn't pay any room or board, and she expects to help like a family member."

If Ella had been offering her own help, Miriam would have turned her down flat, but this suggestion was better. "I'll have to ask Binyamin, but it sounds possible."

"I'll give you the phone number of the secretary at the seminary, and if you decide that you're interested, you can call her directly."

Miriam got her address book and wrote down the number that Ella dictated.

"How was your adventure with the chickens?" Ella asked.

"Oh, awful. I got through the bulk of it, with a lot of time and a lot of help from my neighbor. Then Binyamin walked in while I was skinning the chicken feet and I broke down in tears."

"I never bother with the feet," confessed Ella. "I use the necks and the bones for my soups."

"I wish you had told me that!" said Miriam.

"I must say, the idea of you standing there skinning chicken feet is rather amusing." Ella chuckled.

"Sure," said Miriam coldly. "I break into giggles every time I remember it."

There was an uncomfortable silence. Apparently Ella realized that Miriam was offended. Miriam, for her part, was restrained by a troubled conscience. The big news of the week was the purchase of the car. However, since she never had relayed Ella's objections to Binyamin, bringing up the subject could lead to embarrassing questions.

Ella was the first to break the silence. "How is your husband managing with the daily commute?"

"It's grueling. Two hours each way."

"There are ways to keep that time from being completely wasted," suggested Ella. "*Daf Yomi* tapes with a portable tape recorder, for example."

"He does some of that, but he says that it's not the same as learning the material 'inside' with a group." Miriam took a deep breath in preparation. Here it goes. "He'll be very relieved when we get our own car after Pesach and he'll be able to get home in time to go to a real *shiur*."

"A car? Oh, Mimi." Ella sounded actually hurt that her advice had not been heeded. "Did you tell your husband my objections?"

"No," admitted Miriam, "I didn't. Binyamin and I are adults, Ella. We have been married for five years. We can make our own decisions without outside interference."

"If you were so sure of yourself, you wouldn't have been afraid to tell him."

"Let's just say that I had already been burned too often, for too many years." The effort to stand up to Ella was taking its toll. The hand holding the telephone was shaking.

"You've only been living here for half a year, and of course if my advice isn't welcome, I don't have to give it." Now Ella was beginning to sound offended.

"That might be an idea."

"Listen, Mimi..." said Ella.

"Don't call me 'Mimi'! In fact, you don't have to call me at all!" Miriam slammed down the receiver with a satisfying thud. Then she walked into her bedroom, threw herself down on her bed, and broke into stormy weeping.

Ella sat frozen in her seat, the dead receiver still in her hand. Afraid that phones lines might still be connected, she lowered the receiver into its cradle.

She definitely shouldn't have laughed at the idea of Mimi skinning chicken feet, particularly when she was the one who got her into it. She probably shouldn't have urged Mimi to *kasher* chickens at all. And she shouldn't have called her Mimi instead of Miriam. She was ready to apologize for all those things, as soon as Mimi calmed down. Whoops, as soon as Miriam calmed down.

The car question, though—that was harder. She was sure that her advice was right. All right, so she didn't have to apologize for giving the advice, only for chiding Mimi/Miriam when she didn't take it.

Chaim Ozer's remarks about "bite-sized" advice came back to her. She realized that she was not at all anxious to tell him about this whole blow-up, at least, not right now when she was in the middle of it. She didn't think he would approve of her behavior, and Chaim Ozer's disapproval was hard for her to face. Later, when it was straightened out, when she and Miriam could laugh about it together, then she would tell him rather contritely about the episode and promise to heed his advice better in the future.

She stood up and stretched. She would give it three days. By then, she figured, Miriam would have calmed down. Of course,

Miriam had told her straight out not to call again. She would like to heed that. After two weeks, Miriam would realize that she didn't want a complete break, wouldn't she? And even if she didn't, her husband would surely step in to straighten it all out.

Ella plunged into her housework with her usual brisk step.

As the bus ground up the hill to Givat Saul, Binyamin almost enjoyed the noise. Only a few more weeks and he would be able to make this trip in his own car. No more twisting and turning as the bus poked in and out of every little corner in the area. No more lugging tired children from the bus stop to the house when they had been out in the evening. No more waking up at 5:15 to make sure to synchronize three connections and arrive at work on time.

Actually, when the weather was nice and he didn't have too much to carry, he didn't bother with the bus into Givat Shaul but walked home from the highway. Tonight, though, he had both his computer and an overloaded briefcase. Mitch was returning from his trip to America, and Binyamin, who had been in charge of project management while he was away, wanted to review what all the team members had been doing over the last month and make a written report that would be waiting on Mitch's desk when he arrived. He hadn't been asked to do this, but he knew that it would be a big help to Mitch, and he wanted to justify the confidence his boss had displayed in him even though he was just a new employee.

The bus finally reached his stop, and he gathered up his things. This would not be the appropriate day to lose his briefcase, and with it, the documentation that Rami had grumbled about preparing. He climbed the stairs of their building, humming softly to himself.

When Binyamin opened the door of the apartment, he could tell immediately that something was wrong. It was much too quiet. He finally located the children in the bedroom, standing at the foot of Miriam's bed and staring solemnly at their mother. Miriam had her head buried in the pillow, but from the tremor of her shoulders he gathered that she was crying. He first led the children into the kitchen, gave them cookies, and found each of them a favorite toy.

"Shimmy, you be a big boy and watch Tami for a while. I'm going to talk to Ima, and then I'll give you your supper." He took along a chair and closed the door behind him.

Binyamin just sat quietly at first, hoping that Miriam would say something. He was certain that exhaustion had a lot to do with her moodiness, but he knew that to say that would sound unsympathetic. He would have to deal with whatever had triggered this new fit of crying.

Miriam turned her face on the pillow and looked at him from red, puffy eyelids. "You might as well call up those people and tell them that we can't buy the car."

"Why not?" asked Binyamin, genuinely startled. What had happened while he was away?

"Why not? Because Ella thinks it is a bad idea, that's why not. In the end, everything has to be done Ella's way, so why try to fight it?" She didn't sound sarcastic. That was genuine fatalism in her voice.

"She told you this today?"

"No, she told me this more than a month ago. You remember the night we went to look for apartments, when I didn't let you eat supper at the Wahrhaftigs? That was the night she wanted to talk to you about it, when she saw that she hadn't convinced me. I met you on the stairs and dragged you off, but I should have known it was hopeless." The fatalistic note returned to her voice, and she began sniffling in self-pity. "She got her way about sharing my first very own bedroom, about which bed she would sleep in, and about which route we would walk to school. She'll get her way about this too. Why shouldn't she get her way? She's always smarter and *frummer* and better informed and ... and she's always right." Miriam broke into a new burst of sobs, her face buried once more in the pillow.

"About sharing a room?" echoed Binyamin blankly. He was rapidly revising his initial assessment of the problem. This wasn't just moodiness. These were very deeply buried resentments that were surfacing because Miriam had lost some of her control. In all the years of their marriage, he had never heard a word about this long-ago room-sharing issue.

There had been hints, though, which he hadn't caught, like the day he had suggested that they move to Eretz Yisrael, and she had asked if Ella had suggested the idea. It was apparently good that he had been able to say in all innocence that it hadn't been her idea at all.

Miriam sniffled again. "When Leah got married, I graduated to having my own bedroom. It was that little room to the left of the stairs where we put the children when we stay over at my parents' house. Two months later, when Ella came to live with us, there was no one left in the house except Reuven and me.

"When Mama first told me that Ella would be coming, I figured that the three of us would each take one of the three smaller bedrooms, and the big bedroom would be for my brothers when they came home from yeshivah. Then Ella arrived, full of excellent reasons why she and I should share the big bedroom. I had grown up on stories about how Ella's mother and her sister had shared their tiny bedroom with Mama when she first came from Hungary. It would have been churlish of me to object. So I didn't.

"Then came the question of how to arrange the room. I made a suggestion that involved putting the two dressers in a line to give everyone some personal space, but that was also overruled. Apparently, at the Gutfreund house they leave the center of the room 'uncluttered'"

"Did Ella realize that you resented being pushed around?"

"Probably not. I didn't put up much of a fight, just gave in quietly. It was very important to me that Ella and I should get along."

"Because the Gutfreunds took in your mother when she came from Hungary?"

"That was part of it, but also because four years of conflict would have been four very uncomfortable years."

"And the route to school?" Binyamin prodded.

"I used a roundabout way, to avoid passing an alleyway where some thugs had knocked me down and thrown my books into a puddle when I was eight."

"I remember you telling me about that," said Binyamin, nodding.

"Well, the detour didn't suit Ella's sense of efficiency, but she also didn't feel right about leaving me to walk by myself, so she decided to cure my phobia. For the first two years I still walked the old way if she wasn't with me, but after that I guess I did get 'cured.'"

Binyamin felt that by now he had an adequate grasp of the problem. "First of all," he said, "we aren't going to back out of the car deal. We made an agreement and we will stick to it. If it turns out to be too great a financial burden, then we'll refinance the loan, and in two years we can sell it on the open market."

Miriam looked at him with an expression of growing hope.

"Second, perhaps you and Ella need to take a vacation from each other for a while."

"Oh, I took care of that already," said Miriam with a laugh that held a slightly hysterical lilt. "I told her never to call me again and slammed down the receiver."

"Hmm. Well, I imagine you will both want to straighten this out before Yom Kippur, but you may do a better job if you wait a bit before trying. Right now you should take a nap."

"But I have to feed the children and bathe them."

"I'll do it. You go to sleep," Binyamin told her.

"But it's really my job," Miriam objected.

"They're my kids too, Miriam," he said, smiling. "Just this once I can to feed them supper and give them their baths."

"Thank you," Miriam murmured, closing her eyes and relaxing.

Binyamin set about the tasks he had promised to take care of. Later, as he tiptoed out of the children's room after tucking them in, it seemed clear that he had better pitch in to help his wife with Pesach preparations before she collapsed completely.

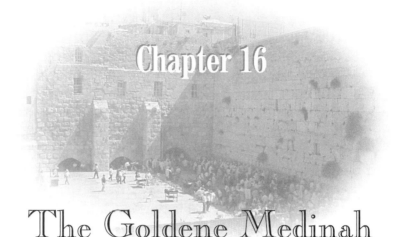

Chapter 16

The Goldene Medinah

"Hello, is this Rebbetzin Wahrhaftig?"

"Yes, it is," answered Ella, puzzled. The voice on the other end of the phone line was not one that she recognized.

"This is Rabbi Feldman, from Marbitzei Torah Yeshivah in Winston. Is your husband available?"

"No, he's out at *kollel* at the moment. Shall I have him call you when he returns?" What did this Rabbi Feldman want with Chaim Ozer?

"I'm afraid that I'm here on business and can't be reached by phone at any fixed place. If you could tell me approximately when he'll be in, I'll call back."

"He's home for half an hour between 8:30 and 9:00. Then he goes out again." Could he want Chaim Ozer's advice about something? It seemed unlikely that, on a tight schedule in one of the Torah capitals of the world, he would need to consult her husband. For all his undeniable talents, her husband was still pretty junior, and was not, to my mind, valued at his true worth.

"All right, I'll try to catch him then."

The phone call came just at nine, when Chaim Ozer had already put on his overcoat and was about to walk out the front door. Ella, cleaning up from supper in the kitchen, could not hear enough of the conversation to judge its content. It did not last long, and then Chaim Ozer was out the door in order not to keep his study partner waiting. If it was some private matter of Rabbi Feldman's, Ella didn't expect to hear any more mention of it. If it was of general interest, he would probably tell her about it when he got home.

Ella was very tired that evening. She had lost more sleep than she liked to admit agonizing about the blowup with Miriam Lerner. She sat at the dining room table grading papers and waiting for her husband.

Chaim Ozer was late. Five minutes late. Ten minutes late. Fifteen minutes late. Ella was ready to give up waiting and go to bed, when Chaim Ozer came in and sat down rather heavily. "You may be wondering about that phone call," he began. "Rabbi Feldman mentioned that you told him when to catch me."

Ella gave a nod of assent.

"He called to offer me a position, teaching the second class in their *beis medrash* program."

Ella was instantly alert. "Did you tell him that we were permanently settled in Eretz Yisrael?" she asked sharply.

"No," said Chaim Ozer. "I told him that I would think about it, and talk it over with you, and discuss it with our Rabbanim. I was late coming home because I was walking around thinking about it, and now I want to discuss it with you. He would like an answer in two days, because if we don't want the post, he wants to offer it to someone else before he leaves Eretz Yisrael."

"How did he hit on you?" asked Ella. "Does he know your father or mine?"

"He does know your father, but I don't think that's relevant. He says that he came and asked some of the rabbinical leaders here for suggestions, specifying that it should be someone fluent in English. As you heard, I was not the only candidate suggested."

"You say you've thought about it. What do you think?"

"I'm interested, but I'm not yet quite sure why. Maybe, as we talk, it will become clearer. I'm surprised at my reaction."

"Why?"

"I never had any intention of leaving *kollel* this early. We discussed the idea that I might have to look for a position when Leah'le was fifteen or so, to start saving up for her wedding. I had never contemplated the prospect with any enthusiasm."

"Why don't we start at the other end," suggested Ella. "Why were you *not* enthusiastic about the idea?"

"First of all, I love learning. I have no lack of *sitzfleisch*, and only in the sort of full-time learning that you permit me to do can I really get to the bottom of a *sugya* and then work it out in all its details. Once I have a position and all its attendant responsibilities, I don't know how much of that I'll be able to manage.

"Second, I think it's crucial for the whole spiritual balance of the world and for the honor of the Torah that there be people doing nothing except sitting and learning, visibly, enthusiastically, and well.

"Finally, there are so many people competing for so few positions. I was afraid that I would feel that I had snatched a job I didn't really want from someone who might have been much better at it because it would have been exactly what he was looking for."

"So why is this job offer in America different?" Ella asked. "Just because they came looking for you instead of your going to look for them?"

"That's exactly the question I ask myself," admitted Chaim Ozer. "Is it simply that this is more dignified than having to scramble among thirty other candidates for a position? Or is it something about the job itself that appeals to me?" He fell silent and Ella allowed him to think.

Chaim Ozer might doubt his motivations, but Ella was depressingly certain that they were good ones. It seemed to her almost a foregone conclusion that they would have to wind up all the threads of their life here in Yerushalayim and move to some out-of-town backwater in the States.

With a sudden burst of insight, Ella wondered if Miriam got this same heavy, hopeless feeling whenever she made some suggestion to her about how things should be done. Well, Miriam had freed herself of Ella by slamming down a phone receiver, whereas Ella had not the slightest interest in "freeing" herself from Chaim Ozer.

After about three minutes, he looked up at her and said, "It's the boys."

"What boys?" She could hardly see how moving to Nowheresville would be good for their own boys.

"The yeshivah boys. I went to a yeshivah like this for two years after high school. It's a feeder school for Lakewood. I understand the kind of boys who go there, and I think that for some of them I could really make a difference. It's not at all clear to me that I could connect as well with Israeli yeshivah boys. The mentality is different."

"Suppose that's true. Why now? Why not wait ten years as we had originally planned?" objected Ella.

"You know that the Rabbanim don't recommend coming on *aliyah* with children over nine. I imagine there's some such problem in the other direction as well."

"But Leah'le is only five."

"There isn't much turnover in the staff of these yeshivos. This position only opened up because the previous *rebbi* for this class passed away. Who's to guarantee that I'll be offered a job like this in four years, particularly if I turn this one down?"

Ella felt another flash of empathy for Miriam. Maybe she shouldn't have given Chaim Ozer a full three minutes to think. For someone of his caliber, that was enough time to work out everything.

"What would I do?" Ella asked dully.

"I imagine that you would teach *limudei kodesh* in the day school. There may even be a girl's high school."

For the first time, Ella felt a glimmer of interest. Here in Yerushalayim she taught English. She sighed. "What happens now?"

"If we decide that we may want to take the job," said Chaim Ozer to Ella, "I'm supposed to meet with Rabbi Feldman tomorrow. Then I go talk to the Rabbanim."

"Rabbi Frenkel?" He was the *Gadol* with whom her husband was particularly close.

"I would talk it all over with him first, but then I would have to go to Rav Margulis. I'm not going to uproot my whole family from Yerushalayim and try to raise them in a small American community without his encouragement and blessing." He looked steadily at his wife.

Ella dropped her gaze to her coffee cup and said nothing.

"Ella?"

"Yes, Chaim'ke?"

"If we go on with this," he said gently, "I'm going to tell the

Rabbanim that the whole idea makes you miserable, but they might ask me to be more explicit."

"Hmm," said Ella noncommittally.

"If you need time to think about it, I can put Rabbi Feldman off for a little while."

"No! Who needs to think? Isn't it all obvious?" Once she finally started to talk, the words came tumbling out. "People talk about a high standard of living in America, but is there any standard of living for a *frum* family higher than what we've got here? The best Jewish schools in the world, with only fifty dollars per month tuition. The best *hechsherim* available right down the block. Shabbos without a car in sight. The greatest *talmidei chachamim* of the nation available for consultation. *Mitzvos* that we can't keep anywhere else. What can America offer to compete with that?"

"Is that a purely rhetorical question?" asked Chaim Ozer.

"No, no, you can answer it," said Ella, subsiding again.

"What America has to offer us is a mission in life. Not the one we prepared for, not the one we planned, but perhaps one to which we are particularly suited. And if so, it may be the one which Hashem planned for us."

"For you. What do I have to do with it?"

"Ella, your redoubtable presence makes itself felt even in Yerushalayim, among some of the most righteous women of our generation. I suspect that that will be all the more true in Winston."

Ella was slightly mollified by the compliment. "Even though my heart will still be in Yerushalayim?"

"*Because* your heart will still be in Yerushalayim. And Ella? So will mine."

Chaim Ozer left the house early the next morning. Ella had prepared him a bag lunch, which he took along. Ella herself was restless all day. As far as she could see, the best possible outcome would be for the Rabbanim to tell him that it was too early for him to leave learning, but they would remember him later when another position opened up. Who knows? She daydreamed — perhaps he could find something in one of the better yeshivos in Yerushalayim. They all had some American *bachurim*. Maybe they would need someone on the staff who felt that he could relate to them.

Chaim Ozer returned as usual at 8:30. His face was serious, but Ella didn't know if that was because he was disappointed at the answer or because he expected her to be disappointed.

"Did you get an appointment to speak to Rav Margulis?" she asked.

He nodded.

"What did he say?"

"'Go up and succeed!'" quoted Chaim Ozer.

Go down and succeed, thought Ella, but she did not say it. Now it was her turn to be silent.

"That doesn't necessarily mean that we're going. Rabbi Feldman's offer is not final. He can recommend me to the yeshivah board, but they have to ratify the appointment. It's not at all a foregone conclusion, because I was not willing to meet all his conditions."

"What conditions?"

"They're trying to fill a vacancy. They wanted me to start before Shavuos."

"Shavuos!" So soon!

"I told him this morning that it was impossible, that you had responsibilities to your school and your students, that we didn't want to move our children into a new school in the middle of the school year, that we all needed time to adjust and to wind up our lives here. I said that we could come for Elul, and that there would be no hard feelings if he wanted to withdraw the offer. He thought it over and decided to let the offer stand, but warned me that he wasn't sure the board would ratify it. Oh, by the way, I asked him about the high school for girls. He said that they have a new one, only a few years old, and that they're looking for experienced staff. Then I made an arrangement to speak to Rav Frenkel after his class in the yeshivah, and went to *kollel*."

"Did you discuss the problems of the children's education in a place like Winston?"

"He said that if we were going for the right reasons, and it seemed to him that we were, then we would have *siyatta diShmaya* with the children's education. We might have to take a more direct role than we would here, but there is nothing bad about that. The rest of the afternoon was spent trying to get an emergency appointment with Rav Margulis, which was not, I assure you, easy.

I reviewed the suggestion with him, and we discussed the main issues as Rav Frenkel and I had formulated them. You heard his answer."

"Did you call Rabbi Feldman?"

"No, I wanted to speak to you again first. I'm worried about the fact that we've always made our decisions jointly, and here we are still not together. I haven't convinced you, and you haven't convinced me."

"Chaim'ke, if you think we should do this, and Rav Frenkel thinks we should do this, and Rav Margulis thinks we should do this, then I also think we should do this. I will *shlep* my feelings along after that decision in the fullness of time. If I have until Elul, that gives me a fair amount of time in which to do the *shlepping*. When does Rabbi Feldman expect to have an answer for us?"

"He says that he'll ask the yeshivah secretary to call an emergency board meeting. He'll be going back in three days, and he expects to call with an answer within a week."

It was Ella who was home a week later when the call came through.

"Rebbetzin Wahrhaftig?"

"Yes, Rabbi Feldman?" She remembered the voice very clearly.

"You can tell your husband that the board ratified his appointment. The formal letter will go out by mail tomorrow."

"Thank you, Rabbi Feldman, I will tell him." As she hung up, it occurred to her that there was one bright spot to the explosion between her and Miriam. At least she was spared the embarrassment of admitting that they were moving back to America.

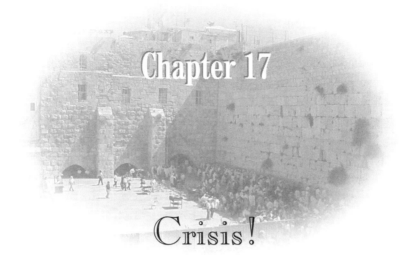

Chapter 17

Crisis!

"**T**here!" said Binyamin proudly, as he stored the last of the frozen chickens in the freezer, already cleaned for Passover. "Now Pesach can come tomorrow. We have the fish, the meat, the packaged foods, potatoes, onions, wine and matzah. Only the fresh fruits and vegetables and the dairy products have to be bought toward the end of the week."

"If you wouldn't mind," said Miriam in a tired voice, "I'd rather have Pesach with the rest of the Jewish people, six days from now."

Binyamin looked around the kitchen with satisfaction. Yesterday evening, after Miriam had finished cleaning up from Shabbos, he had sent her to bed early. Then he had cleared and cleaned out all the upper cabinets in the kitchen and papered the shelves. Today he had done all the shopping, while Miriam finished the living room and the oven.

Tomorrow she was going to do the refrigerator, and he wouldn't be able to help much because he had to teach his *shiur* in the immigrants' hostel. He knew that Miriam was dreading cleaning the stovetop. Tuesday he would surprise her with the new Passover stove that he had bought and hidden at the neighbors', and they would convert the kitchen to Passover mode. That would give her three full days for cooking.

"Admit that the preparations are going well this year. Being ready on time should be a snap," Binyamin said.

"G-d willing," Miriam added.

"G-d willing," Binyamin agreed.

The telephone rang.

Miriam, who was sitting nearest the phone table, reached over to answer it. "Tzippy, what a surprise! ... Oh, dear, when? ... He's right here." She handed the phone to Binyamin.

"Brace yourself, Binyamin," his sister said.

"Why, what happened?"

"Tatti is in critical condition. He had a massive heart attack about an hour ago. The rest of them have gone to the hospital. I'm going to join them soon, but first Mom asked me to call the travel agent and set her to work on getting you a plane reservation. I gave her your number. She'll call you as soon as she has it. Try to leave your line open."

"Tzippy, what kind of chances do the doctors give him?"

"I really don't know anything yet, Binyamin. This has all been so sudden. Tzvi's wife, Channah, is supposed to act as clearing house for information. We'll try to keep her informed as soon as we find out anything ourselves."

"All right, Tzippy. I'll start packing. Tell them I'll be there as soon as I can."

When his sister hung up, Binyamin was left holding the receiver. Tatti. Tatti! He had always seemed so permanent, so indestructible. He was not an old man, barely fifty-eight. The phone in his hand began making that irritating noise indicating that it was off the hook. Binyamin hung up so that the travel agent could reach them.

"Do you want me to pack for you, Binyamin?" asked Miriam. "I could lay out the things on the bed while you say some *Tehillim*, and then you can come see if you want to make any changes."

"Thanks, that's a good idea. I don't think I'd be very efficient right now." He stood up and took a *Tehillim* off the shelf. He found one of the *perakim* usually recited for someone who is ill, and tried to concentrate on the words.

A quarter of an hour later Miriam called him, and he followed her voice into the bedroom. "It's going to be cooler in New York than it is here," he said. "Do you know where my heavy sweaters are?"

Miriam pointed out the high shelf where she had stored their winter things, and he took down a sweater and an umbrella. He opened the shoe drawer to take out a pair of galoshes, and noticed the tennis shoes he always wore on Yom Kippur. With a worried sigh he took them out as well.

"In case I should need them," he said quietly to Miriam, "I wouldn't be in much of a mood for buying a new pair." At this reminder that Binyamin might arrive only in time for a funeral, Miriam's eyes filled with tears. The packing was finished in fifteen minutes, and they returned to the living room to call their sister-in-law.

"Hello, Channah? This is Binyamin. Do you know anything yet about Tatti's condition?"

"There's a major blockage in one of the arteries leading to the heart, and they're going to do a bypass."

"When?"

"As soon as possible, but I don't know when that is."

The travel agent still hadn't called. "I think you should try to sleep," Miriam urged him. "You got only four hours of sleep last night, and you have a long trip ahead of you."

"I'll try," agreed Binyamin, "but I don't know how well I'll succeed."

The phone rang.

"Hello, Binyamin Lerner? This is Feigy Rosenblum, the travel agent. I have you on a flight leaving Ben-Gurion at 10:00 tomorrow morning. It was too late to get a special kosher meal on the flight; sometimes there is an extra. Here's how you get your ticket ..."

Binyamin copied all the information into his appointment book, thanked Mrs. Rosenblum for making all the arrangements, and hung up. He told Miriam about the meal.

"I'll pack you something in the morning," she said.

"There won't be much time," he warned her. "I'm supposed to be at the airport for the security check at 7:30. I won't quite make that because the earliest *minyan* is at six o'clock. I had better order a ride from the taxi service for 7:00."

"All right, so we'll both get up at five, but now you should try to get some sleep."

Binyamin arranged for the taxi, got ready for bed, and was actually drifting into some sort of a doze when he jerked awake and sat up in bed. "Miriam! I'll be away for Pesach!" Even if his father should have a miraculously speedy recovery, his plane ticket would require him so stay abroad for at least six days.

"I know. I thought of that already," said Miriam quietly.

"Perhaps one of the neighbors can *kasher* the counters for you, and—this was supposed to be a surprise—I bought you a Pesach stove. But you can't possibly have the Millmans. Pesach is too exhausting as it is. It could be dangerous to the baby, *challilah*."

"You're probably right," agreed Miriam after some consideration. "Once you leave, I'll call them and explain the situation. One of the neighbors here will take us in for the *seder*."

Binyamin tried to get a bit more sleep, but he simply alternated between worrying about whether his father would pull through this crisis and worrying about how Miriam would manage to make Pesach without his help. What snatches of sleep he did get were not very restful, and it was almost a relief when the clock finally registered five and he could get up to shower and dress

He called his sister-in-law and heard that his father was hooked up to a respirator and all sorts of other machines. The operation would take place tomorrow afternoon, shortly before Binyamin was scheduled to arrive. The doctors gave him a seventy percent chance of survival.

The next two hours were frantic, as he tried to settle as many things as possible before he left. During *davening*, when he should have been concentrating on praying for his father's recovery, he kept thinking of new problems caused by his sudden departure. Just as he got up to the prayer for the sick, he struck his forehead and thought, "The car transfer!" He resolutely tried to banish the deluge of new worries connected with that, and concentrate on what he wanted to say: "May it be Your will, our G-d and G-d of our Fathers, that You send a complete recovery, a recovery of the body and a recovery of the soul, to the patient Meir Simcha ben Chaya Sarah amidst the others who are ill among the people of Israel."

If the new baby was a boy, they had been thinking of naming him Yitzchak Elchanan after Binyamin's grandfather. He desperately hoped that they would not name the baby Meir Simcha.

It was nine o'clock before he got his ticket, checked his luggage, and finished with passport control. If this were a trip for business or pleasure, he probably would have gone to the duty-free shop to buy gifts, which he could pick up when he returned. Instead, he headed straight for a row of telephones. Miriam had gotten him off with some shred of sanity by pointing out that he could call her from the airport and tell her everything he had forgotten to say.

"Hello, Miriam? Did you call Mitch?"

"Yes, it's fine. He says that he'll take care of informing Mr. Livneh."

"Did you cancel my *shiur*?"

"Yes, I managed to get hold of Asaf Almio, and he said that he would take care of it."

"And did you call the Millmans?"

"Yes."

There was something slightly reticent about her tone. Had they been very disappointed? "Did they understand?"

"Yes, of course." Miriam paused and then added, "I agreed to go to them."

"You what?"

"I agreed that the children and I would go to the Millmans in Bnai Brak for the *seder*."

"Will they be able to afford it?"

"I only agreed on condition that they would take some of the meat and other supplies that we had already laid in."

"How will you get there?"

"Mr. Millman is going to come take the things and our suitcase on Wednesday. The children and I will come on Thursday. As for getting back, they'll take us to the bus, and we'll take a taxi home from the bus station.

"Trudy says I can sit like a queen and not lift a finger, as long as I do it in the kitchen where I can give her advice." She paused. "They're very excited about the whole project."

"Yes," sighed Binyamin. "I was also excited about the idea of making my first *seder*."

They went on to the technical details about the car transfer, in case Binyamin did not manage to return during the intermediate days of the Yom Tov. He talked to Shimmy and to Tami, and then said goodbye to Miriam again. He hung up with the feeling that

Miriam was going to manage very well by herself, and that he could concentrate on his father. He took out his *sefer Tehillim* and began reciting *Tehillim* until his flight was called.

From Kennedy Airport in New York, he called his sister-in-law and was told that his father was still in the operating room. No one was meeting Binyamin; he should take a taxi to the hospital.

He found his mother and all his siblings assembled in the waiting room, looking very rumpled. His mother hadn't left the hospital since his father was brought in, more than thirty hours ago. The others had gone to their homes in shifts, always leaving someone with Mom.

Tzvi rose to meet him as he came in, and they embraced. He kissed his mother and shook hands with his other brothers. Then they all returned to their *Tehillim,* and he opened his. It felt strange to slide so easily into the family, after six months of not seeing them.

Every time the door to the operating theater opened they all looked up, but usually only a nurse or intern appeared. Finally, after three-quarters of an hour, a green-clothed surgeon came out and looked about for Mrs. Lerner. She jumped to her feet, and the others followed her.

"Is the operation over, Dr. Matthews?"

"Yes, and he survived it."

This phrasing did not sound very promising to Binyamin. He and the other family members looked at each other.

"As planned, we removed a section of vein from his leg and substituted it for the damaged artery in the heart. Unfortunately..."

Here it was. They all tensed.

"A section of the clot escaped as we were excising the artery, and made its way to the brain, causing a small stroke."

Mrs. Lerner blanched. "How much harm did it do?"

"We won't know until Mr. Lerner wakes up from the anesthesia. You understand that he will be in intensive care for several more days, until the bypass knits correctly with the surrounding arteries."

It was another hour and a half before Mrs. Lerner was called into the recovery room to see her husband. She came out after twenty minutes. She had returned the hospital gown, but she still had the disposable coverings over her shoes and a white disposable cap over her *sheitel*. She sat down looking worn out and glum. "He recognized me," she said, "but he couldn't get any words out. He was very frustrated. I had to tell him not to try to talk, that he should rest and recover now. I told him that he had had a heart attack and that they had done a bypass. It didn't seem practical to try to explain about the stroke yet."

The family had established their headquarters in one of the corners of the waiting room outside their father's ward. They tried not to have more than one person in the room with him at a time. It was hard enough for him to speak with one person.

Tzippy worked out a schedule for the next few days so that one of them would be at the hospital at all times. She divided the day into six four-hour shifts, and wrote everyone into a slot. They all knew that their mother would stay there a lot more than four hours a day, but at least she would be able to go home to rest whenever she was tired.

"Right now," said Tzippy to her mother, "you have to get some sleep or we'll have two patients. Tzvi's house is the closest. The car is at home, right? I'll drive you to Tzvi's."

"Wouldn't ... " Binyamin started to protest, but was silenced by a warning look from Tzippy. It was a few minutes before he got a chance to exchange a few words with her in private. "Wouldn't Mom sleep better in her own bed?"

"No, because as soon as she walked in the house, she'd remember all that she has left to do for Pesach."

Binyamin had an idea. He pointed to their two unmarried brothers, who were studying in out-of-town yeshivos, but were now home for intersession. "Listen, Zevy and Motti and I are going to have our headquarters at home. If Mom stuck to her usual schedule, she has nothing left to do but the kitchen. Why don't we take responsibility for finishing the cleaning?"

Tzippy looked at him suspiciously. "You won't make things worse instead of better, leaving dirty dishes and crumbs all over? I had been about to suggest that at least Zevy and Motti should come stay with me."

"On my honor, Tzippy." Binyamin was offended by the suggestion that they would do more harm than good. "Any *chametz* we eat will be out of the house."

Zevy had the first shift at the hospital, so Binyamin and Motti took a taxi home. Binyamin, jet-lagged and exhausted, wanted nothing more than to shower and fall into bed, but a sense of duty made him dial Miriam's parents first.

"Hello, Mama, this is Benny." He used his "old" name with his mother-in-law. "Did Miriam phone to tell you the news?"

"What news?" asked Mrs. Adler breathlessly. "Isn't this much too soon?"

"No, not that, I'm afraid. My father just had a heart attack, followed by a bypass operation."

"Oh, dear, poor man! How is he?"

"We don't yet know, because he also suffered a stroke as a result of the operation."

"How terrible! Papa! Get on the other line."

Binyamin repeated the story, with some amplification, for his father-in-law. Mr. Adler wrote down Mr. Lerner's Hebrew name so that he could *daven* for him.

"Your poor mother!" said Mrs. Adler. "Are you planning to come to New York?"

"I'm here. I'm calling you from Flatbush," Binyamin announced. "I took the first flight I could get as soon as I was called."

"But then... where is Mimi?"

"She's at home, with the kids."

"At home? What do you mean, at home?"

"At home in Yerushalayim." Wasn't that self-evident?

"Benny Lerner! You mean that you left her there all alone in a strange place to make Pesach?" His mother-in-law was scandalized.

It was all too much for Binyamin to take on the little sleep he had had for the last two days. "Listen, Mama, I came as fast as I could because I was afraid my father might be dead before I got here. There was no time to pack up Miriam and the children to bring them along, nor could they have gotten the same kind of emergency plane reservation that I did." He didn't mention that they also could not have afforded it. He didn't want to hint that his parents-in-law should pay. He barely knew how he would pay for his own ticket. It would have to come out of their fast-shrinking savings.

"You could have tried," Mrs. Adler's voice was accusatory.

"It was a pretty grueling trip, Mama. I'm not at all sure it would have been good for her."

"At least she could have rested when she got here. How in the world is she going to *kasher* the kitchen all by herself? What is she going to do for the *seder*?"

Since Binyamin was almost as worried as Mrs. Adler about the first question, he chose to answer only the second. "She and the children are going to go to this couple, the Millmans, who were planning to come to us. She made the arrangement after I left."

"Outside the family? On Pesach?" Mrs. Adler didn't eat anywhere except her own home on Pesach, not even her children's houses.

"They are very *frum*, Mama. I'm sure it's going to be superkosher."

"Couldn't she at least go to Ella? That would almost be like family!"

"Miriam says that the Millmans are looking forward to having her. They would be very disappointed if she canceled." If Miriam hadn't told her mother about the tiff with Ella, Binyamin didn't want to be the one to do so.

"It seems to me that you're concerned about everyone in the world except my daughter," protested Mrs. Adler in a huff.

Mr. Adler intervened. "Mama, Mama, you're being too hard on Binyamin. He's under terrible pressure because of his father. If you don't like the arrangements, talk to Mimi about them."

"I certainly will!" She slammed down the receiver.

"Thank you, Papa," said Binyamin in a broken voice.

"Go get some sleep," Mr. Adler advised him.

"I will, Papa. Good night." He hung up the phone, buried his face in his arms in despair, and fell asleep on the spot.

Tuesday, after his shift at the hospital, he called Miriam.

"How does your father look?" she asked immediately.

"Just awful. His whole right side was weakened, including the muscles in his face. He can say a few words, but what comes out isn't appropriate, and doesn't seem to be what he means to say. It's very frustrating to him and to all of us. Much of the time he's sleeping or too weak to react to our presence. That's when I try to catch up on the *Daf Yomi*. We're all doing four-hour shifts once a day, and the rest of the time we're trying to clean for Pesach. Did you find a neighbor to help you with the kitchen?"

"I did better than that. I got an American seminary girl who is staying with us and helping out with everything. Her name is Sarah Dinah, and she's a whiz with housework. She comes from a big family and is used to taking responsibility. I don't have to tell her what to do. She just knows."

"That's fantastic!" Binyamin sighed with relief. Maybe this arrangement would mollify his mother-in-law a bit.

"Do you know yet when you're coming back?" Miriam asked.

"I truthfully haven't thought past Pesach, which is coming closer and closer. Zevy and Motti and I are trying to finish cleaning the kitchen, in between duty at the hospital, *davening* and sleeping. My head is spinning from all the running around. For the *seder* we're going to Tzvi."

"Do you think your contribution is important?"

"Surely, yes." He was the one directing the Pesach cleaning since his brothers had only the vaguest idea of what was really involved, and of course he had his shift at the hospital.

"Then perhaps you should stay until after the end of Yom Tov?"

"I'll miss an extra two days work, since there is an eighth day here, and I'll be traveling back against the clock." To have a very small salary check coming right after Pesach was going to be exceedingly difficult.

"I just know that if it were my parents, I would want to stay the extra week."

That reminded Binyamin. "Did your mother call you?"

"Yes," said Miriam curtly. Apparently she hadn't enjoyed the conversation.

"Did she talk you out of going to Bnai Brak for the *seder*?"

"No," said Miriam. "She tried, but she didn't succeed."

The next three days were nightmarish. Of the three brothers living at home, one was usually at the hospital or in transit, while the other two were sleeping or cleaning the kitchen. The first thing they did when Binyamin woke up from his cramped and uncomfortable sleep was to eat everything they could manage out of the refrigerator. Then Binyamin ruthlessly threw away everything else and started cleaning the shelves. The most frustrating job was cleaning out and papering the cabinets; he'd already done that in his own home. He gladly handed that job over to one of his brothers when it was his turn to drive to the hospital.

Bit by bit, in the course of his hospital visits, Binyamin told his father about all their adventures since the beginning of the year. He relived again the awe he felt on Yom Kippur, his fear when the *sukkah* collapsed and he thought that Shimmy might have been under a fallen wall, his frustrations about not getting the security clearance that would allow him to start earning a living.

He did not mention the times he came home from work and found Miriam in despair. The memory of those occasions made him very uncomfortable, and they seemed too private to be shared. Not, of course, that it was clear how much his father understood of what he said.

Friday morning he called the Millmans. It was four in the afternoon in Eretz Yisrael, and the children were very excited to speak to him. Shimmy rattled off the beginning of the Four Questions and would have recited them all had not Miriam restrained him.

"Did the seminary girl come with you?" Binyamin asked when he got Miriam on the line again.

"Sarah Dinah? She helped us get here, but she's staying with some distant cousins for the *seder*."

"Have a *chag kasher vesameach*," Binyamin wished her.

"A *chag kasher vesameach*," Miriam returned, "and don't worry about us. We are being well taken care of."

Although he was sitting in the house where he had spent most of his life, Binyamin felt terribly homesick as he hung up the telephone.

The family was gathering at Tzvi's house for Yom Tov, since it was within an hour's walk of the hospital. Binyamin dropped off Motti with their bags and went cruising around to find a parking space. As he walked back to the house, he was approached by a charity collector.

"Do you speak Hebrew or Yiddish?" asked the man in Hebrew.

"Yes," answered Binyamin with a smile, "I'm from Eretz Yisrael." He was proud to say it.

"Can you help me read this address?" asked the man, holding out a crumpled sheet of paper.

Binyamin gave him instructions for reaching the place, and then turned into Tzvi's sidewalk. The man followed him to the door, perhaps thinking that Binyamin was also collecting charity, and might know where he was going. The Polish maid, Anna, opened the solid wood door and admitted them to the vestibule. The man looked around in awe at the wood paneling, the textured molding around the ceiling, and the fabric on the walls. He reached out gingerly and touched the walls, to see if all this elegance was real or just painted on, as it sometimes was in Eretz Yisrael.

Binyamin looked at his brother's house with new eyes, eyes that had been accustomed over half a year to apartments on a smaller, simpler scale. He had to restrain himself from touching the walls as the visitor had done. Through the broad door leading into the house proper, he could see the living room stretching out like a football field. One part of him rebelled; why does one family need to monopolize so much space? Another part of him estimated whether he could eventually have bought something like this for Miriam.

Tzvi arrived, summoned by the maid. The man from Eretz Yisrael pulled out his letters of introduction and began explaining that he was here with his wife, who needed an emergency operation. Tzvi wrote him a check, made sure that he was set up for the *seder* and walked him to the door. Then he turned to Binyamin. "You, Zevy, and Motti are in one of the second-floor bedrooms. Channah is serving everyone lunch in the regular kitchen. The Pesach kitchen is in the family room in the basement, so that's where we'll be having the *seder* tomorrow night. After lunch, you're welcome to shower in either the second-floor bathroom or the third-floor bathroom."

A Pesach kitchen. That was another thing that had always seemed a little extravagant to Binyamin, but after having done a good part of the work to prepare two separate kitchens for Pesach, he no longer found the idea quite so outlandish.

As he went upstairs to get his towel and Shabbos clothes, he kept marveling at the sheer size of the house. Tzvi must be doing well to be able to afford all this in a city where everything was expensive. There was, he knew, a big mortgage, and Channah also held down a high-powered job to help cover the family's budget, which is why the full-time maid was so essential. Binyamin decided that Miriam would not have wanted a house like this under those conditions.

Binyamin missed the family *seder*, because he was making a

seder for his father in the hospital. His mother took the morning shift on the first day of Yom Tov. She arrived home around two o'clock in the afternoon, looking exhausted, and collapsed into an armchair.

"You look as if you need a long nap," suggested Binyamin.

"Soon," answered Mrs. Lerner, tipping her head back and closing her eyes. "We're alone here in the living room, aren't we?"

"Temporarily," said Binyamin. "With the house so awash with Lerners, the population of any given room is subject to change without much notice."

"You haven't told me anything about how you're settling in Yerushalayim."

That was true. Although he had had plenty of time alone with his father, he had hardly seen his mother since the operation, and this was surely the first time they had been alone since he arrived. Conscious that his mother really ought to be resting, he gave her a very abbreviated account.

"How is Miriam adjusting?"

"Miriam is being a trooper, Mom. What with me working so far away, she has had to learn to manage for herself. By now she runs all sorts of errands in Hebrew and she is getting to be better than I am at dealing with government offices."

"Of course I'm glad to hear that, and I'm proud of her for managing so well, but that's not what I meant." She straightened up in the chair, opened her eyes, and looked straight at Binyamin. "Is Miriam happy?"

"No," admitted Binyamin.

"Then maybe you should come home?"

All the exhaustion of a grueling week washed over him at once, and he sank back against the pillows of the couch, as worn out as his mother. "Maybe," he said in a tone of despair.

Chapter 18

The Inheritance of Our Fathers

"How was the *seder* at your cousins' house?" Miriam asked Sarah Dinah, the seminary girl who was helping her while Binyamin was away. It was the first day of Pesach, and she had walked over to visit.

"Oh, it was nice. Of course, some of the Hebrew went over my head, but the Haggadah itself is familiar. I felt like cheering when we got up to the part where Rabi Akiva and Rabi Tarfon and all the others are having their Pesach *seder* in Bnai Brak."

"I actually did cheer," said Trudy. "A quiet, dignified, 'Yay!'" It was the first time any of them had spent the Pesach *seder* in Bnai Brak.

"But then I felt like crying when I got up to 'Next year in Yerushalayim,' knowing that it wouldn't be," continued Sarah Dinah.

"When are you going home?" asked Trudy.

"The middle of the summer. Then I am supposed to get a job, and after that, start looking for a *shidduch*. It breaks my heart."

"What, looking for a *shidduch*?" asked Miriam.

"No, going back to America and settling there. I really wish my parents would agree to let me look for a job and a *shidduch* here in

Eretz Yisrael."

"Sarah Dinah, the question of who you marry is much more important than where you live. Your parents want to have more input into that than they could be able to manage by long distance telephone."

"They also prefer to have me live nearby."

"So would mine," agreed Miriam, "but they accepted our decision. If you're so much in love with Eretz Yisrael, maybe you and your husband will come here after you get married. There are plenty of English-speaking *kollel* couples in Yerushalayim and Bnai Brak, and many of them stay."

"I still think it would be easier to find such a husband here than in New York." She bounced Tami on her knee, but it didn't elicit the usual delighted squeals. "What's wrong with you, Tami?"

The only answer from Tami, who by now spoke a very cute English, was a whimper.

"She's been under the weather all day," said Miriam, taking her on her own lap.

Sarah Dinah stood up. "Well, I'm off. I still have a second *seder* to make."

"Are you sure you don't want to stay overnight?" asked Trudy.

"No, I want to get the children home to their own beds, and I want to take Tami to our pediatrician in the morning." Tami had not improved. "Don't think, though, that we haven't enjoyed ourselves. The way your husband personalized the *seder* for Shimmy was terrific." The Yom Tov had been very restful, much more so than the large and rather hectic family *Yamim Tovim* that she was used to.

The Millmans got them settled on the 400 bus to Yerushalayim. Tami, who seemed to be running a fever, was very tired, so Miriam let her stretch out on the seat with her head in her mother's lap, and put Shimmy on the seat in front of them next to a plump and cheerful-looking woman in an old-fashioned wig. Miriam leaned her head against the window, and allowed her thoughts to drift.

The next thing she knew, the driver had turned on all the lights, and people were lined up in the aisles to get off the bus. Startled, she looked out the window and saw that they had already arrived at the Central Bus Station in Yerushalayim. The lady who had been sitting next to Shimmy was no longer in evidence; she must have gotten off at one of the stops on the way into town.

Miriam leaned over the back of the seat to wake up Shimmy, but he wasn't there. He had been on the seat in front, hadn't he? Had he stood up already and gotten in line to leave the bus? Gently she lifted Tami's head from her lap and settled her back onto the seat as she stood so she could search up and down the aisle. It was hard to tell with all the adults in the way, but she certainly saw no evidence of him. Could he have slipped off the seat onto the floor? She went around to the seat where he had been sitting and bent down to look under it, as people protested that she was blocking the aisle. Shimmy wasn't under the seat.

Miriam crossed the aisle to the right side of the bus and looked out the window to see if he might have gotten off the bus with the first of the passengers, before she was awake enough to notice. She didn't see him standing on the sidewalk. The aisle was by now more or less clear, so she picked up Tami and began working forward from their original seats, looking under each one. It was awkward bending down with Tami in her arms, and she protested sleepily to all the lurching, but Miriam was not willing to let her out of her sight.

"*Giveret!*" called a man from the back of the bus. "Are you looking for your canteen? Here it is!" He held up a child's canteen with a plastic strap.

"No!" wailed Miriam. "I'm looking for my son!"

Another man who was about to step off the bus turned and asked, "Was he about five years old? With *peyos*?"

"Yes, yes," said Miriam with excitement. "That's him."

"He got off the bus at Castel. Several people got off there. He ran to the door just as it was closing and got off after them. I thought he was with them."

He got off the bus at Castel! A picture of the windswept Castel stop on the Tel-Aviv–Yerushalayim highway forced itself on Miriam. There was a narrow strip of asphalt along a major three-lane highway, with the access road to the bridge in the background. In her mind, she saw a bewildered Shimmy standing there alone, with cars whizzing past, while the other passengers, not noticing that he had gotten off after them, trekked up the slope to the bridge.

She understood perfectly what had happened. Shimmy had woken up when the bus stopped. Looking around in panic and not seeing his mother, he had noticed people getting off at the stop and ran after them, thinking that she had already gotten off. Then he had found himself at the edge of the highway, utterly alone. At the thought of his face scrunching up as he realized that she was not there, her own throat grew tight.

She went quickly forward to the driver. "Excuse me, I have lost my five-year-old son, who got onto the bus with me in Bnai Brak. I am told that he got off the bus at Castel."

"There is a police station here in the terminal. Go report to them and they will call on the radio and send a police car to look for him."

The driver's suggestion that she have the police send a cruiser after Shimmy was such sensible advice that Miriam was somewhat relieved, sufficiently relieved to remember her luggage. "I have a bag and a stroller in the luggage compartment under the bus."

The bus driver realized that in Miriam's condition she needed help. "I'll get you the stroller now and bring the luggage to you at the police station after I park the bus."

Miriam thanked him and got off the bus to show him her suitcase and stroller, which were by now the only items left in the luggage compartment. A private car pulled up behind the bus, and as she was opening the folded stroller Miriam wondered vaguely what it was doing here. This particular section of the terminal was used only by buses letting off passengers. She settled Tami into the stroller.

The door to the driver's seat opened and a woman stuck her head up above the roof of the car. "Excuse me," she asked, "are you this child's mother?"

Miriam looked around in astonishment. There was Shimmy, opening the door of the car and getting out. They ran to each other and he buried his head in her skirt, crying bitterly.

"I saw the bus drive off and leave him standing alone at the side of the highway, so I put him in my car and followed the bus."

"How in the world can I thank you?" said Miriam, now crying herself.

"All I can say is, you are lucky you are in Israel." The woman got back into the car and drove off to her original destination without waiting for further thanks, and without leaving her name.

You are lucky you're in Eretz Yisrael, Miriam told herself as tears coursed down her cheeks.

One of Binyamin's last stops before leaving Brooklyn was his Aunt Toby's house, to visit his cousin Elisha. The entire first floor of the house had been remodeled for wheelchair access, and Elisha's bedroom was in what had once been his father's study.

"I was sorry to hear about your father," said his cousin. "He should have a *refuah sheleimah*."

"Thanks," said Binyamin. "We're all *davening*."

"You don't look in very good shape yourself," continued Elisha.

"You know, hospital visits, Pesach cleaning." Binyamin waved his hand in a vague gesture. "Haven't gotten much sleep."

"How are you settling in Eretz Yisrael?"

"I don't want to discourage you if you're thinking of coming…"

"It's still an option," said Elisha with a nod, "but at the moment it appears to be a very distant option."

"The move is tough. Decidedly tough."

Afterwards, as he was driving to the hospital to say goodbye to his father, he wondered why he had been so negative. He did love living in Eretz Yisrael. Despite the frequent tension at work and his frustrations with the bureaucracy, he still felt privileged to walk on its soil, to eat of its fruits. His concerns, he realized, revolved around Miriam. Something she had said, something relevant, was nibbling at the edges of his consciousness, but he couldn't quite get hold of it.

She had been upset; her voice had had a choky tone. He began reviewing conversations in which she had been upset. And then, if hit him. When she was telling him about sharing a room with Ella, she explained why she hadn't put up a fight to arrange the bedroom as she would have liked it. It had not only been gratitude to Ella's family for taking in her mother when she arrived as an immigrant. "Also, because four years of conflict would have been four very uncomfortable years." And a lifetime of conflict would have been a very uncomfortable lifetime. How much of Miriam's acquiescence to his idea of moving to Eretz Yisrael could be attributed to the same feeling?

Miriam drove to Ben Gurion airport to meet Binyamin in their newly purchased car. One of the things they had accomplished while in the immigrants' hostel was to get Israeli driver's licenses, and Miriam was now glad she was able to drive legally.

She let the children swarm all over their father for a minute or so before she tried to talk to him over their heads. He didn't look well at all. He had dark circles under his eyes, and there was no spring in his step. When they got to the parking garage, she ceremoniously handed Binyamin the keys so that he could take his first drive in the new car. Even that did not awaken the interest she had expected.

He stumbled through the evening routine without saying much about the trip, answering briefly any questions she asked about his father and volunteering nothing else. Because of his mood, she didn't tell him about her adventure on the bus, and Shimmy also didn't bring it up. After all, more than a week had passed since then, and he was more interested in talking about the first day of kindergarten after the Yom Tov.

Miriam put the children to bed as early as possible. She had expected that Binyamin would collapse as soon as he had finished his evening's stint of learning, but instead he came into the kitchen, where she was finishing cleaning the counters and asked, "Do you think we could have a talk? Maybe out on the front porch?"

"Sure," she said, wiping her hands on a towel.

Binyamin brought out two chairs to the enclosed porch and opened the shutters to catch the spring breeze, but he didn't turn on the light and Miriam followed his lead, leaving the porch in semi-darkness. She sat down and waited for him to begin.

"When we moved here," he said, after a pause, "we decided to assume that we were going to stay. Otherwise, we thought, we would be taking our temperature every day. On Monday, some aspect of the bureaucratic hassle makes us feel like throwing up our hands and leaving, but on Tuesday, we notice how much Shimmy is learning and ask ourselves how we could possibly go back, and so forth. As a strategy, I think it was a good one, but..."

"But?"

"But maybe, for all that, we should stop and do some sort of summing up."

"Summing up?"

"Weighing the pros and cons. We know a lot more now than we did eight months ago about what living in Eretz Yisrael means and how well we can adjust."

Miriam was genuinely puzzled. "Are you sure this is necessary? Can't we just go on assuming that if we haven't gone bankrupt and haven't had nervous breakdowns, then we're adjusting perfectly well?"

"I think *it is* important, and I think *this* is the time to do it," Binyamin insisted.

Miriam didn't think this was the time for Binyamin to do anything but get a good night's sleep, but it appeared that he wouldn't be able to sleep until he had said whatever it was that he had to get off his chest. "Okay," she agreed.

There was a silence.

"*Nu?*" asked Binyamin, when the silence had stretched on for a couple of minutes.

"*Nu*, what?"

"What are the pros and cons?"

"I thought you were going to tell me," said Miriam. "You're the one who has been thinking about this."

"No, I want to hear what *you* think. In your own words."

"I think it's a beautiful country, full of concerned, friendly people, at the hub of the Jewish world. I think we should stay," asserted Miriam.

"Miriam, try to be honest with yourself. Don't say what you think I want to hear, tell me what you really think. This is your big chance."

Big chance for what? To have every word doubted? "Binyamin, do you realize that you just called me a liar? Is that what you meant to do?"

"Miriam, I didn't find you crying over onions, I discovered you crying over chicken feet. You found the *frumkeit* here oppressive."

Had she found the *frumkeit* oppressive? There was nothing particularly *frum* about chicken feet. She had found Ella oppressive, but she had solved that with a slammed phone receiver. "I thought your answer to that particular fiasco was adequate. I shouldn't push myself farther than I can manage. So I won't."

"What about your worries that Shimmy isn't adjusting well to Hebrew?" Binyamin pressed her.

"That should be our biggest problem. He'll be running circles around both of us in Hebrew soon."

"What about your mother and father? Don't you miss them?"

Miriam sighed. "Yes, of course I do."

"Do you realize what it would mean to you if one of them were sick and you couldn't spend much time over there because of your responsibilities to your own family? It's all well and good to say that we each have a lot of siblings, but if, *chas veshalom*, something happens, you want to be there yourself to pitch in."

"I would do the best I could."

"What about the reality that in most material respects, the standard of living is higher over there?"

That one rang such a false note that Miriam asked suspiciously, "Are you sure you haven't been hired by the Syrians to disseminate anti-*aliyah* propaganda? Maybe I shouldn't have given such blithe answers to the man who interviewed me for the security clearance."

Binyamin halted his interrogation.

Now it was Miriam's turn to ask a question. "Is this change of attitude because of your father's illness? What exactly happened to you back there in New York?"

It was Binyamin's turn to sigh. "I talked to my mother."

"If you had said that you had talked to my mother, I might have understood, but what did your mother have to say that depressed you so much?"

"She asked me if you were happy, and I had to admit that I didn't think you were."

Was she happy? Miriam didn't usually spend much time thinking about that question, and was sure that was for the best. Happiness was not something acquired by pursuing it, the Declaration of Independence to the contrary. "Before we go on, let me tell you what happened to us while you were away." She told him the whole story of losing Shimmy on the 400 bus.

Binyamin shuddered. "All's well that ends well, but it must have been a terrifying experience."

"That's the point I'm trying to make. I wasn't really terrified. I hadn't been poised for tragedy. I didn't start to worry that perhaps that grandmotherly woman had kidnapped him, nor did I think that the other passengers at Castel would do him harm. Although of course I won't do it again, the very fact that I had been willing to seat him separately from us shows that my general level of trust in the people around me had been high. And Binyamin ... that wouldn't have been true if it had been a New York subway instead of an intercity bus in Eretz Yisrael."

Binyamin looked bewildered. "Every time I try to be noble, it seems to backfire on me. I had decided that it just wasn't going to work out. I came home prepared to get you to open up about your true feelings, ready to declare that we should pack up and go home."

"You came home depressed as all get-out, from which I gather that despite your worries about your father, you also want to stay here."

"Yes," admitted Binyamin without amplification.

"Then there's no problem. We'll stay."

"It's a little more complicated than that. There's still the financial angle and the housing question."

"What is the financial angle?"

"We haven't gone bankrupt yet, but we also are not living within our income. On day-to-day expenditures we're okay, but we keep spending large chunks of cash from savings."

"Like the car?"

"And this trip I just made to America."

"Okay. And the housing question?"

"Well, if we really want to stay, it's much more sensible to buy and assume a mortgage than to rent, where we're just throwing our money down the drain. But that requires a down payment, for which we're about $10,000 short."

"Family loan?" suggested Miriam.

"Even family loans have to be repaid. Car payments and mortgage payments and payments to family probably would be more than we could handle. Also, which family? Yours isn't very enthusiastic about our staying here, and mine is under a lot of financial pressure at the moment. Zevy is going to drop out of yeshivah for the summer term and try to keep Tatti's business afloat, but it certainly won't earn as much as when Tatti was running it." Mr. Lerner was in import-export.

"Tell me, why do you mention all these problems specifically now? Why didn't I hear about them for the last three months?"

"I suppose I was afraid that you would throw up your hands and say we should return to the States," admitted Binyamin in embarrassment.

"Binyamin Lerner! Who is accusing whom of not being open?"

"I'm sorry," said Binyamin.

"It may have been mutual," said Miriam. "Perhaps I wasn't telling you all that I liked about being here because I was afraid of having it thrown in my face if I should decide that I didn't want to stay."

"What do we do now?" asked Binyamin.

Miriam thought about it. "We want to stay; but there are difficulties. Eretz Yisrael is only acquired with difficulty, as everyone hastens to tell us. I think we should look into houses and mortgages. If it turns out to be more than we can handle together with the car payments, then we can wait until we have paid off the car."

"I agree," said Binyamin, who seemed to be perking up. "I just want to add one proviso, after seeing how tangled up I got emotionally over this question. If there comes a point where we find that we're seriously in doubt about whether to go or stay, I think we should discuss it with someone else. Just preparing the question would help us sort out the real issues from the irrelevant ones."

"Agreed."

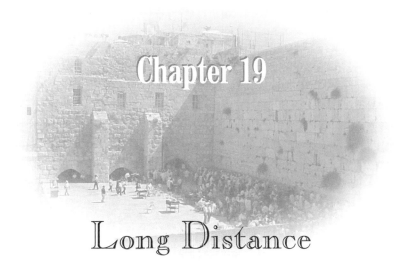

Chapter 19

Long Distance

I t was a mild spring night. The flower garden, or what was left of it after the swath cut by the ramp, was in bloom. The pastel colors were barely visible in the yellow light of the porch lamp, but the scent filled the air. The ramp was not steep, and Elisha pushed himself up, with Mr. Sheinfeld standing behind as a backup in case he should slip. The most awkward part of coming home was opening the screen door and moving it past the axle of the wheel so that he could get his key into the lock.

His mother was waiting in his room as they came through the door. This was unusual. She was usually finishing up in the kitchen when they returned each evening. "May I speak to you in private for a moment?" she asked her husband.

"Sure," he agreed, following her to the kitchen.

Elisha assumed that it was something to do with one of his siblings. His mother did not seem worried, so he didn't worry either. He did wonder where Joe was. His attendant was usually waiting when he and his father returned from shul.

His mother returned almost at once. "Someone has made a new *shidduch* suggestion," she said immediately. "I think we should talk it over. I asked Joe to hold off and come a bit later." Mrs. Sheinfeld made this announcement with much more animation than she usually displayed. Elisha gathered that she considered the suggestion a good one, and found his own hopes rising in response. The three of them adjourned to the dining room table.

Mrs. Sheinfeld consulted her notes. "The girl's name is Naomi Wechsler. She's twenty-three. On the tall side, but that doesn't matter to us. Her father is the principal of a school for Jewish boys in London. The family lived in France for a few years while her father was teaching there, so she speaks French; she works from the house translating from French into English. She is the fourth of five girls; the older ones are all married. Naomi herself is said to be pretty, *frum*, and ..." she paused.

"And ...?" Elisha prodded. He was still waiting to hear why the Wechslers might be interested in them.

"And blind from birth."

Elisha thought it over. It sounded reasonable, much more reasonable than most of the suggestions they had been getting. He could see why his mother was excited. The girl's background was similar enough to his that they should have a lot in common.

"Would I have to travel to London?" he asked. That would jeopardize all the carefully scheduled learning and exercise arrangements, but if the suggestion really were a good one ...

"No, at least not right now. Naomi is staying with her mother's sister in Far Rockaway."

That made sense. There aren't that many possible "special" *shidduchim* in England, where the Jewish community is so much smaller. Elisha noted that she had chosen to come to America instead of going to Israel; if she had an aunt here, that was a good reason for coming. "It sounds pretty good. What's the next step?"

Mrs. Sheinfeld looked pleased. "I get back to the *shadchan,* and we all keep our evening schedules clear for the next few days."

"If that's decided, can I call Joe?" asked Elisha.

"What? Oh, certainly." His mother seemed to feel that prosaic details like getting ready for bed were a bit beneath her notice at the moment.

The first meeting was to be in the home of Mr. and Mrs. Stillman, Naomi's aunt and uncle. The Sheinfelds would all go together in Mr. Sheinfeld's car. Elisha hesitated over whether or not to attend his regular exercise class that evening, but decided to go through with it. There would be plenty of time to get ready afterwards, and a schedule wasn't worth much if every special event cancelled it.

When he and Joe arrived at the gym, someone in a wheelchair was hesitating at the bottom of the ramp. He was young, perhaps eighteen, and wore a plaid shirt and a small yarmulke. Elisha moved his chair beside the newcomer. "It's pretty steep," he said. "I don't usually try it myself. Why don't you let Joe here take you up?"

"Would he? That would be great!"

"Sho' thing," said Joe. He grasped the handles of Elisha's chair, intending to take him up first.

"Why don't you start with my friend, Joe? I can wait." As Elisha sat at the bottom of the ramp watching Joe wheel the new boy up the ramp and negotiate the sharp bend in the center, he realized that that was how he looked to other people. Joe came down the steps and pushed Elisha's chair to the top.

"I'm Elisha Sheinfeld," he introduced himself.

"I'm Danny Trachter," said the new boy. They shook hands.

Elisha motioned in the direction of the locker room. "Let's go change."

"I didn't bring anything to change into," mumbled Danny. "I didn't know that we needed anything, and also, I wasn't really sure I could manage the ramp. If you hadn't come along I probably wouldn't have."

"Most of us change into something loose-fitting, but it isn't compulsory." Danny followed Elisha into the locker room and waited while he removed his white shirt and slipped a sweatshirt over his *tallis katan*. Then they moved out onto the floor of the gym. Elisha moved his chair back and forth as a warming-up exercise. "Your name sounds familiar," said Danny. "Do you suppose we've met somewhere?"

"I don't think so," said Elisha. "Maybe you read the name in the newspaper."

Danny raised his eyebrows as a question.

Elisha laid his palm on the arm of the chair. "I was stabbed. In Yerushalayim. About a year ago."

Danny nodded. "I did read about it." He sighed. "My case is much more prosaic. I was injured in a car crash."

"And the prognosis?"

"I'll probably be paralyzed from the waist down for the rest of my life."

"You're living with your family?"

"My poor family had to pick up and move because of me. We lived in a third floor walk-up, which was obviously impossible once I was in this chair. We had to move to something with street access, but it's both smaller and with a higher rent. That, on top of all the extra expenses, has been a serious blow to the family finances. I try to get grants for the rehab programs and the equipment, but sometimes it takes months 'til they come through, and in the meantime we have to lay out the money."

"Doesn't sound easy."

"The time it takes to fill out forms and get supporting documents and recommendations from my social worker is a real pain in the neck. Before the accident, I hoped to go to school this year, but at the moment I'm employed full time at being disabled. I don't know why I am telling you this. I'm sure that you have the same problems."

"A little different," said Elisha quietly. He didn't want to admit that he had never filled out a single grant application. He had not appreciated how much smoother his life was because his parents could afford the equipment and treatments that he needed. To change the subject, he asked, "What were you planning to study?"

"I wanted to be an accountant. I'm still hoping to get there eventually. And you?"

"I wanted to be a teacher. And I don't know if I am going to make it."

A few hours later, the Sheinfelds, all dressed in their best, were climbing into Mr. Sheinfeld's car. Elisha got to drive, because the crane for lifting the wheelchair to the roof picked it up from beside the driver's seat. He was glad for the chance to practice. Most of the week they used his mother's car, which Joe shuttled back and forth between Elisha and his mother.

Elisha pulled the car out of its reserved parking spot and headed for the nearest freeway. Driving with only hand controls was more demanding than using foot pedals, and he was not yet completely comfortable with them. Driving both of his parents was a responsibility, and he was very conscious of it.

His mother did the navigating, using a book of city maps. She gave him plenty of warning as his exit approached, and successfully guided him through a series of one-way streets until they reached the Stillman's house. After parking the car, as Elisha waited for the crane to lower the chair from its storage box on the roof, he finally had a little time to get nervous about the upcoming meeting.

Elisha wheeled himself up the walk and then Mr. Sheinfeld bumped the chair up three steps to the porch. There was another step up to the house, so Mr. Sheinfeld remained standing behind the chair while Elisha's mother rang the bell.

Mrs. Wechsler had absentmindedly watered her houseplants for the third time that morning. Excess water spilled out of the plate under one of the pots on to the varnished end table. She brought a dishcloth from the kitchen and wiped it dry, glancing frequently at the hands of the clock that were advancing with excruciating slowness. She should have told Naomi to call her as soon as the meeting was over, even though it would have been four o'clock in the morning in England. She sat down on the blue plush couch. Then she got up and walked to the window. She had long since tied back the heavy velvet over-curtains. Now she parted the gauzy under-curtains as well and looked out at the quiet street. Such a bright sunny morning was rare in the early spring. She hoped it was a good sign.

The Sheinfelds had agreed very quickly. She herself had investigated them for several weeks before she had given the *shadchan* her approval to suggest the match. Did that mean that they were a slapdash sort of people? Naomi was a pretty good judge of people, even without being able to read facial expressions. She could hardly wait to hear her daughter's general impression.

Trying to run thorough background checks on both sides of the Atlantic wasn't easy. Of course, she wasn't complaining. It had been so hard to convince the ever-loyal Hindy that she should start going out before her sister. She had pressed, her husband had pressed, Naomi had pressed, and at last Hindy had agreed that when Naomi was in America they could look for a *shidduch* for her as well. She was, after all, twenty-two already and not getting any younger. Mrs. Wechsler was sure that her younger daughter was afraid that the thought of her getting dressed to meet someone would discourage Naomi, for whom they had not been able to find any new suggestions in England for almost a year.

Oh, how she hoped that this Sheinfeld boy was Naomi's *bashert*! It would be so wonderful for both girls if Naomi would get engaged before Hindy. It was after seven o'clock in New York already. She had heard that you could call people at eight in America.

The telephone rang and Mrs. Wechsler pounced on it.

"Mummy?"

For a moment she heard what she wanted to hear, but then she realized that it was not Naomi, but Rachel, her oldest. She tried to empty her voice of disappointment as she said, "Yes, dear?" She wasn't informing her married daughters about possible *shidduchim* for Naomi and Hindy.

"I'm going to be over your way ... shopping, this afternoon. Shall I stop by with the children?"

"That would be lovely. About what time?" She would take a coffee cake out of the freezer to defrost. Did she have enough boxes of juice for the children? She wasn't going out to the store, not until she had spoken to Naomi.

"Around five."

"Wonderful!" After hanging up, she went to check on the juice supply. She was still rummaging around in the pantry, hoping to find some juice, when the phone rang again. She snatched the receiver off its bracket. "Hello?" she said, a bit breathlessly.

"Hello, Mummy. This is Naomi." She sounded very normal.

"How are you, dear?" Mrs. Wechsler didn't want to press for information, in case the meeting had gone badly.

"Fine. The Sheinfelds came last night, as arranged."

"Yes?"

"They seem like very solid and ... decisive people." It wasn't clear if this last word was a compliment or not. However, that took care of her earlier worry. They weren't slapdash, just quick deciders.

"And the boy?"

"Well, Uncle Avner asked him some questions about what he's learning. He seemed to know what he was talking about, and

Uncle Avner told me later that he answered well. However ..."

Uh-oh. "Yes?"

"He's never quiet."

"You mean he talks a lot?" That isn't what she had heard about him. Maybe he was nervous?

"No, I mean that he was constantly moving. I could always hear him."

"Wheeling his chair around the room?" That would be nerve-wracking.

"No, he stayed in one place. He just moved the chair slightly backward and forward, or tapped the arm, or shifted his weight from side to side."

"Listen, they all told me that before the attack he was very active. He played basketball with his friends after school, was a counselor in camp, took long hikes in the mountains during vacations. He probably has a lot of energy to burn and it is hard for him to be cooped up in that wheelchair."

Naomi agreed. "That sounds right."

"What did you talk about?" The boy seemed to have passed the first inspection. Now she wondered how Naomi had fared.

"Now, Mummy, just remember the situation. There were four adults and two young people, all trying to be polite and make a good impression. Uncle Avner felt duty-bound to test Elisha to see how he learns. Aunt Judy kept pressing everyone to eat. Mrs. Sheinfeld complimented Aunt Judy on her house. Mr. Sheinfeld and I could barely have gotten a word in edgewise if we had wanted to. A couple of times I was asked if I had anything to say, but always just when I didn't."

"But you would be interested in meeting him again? Next time without so many people all at once?"

"Yes, Mummy. I'm making it sound worse than it was. They're pleasant people. Very American, but pleasant."

Mrs. Wechsler glanced at the clock as she hung up the phone. Another hour before she could call the *shadchanit*. There was just time for her to go buy that juice for her grandchildren.

"So what do we think?" asked Mrs. Sheinfeld over breakfast, looking pointedly at Elisha. They had agreed in advance that they wouldn't discuss the meeting during the car ride home, but would wait until the morning.

"She's very quiet," he answered. "It's hard to guess what she's really like."

"If you agree to meet her again, you'll have plenty of opportunity to find out." Mrs. Sheinfeld still felt, as she had felt when she had first gotten the phone call from the *shadchanit*, that it was a very appropriate match.

"Oh, I'm willing to meet her again. I was just wondering … did the *shadchanit* say anything about where she wants to live?"

"Not that I remember. Nor did I think to ask. I guess I was just assuming that if they sent her here to look for a *shidduch*, she was prepared to live here as well." Indeed, Mrs. Sheinfeld realized now that she hadn't given enough thought to that issue.

"I just noticed that while her aunt was talking about all the things she had to get used to when she moved from England to the United States, Naomi nodded a few times."

"That could just mean that she's thinking of doing the same. After all, her aunt married an American and came to live here."

"Or it could mean that the idea worries her." Elisha seemed thoughtful.

"Would you be willing to move to England?" asked Mr. Sheinfeld.

Elisha sighed. "Could be. We'll see what happens."

Elisha pushed the chair back and forth within the closed confines of his room. It was the closest outlet he had to pacing. He replayed the conversation in his head again, trying to figure out what seemed to be wrong. All he had done was tell an innocent story about some misbehavior when he was five years old. Why had Naomi frozen up as if he had revealed that he had a criminal record?

He had tried to explain to his mother that there was some problem he didn't understand, but she hadn't been ready to hear him. Everything had seemed to be moving along so smoothly. It had already been agreed between the sides that if there was to be an engagement — and they really meant *when* there was to be an engagement — Elisha and his parents would fly to London to formalize everything there.

The biggest stumbling block in the *shidduch* had been the question of where the young couple would live; but once Naomi had dropped her reserve enough to let him understand what a frightening place she found the world, Elisha had realized that it would be much easier for him to adjust to England than for her to adjust to the United States. That was when he had had to make a really tough decision, because deep down he still harbored hopes of moving to Eretz Yisrael.

However, Naomi was clearly not a candidate for moving so far from everything familiar. He had made the decision and was content; making a good marriage and raising a family was more important to him than where he lived. Everything seemed to be fine, and now ... this!

What had happened? He couldn't even remember what had led him to tell that story. Had he been trying to say something in praise of his mother? She had been telling Motti and Elisha the old fairy tale about the gingerbread man, who jumped up off the pan and ran away, calling, "Catch me, catch me, if you can," to all the people chasing him.

The two boys had thought this was very funny, so when their mother said that it was time to turn out the light and say *Krias Shema*, they started bouncing from bed to bed in their pajamas shouting "Catch me, catch me, if you can!"

She had stood watching them for a minute or so without moving and then had said, "I know two little boys who are going to 'catch it' if they aren't in bed and under the covers by the time I count to five." They had believed her and had gotten into bed.

What, in that story, had upset Naomi so much that afterward she hardly said another word?

Naomi was waiting for the grandfather clock to chime. She was sitting up in an armchair, with a blanket over her shoulders for warmth. By three o'clock in the morning, New York time, she figured that she could call her mother. It would be eight in London. Her mother was usually up by then, and Hindy would not yet have left for work. She would have a hard time explaining her decision to her mother, but she thought Hindy would understand.

It was difficult to explain to outsiders how important Hindy was to her. It had started accidentally. Their family had moved to France just as she was entering second grade, and her sister Hindy was starting first grade.

It had seemed natural to leave Naomi back a grade so she would have a better chance to pick up the language. The entire school experience had been so much more pleasant without a daily crisis over how to get the homework, that she had stuck with Hindy throughout their school career. Although she was a full year older, they were nearly as close as twins.

As soon as the clock chimed the hour, Naomi dialed home but the line was busy. Bother. She hoped to get through before Hindy left. She tried again at two-minute intervals and was finally rewarded with a long ring.

"Mummy?" she asked.

"Naomi? This is Hindy. What are you doing up so late at night?" Her sister was clearly worried by the unusual timing.

"I need to talk to Mummy and to you. Stay around if you can. Is Mummy there?"

"I'll call her."

A moment later she heard her mother's worried voice. "Naomi? Are you all right? What's the matter?"

"Mummy, I've decided to call it all off."

"Call it all off? Such a fine boy, and we've gotten so far along! What in the world are you saying?"

"We had a meeting this evening." Naomi repeated the story about the gingerbread man.

"I have no idea what you're talking about, Naomi! So he was a little rambunctious when he was five. You're going to hold this against him twenty years later?" Her mother was so upset that her voice was shaking.

"No, of course not. It just made me realize that maybe our disabilities are not so complementary, after all. Neither one of us could deal with two little boys like that."

"The way you told the story, his mother needed neither her eyes nor her legs to bring them back in line. All she used was her voice."

"Yes, she conveyed authority, because she was tolerably certain that her sons would do as she asked. If I tried that, I would know that it was a bluff … and so would they."

"If you're worried that you'll have trouble with discipline, then you can get a nanny. A good, solid English nanny who brooks no nonsense. Naomi, have you said anything about this idea of breaking it off to anyone?"

"No. I haven't had much time. I only got back a few hours ago."

"Naomi, please, don't say anything to anyone. I'm calling a travel agent to get a ticket to New York this very afternoon. We'll straighten everything out when I get there."

"No, Mummy, don't! It's no use. Now that I've had time to think, I'm sure this is the right decision. If we got engaged he'd have to move to a place where he doesn't want to live and take a job that doesn't appeal to him. Let me speak to Hindy. I'll try to explain myself to her."

It was a long, wearying phone call.

Elisha was pushing himself listlessly back and forth across the floor of the gym as he waited for the class to start. A clap on his shoulder startled him. He glanced around to see a cheerful-looking Danny. Lucky thing he had never told him about Naomi. It spared him the embarrassment of trying to explain that it was all off.

"Hi!" exclaimed the younger boy. "How's it going?"

"Not so well. Had a set-back in something that was important to me." Elisha's lips twisted in a rather bitter smile. Just a week or two ago he had been sagely telling Danny all the disadvantages of the catch-as-catch-can method of hunting for a wife. If Danny knew what a disappointment Elisha had just been dealt by the *shidduch* system, he would think that after all was said and done, he had had the last laugh.

"Will moping help?" asked Danny.

"No," admitted Elisha, smiling in spite of himself.

"Have any idea what you should have done better?"

"Nope," said Elisha. "I'm totally clueless." But he was slightly consoled.

Chapter 20

Loose Ends

N othing was getting done. The Wahrhaftig apartment was a disaster area, with boxes all over the place and stray items covering all the surfaces. Occasionally Ella picked up one of the items, carried it somewhere else, and put it down again.

Most of the packing had actually been done by Chaim Ozer; but, of course, he wasn't the expert she was at keeping the house neat while turning it upside down. Ella didn't have the heart to pounce on the project with her usual energy, leaving aside the fact that she didn't have her usual energy.

One evening, as he was transferring stacks of winter clothing from the high cabinets into cartons, he said, "We haven't heard from the Lerners for a long time. Since before Pesach. I remember you told me that you and Miriam Lerner had some sort of disagreement; but was it really so severe that you couldn't make it up in three months?"

"Ummm," answered Ella noncommittally.

Chaim Ozer stopped what he was doing and looked at her. "You know, you won't be here the day before Yom Kippur."

"I know," agreed Ella. "I mean to take care of it before we leave."

"Good," said Chaim Ozer.

Ella honestly meant to get to it within the next day or so. Somehow, though, she kept putting it off from day to day. There was the difficult question of how to approach her former friend. A letter? A phone call? A personal visit? If she showed up at Miriam's door, would she get it slammed in her face?

Ella felt a flash of resentment. What was this horrible crime for which Miriam was punishing her so drastically? Ella had offered advice. Not misleading advice, not malicious advice, not demeaning advice. Solid, useful, practical advice. Advice that Miriam herself had often solicited.

Ella was willing to admit that the advice about the car had not been "bite-sized." She realized that it might have been intrusive. That was why she had never explained the details of the argument to Chaim Ozer. But Miriam had overreacted. If she didn't like the advice she didn't have to take it. But to hold a grudge for months afterwards? Ella was willing to apologize, but she didn't think she should have to grovel. And since she was not enthusiastic about the possibility that her apology would be thrown back in her face, she kept putting off the attempt to contact Miriam.

Chaim Ozer took down the last stack of winter clothing from the high cabinets in their bedroom. Suddenly, he more fully appreciated all that his wife did to prepare before every Pesach. Although he had always pitched in during the last frantic week, Ella had quietly sorted these piles at least a month earlier.

At the thought of Ella, he sighed. Their scheduled departure was only three weeks away, and as far as he could tell, she still hadn't contacted Miriam Lerner. He had mentioned the subject once, and she had agreed to take care of it. He didn't like mentioning it again, but it seemed that the problem was deeper than it appeared. This feeling was strengthened by the fact that Binyamin hadn't been in contact with them since the argument, not even to clarify some point for his *shiur*.

It seemed that he would have to speak to Binyamin. It was too delicate a matter to handle by phone, and he didn't want to go to their house. He didn't know which shul Binyamin *davened* in, and he hardly wanted to hang around the entrance to the building trying to waylay him. Besides, today was Monday and he would be coming home late because of his *shiur*. That gave Chaim Ozer an inspiration.

He dialed the number of the immigrants' hostel, which he still remembered from seven years earlier. A recorded voice told him that the number had been changed to seven digits and he should add a five at the beginning. On his second try he got the clerk and persuaded him to look on the bulletin board. Binyamin's *shiur* was scheduled for 7:15 in the shul. He called up the bus company to find out what bus would get him there on time.

Chaim Ozer actually arrived in the hostel at 7:30. He went to the shul and sat down with the others to enjoy the *shiur*. Binyamin's face registered surprise when Chaim Ozer came in, but he did not pause in his explanations. Binyamin was contrasting the different opinions with regard to the rules against wasting the produce of the *shemittah* year, trying to explain why *shemittah* observers in communities outside Yerushalayim did not throw away edible vegetable peels until they had spoiled. Chaim Ozer felt a pinch of unhappiness over the fact that soon they would have no active part in keeping these special *mitzvos*.

When the class was over, Chaim Ozer came up to him. "Nice presentation," he said, "and a respectable-sized group."

"Shrinking, I'm afraid," said Binyamin. "With the recent decline in *aliyah*, this immigrants' hostel is being phased out. I have two *baalebatim* from the surrounding community, but I don't think there is a large enough base there to support a *shiur* once the hostel has emptied out."

The question of what had brought Chaim Ozer to Mevasseret was still hanging in the air. "Are you going home now?" he asked.

"I usually *daven* with the *minyan* here at 8:15. They're also beginning to have trouble gathering ten men every night."

Chaim Ozer glanced at his watch. It was nearly 8:15, and someone had already stepped up to the lectern. "Then you're going back into town?"

Binyamin nodded. "I can give you a lift if you want."

After the *minyan*, they walked out to the car in silence. Binyamin was very clever. He must realize that Chaim Ozer had sought him out to speak about something, and he presumably guessed that it involved the rupture between the two families. It would help if Binyamin would bring up the subject himself and give Chaim Ozer an indication of his attitude, but if he chose to leave the initiative to the person who had arranged the meeting, it was hardly surprising.

Chaim Ozer broke the silence after Binyamin had pulled the car out of the parking lot and was headed for the overpass crossing the highway leading into Yerushalayim. "It's been a long time," he said.

"It has," agreed Binyamin. "My father had a heart attack just before Pesach, and I spent Yom Tov there."

"How is he now?"

"Well, they did a triple bypass which was pretty successful, but he had a stroke during the operation. He's been getting intensive physical and speech therapy, but he's still far from a complete recovery."

"*Refuah shcleimah*," Chaim Ozer wished him. "Tell me his name." None of this, of course, was getting him any closer to the purpose of his visit.

He would have to be more direct.

There was a pause, but before they could lapse into actual silence, Chaim Ozer inched closer to his subject. "Did your wife go back with you when your father had the heart attack?"

"No, she stayed here with the children."

Chaim Ozer winced slightly. Even in an emergency like that, the Lerners hadn't turned to the Wahrhaftigs for assistance. The rift was even deeper than he had realized.

Binyamin must have caught something of what Chaim Ozer was thinking, for he added, "Miriam went to the Millmans in Bnai Brak and seems to have had a wonderful time. They enthroned her as queen and did everything just the way she told them."

Chaim Ozer imagined Miriam Lerner sitting on a throne giving instructions to her loyal subjects. It was not a role he would ever have associated with her, but she had surprised him several times over the last year. "How has she been, other than that?"

"It was a hard winter. Actually, since Pesach she's been feeling somewhat better."

They were getting closer to town, so this leisurely sidling up to the subject might not get him what he was trying to accomplish in time. "How much do you know about this disagreement between our wives?" asked Chaim Ozer.

"How much do you know?" Binyamin countered.

"Hardly anything."

"Then I'm probably better informed." He continued watching the road and did not glance at Chaim Ozer.

He thinks there is a right and wrong side to it, and that his wife is in the right. That was unpromising for Chaim Ozer's hopes of enlisting Binyamin to help break the stalemate. "Perhaps it would help if I were better informed than I am?" he suggested gently.

"Isn't your wife the proper address for that request?" suggested Binyamin, equally gently.

Was she? That depended on why she hadn't told him what was going on. "How certain are you that my wife understood what your wife was upset about?"

That gave Binyamin pause. "Not completely. In fact, some of it was never mentioned."

"Then, perhaps, my first address was the proper one after all?"

"Does your wife speak much about her high school years?" asked Binyamin with a sigh of surrender.

"Yes, rather often. It was her introduction to the big world. She is always lavish in her praise for your parents-in-law for taking her in so graciously and making her feel a part of the family."

"Does she ever mention Miriam sharing her room, and changing a lot of her habits?"

Memories of that conversation between Ella and Miriam, on the way to the Millmans' *sheva berachos,* came back vividly.

"Brrr," said Ella. "I'd forgotten how cold New York gets in December."

"On the other hand," said Mimi with an edge in her voice, "the houses are well heated. Once you get inside you can unknot your muscles."

Ella laughed. "Still the local patriot, I see. Remember how we used to argue the relative merits of living in New York or living out of town."

"I surely do," replied Mimi. "I remember that when you first came to stay with us at the beginning of high school you would be offended that perfect strangers didn't all say 'Gut Shabbos' to you in the streets."

"Those first few months were terribly hard," Ella reminisced. "To go from being a graduating eighth-grader in a small day school to being a lowly ninth-grader in a huge high school was one of the most humbling experiences in my life."

"I would never have guessed it from the way you walked into the building on the first day of school. I was nearly shaking with nervousness,

even though I knew nearly a third of the girls in our class, and you sailed in as calmly as if you had been going to the school for years, although you didn't know a soul."

"It was sheer bravado," admitted Ella, "but I didn't realize that I had pulled it off well enough to fool you as well."

"That's interesting," said Chaim Ozer to his wife. "You often told me how scared you were, and you never told me what a brave front you put up. Do you think it helped?"

"Can't tell you," said Ella with a shrug. "I never tried the experiment of creeping into a new place with my eyes on the floor."

"You must have been doing something right, since you were put in charge of organizing our class booth for the Chanukah bazaar."

"I'm sure at least part of it was trying to make the outsider feel welcome. I considered it thoughtfulness on the part of the teacher."

At that point, since Miriam seemed upset, Chaim Ozer changed the subject.

"I think I begin to get the idea," said Chaim Ozer. "It's strange, when we're invited out we always remember to thank our hosts, but often forget to thank the children of the family for the inconveniences they put up with."

"You shouldn't get me wrong," Binyamin hastened to say. "Miriam understood that her mother was under a strong obligation to Mrs. Gutfreund."

"You're telling me that she wasn't grudging, just overwhelmed?"

"That's the word," said Binyamin with relief. "Overwhelmed." He pulled up the car in front of Chaim Ozer's apartment building.

"But this part was not actually mentioned in the argument?" Chaim Ozer asked.

"No, I don't believe so. I think it was ostensibly about chicken feet and our car. You can get the details from your wife."

Chicken feet? Their car? "There isn't much time for dealing with anything that goes ten years back," mused Chaim Ozer out loud. He looked up at Binyamin. "We're leaving for the States in two weeks, *im yirtzeh Hashem.*"

"Vacation?"

"No, we're moving back."

Binyamin widened his eyes in astonishment. "Is someone ill?"

"No. I accepted a job teaching in a yeshivah."

Binyamin looked up at the apartment building and back at Chaim Ozer. "I find it hard to imagine you living anywhere except Yerushalayim."

"You understand, at least, why I think something has to be done. I don't think it would be healthy for either your wife or mine to have this dragging on after our departure."

"Of course not," agreed Binyamin. "What do you suggest that we do?"

"I'll speak to my wife and you speak to yours. I think it would be best for you to call me, say in two days."

"You're on ... and, Chaim Ozer?"

"Yes?"

"I may not have shown it, but I really appreciate the effort you made in coming to search me out at the *shiur*."

"I enjoyed it. It was a good *shiur*." They shook hands.

As Chaim Ozer went up the steps toward his building, he tried to figure out how to speak to Ella. She had given him so few details of an argument that turned out to be very serious, so she must consider it unflattering either to herself or to her friend. He would have to let her tell it in her own words, after explaining why he thought he needed to be informed. Then he would deal with Binyamin's revelations as gently as possible.

Chaim Ozer looked at his watch as he climbed the stairs. It was after nine. He hoped Ella wasn't worried about where he had been. He knocked on the door and turned the handle, but it was locked. That was odd. Ella didn't usually lock the door when he was expected home. He tried to put his key in the hole, but it wouldn't go in.

Where could Ella have gone with all the children at this time of night? If she had gone out, why would the key be in the lock on the inside. Unless ... when he had left for *kollel* at 3:45, he had left a neighbor's daughter in charge, because Ella wasn't due back from the doctor until 4:30. He knocked again, harder, and was rewarded by sounds from inside the apartment, and the click of the latch. The same neighbor's girl, looking groggy, opened the door.

"Mrs. Wahrhaftig went to the hospital," she announced. "My mother fed the children supper, put them to bed, and told me to stay for the night. You're supposed to take this to the hospital." She handed him an overnight bag for his wife. "You had better ask my mother for the details."

Chaim Ozer didn't pace. On the other hand, it was impossible to concentrate on his *Gemara* either. So he was reviewing *mishnayos*. They had already told him that the baby was a girl and that she and the mother were healthy. Now he was waiting to be allowed inside to speak to Ella. At last, the nurse appeared in the door of the waiting room and motioned for him to follow her. Slipping his *sefer* in his pocket, he picked up the overnight bag and strode down the corridor.

Ella was lying with her eyes closed, her face completely drained of color. Chaim Ozer wondered where she had gotten the strange looking vermilion snood that emphasized her pallor. Through the bed's raised side bar, he gazed at the baby who, swaddled in the institutional garments provided by the hospital, was cradled in the crook of his wife's arm.

"*Mazal tov*," he said softly. "She's beautiful."

Ella half opened her eyes and smiled weakly. "When Leah was born, you thought she looked like a dried apricot," she teased.

"Since then I've had a lot of practice looking at newborn babies. Your newborn babies are beautiful. The rest of them, I admit, still look like dried apricots." He raised the overnight bag into her range of vision. "I brought your things."

"About time. I arrived here in a *sheitel*. I exchanged it for one of those operating room things that looks like a shower cap, and after I was out of the delivery room someone lent me this purple thing from one of the other *frum* women. Can you get me my snood from the bag?"

Chaim Ozer fumbled around in the bag until he found it. He draped it over the bar of the bed and went to the sink to bring her a damp washcloth. When he returned, the vermilion snood was still clutched in his wife's hand, as if the effort of placing it on her night table was too much for her.

"Where were you?" she asked. "I went to the hospital straight from the doctor's office. About 7:15, I asked Mrs. Lichtenstein to send one of her boys to call you from *kollel*, and they said you were gone."

"I had an adventure," said Chaim Ozer. "I'll tell you about it later. I got home just after nine, and of course the Lichtensteins sent me straight here."

"Listen, Chaim, could you call the Lerners tomorrow evening to tell them about the baby?"

Tomorrow was Wednesday. "Perhaps I should wait until after we give her a name on Thursday morning?"

"I'd like them to know early enough for them to come visit if they decide to."

So that was what she had been waiting for. The idea had its merits, even though it diverged from the script he and Binyamin had set up. He narrowed his eyes as he considered it, and paused just a bit too long.

"Does this adventure of yours have something to do with the Lerners?" Ella asked suspiciously.

He might as well confess. "Yes, I went out to Mevasseret to catch him at the end of his *shiur*."

Ella bit her lip and closed her eyes, as if bracing herself for something unpleasant, but said nothing.

"I originally meant to speak to you this evening," continued Chaim Ozer, "but I think this isn't the right moment. You haven't an ounce of energy, Ella, and any moment a nurse will burst in and scold me for exhausting you. Just believe me when I tell you *s'iz nisht azoi geferlich*— it's not so awful. I think we'll have it all worked out in a day or so."

Ella seemed to relax, though the snood remained clutched in her hand.

"If you'll let go of that purple thing," he added, "I'll try to get it returned to its owner."

"Levy," murmured Ella in a barely audible voice. "Chedva Levy."

Brrngg. When the nurse had taken the baby away, Ella had asked her to set the alarm clock for five of eleven. She had been afraid that if Chaim Ozer came at the visiting hour and found her asleep, he would quietly leave. He hadn't told her when he was coming, but she wanted to be ready.

Ella raised her arm with great effort, shut the alarm, and let her arm drop back onto the bed. Something was bothering her, but she found it difficult to focus her thoughts. Something to do with

Chaim Ozer. He had come last night while she was wearing that horrible purple snood, but that wasn't the problem. He had come home late because he had gone out to Mevasseret to speak with Binyamin Lerner.

Ella winced.

Binyamin had probably told him that the argument was about the car, and Chaim Ozer was not likely to think that she had been justified. She remembered the letter she had sent Miriam last year, the one Chaim Ozer had said contained advice that had not been sufficiently "bite-sized." He had warned her, and she hadn't taken his warning seriously.

It was odd how, when this argument had been between herself and Miriam, she had found it easy to contain the crisis. She had decided where she had gone wrong and for what she would have to apologize. Then she had allowed herself a little indignation at Miriam for blowing it up out of proportion.

Now that the husbands were involved, it all looked different. Now the argument was being viewed from the outside, and of course, it was very easy for them to wonder what business it was of hers whether or not the Lerners bought a car.

She surely had only herself to blame that Chaim Ozer had taken this initiative. He had given her a gentle hint, and she had said that she would take care of it. But she hadn't followed through. Just thinking of the whole mess left her weary and depressed.

Ella had intended to spruce up a bit and adjust her robe before her husband's arrival, but she simply didn't have the energy to do so. She didn't remember being so wiped out with Leah and the other children. She struggled to keep her eyes open, but the effort was too much for her.

Ella was jolted awake again by the sound of someone sobbing next to her bed.

It couldn't be Chaim Ozer. He wouldn't be sobbing. She managed to pry one eye half open. Miriam Lerner was sitting next to her bed, tears running down her face.

At this sign of returning consciousness, Miriam took Ella's limp hand between both of hers. "Ella, can you hear me? It's me, it's Mimi."

Ella managed a nod. The hard lump of her own anger began to soften at the sight of Miriam's evident distress.

"You look ... you look the way you did that first winter when you got that intestinal infection."

Ella nodded again. She had been unable to eat for almost a week, and had lain in her bed looking wan. Mrs. Adler had been distraught with concern, worrying about whether she should summon Rebbitzen Gutfreund to her daughter's sickbed. The doctor had recommended chicken soup, and it was Miriam who had had the patience to sit by the bed and feed Ella one spoonful every five minutes. In between spoonfuls, she would tell her the news from school.

Ella managed a faint smile. "Sorry I was such a nuisance."

Miriam leaned forward. "Really, Ella, I think Binyamin may have painted the picture a bit too black. Life was more interesting with you there. I didn't feel pushed around all of the time. It was only that everything always seemed to be done your way."

She doesn't realize that Chaim Ozer hasn't spoken to me yet, thought Ella. She took my comment about the chicken soup as an apology for ... for what? For four years of "pushing around." Not *all* of the time. Just some of the time. Or most of the time.

Formulating a true apology seemed beyond her, so taking refuge in her very real physical weakness she closed her eyes. Miriam's last statement echoed in her mind. Everything *always* seemed to be done your way. *Everything* always seemed to be done your way. Everything always seemed to be done *your* way.

Miriam squeezed her hand, and with a strong effort of will Ella returned the squeeze. "I see that you're too tired for a visit now. I hope we'll see each other again before you leave, though I don't know for sure that that will be possible. If not, let's just regard the whole episode as forgiven and forgotten."

Ella's sense of honesty prevented her from letting that pass with just a superficial nod. "Forgiven," she agreed. She did not, however think that she would forget. Something had changed irrevocably.

"May you raise her *l'chupah u'l'maasim tovim,*" Miriam wished her as she stood up.

"*Amein.*"

Chaim Ozer arrived at ten minutes to twelve. After a glance at his wife's face, he went to the foot of the bed to check her chart. "Seven!" he announced with a wince. He was talking about her hemoglobin count, which was usually around thirteen. He sat down in the chair Miriam had vacated half an hour earlier and smiled at her. "Maybe I had better have Mrs. Lichtenstein make you some of her famous chopped liver. That's guaranteed to bring your iron up!" When Ella didn't smile back at him, his own smile faded. He leaned forward and asked, "Would you rather that I not bring the children to visit you at three? You still look as wiped out as you were last night."

Ella gave a noncommittal shrug.

"I'm going to track down your doctor and talk to him. Unless I hear something very encouraging, I won't bring the children this afternoon." He remained seated, quietly telling her what was going on at home, until visiting hours were over.

When the nurse brought her the baby, Ella looked down at the tiny form. When this little one grew up to be a teenager, would she think that her mother pushed her around, and always wanted things her own way?

Ella was usually fiercely possessive of her newborns, but today she was relieved when the nurse came and took the baby away again.

As their departure drew closer, Chaim Ozer was suffering withdrawal symptoms. In the wake of Ella's anemia and depression he had left *kollel* before the end of the *zeman*, in order to tie up all the loose ends of their seven years in Yerushalayim. He had frozen their sick fund membership and national insurance, found tenants for their apartment, sold the small appliances, and taken care of many similar details. Whenever he walked past the bookshelves on the way from the telephone to the children's room or from the kitchen to the bedroom, his hands would twitch and he would glance longingly at his beloved *sefarim*. He made time for his regular "extras," but for the sort of "in-depth" learning on which he usually spent most of his energy, there was now neither time nor opportunity.

On his next trip past the bookcase, Chaim Ozer gave his *Shas* a stroke of farewell. Tomorrow the movers were coming, and for at least six weeks he and his *sefarim* would follow different paths.

Ella sat at the airport holding the baby. The rest of the family was waiting in line for the security check and Ella didn't like exposing her newborn to so many possible sources of infection. She had folded the blanket so that it formed a hood around the baby's head.

"Hello! We came to say goodbye." It was Miriam Lerner's voice.

"Hello," said Ella dully.

Miriam sat down beside her and peered into the bundle. "What did you name her?"

"Chanah. Chani. After Chaim Ozer's grandmother."

Miriam smiled down at the baby. "It's good to hear you speaking in full sentences again. You were at the one-word level when I came to visit you in the hospital."

"My blood count was very low."

"I ... I wanted to make sure you understood. I'm sorry that I slammed that phone down on you. I was under a lot of stress. And then ... it dragged on. The moment Binyamin told me that you were moving, I felt terrible about having made such a *tzimmes*."

Of course. Once there was no danger that Ella would continue pushing her around, why shouldn't they make up? At this point Ella's own conscience fluttered in protest. Apparently you did push her around for four years. Maybe ten years. Shouldn't you make some effort to make that up to her? This is your last chance for a long time. Ella shifted the baby so that she could be held in one arm, and laid her hand on her friend's hand. "Miriam, I'm sorry."

Miriam burst into tears, and once again clasped Ella's hand in both of hers as she had in the hospital. "No, Ella, don't. Don't apologize. Let's just let it all be forgiven and start over again."

Ella leaned over and kissed Miriam's wet cheek, but she kept to herself the feeling that things could never be the same as they had been before this blowup. Not because of some change in Miriam or how she viewed Miriam, but because of a change in how she viewed herself.

Chapter 21

A View of the Hills

Miriam was lying in her bed in Em Vayeled, the convalescent home for new mothers in Telz-Stone, just outside of Yerushalayim.

"This was easy to get to!" exclaimed Binyamin from the doorway. He had dropped by on his way from work to his *shiur* in Mevasseret, which was further down the highway. "They should put up one of those, 'If you lived here, you would be home by now' signs."

"I don't know how many people commute from Tel Aviv to Yerushalayim."

"Judging by the traffic jam at the entrance to the city at rush hour, quite a few." He sat down near the bed and told her about his day, which had been complicated. Mitch Weissman was in the States on a business trip, and Binyamin was coordinating the different parts of their current project while he was away.

Rivka Weissman, Mitch's wife, appeared in the doorway. "Can I visit, too?"

"I'm afraid that in a moment you will be the only visitor. I have to run out to my *shiur*."

Rivka sat down on the chair he vacated. "How are you managing?"

"We're looking for an apartment, and it's not easy. Yerushalayim is terribly expensive."

"Because lots of people want to live there. We might have lived there ourselves, except that Mitch had work in Tel Aviv." She looked around the room. "Who is taking care of your children? I know it can't be your husband, because my husband has tied him up at work."

"An American seminary girl who stayed with us for Pesach. She's taking care of the children until my parents arrive for the *bris*. Binyamin is sleeping at the neighbors' in the meantime."

"I took a nurse for the baby we had shortly after we arrived. She was Dutch and spoke no English. I had to struggle to communicate with her in Hebrew. One day, I came home and she told me that she had hung out three *chitulim* on the line. We had had a terrible plague of cats that year. If you left the door to the porch open, they would streak through the house, snatch something edible off the table, and plunge through the window. I had an instant mental picture of three of these scruffy cats, spitting and scratching, hanging by their tails from the clothesline.

"'Why did you do that?' I asked, with a rising note of hysteria in my voice.

"'Because they were wet,' she said matter-of-factly.

"Now I pictured three wet cats hanging in a row by their tails.

"The nurse picked up her purse and said, 'I am going now. You can take them down when they are dry.'

"'No, you are not going!' I shouted. By then I was really hysterical at the prospect of having to deal with these furious animals by myself. 'First you are going to take them down.'

"Finally, she seemed to grasp that there was some misunderstanding. '*Geveret*,' she explained patiently, 'there are *chitulim*, diapers, and there are *chatulim*, meow, meow.'

"I was both very relieved and very embarrassed."

The next morning, Binyamin, a bit groggy from dealing with extra responsibilities at home while carrying a full load at work, was checking several recently completed modules against the specifications. He was sitting at Mitch's desk, because it had the computer with extra functions. He hit the button on the intercom. "Rami, there's something wrong with the last module you wrote.

Come look at it."

"Stuff and nonsense," growled Rami belligerently. "I ran five sets of test data through that module. It works like a dream."

"It may work like a dream, but it doesn't do what it is supposed to. Cut the guff and come here."

Rami slouched through the door five minutes later, glowering. Binyamin, who had been tapping his fingers impatiently, sent the specifications skidding across the desk with a flick of his wrist. "Here! The part I underlined in red. You're supposed to change the color every time you draw another line on the screen."

"What a silly idea! The screen will look like a clown suit."

"We're doing the project for the aerodynamics division. Maybe they are into clown suits. Maybe it helps them tell which line goes where. Our job is to produce the program according to the specifications, and if, when it is done, they think it looks silly, then that's their worry."

"You want me to bring in a random number generator for a dinky module like this?" Rami sounded outraged.

"Of course not. There are 256 colors, right? So use a linear function with large coefficients and reduce modulo some prime less than 256, say..." Binyamin thought a moment, "251."

Rami picked up the specifications, but continued to glare at Binyamin. "I think there's something pretty fishy going on here that Mitch keeps asking you to cover for him. I don't know if it's because you are both *dati'im* or because you are both Americans, but one way or another, I am going to object."

The next morning Binyamin was late for work because he stopped in Telz-Stone to make a down payment on the *seudah* for the bris. When he got in, he found a note on his desk that Livneh was looking for him. With a heavy heart, he dropped his briefcase and portable computer next to his desk, took off his jacket and hat, and went straight to personnel.

"What kept you?" grumbled Livneh when he saw Binyamin standing in the door.

"I arrived late," admitted Binyamin.

"The cat's away, the mice will play, huh?"

What was Binyamin supposed to answer to that? No, I'm late all the time, even when my boss is here? He just stood and waited to see why he had been called.

"Listen, I received a complaint about you. Something about unjustified interference and absence from work. Since it doesn't originate from your superior I won't put it in your official personnel folder, but I am opening an unofficial folder in which I will keep it."

"I think the complaint is unjustified, and I think I would prefer to have it investigated now," Binyamin replied.

"Believe me, Lerner, it won't be to your advantage to have a public *tzimmes* made of this. You don't have tenure yet, and that sort of thing will leave an unpleasant impression in the minds of those who will have to make the decision. Just shape up and none of this will ever become public."

Binyamin left with a very uneasy feeling. The idea of Livneh collecting a private folder of uninvestigated complaints about him was very disturbing. Should he ask Mitch not to put him in charge the next time he wanted to travel? Of course, that was just what Rami wanted. He had chosen to complain about Binyamin rather than Mitch because Binyamin was much more vulnerable.

Furthermore, what did "shaping up" mean? His parents-in-law were arriving this afternoon. Was he not supposed to meet them? Was he supposed to skip his son's *bris* tomorrow morning? Mitch wouldn't have made a fuss about any of these absences, but now he had to worry about how they would go over with Livneh or some group of people who would decide at some unspecified date whether he could keep his job.

"How would you like to take a walk?" asked Miriam's roommate, Tova, a resident of Telz-Stone and, like many of the local residents, an American immigrant.

"To see your house?" asked Miriam.

"No, to see my *sheitel macher*. The kids took my good *sheitel* to get it done for the *bris*, and I want to try it on." Tova's son was one day younger than Miriam's.

Since Miriam was in despair over the fact that none of her regular clothes fit her yet, the idea of getting a little exercise seemed appealing.

As they walked down the hill, Tova pointed out the "sights." The new shuls that were being built; the grocery store that carried everything, including anything you could want from America; the playground that was crowded with children. "They're building a new one across the road, but it isn't ready yet."

They turned down a small lane and reached a set of steps. Miriam paused at the top. "What a beautiful view!" she said, pointing toward tree-covered hills across a small valley.

"Yes, it is. This is the far side, away from the main highway, and the hills over there have not yet been developed."

They walked down a street lined by a row of two-story houses, and Tova turned in at one of them. Her *sheitel macher*, Chavy, lived on the first floor and seemed to have a private yard. Miriam was introduced, and she looked around curiously as they walked through the house to the hairstyling room. The picture window in the living room gave the same view of the valley that had enchanted Miriam before.

Tova sat down in a swivel chair in front of the large mirror, and Chavy set the freshly combed wig on her head. She began making deft adjustments of the style with her comb.

"Any luck with your plan to move up the hill?" asked Tova, as Chavy worked.

"No!" answered Chavy with distress in her voice. "The place we bought is finished, the bridge mortgage we took has almost expired, and we still haven't succeeded in selling this place. We've gone down another ten thousand, to $120,000."

"That's a good price for a three-bedroom apartment. I should think you would find a buyer pretty quickly."

"We thought that the last time we advertised, too," said Chavy, disconsolate.

To Miriam it was instantly clear that this was the apartment she hadn't even dared to dream of: It had a view, and a yard, and was relatively close to Binyamin's work, in a community full of Americans. She would almost have blurted something out on the spot, but she felt that wouldn't be fair to Binyamin. Besides, it might compromise their bargaining position.

The wig was decreed to be finished, Chavy sprayed it with a suffocating amount of hair spray, placed it on a styrofoam head, and covered it with a plastic bag to protect it from breezes. Miriam contended with a fierce inner debate about whether she should mention her interest in the house. In the end, she decided not to.

The next time she'd see Binyamin was when he brought her parents from the airport, and that surely wouldn't be the proper moment to pull him aside and bend his ear about some apartment she had seen. Better to call him at work now and try to catch him before he left for the airport. She took her phone card and went out to the public phone.

"Hello, is Binyamin Lerner there?"

"Just a moment, I will switch you over."

"Hello, Binyamin?"

"Miriam? Is something wrong? Is the baby okay?" Binyamin's voice was worried.

"No, everything's fine. I'm sorry to disturb you at work. I just called because I saw the most fantastic apartment. Not expensive either."

"Listen, Miriam, this is neither the time nor the place for this discussion." The worry was replaced by irritation.

Miriam forged ahead, although the conversation was not going as she had planned. "I want you to go look at it, tonight or tomorrow after the *bris*. I'm afraid it will be snapped up."

"How can I possibly make your exhausted parents wait while I go look at an apartment? They are dissatisfied enough with me for making you move to Eretz Yisrael. Making them hang around when they're exhausted from a trans-Atlantic flight would be the capper."

"My parents are very fond of you, Binyamin," asserted Miriam. "They always have been."

"They always had been. You mother expressed a different opinion over Pesach. As for tomorrow morning, I remind you that I am filling in for my boss. I can't afford to take a minute more off from work than necessary."

"Excuse me for having disturbed you while you were so busy," said Miriam quietly, and hung up, feeling snubbed.

Miriam managed to subdue her worry about losing the apartment during the reunion with her parents. Her genuine joy at seeing them again after a year's absence surely helped. After they visited a while with Miriam and the baby, they drove away in their rented car, following Binyamin to the Lerners' apartment.

Only after their departure did all her frustration surface again, making it hard for her to fall asleep. Binyamin hadn't been willing to listen at all. He hadn't asked about the price, or the size, or the location, or anything. Was he so certain that Miriam didn't know anything about choosing an apartment?

Miriam tried to control her pique. Being angry would only get her into a fruitless argument with Binyamin. It wouldn't help her get the apartment she loved. Binyamin had told her in a few snatched sentences about being called in by Livneh this morning. He wasn't taking any interest in the apartment because he was too worried about other things: His problems at work, his relationship with his parents-in-law, the *bris* tomorrow.

Miriam was still convinced that those were, in a sense, temporary problems, and that the apartment was a decision that would have serious consequences for the future. Having half an hour cut from his commuting time in each direction could make a tremendous difference to Binyamin, and having a lot of American friends would probably do a great deal for Miriam's adjustment to Eretz Yisrael. Think how nice it would be to be able to send the children out to play in the yard, without having to worry that the youngest might toddle into the street!

Miriam took a deep breath and resigned herself to the probability that they would not buy this apartment. Acceptance brought relief. Her muscles relaxed, and she realized that she was incredibly tired. Her last thought, as she sank into sleep, was that she would try once more to get him to look at the apartment.

The *bris* for the Lerners' new son was to be held in the convalescent home in Telz-Stone. The night before the *bris*, a troop of some fifteen young *cheder* boys came to recite *Krias Shema* for someone else's new brother. Miriam asked them to say *Krias Shema* for her baby as well.

In the morning, when Binyamin came to speak to her before the ceremony, he was in a much better mood than the day before. "You're sure you're happy with the name?" he asked.

"Sure," said Miriam. "Shimmy was named after my grandfather, so it's only natural that his brother should be named after yours."

"That's what your parents said, too," Binyamin said with a grin.

He had apparently gotten along with Mama and Papa better than he had expected. That would explain his buoyancy. Miriam seized her opportunity. "Binyamin, maybe on your way home from work you could just take a quick look at this apartment I saw."

"You really liked it didn't you? All right, give me the address and I'll try to fit it in."

Miriam felt new hope, but along with it came new anxieties. "Can I tell them that you're coming? Also, I should check to see that it hasn't been sold already."

"If it has, call me at work and let me know so I won't have to bother to stop by." He glanced at his watch. "I'm going downstairs to greet our guests. You should come down too, since the *mohel* will want to check the baby."

"I'll be down in about ten minutes," Miriam promised.

A few of their friends from the immigrants' hostel had come, including several of the men from Binyamin's *shiur*. Two of their neighbors from Givat Shaul had come in the car with the Adlers. A couple of the women she had met here in the home attended, and Sarah Dinah, their loyal seminary guest-helper, came as well. She felt the absence of the Wahrhaftigs, who would surely have made every attempt to come, had they been in the country.

Miriam settled the baby on the embroidered pillow. Binyamin had put on his *tallis* and *tefillin* and was waiting next to the table with the wine and the *mohel's* equipment. Sandra and her husband were the *kvaters*. "*Baruch haba! Baruch haba!*" announced the *mohel*.

Papa was to be the *sandek*. For Shimmy, it had been Binyamin's father. Miriam picked up Tami and moved back, bracing herself for the moment when the baby would start to cry. Mama came and held her arm. First came the *berachos*, followed by the baby's wail. Miriam bit her lip and looked away. Mama squeezed her arm and handed her a tissue. The baby calmed down as the *mohel* gave him some of the wine.

Binyamin, still beaming, scooted out to work immediately after the catered meal, leaving to his parents-in-law the privilege of conveying Miriam home with the newly named Yitzchak Elchanan.

"What will you call him?" asked Sarah Dinah, cooing at the baby.

"Itzik, I imagine," said Miriam.

"Are we ready to go?" asked Mr. Adler, hefting Miriam's bag.

"Well, uh, if you wouldn't mind, Papa, there is just one little stop I'd like to make before we leave Telz-Stone. You can all wait in the car with the children while I run down myself."

"I imagine that there's time for you to *walk* down, since we're not rushing anywhere. Can we know what it's about, or is it a secret?"

"No, it's not a secret. It's just," Miriam braced herself for a hurt reaction from her mother, "an apartment I want Binyamin to look at."

Mrs. Adler exchanged a look with her husband. "If it's something you're considering buying, I think Papa and I would also like to see it."

"I don't know if that's worthwhile, Mama. Binyamin isn't very enthusiastic."

Mrs. Adler exchanged a second look with her husband. "We'd like to see it."

In the end the entire family made the tour, including Sarah Dinah, Shimmy, and Tami. Everyone admired the view. "You can even see those beautiful hills from the kitchen," Mrs. Adler pointed out. Mr. Adler took particular interest in the storage room one floor down, which, he pointed out, could be made into a fourth bedroom. Miriam ascertained from Chavy that they had not promised the apartment to anyone else, and she told her when to expect Binyamin.

Mrs. Adler cooked supper that evening. Miriam had nothing to do but take care of the baby, pay attention to the other children, and worry about what Binyamin would think of the apartment.

Binyamin arrived home at eight. He was well fed by Mrs. Adler before he came in to speak to Miriam. "Did you go?" she asked him, as soon as he arrived.

"Yes," said Binyamin.

"What did you think of it?"

"Quite frankly, I wasn't very impressed. It's very hard to get to, down those steps and along that walk. It's not just a matter of getting the furniture in. It will be a problem every time you come home with packages from food shopping pushing a stroller. It's on the north side of the hill, which means there probably isn't all that much sun in the winter. As for this idea of turning the storage room into a bedroom, putting in steps takes up a lot of floor space from both floors. Although the price is reasonable, even something of a bargain, I just don't think we can afford to pay it right now. I am more and more certain that we'll have to finish paying off the car before we can think of buying an apartment."

Miriam felt a second stab of disappointment, but it was not as intense as it had been yesterday, and she really had resigned herself to giving up the idea. "Okay," she said quietly, "if we can't buy now, then we can't. You have a better grasp of our financial situation than I do."

Mr. Adler appeared in the door of the bedroom. "Isn't it time for *Maariv*, Benny? This is when we went yesterday."

"Oh, you're right, Papa," said Binyamin, glancing at his watch.

Miriam felt a rush of empathy for Ella. She was an expert at taking the long view. When Miriam was just barely coping with the challenges of that same day, Ella would be talking about things that might happen two years or ten years down the road. It came from being organized and self-confident. Frankly, the fact that Miriam now found herself in Ella's position was an indication that she now felt more competent, more ready to take the initiative than she had a year ago.

This whole comparison with Ella gave Miriam pause. After all, she still thought that Ella's advice not to buy a car had been wrong. She had predicted correctly that it would be a terrible burden financially, but she hadn't given enough weight to the strain commuting by bus caused Binyamin. It was not a problem that she had seen from within, as Binyamin and Miriam had.

Perhaps Miriam was also giving inadequate weight to some factor because she didn't see it from close up. Binyamin was quite concerned about his problem at work, which seemed trivial to Miriam. Perhaps he was right that he must be punctilious about spending enough time at his job.

Miriam picked up Itzik. He was more important than any possible apartment.

Binyamin and his father-in-law walked down the stairs and out into the balmy Yerushalayim night. At this hour the children had already gone inside, and most of the pedestrians were other men like themselves in suits and hats, either coming home from *kollel* or work, or going out to shul or to a *shiur*.

"Much nicer weather than we get in New York this time of year," Mr. Adler commented.

"Huh? Oh, yes." Binyamin was still distracted by a vague feeling that he had let Miriam down.

"We didn't get much time to talk yesterday," said his father-in-law. "We were tired from the flight and you were busy with the children."

"True," said Binyamin.

"How is your learning going?"

"Not perfect. I keep up with the *Daf Yomi,* but I haven't found a *shiur* that fits into my schedule, and learning alone is not as interesting. I have this *shiur* I teach in Mevasseret, but it's shrinking because people are moving out into apartments and they aren't accepting new immigrants."

"Speaking of apartments, Mimi said that you were going to look at the one in Telz-Stone on your way home. Did you?"

"Yes, Papa. I'm not nearly as enthusiastic as Miriam, but that's not the point. After looking at prices and mortgage terms, I've decided that we can't afford to buy until we finish paying for the car. We'll just have to hope that there isn't a big jump in prices by then."

"Hmm." Mr. Adler lapsed into silence, which he maintained until they walked out of shul after *Maariv.* Then he raised the subject again. "Binyamin, Leah and her husband recently paid back the $10,000 that they borrowed from us when they bought their place. Mama and I thought we would offer it to you and Mimi. You would only have to pay back $5,000, and you could wait until you finish with your car payments."

Binyamin was overwhelmed. "That's terribly generous of you, Papa. I really don't know what to say."

"You can say 'thank you' and buy Mimi that apartment."

Binyamin took a deep breath. "There's another problem with that particular apartment. The family needs the money very quickly to pay off a bridge mortgage. To buy it would require frantic running around to lawyers and banks. I have a problem at work right now and can't take time off, and Miriam can't do it either, so soon after giving birth."

"Hmm." Mr. Adler lapsed into silence again, which he broke only when he got close to the Lerners' building. "This girl, Sarah Dinah, seems right on top of things, and I understand that her school is finished. Suppose she and I do it, while Mama takes care of the baby and the house and Mimi."

Binyamin wasn't following at all. "Suppose you and Sarah

Dinah do what?"

"All the running around to lawyers and banks and things. We'll bring the papers home for you and Mimi to sign. By the time Mama and I leave in two weeks, Mimi should be back on her feet."

"I'll tell you what, Papa. Let's not say anything to Mimi. In the morning, I'll go straight from shul to Telz-Stone and look at the place again on my way to work. I really wasn't taking it seriously before because of all the other problems. If I change my mind and think we should buy it, I'll call you all from work and you can explain to Mimi and Mama."

At 7:15 the next morning, Binyamin pulled through the main gate into Telz-Stone. The marigolds in the flower beds and the pine trees in the park had the clean, washed look of early morning. He paused in his drive to look down at the new playground under construction. He parked the car and admired the view. He walked along the sidewalk and looked over the front yard.

The neighbors had built steps down from their balcony to the yard; it wouldn't be hard to do that here as well. The patio intended for the *sukkah* was at the side of the house, with the same dramatic view of the hills. The front yard had grass and flower beds and a pomegranate tree.

Binyamin didn't know whether it was just the bright light of morning or simply the fact that the other obstacles to buying had been cleared away, but now even the fact that it was hard to reach seemed like an advantage, because it would keep the children far from the street. Suddenly he wanted the place very, very much.

Perhaps, while he had been dithering around, the family had sold the apartment to someone else. Binyamin looked at his watch. He had to get to work and he wasn't willing to knock before eight o'clock. What should he do? He pulled out a piece of paper, wrote a note to the owners of the apartment, and tucked in into the door handle. Then he turned and went back out past the pomegranate tree. When he got to the steps, he paused once more to admire the view.

Mr. Adler was playing with Tami and wondering whether his intervention with Binyamin had been the right thing to do. He was the one who usually told his wife not to interfere in the children's decisions. This particular bit of interference had been of a most dangerous kind, taking the side of his own child.

The offer of the ten thousand-dollar loan was one thing. That had been okay. The problem had come when he had told Binyamin to take the money and buy Mimi the apartment. The more he thought about it, the sorrier he was that he had budged from his usual policy — especially since it was unlikely that anything would come of it except hard feelings.

The phone rang. Mimi was sleeping, and his Hebrew, while not good, was better than his wife's, so he decided to answer.

"Hello, this is Chavy Goldberg. Is this the Lerner family?" She was speaking English.

"Yes, but my daughter isn't available now."

"Could I speak to her husband?"

"He's at work. Wait, you have that apartment for sale?"

"That's right."

"I'm Miriam's father. We toured the place with her yesterday, but I'm afraid we don't have an answer for you yet."

"Then that note was a mistake?" asked Chavy.

"Note? What note?" Mr. Adler was glad that they were speaking English, because otherwise he would have been sure that something had slipped past him because of the language barrier.

"The note that was left on my door handle this morning."

"What did it say?"

"Something about wanting to meet this evening to work out the details of the purchase. It had this phone number."

"Who signed it?"

"Binyamin Lerner."

"Hang on, don't go anywhere. Better yet, give me your phone number and I'll call you back. I'm going to get my daughter!" He still thought that interfering had been a foolish thing to do, but apparently it had been a lucky *narishkeit*.

"All right," said Binyamin, "let's go over this payment schedule once more. Five thousand dollars when we sign the contract, the mortgage money as soon as we can get it, and the rest of the cash when you hand over the keys." It was that same evening. The Lerners and the Goldbergs were seated around the Goldbergs' dining room table, signing the draft agreement for the house purchase. Mr. Adler was hovering in the background, looking pleased with everyone. Mama was back in Yerushalayim baby-sitting for Shimmy and Tami.

Both couples signed the handwritten draft. Binyamin and Mr. Goldberg shook hands. Miriam, holding the baby, looked a little dazed. Binyamin got up and went to look through the picture window at the back yard, with its fruit trees, rocks, and pines. "Each man under his vine, and under his fig tree," he quoted softly to himself. "Our own personal piece of Eretz Yisrael."

Chapter 22

Elul

Ella and Chaim Ozer had been staying with her parents, but Chaim Ozer was now on his way to Winston to get oriented and find them housing.

Ella began to miss Chaim Ozer intensely on the third day after he left. It was the first intense emotion she had felt since the baby was born.

She had felt the consequences of his departure immediately, thanks to the fairly simple rule for dealing with the ebb and flow of guests in her home instituted by Rebbetzin Gutfreund, Ella's mother. Each family was responsible for feeding and clothing its own children. The kitchen and laundry room were open, but it was the parents' job to find something that their offspring would eat and to keep the washing machines going. During the week they had all spent together, first at his parents' house and then at hers, Chaim Ozer had done much of that. Now it fell on Ella.

Dressing the children was the hardest. They were living out of suitcases and laundry baskets. Finding a full set of clean clothing every morning for every child might have been a challenge even if Ella had been in top form, which she wasn't. One morning, Rebbetzin Gutfreund came into the room as Ella was asking her three-year-old, "Do you want these green pants or the blue ones?"

"Mercy, Ella! Pick out something yourself and help him put it on. When he's old enough to dress himself, he can get to choose."

In the morning, Ella initiated her children into the mysteries of American breakfast cereal. For lunch she made them soup and a sandwich. Her mother cooked one big family meal each evening. Fortunately, it was summer vacation, so her teenage sisters kept the children occupied during the day, which gave Ella much-needed time to rest and care for the baby.

What she missed so intensely with Chaim Ozer gone was the casual conversation, the possibility of expressing her frustrations as a light aside and then getting on with life. Her husband had also been her sounding board on those once rare and now too common occasions when she wasn't quite sure what to do. Although he called every evening, it wasn't the same.

He had spent the first two days meeting the other Rabbanim in the yeshivah and familiarizing himself with the community and the locations of the shuls and schools. Today he was supposed to start house-hunting. Ella was restless as she awaited his call. She might live in the house he chose for many years, and she would have no part in picking it out.

"Did you find anything interesting?" she asked as soon as he was on the line.

"No, I got nowhere at all. I called three real estate agents. I explained to the first one who we were and exactly what we wanted. She said politely that she couldn't help me and hung up. Okay, I thought, maybe I had been too restrictive. To the second agent I just said that I was looking for a place to live in the northwest section of Winston. When she asked if we had any pets, I told he we had an aquarium and would probably buy goldfish unless the landlord objected.

"She seemed okay with that, but then she asked whether we wanted an apartment or a house. When I cagily asked her which she had, she said, 'Oh, we have both.' But when I asked, 'Have anything with three bedrooms?' she said, 'Oh, dear, you mean that you have ... children?'

"'Well, yes, we do,' I answered, trying not to sound apologetic.

"'More than one?'

"'Yes, more than one.'

"'Two?'

"'Well, actually, more than two."

"'How many more?'

"'Three,' I said.

"'Three children?'

"'Three more than two. We have five children, thank G-d.'

"'I'm afraid I can't help you.'

"I made myself a cup of tea to steady my nerves and tried the last name on the list. 'Hello?' I said.

"'Are you the Roman Catholic fellow with all the kids?' she asked me.

"'We're not Roman Catholics,' I said, 'but I am probably the person you're talking about.' Apparently one of the other agents called her to warn her about me. So there you are; we're blacklisted."

"This is terrible, Chaim Ozer. Where will we live? The lift will arrive from Eretz Yisrael and we won't have where to put our things." Ella was torn. One part of her was casting about for ways out of this fix, while the other was glad to leave the problem to Chaim Ozer.

"Tomorrow I'll check the newspapers and talk the problem over with the Rosh Yeshivah."

Two weeks dragged on, with Ella growing more and more restive. There were a few houses for rent, but no one was willing to rent to a large family. Chaim Ozer tried in neighboring communities, even though that would mean a commute every day to school for the children.

Finally, one evening he called up and asked to speak to Rebbetzin Gutfreund. "Mother, I have to make a decision between two possibilities that are far from ideal, and I need Ella's reactions, if not her actual help with the decision. Can you spare her for a few days?"

Ella packed with more enthusiasm than she had shown for anything in a long time. After her parents drove her and the baby to the train, the children stood on the platform and waved them both good-bye. Although Ella's father's yeshivah was as far from New York as Winston was, it was in the other direction, so she would have a five-hour train ride. She took along very little luggage. When they reached Winston, Chaim Ozer picked them up in the old-fashioned station wagon he had bought.

Ella, who hadn't driven since they moved to Eretz Yisrael, didn't have a valid license. Her Israeli friends in Yerushalayim hadn't driven either, and she hadn't missed it at all. But if they were going to be living in the suburbs, she would have to get a license, or else Chaim Ozer would be spending a lot of time as a chauffeur.

Ella strapped the baby into the car seat Chaim Ozer had bought and slid into the back to sit beside her.

"Look how many trees there are," Chaim Ozer said as they moved out of the commercial area near the train station into a residential neighborhood.

Trees? They had trees in Mattersdorf too.

Chaim Ozer had been staying with Rabbi Feldman since he arrived in Winston, and now the Feldmans made room for Ella and the baby as well. After feeding the baby and putting her down for a nap, Ella also rested. At dinner she would have to meet all these new people, but for now she could put it off.

"As your husband has already explained," said Rabbi Feldman when they sat down to discuss the housing problem after dinner, "we have not found a house for you to rent."

Meeting these new people hadn't been as bad as she had feared. Ella thought back to the days when she had enjoyed having guests she had never met. Now she had to do something even harder — make a complicated decision. Chaim Ozer had not brought her all this way so that she could say, "Do whatever seems best to you." She was expected to focus on the problem. Ella tried thinking back to the old days. What information would she have wanted?

"What do the other *rebbeim* do?" she asked.

"They own their own homes, near the yeshivah. Now I understand from your husband that your lift is arriving in three weeks, and that if you don't accept delivery right away, you'll be penalized with heavy storage fees."

Ella nodded, vaguely recalling Chaim Ozer mentioning some such problem.

"I can see only two possibilities. One is that you will have to buy instead of renting," said Rabbi Feldman.

Ella winced.

Rabbi Feldman continued, "We've looked over the houses on the market, and two are available reasonably close to other yeshivah families."

Ella shot a glance at Chaim Ozer. He hadn't mentioned that he was looking into houses for sale. "What's the other possibility?"

"There is a property that belongs to the yeshivah, next to the dormitory. We bought it cheaply because it was run-down, and we're holding it in case we'll want to expand the dormitories. There is a house on the property. Seventy years ago it was a small mansion, but when property values in the area started to decline, it was converted into a two-family house. The yeshivah's cook lives in one side, and for a while we rented out the other side to someone who was doing fund-raising for the yeshivah. But for this past year it's been empty."

"How many bedrooms does it have?" asked Ella.

"Only two."

Five children in one bedroom. Stacking them up like sardines, the way they had done in Eretz Yisrael. The one thing she had hoped to get out of this move was more space for the children to sleep in. "Could we go see this place tomorrow?"

"Should we make appointments to see the ones for sale as well?"

Ella shrugged in acceptance.

In the morning, Rabbi Feldman accompanied them to see the yeshivah property. The house was hidden from the street by a tall, tangled hedge. As they walked through the squeaking iron gate, they got their first good look at it. A tower rose to a conical roof on the front corner of the building. The house itself was of gray stone, but the broad porch around two sides was of weathered wood. The front door faced the yard, not the street, and a long walk led up to it. They climbed up the wooden steps, crossed the porch, and waited as Rabbi Feldman unlocked the front door.

"Stained glass?!" exclaimed Ella, as she entered. In front of them was a broad staircase of polished wood, and at the landing halfway up was a bay window with a stained glass design of flowers. The dining room to their left had a curved wall and curved windows at the corner with the tower. The rest of the downstairs was not very impressive. A narrow kitchen had been installed at the back of the dining room, and a bathroom had been set in under the staircase, next to the steps leading down to the basement.

Upstairs, the master bedroom, the one with the tower in the wall, was huge, whereas the other bedroom was about the size of an Israeli bedroom. It would hold two beds and some minor furnishings, but three beds would be a squeeze. Both rooms had built-in closets with hanging space and one broad shelf above. The house came with the major appliances, a dining room table and chairs that had obviously come from the yeshivah dining hall, and two beds.

As they walked out of the house Ella surveyed the huge, over-grown yard, surrounded on all sides by the hedge. Only a strip of sod alongside the house had been mowed; the rest was a waist-high tangle. Ella stepped off the sidewalk to peer at one of the trees. "Rav Feldman," she called. "Do you know what this is?"

The Rosh Yeshivah shook his head. "I'm afraid that it's been a long time since I took nature walks in my camping days."

"This vine, the green leaves with the red underneath. It's poison ivy."

The other two houses, the ones for sale, were much more prosa-ic. Each had a living room, dining room, and kitchen extending back from the front door; the stairs ran up a wall joining the house to the other side of the duplex, and there were three bedrooms and a bath on the top floor. Ella paced off the bedrooms. One of them was quite small. It was a nuisance trying to measure a room with-out the standardized Israeli floor tiles.

As they walked out of the second of the two houses that were for sale, Ella looked back at the small front lawn, half of which sloped to the sidewalk. Ella could imagine herself living in one of these houses. She couldn't imagine herself loving them the way she had loved her own compact apartment in Yerushalayim.

When Chaim Ozer and Ella got back to the Feldman home, they adjourned to their room to make their decision.

"If we want to take the yeshivah property," said Ella flatly, "Rav Feldman will have to get this maintenance people to mow the lawn, cut the hedge, and get rid of the poison ivy."

"But where would we put the children?" asked Chaim Ozer.

"I thought that was obvious," said Ella. "We'd have to buy two tall free-standing closets and use them to divide the master bed-room into two rooms, one for the girls and one for the boys."

"You would still rather rent than buy, wouldn't you?"

"Yes," said Ella decidedly, "at least for the next two years, until we see how everything works out. I want to have our own apart-ment in reserve to go back to, and I'm afraid that if we get tangled up in loans and mortgage payments before we really understand how much it will cost us to live here, we might endanger that."

Chaim Ozer breathed a heavy sigh of relief. "Ella," he said, "I can't tell you how relieved I am to have you back in decision-making form. It's been a heavy burden, making decisions alone for the last month or so. What you say about renting makes sense." He stood up. "I'll go talk to Rav Feldman about the lawn and the hedge."

"And the poison ivy."

The lift was due to arrive the second week of Elul. Chaim Ozer remained at the Feldmans' so that he could take up his teaching duties when the new term began at the beginning of Elul, and Ella and the baby returned to the Gutfreunds'. Before she left Winston, they had ordered the two tall closets, bunk beds, and desk sets for the children, so that they would be in place before their personal possessions arrived.

Ella chafed under the enforced wait. She began to wonder if she had been right in refusing a teaching position in the new girls' high school. At least she could have been working out lesson plans for the year. She did shop for the children, to get them ready for school. She had asked Chaim Ozer to find out just what sort of book bags and lunch boxes were "in" at their new school.

One evening, Ella got a phone call. "Rebbetzin Wahrhaftig? This is Yehudit Ullman. The principal of the high school."

"Yes?"

"The woman who was going to teach *Navi* for us was forced to cancel because her mother just had a stroke. Your husband thought that you might be willing to reconsider. It's for four hours each week, spread over two days."

Ella was indeed tempted. "How would I get to the school? I don't drive, and I wouldn't want to take my husband away from his learning to get me there."

"The school will provide your transportation for the first six months. After that, I imagine that you'll have had time to get your driver's license in order."

"I'll talk it over with my husband and get back to you."

Moving day was just as hectic as Ella had feared. Her mother drove Ella and the children to Winston the day before. The children, thrilled by the huge lawn, whooped and ran and played hide-and-seek. Ella and Chaim Ozer had trouble getting them into the house and bedded down on borrowed sheets. The next day, Rebbetzin Feldman kept the children while the movers brought in the boxes and set up the bookcases. Chaim Ozer spent the evening unpacking his *sefarim* and arranging them on the shelves, while Ella, who had a relapse of depression at the sight of all the unpacked boxes, went to bed early. Now she was sorry she had taken the teaching job.

After feeding the baby, she lay in bed staring up at the ceiling. It all seemed so terribly permanent, having their *sefarim*, and clothes and dishes here. Because truthfully, she didn't want to be here. She had always given Miriam a lot of hype about the positive sides of living out-of-town: Knowing a broad spectrum of people, more parental involvement in the children's education, friendly neighbors.

However, there was a down side that she had never mentioned. Having been raised out-of-town, she knew firsthand just how hard her parents had struggled not to compromise their principles. She remembered all the things her mother had cooked or baked by herself because they weren't available locally, how many hours her father had put into tutoring her brothers so that they would be well-prepared for the best yeshivos, all the delicate decisions about which activities the children could share with their school friends and which they had best skip.

Ella thought she had finessed the more uppity of her New York classmates by moving to Yerushalayim, the capital of the Jewish world. Now, here she was, reliving her mother's life. Her mother's life had been successful, but hard. If that was really the task she had been given, she would try to do it well, but it was difficult for Ella to work up enthusiasm.

Take Elul, a whole month of soul-searching in preparation for Rosh Hashanah. In Yerushalayim, Elul had been felt in the very air. Special lectures on the theme of *teshuvah* had made everyone aware what Elul meant. Now here she was, with less than three weeks remaining until Rosh Hashanah, without having given one thought to how she should be improving herself spiritually.

Ella turned over, wondering how much longer it would take Chaim Ozer to finish with his *sefarim*. She wanted to talk to him about Elul. Of course, she didn't have to wait. She wasn't falling asleep anyway. She could go downstairs and look for him. Ella got dressed, walked through the doorway, rested her hand on the *mezuzah* and then kissed her fingers, as she had been doing since she was old enough to reach up that high on the doorpost. She did this automatically, but then she paused. The same words were written on the parchment inside this case as were written on the parchments in their home in Yerushalayim. Chaim Ozer would be learning the same *sefarim* that he had learned in Eretz Yisrael. Some things they took with them wherever they might wander.

Ella started slowly down the broad staircase, her hand resting lightly on the wooden banister. Perhaps she didn't need to speak to Chaim Ozer about Elul. She actually knew what she had to do. She had to find more positive ways of dealing with this new turn in their life.

The coming month would be very hard. The children had to get settled in their new schools, she had to unpack, she had to start a new school year, all at a time when Chaim Ozer should be putting all his effort and energy into learning to become a good *maggid shiur*. No one in the family could afford to have her sink into depression again. The medical causes of her depression were clearing up. Although Chaim Ozer had been fantastic about protecting her when she needed it most, it was time for her to make some effort of her own to pull out of this slump.

"How are you coming along?" she asked, as she turned the corner at the landing.

"Pretty well. I have the *Shas*, the *Tur*, and the *Shulchan Aruch* out already, together with lots of smaller *mefarshim*. Actually, I'm about to call it quits for the night."

"I had trouble sleeping," said Ella, removing a pile of *sefarim* from a chair and putting it on one of the boxes.

"New bed," said Chaim Ozer, "and new night sounds."

"I'm sort of sorry to have to give up the room with the tower to the children. I used to dream of living in a castle when I was a little girl."

"That's an odd dream for the daughter of a Rosh Yeshivah."

"We didn't have that much in the way of English language Jewish books back then, particularly not where my parents live. We got our reading material from the public library, and I liked books about princesses."

"Is that why you insisted in putting the girls on the side with the tower?"

"I suppose so, though I wasn't thinking about it consciously. Who knows, maybe living in a room with a curved wall will make them well-rounded."

Chaim Ozer turned around with a broad grin, "Now that's my Ella back."

"It was a pretty feeble joke, Chaim'ke. Are you sure you want to encourage me to make more?"

"To the best of my memory, Ella, that is the first attempt you have made to be humorous since you teased me in the hospital about calling Leah a dried apricot."

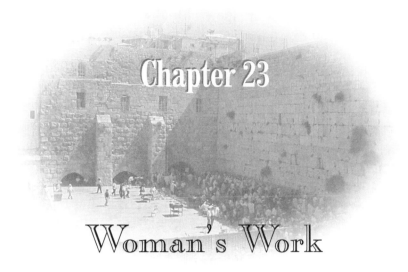

Chapter 23

Woman's Work

"I'm thinking of going back to work," announced Miriam to her friends. They were all sitting on a bench in the park, watching the children play.

"What did you do?" asked Shifra, who was a nurse.

"I was a secretary for two years until I got married. Then I worked from the house doing typing for a Jewish publisher until Shimmy was born. Since then I've been raising the children."

"One of the big problems with office work is finding a good baby-sitter," said Shoshy. She was a computer programmer for a bank in Yerushalayim. "In addition, it's terribly expensive."

"They have those family-care arrangements through the municipality," suggested Shifra. "Those are at least subsidized, so they aren't as expensive. They allow a maximum of five children per family, so it is not as impersonal as a regular day care center, and the caretakers get training through the municipality."

"How do you know so much about it? Have you ever used it?" asked Miriam.

"I looked into it," said Shifra, "but as long as I'm only working part-time, we decided to stick to our current system of having me work evening shifts and Fridays, when my husband can be at home with the children. The hospitals are glad to get someone for those unpopular times."

"The other problem with baby-sitting arrangements is that they make it hard to keep up the children's English," pointed out Shoshy. "You know, we all want them to be able to speak to their grandparents."

"If you could find some way to work from the house, that might be the best," said Shifra. "In my profession I can't, but you say that you did it once."

Sarah, who had been sitting on a different bench, chimed in at this point. "It's not quite as simple as all that. When you work at home, it is hard to keep your business and family life separate. Now that Chavy has moved, she does her *sheitel* business from the storage room, in order not to have women traipsing through her house all the time and snippets of hair all over the floors.

"Also, there is a lot of overhead. My parents gave us a fancy computer set-up when we got married, and for a few years I did graphic design from the house. But after a few years the hardware and the software had to be updated, and it simply wasn't profitable. When you work for someone else, that sort of problem is something for the boss to worry about."

Miriam felt her head beginning to spin. "You're all giving me a lot of contradictory advice. You don't make going to work sound very practical, but I see that almost everyone does it."

"It's hard to get by comfortably on one income."

"I've noticed," said Miriam. It was hard, though, to imagine how she could manage working and taking care of the children. Unless ...

Miriam fidgeted as she waited. She wasn't comfortable about the fact that she hadn't yet discussed this with Binyamin. On the other hand, as soon as she broached the subject, if he didn't reject the idea out of hand, he would want all sorts of details that she would be unable to give him without some sort of a meeting like the one she was about to have.

"Mrs. Lerner, you can go in now." Miriam stood up, clutching the folder with her diploma from high school and her references. They were all in English, of course, and she hoped that it wouldn't make a difference. She walked into the office and took the seat that was offered to her.

"On the phone you told me that you're interested in opening a family-care center in your home."

"I wanted to find out what's involved. I'm not actually applying yet."

"You're a recent immigrant?"

"We arrived a year ago."

"Perhaps it's a little early to consider employment like this. After all, much of the Hebrew that the children will be hearing will be from you, and it would be a shame to get them mixed up."

"No, that's the point," said Miriam. "I want to open a family-care center in English. I think that there's a genuine need for this in our community."

The social worker behind the desk looked dubious. "We offer lectures in the evenings now and then that you're expected to attend. Those are all in Hebrew."

"That's no problem. Will my sitting in the audience corrupt the lecturer's Hebrew?"

It took the woman behind the desk a moment to realize that Miriam was being ironic. When she finally caught on, she gave a dutiful smile. "We've never authorized something like this. I would want the names of at least two families interested in an English family-care center before we'd agree to it."

"As I said, I am not applying yet."

"I'm thinking of returning to work," Miriam announced to Binyamin, who was bent over his portable computer, trying to balance the budget.

He looked up at her, startled. "Why do you want to do that?"

"We need more money."

Binyamin looked hurt. "Your father supported your mother. My father supported my mother, at least until we were all in school. Am I not allowed to support you?"

"Somehow things are different today, Binyamin. Most of my friends work, at least part-time. They don't do it because they're bored at home, they do it because the extra money helps. You see how strapped we are at the moment, and I feel partially responsible. I'm the one who urged you to buy this apartment before the car was paid for."

Binyamin looked unhappy. "I do not want our children raised

by strangers, I want them raised by you."

"I want that, too, Binyamin. That's why I want to work at home."

"Doing what?"

"English-language baby-sitting for working mothers."

"Baby-sitting is usually at the very bottom of the economic scale, with no social benefits at all."

Miriam showed him the photocopied sheets describing the financial arrangements and regulations. He sat down and read them through, a project that Miriam had not yet tackled. "Well, you're right that this doesn't sound as if you would be exploited, but it also requires a greater commitment than usual baby-sitting. It says you have to be willing to keep the children until four o'clock. Also, when would you go shopping and run errands?"

"Does it say that I can get a substitute sometimes?"

"One day a week."

"Then that's what I'll do when I have errands I can't take care of after four."

"Miriam, I'm not going to stop you. Just take it from someone who works forty hours a week, the constant time pressure is very tough."

"Take it from someone who works a hundred hours a week," said Miriam with a slightly dangerous glint in her eye. "I know all about it."

As soon as Miriam got official approval for her family-care center, she began soliciting customers. Her first announcement was to the other women she sat with at the playground. Shoshy, who had signed a letter to the municipality saying that this would fill a need in the community, said that she was interested. Shifra suggested that Miriam place an English-language ad in the Telz-Stone bulletin. If she called in her ad right away, it would appear in the edition coming out on Wednesday. Her other friends promised to ask around among their English-speaking friends and neighbors.

That evening, there was a knock on the door. When Miriam opened it, she saw a woman she recognized vaguely from the grocery store standing on her doormat. "Please, come in," she said, holding the door open. "You're Terry, aren't you?"

"Right," said the other woman, obviously pleased to be recognized. "I heard from Shoshy about this family-care center you're opening. I have a daughter who started kindergarten this year, but she isn't adjusting as well as I had hoped. If she doesn't settle down within another week or two, I might want to move her back to playgroup. Would you consider taking her?"

"It's not as if I am swamped with applicants yet," Miriam said with a smile. "I only just started advertising this afternoon."

"It's not quite that simple," said Terry. "Yocheved is five."

Five? And just starting kindergarten? Miriam waited for more information.

"She has Down's syndrome," explained Terry.

Well, here was a challenge, right at the outset. Could she do it? Would the other mothers think she could do it? She hated to be another in what might be a long string of rejections Terry had had to absorb. "I suppose I should meet her," said Miriam uncertainly. "I have no training at all in special education."

Terry smiled. "Why don't you get your group started and get used to managing several children at once? Then, if Yocheved still hasn't adjusted to *gan*, I'll bring her over and we'll see if you think you can manage her too."

Miriam's next problem was to find some way for Shimmy to get to and from his school. A boy in his class lived a few houses down. His mother and Miriam occasionally traded the task of walking the boys to school. Perhaps, in return for some other form of child care, she would be willing to take Shimmy regularly.

The opening day of Miriam's new family-care center began inauspiciously. The mother of the boy who was supposed to walk Shimmy to *mechinah* called up to say that her son had chicken pox, and Binyamin had already left for work. Shoshy was bringing her baby at a quarter to eight. What should she do?

She called Shoshy and told her that she would be coming by in a few minutes. Strapping Itzik into the baby carrier on her chest, she took Tami by the hand and dragged the double stroller behind her until she was up the steps. Then she fastened Tami into the stroller and had Shimmy hold onto the other side. As they passed Shoshy's house, they added her baby, Elisheva, to the stroller. The entire procession moved slowly, and the eight o'clock bell was ringing by the time she got Shimmy to the *cheder's* gate. Then she had to cover the same distance back. By the time Miriam arrived home, her second client, a woman she barely knew, was tapping her foot impatiently outside her locked door. A flustered Miriam tried to make the two toddlers feel comfortable in their strange surroundings, while simultaneously apologizing to the annoyed mother.

At 12:30, Miriam found a neighbor willing to watch the four children while she ran to get Shimmy. Coming back was somewhat slower than she liked, because Shimmy was rather listless. However, it was not until he had already been playing with the new children for half an hour that he thought to say, "Mommy, I itch."

With trembling fingers, Miriam unbuttoned his shirt, moved aside his *tzitzis*, and lifted his shirt. There they were, sprinkled here and there on his chest — the first red bumps of chicken pox!

"I think I should abandon the whole plan," grumbled Miriam to Binyamin as he walked in the door. It was three weeks after the family-care center had opened. The second mother had yanked her child out immediately after her son caught chicken pox, but Terry's Yocheved had already had the disease.

"I thought it was going to get easier, now that Shimmy is well enough to go back to school," said Binyamin with sympathy.

"I thought so too," wailed Miriam, "but now Tami and Elisheva have broken out in rashes. And I promised Shoshy that if Elisheva caught chicken pox from Shimmy, I would take her even while she was sick."

"Are you really planning to quit?" asked Binyamin.

Miriam remembered sitting on the bench at the immigrants' hostel, with the words "Quitter, quitter, QUITTER!" reverberating in her mind. She hadn't quit then, and she didn't want to quit now, either. "No, not really. I was just grumbling a bit as an outlet for my frustrations. I'm going to hang on."

"You're a trooper, Miriam," said Binyamin with approval.

Miriam answered the expected ring of the doorbell.

"All right, here it is," said her friend Terry, holding out two type-written sheets. "Shall we go into the kitchen to look it over?"

"I don't quite know how you talked me into this. I never acted in high school."

"It's not as if it were a full-scale play. It's just a short skit for the N'shei Ahavas Chessed. You don't even have to learn your lines by heart. You can read them off the paper."

"Did you write this yourself?"

"The idea was mine. I have a friend who's a writer, and she helped me polish it."

Terry, who was playing the mother, settled herself down at the dining room table, struggling to write a skit for a N'shei Chanukah party, but encountering difficulty because she was by now only semiliterate in English.

"I spelled 'which' as 'W-I-C-H," she complained to her 'daughter' Dina, "but it doesn't look right."

"My teacher spells it 'W-I-C-H-E,'" Miriam read off the sheet.

"You have an Israeli English teacher this year, don't you?" asked Terry. "How is it going?"

"Well, it was a little hard at first. I had to learn to say 'I leeve een Telz-Stone, and I write on the bleckbord,' but I've gotten used to it." Following the stage directions, Miriam stood up to go.

"Well, thank you for your help." Terry bent over her 'work' again.

"Uh, Mummy, my friends are coming soon. You will speak English, won't you?" read Miriam, lingering in the doorway.

"Sure," answered Terry off-handedly, without looking up. "I always speak English at home." A moment passed in silence, and then she looked up with a startled expression and called her 'daughter' back. "Dina! Come here!"

Miriam reappeared in the doorway, trying to look innocent. "Yes, Mummy?"

"Why do you want me to speak English in front of your friends?" asked Terry with a suspicious intonation.

"Why, Mummy, you speak it so well. You always sound so smart in English!"

Terry folded her arms on the table and buried her head in them, while Miriam made a second exit.

Miriam and Terry folded up their copies of the skit. "There I go, a few years down the road," commented Miriam wryly. "I'll probably be treated as a new immigrant for the rest of my life, and I may feel like a new immigrant for that long."

"Culture shock getting to you?" Terry asked.

"I don't know if I would call it culture shock, exactly. I still make an occasional mistake, though not so mortifying anymore. I also miss my family. That part is better since my parents were here. They were so helpful in getting us organized to buy this place. My father and my friend, Sarah Dinah, did most of the running around to banks because I had just given birth to Itzik and Binyamin was tied down at work. I felt useless."

"Surely no one expected you to do anything at that point!"

"Of course not, but I feel that I'm not doing my share in the extended family. Just before we left, my younger brother Reuven told me he had been expecting my help in finding a *shidduch*, and truthfully, my mother is having trouble with it. He wants a girl who would be willing to spend a year or so in Eretz Yisrael, and there don't seem to be many of those in my mother's circles."

"Maybe you can help," suggested Terry. "Yerushalayim is flooded with seminary girls studying here for a year. Maybe if you were to go out of your way to meet some of them, you would find someone suitable for your brother."

"Terry! That's a brilliant idea."

Miriam was picking up toys. Now that she ran a family-care center, she spent a lot of time picking up toys and she was becoming very efficient at it. The first trick was to get the kids themselves to do as much of it as possible. The second was to sweep them into a pile near a low stool, on which she could sit as she sorted them into three bins. She had just scooped up a handful of the small metal cars that are so important to four-year-old boys when the phone rang.

"Hello, Mrs. Lerner?"

The voice was not familiar. "Yes?"

"My name is Bitya Cooper. I am calling on behalf of Da'as Tevuna seminary. We're having a *Shabbaton* in Telz-Stone in two weeks, *Parashas Mishpatim,* and I was wondering if you could host two girls?"

"Let me check." Miriam put down the receiver and found the appropriate square on the wall calendar. Fine, it was empty. "Yes, we're open that week."

"For sleeping and the evening meal?"

"Yes, that would be okay."

"Wonderful! Thank you so much!" She took the address and hung up. Miriam found a pen and wrote in 'two girls, evening meal' on the calendar. Who knows, if her first try at finding someone for Reuven didn't work out, perhaps she could make additional contacts through these girls.

The guests, Rina Schneider and Pessie Rotstein, turned out to be rather quiet. Miriam accepted with thanks the wafers they brought as a hostess gift and offered them a cold drink. Then she showed them to the guest room. Nothing more was heard from them until half an hour before Shabbos, when Pessie emerged, dressed for Shabbos, to ask if she could help. Miriam set her up to cut the salad and asked her about the seminary, but Pessie answered all her queries in a decidedly distracted manner. Maybe she was shy. After Miriam lit the candles, Pessie vanished into the guest room again and did not emerge until Binyamin returned from shul.

"Uh," she said hesitantly, "my friend isn't feeling well. She doesn't think she can come out for *Kiddush*."

Miriam exchanged concerned glances with her husband. "Maybe I should see what's the matter," Miriam said to Pessie as she followed her into the guest room. Rina was lying on her side, her arms clutching her stomach. Miriam pulled up a chair and felt the girl's forehead with the back of her hand. She might be running a fever. Miriam took the coverlet from the end of the bed and spread it over the girl. When Rina didn't open her eyes in response to Miriam's ministrations, Miriam turned to Pessie for information. "What happened?"

"Well," said Pessie, "she felt sort of queasy on the bus ride here, so she decided to lie down a bit before getting dressed, thinking she'd feel better after a while. But it just keeps getting worse. She thinks it's either an intestinal virus or food poisoning."

Miriam felt Rina's forehead again. It did seem hot. "You sit here with her," she told Pessie. "I want to talk to my husband."

Together they decided that Binyamin had better go for the doctor. Though they hated to pull him away from his Shabbos table right before *Kiddush*, they were afraid it might be an emergency. Miriam brought a basin to the door of the guest room. She didn't go in because by now the children were clinging to her skirt and she didn't want to expose them if it were a virus.

"May I go get my counselor?" Pessie asked.

"As soon as my husband gets back," Miriam told her. "I can't care for her properly while I'm solely responsible for the children. You know where she's staying?"

Pessie nodded. "About a block away."

It was nearly half an hour before she heard Binyamin return. The children had eaten earlier, so she had filled in the time alternately reading them stories and checking on Pessie and Rina. Binyamin opened the door, and she was relieved to see that he had persuaded the doctor to accompany him.

"Okay, Pessie, go get your counselor. Binyamin, would you please watch the kids while I help the doctor?"

Dr. Ross, a South African immigrant, took the girl's temperature. "Thirty-nine and a half," he announced. Miriam had never gotten used to making conversions from Celsius to Fahrenheit, but this fell into the range of fevers her children had had, so she knew that it was around 103.

As soon as the doctor began examining his patient, Rina gave a sharp squeal, the loudest sound she had made since she arrived.

"Uh-oh," said Dr. Ross, shaking his head. He tried again, more gently, and elicited another gasp from Rina.

"Looks like appendicitis. Have your husband get Raphael here as fast as possible, with a stretcher!" Raphael was the nearest Hatzolah medic, who lived two houses away. "Also, make an ice pack and prepare some more ice for the trip."

Miriam dispatched Binyamin on this new errand and went into the kitchen to break ice out of their trays. There was enough for one ice pack, which she took to the doctor. The children were still on the couch, where Binyamin had been entertaining them. They were watching all the unfamiliar bustle with wide eyes, so Miriam didn't want to leave them to fetch ice from the neighbors.

She prepared another plastic bag and was about to call the children to go with her when there was a knock on the door. Pessie and a second girl burst in.

"Oh, wonderful!" said Miriam with relief. She thrust the plastic bag at her guest. "Pessie, Rina has appendicitis, and the doctor is sending her to the hospital. Can you go around to the neighbors and ask for ice? Most of them speak English, and the Hebrew work for ice is *kerach*."

"*Kerach*," repeated Pessie, and then crossed the hall to knock on the neighbor's door.

"Where is she?" asked the newcomer, her eyes opened wide with concern. "Can I go with her?"

Miriam nodded. "They usually allow one accompanying person in addition to the driver. You'll be stuck there for the rest of Shabbos, but there are kindhearted people who provide food for stranded family members."

Binyamin and Raphael returned, carrying the folded stretcher. They set it up next to the bed, and Rina was moved onto it, clutching an ice pack. "Go quickly," the doctor said. "You have to get her into the operating room before the appendix bursts."

The two men carried the stretcher out to the car, with the counselor, Bitya, walking alongside to keep the ice pack in place. Raphael didn't have an ambulance, only his own private car, so they settled Rina in the back seat, lying on her side with her head in Bitya's lap. "*Refuah shleimah*," called all the others, as the car backed down the drive. "*Shabbat shalom*," returned Bitya, with a feeble wave. Dr. Ross returned to his Shabbos meal and the Lerners went to make a belated *Kiddush*.

As she was putting the children to bed, Miriam thought that she had learned a lesson from the whole experience. Looking for a *shidduch* for her brother was a *mitzvah*, and so was hospitality, but she shouldn't try to mix them.

Miriam checked her watch ... again. She was waiting until it would be possible to call the United Sates without waking her parents. Finally, at three o'clock Sunday, she was ready to risk a call.

"*Nu*, Mama, did they meet?" Miriam was very curious.

"Yes, last night, just as planned. Reuven went over to her house, her father talked with him a bit in learning, and then he met her. They didn't go out, just stayed in and talked."

"What did he think? Did he like her? Does he want to meet her again?"

"I think so," Mrs. Adler answered. "I told him to leave after an hour, but he ended up staying for two. He says he wants to see her again. I still haven't heard back from the other side."

"Let me know as soon as you hear. We had some excitement over Shabbos. Our guest got appendicitis and had to be driven to the hospital. They operated in time and she's okay. Her counselor called right after Shabbos to let us know."

"Listen, Mimi, I just got a 'call-waiting' beep. I'm going to take it, in case it's the *shadchan.*" Mrs. Adler hung up, leaving her daughter just as curious as she was before the call.

Miriam was walking briskly down Malchei Yisrael Street, trying to do some quick shopping. She had left Terry's teenage daughter Malka baby-sitting, and the bus back was leaving in half an hour. Miriam hurried into an electrical appliance store called Electro-Weiss. She had already been in Electro-Schwartz, but they hadn't had what she needed.

Her mother had been calling her so often lately about the *shid-duch* she had suggested for Reuven that it was cutting into the time she had for housework. She was hoping to get either a cordless phone or one with a long cord so that she could continue working while talking.

"What do you have in push-button phones?" she asked, proud that she knew the Hebrew word for push-button. She didn't know the Hebrew word for cordless, but if he didn't offer her one, she would try English or a pantomime.

"This has been reduced," said the salesman, bringing out a box with a picture of a beige phone and the caption, "Slime-Phone." Miriam reread the name. Was it supposed to be "Chime-Phone?" Or perhaps "Sly-Phone?" She stared blankly at the box and made no move to touch it, as if it might actually be slimy. The salesman opened the package and held out the phone, "Only three hundred shekels."

It was a good price for a cordless, if only she could forget the name, "Uh, what do you call it?"

The man held out the package. "I'm sure you read English just as well as I do. It's called the 'Slim-Phone!'"

The storeowner's mistake explained why the Far Eastern company that had manufactured tens of thousands of these things had decided that Eretz Yisrael might be an appropriate place to dump them. Turning the receiver over, she saw that the words "Slime-Phone" were embossed in the plastic. There was no way she would have such an object in her house. She would start giggling every time she tried to make a phone call. She handed it back. "I'd like to see something else, please."

The man put another box on the table. "Maybe this cordless

would interest you more?"

A glance at the price tag showed that it wouldn't. Perhaps, if this match for Reuven went through, she would soon be on her way to America for the wedding. She'd wait to buy a cordless phone in Boro Park.

Binyamin and his co-worker, Rami, were working at the same computer screen, putting the finishing touches on the documentation for the project they had just completed.

"Listen," suggested Binyamin, "this warning is really important. I think we should put it in a box in 'sanctifying the moon' letters." He hesitated, wondering if he had made a *faux pas*. Had he ever heard a secular Israeli speak about "sanctifying the moon" letters? "We always sanctify the new moon outside in the dark, so the text is written in very large letters."

"I don't care if you sanctify the moon standing on your heads waving your feet in the air. I know that 'sanctifying the moon' letters are large, and I don't need a new immigrant with a thick accent to teach me to speak my own language."

Binyamin was stung by the irreverence and, more than he liked to admit, by the jibe at his accent. "Suppose someone tells you that an insurance contract is written 'with Rachel your youngest daughter.' Shouldn't an educated person know where the expression comes from? You can't decree a divorce between language and culture!"

"We can and we have."

It was two months later, long after the Chanukah skit had been successfully performed, that Miriam dropped in at Terry's house and presented her with a gift-wrapped package. Terry unwrapped it and found a Japanese vase.

"What's this for? Are you that grateful that I got you that part in the play?"

"Nope, this is for *shadchanus*. Your idea for my brother worked out, and he just got engaged to the girl I set him up with, my friend, Sarah Dinah."

"*Mazal tov*! When is the wedding?"

"They're getting married in the summer and coming to live in Israel, at least for a year. I'm going to have real family right here in

Yerushalayim with me!"

"That's terrific. Shall we celebrate with a cup of coffee?" Terry picked up the kettle and began to light the stove, but then stopped. "Just let me get these spills off the stove before I burn them on. Could you reach under the sink there behind you and get me the Fantastik?"

Miriam rummaged around in the cupboard under the sink and emerged empty-handed. "I don't find any Fantastik," she reported.

"Oh, you're right. It's not really Fantastik ... it's a cheap substitute under some other name. You can tell that it's supposed to be Fantastik because it's in a yellow bottle."

This time Miriam emerged with a plastic container in her hand, but she was slow to hand it to Terry. "You never looked at the name on this?" Miriam asked.

"No, it didn't particularly interest me. Why?"

"Well ... If we were giving out prizes for creative use of English, I think this company would get one."

"Come on, Miriam. Cut the suspense and tell me the name."

"I wouldn't want to spoil it for you, Terry. Read it yourself." She held out the container of all-purpose cleaner. Blazoned across the label, in bold balloon letters, was the word "*Bombasti*."

Chapter 24

A New Niche

"Hello, Mrs. Wahrhaftig? This is Devora Rothman. My husband is the rabbi of the shul in Stafford." That was the next community over. "I'm putting together the fund-raising dinner for the day school, and I was hoping that you could serve on the committee."

"No, I'm afraid I'm not getting involved in any community projects this year," said Ella firmly. "Getting the children settled and managing a few hours of teaching is about as much as I can handle."

"It's only for a few weeks," coaxed Mrs. Rothman. "It would give you a chance to meet some of the other women in the community."

"I've met the other teachers at the high school and the *rebbetzins* at the yeshivah. Since I haven't got any way to get around, that's probably about as much social life as I can manage at the moment."

"Well, if you should change your mind, we're in the *heimish* phone directory under Rabbi Nathan Rothman. I'm sure that there will be plenty to do up to the last moment."

"Rothman. I'll remember, but I don't think I'm likely to change my mind."

Ella hung up the phone. Chaim Ozer, who was sitting at his *shtender*, put a bookmark in his *Gemara* and closed it. "There was something uncharacteristic about that exchange."

"I've never liked fund-raising," Ella pointed out.

"True," said Chaim Ozer, "but I would have expected you to be tempted by the chance to get to know the other women in the community."

Ella took a deep breath and then exhaled slowly.

"What did that sigh mean?"

Ella hesitated, then asked, "I wouldn't expect you to remember this, but when we were going to the Millmans' *sheva brachos*, Miriam mentioned with a certain amount of resentment that I had been made class chairman for the Chanukah bazaar my first winter in New York. I only found out years later just how deep that resentment was."

"And so?"

"And so, I'm coming into a new community. Everyone here has a niche of her own, and I don't know what they are. If I just sail in and take over this and that job that's offered to me, I could easily be moving into someone's territory, and I might not find out whom I've hurt until ten years from now."

"I hear. Still, it's very different from the situation in a large high school in Brooklyn, where there are hundreds of girls and only a few positions of responsibility. Here, there are a few religious families trying to maintain a full gamut of organizations. There's a calendar up in the yeshivah office for these fund-raising events, so that they won't conflict. There's the day school dinner, the *mikveh* association dinner, the Agudah dinner, and the dinner for the outreach organizations. We are, you should know, expected to attend all of these affairs, and I believe that they can use all the help that they can get in organizing them."

"Not this year, Chaim'ke."

"I also think you would enjoy getting to know Rebbetzin Rothman. She's older than you, like most of the *rebbetzins*, but I think you would have a common language."

"Why?" asked Ella, her curiosity piqued. It irritated her that he knew the people in the community so much better than she did. In Yerushalayim, she had usually kept him informed of the background of various people with whom they came in contact.

"I'll let you find out for yourself, all in good time."

Ella walked into the school office to pick up her paycheck. She enjoyed teaching, especially subjects connected with Torah, but she still would never do it if she were not being paid. In fact, she wouldn't be able to afford baby-sitters if she were not being paid. The secretary was out and another woman was standing and waiting. She was short, with hair reaching to her shoulders.

"Do you know if the secretary is likely to be back soon?" the woman asked.

"I'm sure she's just down the hall," Ella reassured her.

"Good, because I have to get back to the day school to pick up my children."

"They don't go by bus?" The day school had an arrangement with the county, which provided busing for the students.

The woman smiled sadly. "There's no bus to where we live. We're from Medborn." This was a community an hour's drive away.

"Good heavens!" exclaimed Ella. "How do they get here every day?"

"The same way they got here today. I drive them."

"An hour's drive each way? What do you do for the eight and a half hours in between?"

"Three days a week, I go back home to take care of my household. Twice a week I stay in the Winston area, shopping and sitting in the park feeding the ducks."

"You never think of moving closer to the school?"

"My husband puts up with my doing this, but he doesn't see why it's important to send them to Jewish schools. He surely doesn't want to move because of that."

Ella gazed at the woman in awe. She could not imagine herself making the kind of sacrifice that this woman was making to give her children a Jewish education. She would never be called on to do so; they would never live far from a Jewish school. Still, it was inspiring.

Devora Rothman called her again just after the day school dinner. "Listen, I know you have a new baby and that you don't get around much, but I have something you could do right in your own home."

Ella braced herself. "What do you have in mind?"

"A woman named Daisy Schwartz from Medborn became religious a couple of years ago, and she placed her children in the day school. She has a lot of time on her hands, and is interested in learning something. Would you be willing to tutor her for a couple of hours a week? You could do it in the mornings when your children are in school and kindergarten."

"Probably, but I have to check with my husband." The mention of Chaim Ozer reminded her of what he had said about the Rothmans. "I believe he knows your husband."

"Actually, we had him over to Stafford for a Shabbos before you came to town. He and my husband spent the meals reminiscing about Yerushalayim."

"You used to live in Yerushalayim?"

"Yes, we lived there for fifteen years, before my husband took this position. I still dream of returning, but there is so much more that he can do here than there, so I don't think it is going to happen soon."

Ella had a strong feeling that this woman she barely knew would soon be one of her best friends. It seemed so inevitable that there was no need to push it.

Daisy arrived for their first session modestly dressed, wearing a hat on her head. She was interested in learning the weekly Torah portion, so they spent most of their time reviewing it in English, though Ella coaxed her into working through a few carefully selected verses in the original Hebrew. Afterwards, they adjourned to the dining room for coffee and cake.

"This is quite an unusual house," commented Daisy, looking at the rounded windows.

"Yes, it is," agreed Ella. "I was fond of it from the moment I saw it. I keep thinking that there must be some kind of lesson in its decayed grandeur. It's something that can only be appreciated if you keep it up."

"Sort of the opposite of our throw-away age," suggested Daisy.

"Exactly. We had a stained-glass window in the bathroom, but it was buckling and the cold air was coming in. I called all over town trying to find someone willing to repair stained glass and failed. In the end we had to remove it and replace it with regular glass. I don't know what we'll do if anyone breaks one of those curved windows."

They finished their coffee and Daisy rose to go. "Thank you so much, Ella. This was much more interesting than feeding the ducks." They walked through the living room, and Daisy looked with appreciation at the large fireplace, the grand stairway, and the stained-glass window on the landing, through which the sun was streaming. "This house really does have character. You know what it reminds me of?"

"What?" asked Ella.

"Judaism."

A month or so later, Devora Rothman called again. "I hear from Daisy that you two are getting along famously."

"I'm glad that she thinks so. I wasn't quite sure. She's fairly passive about what we should learn, and I wasn't sure that I wasn't pushing her past the bounds of her interest."

"No, she really thinks she's getting a lot out of it, and she appreciates that you're giving her so much of your time. I'm calling now to wheedle a bit of that time for myself."

"Yes?" Ella said warily. She remained firm in her intention to avoid committee work.

"I'll be in your area this afternoon to meet with the caterer. I was going to suggest that you come along so we can get acquainted on the way. I'll bring one of my daughters to baby-sit for your children."

Ella suspected that this was the *rebbetzin's* way of getting her involved in the banquet through the backdoor, but she was also pretty sure that the underlying impulse was a friendly one. She had already decided that she would eventually be friends with Devora Rothman, but it wasn't going to happen very quickly, as long as she remained in her own house and only poked her head out four hours a week to teach. "Okay. When will you arrive?"

"Around four."

"I'll prepare the children. They haven't had baby-sitters for a while."

Dina Rothman was nineteen years old and seemed fully competent to manage the five Wahrhaftig children. Two of the younger ones exhibited a tendency to cling, but Dina distracted them and took them into the house while the two mothers left by the front gate.

"You have to understand that kosher catering is sort of a problem around here. For weddings people often just take the whole affair to New York or Baltimore, and there's a hotel in the city that has kosher dishes locked up in a closet, but the kitchen has to be *kashered* afresh each time. For a small fund-raiser like this, it wouldn't be practical."

"Believe me, I understand perfectly. My mother went through this all the time. My father is Rosh Yeshivah of an out-of-town yeshivah." Ella related some of Rebbetzin Gutfreund's more creative solutions.

"Well," said Devora, "we hold the dinners in the day school auditorium, and we used to alternate between hiring a caterer from one of the big communities and having the women of the community cook the food in the school kitchen. Neither solution was very good. You can imagine what the caterer and the staff charge for the four-hour drive each way, and the local volunteers suffered from burnout. It got harder and harder to find someone to organize the project."

"I can imagine," said Ella, and indeed she could.

"Finally, one of the older women, a widow, suggested that she could do it professionally. She had already been baking and selling challos, since there is also no kosher bakery in the area. So my husband helped her apply for and get rabbinical supervision from the local rabbi in charge of kashrus, and now we're in business."

For as long as this woman keeps her health and strength, thought Ella, but she was not about to make a remark. "So why do you have to consult with her?"

"She still needs assistance with all the chopping, checking, slicing, and grinding a day or so before the event. It was part of the arrangement that we would find volunteers to help with that. I'm going to approve the menu, and find out what sort of help she needs, and when. Usually two girls the afternoon before, and two women the morning before the event is adequate, and I don't have much trouble rounding them up."

They arrived at the home of the caterer, Mrs. Weingrove. It was a large colonial style house with sideboards painted white, and green shutters. Several neatly clipped spruce trees graced the well-tended lawn. Looking over the establishment, Ella doubted that money was the real motivation behind Mrs. Weingrove's business venture. More likely this visit from Rebbetzin Rothman and a wish to be productive were also factors.

"How nice to see you, dear," said their hostess, greeting Devora with a kiss on the cheek. "Come in, come in. And who is this?" She turned to Ella with a smile.

"This is Ella Wahrhaftig. Her husband is a new *rebbi* at the yeshivah. They moved to Winston this summer. "

"We're pleased to have you." After a ritual offer of cake and tea, Devora and Mrs. Weingrove buried themselves in menu choices and estimates of attendance, while Ella sat back in a comfortable armchair and examined the room at her leisure. The honey-hued couch, with throw pillows in fall colors, blended with beige walls and golden drapes, gracefully pulled back by knotted cords.

"Do you like the room?" asked Mrs. Weingrove, looking up from her lists and following the direction of Ella's gaze.

"Very much. It is very tastefully decorated." Ella gave the compliment with complete honesty.

"And what do you think of Winston as a place to live?" asked Mrs. Weingrove.

Ella was struck dumb. She must say something polite and positive, but she could not formulate the proper phrases. The awkward silence dragged on, with both of the other women looking at her. She had to say something, anything. "It's—uh—not quite what I'm used to," she mumbled. Then she flushed with embarrassment.

After leaving the Weingrove home, they traveled in silence for a minute or two before Devora said, "If you grew up near an out-of-town yeshivah, then Winston cannot really be that different from what you're used to." It was a statement, not a question.

"Of course not," agreed Ella, "but it is very different from Mattersdorf."

"I lived in Ezras Torah," said the older woman. "Down the road from Mattersdorf. You don't have to list the differences for me, but I may look at them differently."

Ella struggled with the choice between a conservative silence and an attempt to reach an understanding with Devora. The other woman had offered to discuss the subject, but she wouldn't force her. The urge to talk about her unhappiness welled up in Ella. "I feel as if I've been demoted. Not just one rung but two."

The car was approaching Ella's house. Devora sped on past,

turned left at the corner, and parked under a maple tree about halfway up the next block. "Do you really think that?" she asked. "Do you really think that all possible places to live are ranked? That there's a best place, and a second best place, and so on down the line?"

Ella smiled at the image of all sorts of towns and cities set out in a row. In front of each one was a large signpost: No. 43, No. 44, and so on. "No, not really."

"Good," said Devora, "because if you did, you wouldn't be leaving much room for different families to have different *tafkidim* in life."

Ella inclined her head slightly in acknowledgement. Was she indeed stuck in some sort of schoolgirl view of the world? Tests are handed back with marks on the top that can be placed in a linear order? Once one gets out of school, or just out of the classroom, there is no such simple ranking system.

"I really enjoyed living in Yerushalayim," continued Devora. "The schools, the stores full of modest clothing, the high level of *kashrus*, the variety of shuls. I enjoyed it, but ..."

"But?"

"But I have no doubt at all that the place where my husband and I should be right now is in Stafford. Furthermore, I doubt that you and your husband got to Winston without asking some sort of *she'eilah* of your Rabbanim."

Ella nodded in acquiescence.

"So there is a strong presumption that you are also exactly where you should be," said Devora.

Ella didn't respond. Was that true? She understood that this was where Chaim Ozer should be. The teaching had brought him a new dynamism, had put a new excitement into his voice. And the yeshivah boys were also reacting well. Of course, the first year of teaching is very hard, but he loved it. If Winston was where Chaim Ozer should be, then of course it was where she herself should be. She knew that intellectually, but she still hadn't made peace with it.

"All right, let's leave your feeling aside for the moment while I tell you about some of my friends. There was a whole group of us, bright New York girls who had planned out exciting careers—and then we became *frum*."

Ella looked up, startled. She had not realized that Devora was a *ba'alas teshuvah*.

"I had finished my first year of medical school and was a bit disillusioned with the lives of the doctors I had met. I think that was what made me open to a new direction. I came to Eretz Yisrael for a summer and quickly ended up in a seminary. Almost from the first moment that I decided that the Torah was true and that I was going to try to shape my life according to Hashem's will, I also decided that I would leave medicine. I've never looked back. I would have been happy if we could have stayed in Yerushalayim, but when this opportunity came, I understood that it was right.

"On the other hand, my friend Beth became *shomer Shabbos* when she started college, and grew in *Yiddishkeit* as she continued her very successful scholastic career. I don't think that giving up medicine is something that she ever considered for a moment. She spent a few months in seminary and then went straight back to the States to finish her medical degree. She ended up having a career not so very different from the one she probably would have had if she had never become *frum*. It must be somewhat different, because she surely wouldn't have had the challenge of raising eight children if she had never become religious, but not all that different. She still does research and works in a prestigious hospital. She's very comfortably settled in New York."

"So you're trying to tell me that there's no one 'best' way to become *frum*. There are different possible paths for different kinds of people?"

"Exactly."

"And then I'm supposed to conclude that there's also no best place to live?"

"For us, that was just one part of the puzzle, together with whom we would marry and what we would do with our education. There was Leah, who was a lawyer, or, at least, was licensed to be one in America. She stayed in Eretz Yisrael and turned her degree into something she could use from the house while raising a large family.

"On the other hand, Nancy, who was an architect, got herself licensed to work in her profession in Eretz Yisrael while she was looking for a *shidduch*. She finally got married at thirty-one, to a paraplegic; I think they have five children."

Ella sat up straight, her own unhappiness instantly forgotten. She had been listening to Devora's stories without paying much attention, but the last one gave her a new idea. Devora knew an older *ba'alas teshuvah* who was willing to marry a paraplegic. If it happened once, maybe it could happen twice. "Maybe you can help us!" she exclaimed. She poured out, in a few sentences, the story of the attack on Elisha, his rehabilitation, and his *shidduch* problems.

Devora looked thoughtful as she restarted the car and drove around the block. "I'll have to think about this case," she said as she pulled up in front of Ella's hedge. "It's not the sort of thing you can suggest to just anyone. We're both a bit late right now, and I'm sort of snowed under with this dinner I'm organizing, but when it's over, you can fill me in on more of the details. I'll see if I have any ideas of my own, or if I can figure out to whom to send you."

Ella got out of the car and leaned down to look through the window. "Thank you, both for the expedition and for the talk."

"My pleasure."

Ella passed through the gate and went into the house. She found Dina sitting in a straight-backed chair with the baby in her lap, watching the other children as they built a town with their Lego set. "Your mother is waiting outside. Thank you very much for watching them, Dina. I appreciate it."

"Oh, it was nothing. They're cute, and I brushed up on my Hebrew by talking with them." Dina handed the baby to Ella and walked out the door. Ella looked at her watch. It was 6:15 already!

"Come children, it's late, and we have to get you some supper."

"Oh, we've eaten already," said Shloimy angelically.

"You've eaten already?"

Leah nodded. "We told Dina that we always eat at 5:30, so she made us eggs and toast."

"Well, then, we'll have time for a story. Upstairs, *kinderlach*. We'll have the story as soon as everyone is ready for bed." She was sorry Dina lived so far away. She was obviously a top-notch baby-sitter.

The bedtime ritual took Ella's full attention until after she had said *Shema* with the last of the children and came downstairs again. She looked around the lower floor, contrasting it with Mrs. Weingrove's. This house had a distinctly temporary, no-frills look, as if they would pull up stakes any moment and move on. That was the look she had been comfortable with, but was it fair to the children? Wherever they lived, even for a few weeks, was home to them. Shouldn't it be more homelike?

For the first time Ella noticed that there were curtain rods over the windows. She could probably get three sets of matching curtains for a very reasonable price at the thrift shop. There were no comfortable chairs to offer guests, and reading stories to the children would be a lot more comfortable if there were some kind of couch. She looked next at the bare, Formica-topped table from the yeshivah dining room. At home they had a solid wood table, which she had always kept covered with a cloth to protect the finish. If this one were covered, it wouldn't look much different.

She went upstairs, with an unaccustomed bounce in her step, to look for her favorite tablecloth. And if that didn't match the new curtains, then she probably had others that would.

Ella attended the day school dinner, and even allowed herself to be roped into taking tickets at the door. The auditorium, filled with elegantly set round tables, had a very different look than it did during school assemblies. One man arrived, glanced into the room, and said to his wife, "You guessed right. Red and white." He was obviously referring to the tablecloths, a white undercloth with a rectangular red covering.

"They're probably saving the gold and green for the outreach dinner," said his wife. Apparently, there were two sets of tablecloths that everyone knew infinitely well.

Mrs. Weingrove was standing near the door to the kitchen, directing the waiters. Devora, usually so calm, wore a distinctly frazzled look as she bustled about giving last-minute instructions and solving crises. The main events of the evening were to be the distribution of the advertising journal and a raffle for a trip to Eretz Yisrael. Both the copies of the journal and the box with the raffles were locked in the main office, and no one had arrived with a key.

Devora, pushing a stray strand of her blond *sheitel* back into place, paused for a moment beside the table at which Ella was collecting tickets. "I had an idea for your friend. I don't know if it's a good one. We can talk more tomorrow."

At nine the next morning Ella was on the phone to the

Rothmans. "*Nu*? Who is she? Why do you think she might be interested?"

"Her name is Diane Haskins. She stays with us sometimes for Shabbos, because her parents live in Sherbourne."

That already told Ella that Diane's parents were not religious.

"She's thirty-two and a convert. She is also about forty pounds overweight, and doesn't seem to manage to do much about it. I can't discuss this with her, because I'm some thirty pounds overweight myself, and don't seem to get rid of the extra weight. She's been looking for a *shidduch* for about eight years and doesn't seem to be getting anywhere. I asked her, just to test the water, if she would consider a younger man with a disability. She said that it might be possible, depending on the details. I asked her to inform me the next time she was planning a visit, and left it there for the moment."

As Chaim Ozer went about the house getting ready for Shabbos, he kept stopping to listen for a honk. When it finally came, he raced out of the house, down the walk, and out through the gate.

"*Baruch haba! Baruch haba!*" he called out, going around the parked car to the driver's window and shaking Elisha's hand. The last time they had seen each other had been in Yerushalayim.

"Thanks for having me. Watch out! I already pressed the button for the crane." The lid of the box on top of the car was opening slowly and a mechanical arm was reaching down into the box. It emerged slowly, drawing with it a folded wheel chair. When the wheels hit the pavement, the crane pulled the chair open. Chaim Ozer got out of the way so that Elisha could open the door to the car. Elisha dropped the arm of the chair closest to the driver's seat, took hold of the other arm, and swung himself into the wheel chair.

"Pretty impressive," Chaim Ozer said.

"I don't get to use it that often. My father decided to put the crane and the hand controls on his car, which is newer. My mother and I share the other car, and my attendant, Joe, shuttles it back and forth between us. On Sundays I can take it, and also on a trip like this when I'm trying to manage alone." Elisha settled himself into the chair.

"Now you have to make a decision," he continued. "In the back seat I have a folding lift, which I can use for getting in and out of the chair in the house. It's a bit of a nuisance to use, and you might think it would be easier to move me yourself."

"Fine by me," said Chaim Ozer.

"Well, that means you'll have to wait up for me tonight until I get back from this meeting." Elisha was supposed to meet Diane at the home of one of the other rabbis from the yeshivah. An elderly father lived with them, so the house was wheelchair accessible.

"I'll wait up," promised Chaim Ozer. "I have to wait up anyway, because there are five steps leading to our front door."

Elisha pushed himself to the back of the car and opened the trunk. He pointed to his overnight bag, overcoat, and Shabbos suit, still in its cleaner's bag. "I need those three things," he said, "but I also need help getting up this curb. It will probably be easier to do that first."

Chaim Ozer obligingly pulled the chair up the curb and parked it on the sidewalk before going back to get the bags and slamming the trunk closed.

"I can take those if you like," offered Elisha. "I imagine that it's smooth going from here."

"Not so very smooth," corrected Chaim Ozer. "Tree roots have been growing under our sidewalk, and several of the sections are tilted. I'll take the luggage and you concentrate on getting yourself to the house."

"You're right," agreed Elisha, as he followed Chaim Ozer to the house. "It's not so easy to steer on this walkway." Each of the concrete sections of the walk was at a slightly different angle, and the slabs often overlapped each other by an inch or two.

"The children often stub their toes on those slabs. That's one of the disadvantages to renting," said Chaim Ozer. "If it were our own place, we would probably take care of the worst of them." When they got to the porch, he pulled the wheelchair up the five steps.

The two older children remembered Elisha, and he spent the first few minutes giving them rides around the living room. Then Ella called them off so that their guest could get ready for Shabbos. It was a very pleasant meal, making them all nostalgic for the good old days.

After the meal, while Ella was upstairs putting the children to bed, Chaim Ozer bumped the chair down the steps again and along the walk between the flower beds to the front gate. "Up the hill about half a block, number 6072. They're expecting you."

"How will I let you know that I am back?" asked Elisha. "I don't want to wake up all the neighbors shouting."

"And I don't want you waiting a long time outside in the cold," said Chaim Ozer, pointing to one or two patches of snow that had survived the recent thaw. "When you get back, stop your chair right here. I'll look out every few minutes to see if you've arrived, starting about an hour from now."

It was almost exactly an hour and a half when Elisha returned. He let himself in at the gate, still thinking about the *shidduch,* trying to formulate his feelings. When the Wahrhaftigs had made the arrangement, they had left open the possibility of a second meeting on *motzaei Shabbos.* Was he interested? Would she be interested?

Elisha began rolling up the sidewalk, absentmindedly struggling to keep the chair moving straight ahead on the undulating pavement. What bothered him the most, he decided, was the sense of weariness, almost despair, that she projected. Was it something that would clear up if her situation improved, or was it engrained? Would marrying him seem like an improvement to her?

At a particularly sharp dip in the pavement, his right wheel slipped sideways. Jerked back to the present, he clamped his hands tightly on the bars to brake his momentum, but it was too late. The wheel sank into the soft earth of the flowerbed, pitching him off the chair, into a patch of snow.

Elisha skidded a foot or two across the slushy grass and came to a halt lying on his right side. He pounded the ground with his left fist, frustration welling up inside him. It was not enough that just moving around the house was a struggle, that he was barely considered employable, that the only girls who would consider meeting him had mountains of troubles of their own! He couldn't even return quietly from a *shidduch* without getting tossed into the mud! A little over two years ago he had been so carefree, and hadn't even appreciated how lucky he was!

Who knows? Maybe he would develop pneumonia and that would solve his problem about whether or not to meet this girl again.

After a bitter sob, he choked back his frustration and tried to take stock. His right arm and shoulder hurt; was anything broken? He could move his fingers. He felt along his right arm with his free left hand. Nothing seemed particularly painful. Placing his left hand close to his chest, he managed to lift his body enough to free his right arm and roll onto his stomach. His overcoat and Shabbos suit were streaked with mud, and this just spread it a little further. With a sad smile, he remembered his mother's despair at his inability to keep his Shabbos pants free of dirt for more than an hour when he was a boy.

Elisha rested his chin on his left forearm and flexed the muscles in his right arm, convincing himself that no bones were broken. Ignoring the protest of his bruised muscles, he raised himself on both elbows and looked around.

Fortunately, Chaim Ozer was waiting up for him. Had the building been wheelchair accessible, he might have been tempted to dispense with help, and then he would have been out here until the morning. He shivered at the thought.

He was about twenty feet from the steps. A large bush obscured his view of the front door, which meant that he wouldn't know when it was opened. The chair was on its side across the walkway. It was of no use to him at the moment, and the bush would also prevent Chaim Ozer from seeing that something was wrong if he came out and glanced in that direction. He had to move close enough to have an unobstructed view of the door. He wasn't even sure that Chaim Ozer would open it. He might just glance through the diamond-shaped panes to see if the wheelchair was in front of the door.

"This is what Ted has been training you for," he told himself grimly. "Do him proud." Elisha clasped his hands in front of himself, moved each elbow forward, and dragged himself a few inches. Ted's voice echoed in his head. Right, left, pull. Right, left, pull.

When he was about ten feet from the steps, he could see the door. The light in the glass panes was blocked briefly. That must be Chaim Ozer checking to see if Elisha had arrived. Unfortunately, he was looking for a chair parked on the sidewalk, not for a dark form on the grass.

The next time I'll shout, Elisha decided. He continued inching forward, but this time with his head turned toward the door.

Right, left, pull. Right, left, pull. He was watching for the light to be blocked and was so caught by surprise when the door actually opened that he forgot to call out. Chaim Ozer, in a white shirt that was easily visible, crossed to the side of the porch and stood looking toward the gate. From where he was standing, he could probably see the overturned chair, though he might not realize what it was. He had just come out of the light, and his eyes probably hadn't adjusted yet.

"Elisha?" called Chaim Ozer tentatively.

That finally shook Elisha free of the confusion that had held him silent. "Chaim Ozer! I'm here!"

"Where?" His friend came clattering down the steps. He stood on the sidewalk, straining his eyes to see as far as the gate.

"Here. On the lawn. I fell." Now that rescue was near, he was able to say this in an almost matter-of-fact tone.

Chaim Ozer gasped and turned toward Elisha. He hurried across the soggy grass and knelt next to his friend. "Are you okay? Did you break anything?"

"I don't think so. I took the fall on my right shoulder, but it seems to be working all right. The ground was soft."

Chaim Ozer checked him and became convinced that nothing was seriously wrong. "If you can be moved, then I think that the easiest way to get you back into the house is to return you to the chair."

"Probably," agreed Elisha.

Chaim Ozer went down the walk to where the wheelchair was lying on its side, righted it, and wheeled it as close as possible to his friend. He set the brake and removed the leg rests. "How did you get from there to here?"

"Dragged myself. I have rehabilitation with a Marine drill sergeant. He's been preparing us for emergencies like this one." Ted was going to be interested in hearing about this adventure.

"I think it would help if we moved you closer to the chair before I try to pick you up."

"I think you should change first. My overcoat and suit are covered with mud. We don't have to ruin your Shabbos suit, too."

Chaim Ozer looked down at his dress pants. "These went when I kneeled in the grass. I have other black suits that I can wear tomorrow."

Elisha inched his way close to the chair, then turned himself over, slipping his arms out of the sleeves of his overcoat as he did. He braced himself on his elbows in a half reclining position. Chaim Ozer, grasping him under the arms, first pulled him into a full sitting position on the abandoned overcoat. Elisha rested his weight on his hands.

Chaim Ozer took a firmer grip, heaved Elisha up, and deposited him in the chair. The brake held and he managed to get him settled in properly. Then he restored the leg rests and released the brake. "Whew!" Chaim Ozer exclaimed. "I was afraid the chair would skitter backwards as I tried to get you into it."

"So was I," admitted Elisha.

Chaim Ozer bumped him up the five steps to the porch. He ran the chair back and forth a few times to make sure that the wheels were clean. Then he wheeled it into the house and began the complicated process of dealing with all the mud without violating Shabbos. It was almost a full hour until Elisha was settled in a borrowed folding bed in a corner of the dimly lit living room, with a basin and *nagel-vasser* on a stool at his bedside.

"I'm afraid we don't have a Shabbos clock, so the lights won't close," said Chaim Ozer, "but you can use this eye-shade." He held it out, dangling it from its elastic band, and Elisha took it from his hand. "You know, with all this excitement, I forgot to ask you about the *shidduch*."

"I don't think it will work," said Elisha. "I realized that as I was lying there in the grass. I'm not such an optimistic person that I could counteract all her pessimism."

"So where do you go from here?"

"Perhaps to Eretz Yisrael. My mother is beginning to come around to the idea that we should at least research possibilities in Israel. Of course, she isn't yet ready to consider my settling there."

"If you do move there, you can take my place," suggested Chaim Ozer.

"That would be a bit more than I think I could handle," Elisha said.

Ella closed the door after Chaim Ozer, who was pushing the chair. The doctor who had seen Elisha this morning had agreed that there was nothing obviously wrong, but had still told them to have him take X-rays of the bruised spots as soon as Shabbos was over. Chaim Ozer was driving Elisha to the nearest emergency room.

The children were in bed, and as Ella began straightening up from Shabbos she remembered another evening when she had sent Chaim Ozer and Elisha off together. The night of the attack was, in fact, the last time she had seen Elisha before this visit. How much had changed since that evening!

She would have to call Devora soon. They had left open the possibility of a second *shidduch* meeting tonight that would have to be canceled. Elisha had asked her to try to let Diane down gently, insofar as she had ever been up. He also preferred that she not be told about the fall.

The phone rang. Was that Devora? Ella didn't feel that she was quite ready with a proper answer, but she also didn't think it fair to Diane if she was waiting to hear what Elisha thought. With some trepidation, she lifted the receiver.

"Hello?"

"Hello." It was Devora's voice on the line.

"Hello," repeated Ella inanely.

"I have a report from Diane," said Devora.

"Yes?"

"She thinks that the age difference is too great. She said that she felt as if she were twenty or thirty years older instead of ten. As if he were in the spring of life, and she was already moving into fall."

"Chaim Ozer and Elisha went out, but I'll pass on the message when they return." Ella put down the phone with a great sense of relief.

When the snow had melted, green shoots had poked their way out of the sodden earth, and soon the entire walkway was lined with white and yellow daffodils. The original bulbs had surely been planted when the house was still a mansion, but they had grown wild for at least a decade and there were hundreds of them. The children, both their own and the neighbors,' gathered great bunches of them before Shabbos and filled all the vases in the houses, bringing the scent of spring indoors.

There were several yeshivah families living on the block, in semi-detached houses. None of them had a yard as extravagant as the Wahrhaftigs,' and the neighborhood children came over to play as often as possible. Ella had refurbished the swing set, hanging two new swings. Whatever else was going on, the creak-creak of the swings was heard in the background, as the children took turns by some complicated system based on the number twenty, that only they seemed to understand.

Today was warm, and Ella had brought her work outside to the table on the porch. The baby was crawling around at her feet. Both the porch railing and floor were covered with peeling gray paint, but the yeshivah maintenance staff had found a roll of old linoleum for the floor so that the baby wouldn't get splinters in her hands.

Ella was preparing the chapter of Yechezkel about the stream that would burst forth from the third *Beis Hamikdash*, broadening and deepening as it flowed, until it would refresh the Dead Sea. She was trying to figure out how to get the girls to see that this river, while contradicting all physical laws, was right in line with common spiritual effects. "One candle lighting a hundred," she wrote in her notes, "A teacher lecturing a class. The *ba'al teshuvah* movement."

"... Eighteen, nineteen, twenty. Off you go! It's my turn!"

Ella looked up to see Leah sail off the swing and land with a light stumble. One of her friends took her place. Ella noticed that the shadows were getting longer as the sun sank toward the horizon. The clouds were already slightly pink on the underside. Soon it would be chilly outside. She closed her books, picked up the baby, opened the baby gate at the top of the steps, and went down to fetch her toddler. "Leah'le, Shloimy, Natty!" she called to the older children. "We'll be eating in fifteen minutes. Faigy, Tzippora, Eli, Dovid'l, its time to be thinking about going home."

As she walked into the house to put supper on the table, she remembered her mood nine months ago. She would have been amazed then, had she known how settled she would be by spring.

"Chaim Ozer," began Ella that evening, as she brought him his supper.

"Yes?"

"Do you think we'll ever get back to Yerushalayim?" She put down the serving dishes and sat down across from him, though she herself had eaten with the children.

"Maybe and maybe not. I don't think I would go back without having a position. Not after we've all gotten used to being less cramped."

"Why not?"

"Well, first of all, I enjoy teaching, difficult though it sometimes is. Second, ... I think our old life was too hard on you. You were doing everything yourself, including being the family's main breadwinner. With each new child, it was getting a little harder, and I'm not surprised that you eventually broke under the strain."

"It wasn't just that," protested Ella, wincing a little at the idea that she had "broken." Now that she was sharing the decision making with Chaim Ozer, she had begun to suspect that her insistence on doing everything herself had had something to do with having everything done her way, a privilege she was now ready to renounce. "I'm not sure the same thing would happen again."

"Agreed. A lot of things came together, but the strain was there."

"How would we know if we should go back?"

"I can tell you what the Rav of Ramat Elchanan did when he took a position in Europe. He and his Rebbetzin decided that they would stay until they got some kind of offer in Eretz Yisrael, even if it wasn't very appropriate. At that point, they would look for something that seemed right."

"All right. That gives me some hope. Next year in Yerushalayim!"

"You're finding it very hard to adjust here, aren't you?"

"It's getting better, I admit. At first I felt as if I had been demoted two grades, sent back to live my mother's life over again, and I wasn't sure I could carry it off as well as she did. Now ... I'm beginning to see that this is different. The schools and the kosher food are easier to manage than they were in my mother's day, and there are new challenges. Like Daisy."

Chaim Ozer just smiled.

Chapter 25

Obstacle Course

"**S**o how is Rabbi Yehuda *cholek* on the *Chachamim*?" Elisha asked.

His friend Danny stared down at the volume of *Mishnayos* open in front of him and tried to summarize the differences of opinion. With some stumbling, he managed to do a fairly creditable job. Danny, who had lost the use of his legs in a car accident, had been together with Elisha in the rehabilitation program. Elisha had coaxed him into setting up a learning *seder*.

"Terrific!" Elisha praised him. It appeared to him that Danny was reaching the limit of his concentration span for rabbinical Hebrew. Danny had a day school background, but had never done much serious learning. That's why Elisha had started him out with *Mishnah* rather than *Gemara*. Elisha spun his chair around and wheeled it over next to Danny's. "Shall we take a break and get some water to drink?" he suggested. When Danny nodded, they both propelled themselves over to the water cooler.

"Can we meet this afternoon at the gym for basketball, as usual?" asked Danny.

Elisha nodded. "I finish with my *chavrusa* at six." Basketball workouts were one of the incentives he used to keep Danny interested in learning. Besides, he himself needed some form of regular exercise, as his therapist constantly stressed. "Basketball sure beats all that dreary weight lifting that they had us doing at first."

"Of course it does. I don't know what I'm going to do if you really carry out this crazy plan of yours to go to Israel."

"Well, whatever happens, do find a way to get exercise. You remember what Teddy told us. Other people get all sorts of exercise we miss out on. Just standing up for *Kaddish* ten times during the *davening* is exercise."

"Huh? Just which lesson was it during which Ted O'Brien explained the benefits of standing up for *Kaddish*?"

"You know what I mean. I think he talked about people heaving themselves out of an armchair to go get a snack from the refrigerator; I just translated it into something closer to home."

"What will you do for exercise if you move to Israel?"

"I hope I'll find something. There are, unfortunately, a lot of paraplegics in Eretz Yisrael, because of the wars and the terrorist attacks. There must be exercise clubs with proper facilities."

"When are you leaving on this pilot trip?" Danny asked.

"In a couple of weeks. As soon as my mother gets finished with some charity benefit she's involved in."

"Aren't you nervous about going back? I still tense up whenever we drive down the freeway where my car crashed."

"I don't think so. I'm looking forward to going. There were a couple of policemen who worked hard to catch the guy who attacked me. My mom agreed that we could invite them for dinner. I think it would help me close off that chapter of my life. Come, we have another three *mishnos* to go."

Miriam was in Geula, on Malchei Yisrael Street, shopping for clothes for herself and the children. She almost bumped into the woman with the double stroller before she recognized her. "Trudy! What are you doing here in Yerushalayim? *Mazal tov* on the new baby!"

"Thank you. We moved back a month ago," said Trudy. She looked and sounded tired. "We just couldn't make it in Tzefat. It was cheap to live there, but there were too few possibilities for earning a living. It's a long and rather sad story."

"I'm running at the moment because I have to catch a bus that comes only once an hour, but Binyamin and I would like to hear everything. Are you still mobile enough to come for Shabbos? We don't have anyone this week, and you've never been to our home in Telz-Stone."

"I really would like that," agreed Trudy. "I'll ask Michael. Give me your phone number and I'll try to get back to you this evening."

When Miriam got home, there was a message on the answering machine from her mother-in-law. She dialed back and announced, "Guess who I just saw! Trudy and Michael Millman are back in Yerushalayim."

"If you see them again, please give them my regards," responded Mrs. Lerner.

"I hope to see them. I invited them for Shabbos." Miriam did a quick mental inventory of her freezer and decided that she would have to bake another batch of *kugel*.

"Now, you're probably wondering why I called," said Mrs. Lerner.

Miriam hadn't gotten around to wondering about that yet but said, "Let's hear!"

"Toby is planning a trip to Israel."

"We'd love to have her spend a Shabbos with us. Except for Trudy and Michael this Shabbos, I haven't got any guests scheduled. Tell me when Aunt Toby is coming and I'll make sure not to invite anyone else."

"It's not quite that simple," said Mrs. Lerner. "She's coming together with Elisha."

"Oh, my. I'm afraid our place is really not wheelchair accessible." Miriam was genuinely disappointed.

"We heard that from your parents. They're going to stay in a hotel. You know that money isn't really a big consideration with them. They're planning to invite the two policemen who helped with the case to dinner one night, and they'd like to invite you as well."

"We'd be thrilled to go!" agreed Miriam on the spot.

"Well, I should tell you that Toby has a bit of a hidden agenda here. Elisha has this idea of moving to Eretz Yisrael. He thinks it may provide a way out of his problems with finding a *shidduch*. As far as he's concerned, this is a pilot trip. His parents don't think he's being sufficiently realistic about the difficulties. I know that you two have been having a rough time. I don't think she means for you to argue with him, just to be honest about what's involved."

"I don't know, Mom, if I'm the right person to invite. I'm settling in very nicely. Perhaps she should invite the Millmans."

"What's the heart of their problem?"

"Making a living, apparently."

"Well, that's not so relevant. As much as Elisha talks about wanting to be independent, his family is perfectly ready, and perfectly able, to support him for the rest of his life. Toby is worried about having him live by himself."

"The popular thing to do nowadays, for someone who needs assistance, is to import a foreign worker from the Philippines," Miriam said.

"Elisha doesn't like the idea. He doesn't need all that much help, he claims, so the job would be deadly dull. He would like someone to come in for an hour or so every morning and evening. Toby doesn't agree. In short, they haven't found any plan they both think is workable."

Miriam, being a mother herself, understood Aunt Toby's worries. For all that, she found that her sympathies lay with Elisha.

Grisha stopped his car in front of Nachum's apartment building, and called his partner on his cell phone to let him know that he had arrived. His mind went back ... how long was it, now? More than two years. The stabbing had taken place in the middle of the winter, and now it was spring.

"Here I am!" said Nachum, as he pulled open the car door. He had spruced himself up. Instead of the tee shirt and jogging pants that were his usual off-duty wear, he wore a sports shirt, open at the collar, and a pair of blue pants. Grisha had put on khaki slacks instead of jeans when he changed out of his uniform. Both were aware that the hotel to which they had been invited was a very ritzy place.

"It hardly seems like two years, does it?" commented Grisha. He pulled the car away from the curb and out into the Yerushalayim traffic.

"What happened to Ahmad's wife?" Nachum asked.

"The East Yerushalayim police department has people keeping

an eye on her. They want to know if she's getting money from any terrorist organization. She has started working part time. As far as they can tell, she's being supported mainly by Ahmad's extended family, with a few handouts from her mother."

"So that story he told at his trial is probably true? He did it on impulse and only contacted Hamas after the fact?"

"Yeah," said Grisha, "and Hamas seems to have washed their hands of him after he got both himself and their operative arrested."

They reached the towering, stone-faced hotel, and Grisha drove his car around to the underground parking lot. They rode the elevator up to the spacious lobby and found signs pointing to the dining room. "How will we find our hosts?" Grisha asked.

"That's pretty obvious, isn't it?" returned Nachum. "How many young *chareidi* men in wheelchairs are likely to be there? Besides, I think I would recognize his mother. I saw her a couple of times when I dropped by the hospital to question Elisha."

It was, indeed, easy to spot their party. It included another young couple, introduced as Elisha's cousins. Elisha occupied the end of the table, which was easiest for him. After he had dropped the arms of his wheelchair and placed himself at a normal distance from the table, it was easy to forget about his disability. He looked much better than he had when Grisha had last seen him at the trial. Then he had been easily tired and pale from months spent indoors. Now he looked tanned and fit.

Grisha shook out the elegantly folded napkin and examined the appetizer. It looked too artistic to spoil by eating it. There was an orange item that he finally identified as half a mango, cut crisscross and turned inside out. Also, some honeyed walnuts nestled in the hollow of half an avocado.

"I was hoping," said Elisha, "that we could review the whole story of the night I was stabbed. My cousins here can be the audience. They know very few of the details." He spoke English for his mother's benefit, having earlier checked with Grisha that he and his partner could manage the language. After a murmur of agreement from his guests, he launched into the beginning of the story after *Havdalah* at the Wahrhaftigs', parting from Chaim Ozer at the bus stop, the battle with the umbrella, the sound of footsteps, and the quick glance over his shoulder at a hate-filled face.

Nachum, who had been summoned by the night-duty officer as soon as the victim had been found, told about the chaos at the scene of the crime. He arrived just as Elisha was being loaded onto the Hatzolah stretcher. About fifty spectators had gathered by this time; the police and the men from ZAKA were trying to keep them back while the blood was being sponged up and they searched for evidence of the identity of either the victim or his assailant. Nachum did manage to get a good look at Elisha's face and clothing, as did Grisha, who arrived shortly after him.

The umbrella had been found by the same two *bachurim* who had found Elisha. The two detectives had zipped the umbrella into an evidence bag and taken charge of it as the best lead they had. They had followed the ambulance to the hospital, hoping that more clues would turn up as the wounded man was prepared for surgery, but they were disappointed. Then they set off together for the Wahrhaftigs' house.

The story rolled on: Micha the forensic expert, the "arrest" of Itzik the cook, Grisha opening Ahmad's closet and seeing two eyes, Nachum's argument with Chaim Ozer.

Mrs. Sheinfeld added her own bit at the proper point in the story. "We had had a quiet Shabbos, just the two of us for a change. I was wondering what I would do with my evening once I finished the dishes when the phone rang. I picked it up without the slightest premonition that something might be amiss.

"The moment that the man on the other end identified himself as Elisha's Rosh Yeshivah, I knew that this was something serious. It was nearly one in the morning over there. They wouldn't get the Rosh Yeshivah involved just to tell me that my son was down with the flu.

"'Mrs. Sheinfeld,' he said, 'someone has been wounded, and we believe that it's your son Elisha.'

"I'm afraid I was neither very polite nor very respectful. 'What do you mean, you believe he is my son. Can't someone go identify him?'

"'Not yet. He's still in the operating room. Someone is waiting in the hospital to make the identification as soon as the surgery is over. I'm calling now because I thought you and your husband might want to start making arrangements to travel this evening.'

"At that moment, my husband came in. As I tried to give him the information, I choked up, so I just gave him the phone. The Rosh Yeshivah filled him in on the situation.

"We decided right away that we would try to get on a midnight flight to Israel, and from then on I was too busy to cry. When we got through customs, the first thing we did was to call the Wahrhaftigs to find out if Elisha was still alive." Mrs. Sheinfeld paused, tears in her eyes, unable to continue. After a deep and rather shaky breath, she managed to finish, "And then we took a cab straight to the hospital."

Elisha had a similar difficulty describing the moment when he learned that he would never walk again. The entire recital was not finished until after the main course, and was followed by a moment of silence.

Mrs. Sheinfeld, sitting at the table opposite Elisha, broke the silence. She turned to Nachum and Grisha. "You don't know that Elisha has an idea that he is going to move to Israel. We have no family here except the Lerners," she pointed to the young couple, "and they live in an apartment that is not wheelchair accessible." The husband and wife looked at each other guiltily.

"After all that was said tonight," she continued, "can you understand why my husband and I are unhappy about this plan?"

Now Nachum and Grisha looked at each other. Grisha saw his own perplexity reflected in Nachum's face. How could he put his thoughts across, in English, to this worried mother?

Nachum made the first try. "Mrs. Sheinfeld, after all Elisha suffered here, after all he lost, don't you think that he has become a part of this country? That he sort of, well, belongs here with the rest of us? It's true that we all face dangers, but we try to face them together."

Elisha gave Nachum the 'thumbs up' sign, and Mrs. Sheinfeld looked at him sternly. "Elisha, did you put him up to saying that?"

"Believe me, Mom, I didn't say a word to him. You got his honest reaction."

Now it was Grisha's turn. "Mrs. Sheinfeld, I'll say more. We may need Elisha here more than you need him there. My family brought me here from Russia when I was seven. There we had tried to be Russian *goyim*, and it hadn't worked. The Russians reminded us that there was a difference. Here we try to be *goyish* Jews, and that doesn't always work out quite like we want it to either.

"People like Elisha, who have been badly wounded by our enemies and have put their lives back together, become symbols of hope for the rest of us. I think it's good if some of those symbols are religious Jews. It's a reminder of where we came from."

"This program that I signed up for," Michael explained, "is meant to take two different problems and make each the solution of the other. The first problem is to find a suitable livelihood for those *ba'alei teshuvah* who haven't been absorbed into the mainstream and who haven't found a position in the network of organizations dealing with *ba'alei teshuvah*. People, in short, like myself. The second problem is to find trained personnel willing to go to out-of-the-way places to do outreach work, or to teach in Jewish schools. I will take the course twice a week and get a stipend as I'm learning. In the summer there will be a teacher's training course. When we finish, we're committed to going abroad for at least two years, and taking some sort of position in outreach or education."

"How do you feel about going back?" Miriam asked Trudy.

"Frankly, I'm scared stiff. You know, Michael became *frum* in America, but my entire experience with *frumkeit* is here in Israel, and for me the two are almost synonymous."

"Not for me," said Binyamin, "at least, not any more." He told them about his latest encounter with Rami. "What's the point to having a whole nation of Hebrew speakers with no interest in their Jewish roots?"

Binyamin continued. "In Israel the ignorance extends to people who think of themselves as scholars. My Hebrew-English dictionary includes the expression, 'He knows that the way a Jew knows *Ashrei*,'" Binyamin turned to Trudy, "Do you know what that means?"

"Sure, it's talking about the alphabetical psalm you say three times a day. Even I know that."

"Right, Psalm 145. Except that the author of the dictionary identified it as Psalm 1. He's explaining the language to us, and he himself doesn't know '*Ashrei*!'"

The plan came to Miriam as she was cutting pieces of cake and arranging them on a platter. As she served the dessert, she made some frantic hand signals to tell Binyamin to meet her in the kitchen, but he failed to interpret them correctly. Only when they were clearing up from the meal did she succeed in having a private conversation with her husband.

"I have it! The solution to everyone's problems."

"We'll put the Palestinians in charge of global nuclear disarmament," guessed Binyamin, "and this will keep them so busy that they won't have time to bother the Jews."

"Binyamin! Be serious."

"I find it difficult to imagine two subjects more serious than nuclear war and the Middle East situation, but let's hear what you have in mind."

"Elisha should move in with the Millmans."

"I think Michael said that they live on the third floor. Also, they've fallen behind in their rent and the landlord wants them to leave."

"No, I mean that the Millmans should move in with Elisha, in a divided apartment. Trudy can take care of the cooking, and Michael can help with the dressing and such."

This time Binyamin got it. "Brilliant idea, Miriam! You and I can think over the details and talk to the Millmans about it immediately after Shabbos. If they like the idea, then we'll call Aunt Toby and Elisha.

Aunt Toby and Elisha were sufficiently interested that they immediately wanted to speak with the Millmans. Leaving Miriam in Telz-Stone to baby-sit for the sleeping children of both families, Binyamin drove his friends into Yerushalayim. Michael and Trudy discussed the entire situation on the drive into town, and decided that the program he was on was still the best chance he had of getting a solid *parnassah* and being able to pay off their debts, so they would commit themselves for only two years. The five of them sat around one of the glass-topped tables in the hotel lobby, as they tried to hammer out details of a fair arrangement.

"What do we do when I get engaged?" asked Elisha. "I think we should guarantee the Millmans some sort of safety net, maybe pay their rent elsewhere for half a year, until they can get settled in some other fashion."

"I'm more concerned," his mother said, "about what happens at the end of two years. Do we bring Elisha home when we return to the States?"

Elisha made a face.

"I think we could find some other family in a situation similar to our own who would be interested in taking our place," Michael said.

"What I think we should do," Mrs. Sheinfeld said at the end of the discussion, "is that Trudy and I should go house-hunting tomorrow. I think we'd rather buy than rent. Having been through this already in my own home, I know that Elisha's life will be much easier if we make various changes that no sane landlord would agree to. In Elisha's apartment, for example, we'll want one large room with as much as possible attached to the walls. We'll have to extend our stay for another week or two. Then we'll go back until we take possession of the house and the contractors have made the necessary alterations for wheelchair access."

Elisha's eyes widened in shock. "You're serious, Mom? You're really going to make your peace with my living in Israel?"

Mrs. Sheinfeld looked at him with asperity. "Elisha, though it apparently wasn't obvious to you, I am perfectly aware that you're twenty-five years old and can make your own decisions. I didn't think you were being realistic about the difficulties and dangers. Now that we have a satisfactory arrangement, where you'll be living with people I know and trust, I'm willing to go along with it. Obviously, I'll have to talk this all over with your father once I can call America, but I imagine that he'll agree."

"Are you planning to come as an immigrant?" asked Michael, turning to Elisha.

"Of course," answered Elisha.

"Well, I think taxes and everything on buying the house will be much lower if you're already an immigrant when you buy it."

"On the other hand, don't I get more help with moving if I apply in America?" countered Elisha.

"We could go down to the Absorption Ministry and inquire, while the ladies are looking at apartments," suggested Michael.

"Whoa!" objected Trudy. "I remind you that we have two children, and one of us has to be free to watch them."

"Let me call Miriam," said Binyamin. "You're obviously staying over at our house tonight anyway, and I think she only has three children in her family-care center at the moment. Maybe she can absorb your two as well for one morning."

Miriam, who was thrilled to hear that her proposal was working out, agreed immediately. "It's probably something like a *shidduch;* you have to keep up the momentum. I think it's a wonderful idea that Michael and Elisha should tackle the bureaucracy together. That's the sort of thing that a Philippine foreign worker wouldn't have been able to help him with at all."

As Binyamin returned with his news, Elisha was just saying, "Who knows? If I do find a *shidduch* quickly, maybe my friend Danny will want to take my place. I'd love to have him come."

"Who is Danny?" asked Michael. "Your *chavrusa?*"

"Yes," said Elisha with a smile, "and also my partner in paraplegic basketball."

The car labored up the hill as it approached Yerushalayim. Miriam loved the moment when they came around a bend and the city stretched out in front of her, gleaming white in the late afternoon sun. When they stopped at a red light at the entrance to the city, she checked the three children to see if they were all right. Shimmy was looking out the window, and Itzik was asleep in the car seat. Only Tami looked as if she might be getting queasy.

"Here's Yerushalayim, right in front of us," she said to distract her daughter. "Soon we'll be at Aunt Toby's hotel and you'll all see her. Now, who remembers who Aunt Toby is?"

"Savta's sister," said Shimmy. "Why didn't Savta come too?"

"Because Saba is sick and she has to take care of him." This was all ground that they had been over several times. "Who else is here with Aunt Toby?"

"'Lisha," contributed Tami.

"Right, very good. And who is Elisha?"

"Abba's cousin," said Shimmy.

"And what is special about Elisha?"

"He has a chair with wheels," said Shimmy. Shimmy had a passion for anything on wheels.

"And you're not going to ask him for a ride, right?"

"Right," agreed Shimmy with resignation.

"Nor stare?"

"Nope," said Shimmy, shaking his head in a vigorous assertion of innocence.

Miriam somehow managed to negotiate the complicated traffic

patterns around the central bus station and could see Aunt Toby's hotel looming in front of her. She parked in the lot, unstrapped the children, and took out Itzik's stroller. Then she led her little convoy toward the lobby. Elisha was already waiting for them. "Mom will be down in a moment," he said.

Shimmy was looking down at the floor, taking occasionally quick sidewise glances at the fascinating chair with all the wheels.

"And you must be Shimmy. You've gotten very big," Elisha said, wheeling himself closer. "Do you suppose that you're as tall as my chair already?"

"I'm in *cheder*," said Shimmy proudly, looking up at his interlocutor.

"Would you like me to give you a ride around the hotel?"

Shimmy turned on his mother a glance of intense pleading. "Okay," she said indulgently.

"Me too, me too!" importuned Tami.

Elisha nodded. "One at a time." He reached down and lifted Shimmy up into his lap.

Aunt Toby arrived just as they were setting out. "Elisha, meet us in the room. I have to give Mimi the clothes her mother-in-law sent for the children." She pushed Itzik's stroller while Miriam took Tami by the hand.

As she was unpacking the suitcase filled with adorable outfits, Toby switched to a more serious tone. "Mimi, I'm hoping that you will be able to help me organize this project of looking for a *shidduch* for Elisha." She gave a brief rundown of the sorts of difficulties they had encountered so far.

"How can I help?" asked Miriam. "I have no experience with investigating girls."

"I simply don't know the seminaries in Yerushalayim. I would appreciate it if you'd ask around among your friends, and maybe find me the phone numbers of those that seem most appropriate."

"Are you planning to do this from the States?" asked Miriam.

"I'm hoping to come in the summer."

"A lot of the American girls will be home then," Miriam pointed out. She had been arranging the clothing into neat piles all over the bed, in order of size.

"Let me give you two bags for packing those up," Toby pulled two heavy shopping bags with handles out of her hand luggage and they began to bag the piles of clothing. Elisha and Shimmy came in.

"We came in the elevator and I pushed the button," Shimmy announced.

Tami sidled up to the chair, waiting for her turn to take a ride. Shimmy slid down and Elisha picked up Tami in his place.

"We're finished here," said his mother. "Why don't we all ride down together in the elevator. Mimi and I can say our good-byes as you give Tami her turn around the lobby."

While Elisha and Tami were taking their ride, with Shimmy walking alongside to "push" in a way that surely must have made it difficult to steer, Aunt Toby turned to Miriam and said, "Do you think you can get back to me with those phone numbers in a couple of weeks?"

"I'll try. Aunt Toby, I thought one of Elisha's main reasons for coming was to look for a *shidduch*. Why do you only discuss it when he is out of earshot?"

"I don't like him to know just how much *hishtadlus* we put into this. I'm afraid it would be discouraging."

Miriam looked down at her list, with all her notations penned in the margin. For a while she had actually been using "NA" both for "No answer" and "Not appropriate," but she had caught herself quickly and had managed to sort those out and label them correctly. She had two more seminaries to check out. She was beginning to understand why Aunt Toby wanted to shield Elisha from some of the dreary parts of this project.

"Hello, could I speak to the housemother, please?" She explained, as she had several times before, that a relative was looking for a *shidduch* for her disabled son, a personable and successful *yeshivah bachur*. Toby had instructed her to hang up politely if she noticed icicles forming on the telephone receiver as soon as she mentioned the word "disabled." If the person on the other end remained cordial, then she could go into more detail. Miriam had already encountered a few of the "icicle" reactions, and agreed with Aunt Toby that they weren't likely to be helpful.

This time there was a pause on the other end. "What sort of disability?" the housemother asked.

"He was wounded in a terrorist attack. He is confined to a

wheelchair," Miriam explained.

"How old is he?" she asked.

"Twenty-five."

"We might have someone to suggest, one of our second-year girls. She was born with one arm missing from the elbow. She wears an artificial hand."

This didn't sound like a very serious disability. Miriam decided to probe a bit farther. "Do you think she would be willing to meet our cousin?"

"It could be," said the housemother cautiously. "She's been looking for a match all year, and hasn't found anything yet."

"And her family background?"

"Well, her mother was divorced, but she remarried to a *ba'al teshuvah,* and raised a wonderful family. Bitya had a complete Bais Yaakov education."

"The mother became *frum* after the divorce?"

"Yes."

"And her natural father, is he Jewish?"

"No."

Now it added up. "Okay, I'll pass the idea on to my husband's aunt. If she's interested, she'll contact you for more details."

After the Sheinfelds returned to the States, the Lerners returned to their ordinary routine.

Miriam had just given over the last of her day care charges to a tired mother when the doorbell rang again. Who was likely to be visiting her at this time of day? She opened the door to find Rivka Weissman, Mitch's wife, waiting on the step.

After Miriam gave her a tour of the house, they sat in the kitchen over a cup of coffee, swapping stories about culture shock. "We came on *aliyah* in '69, during the War of Attrition," Rivka told her. "In *ulpan* we were practicing reading the newspaper, which was full of terrorists, shellings, and border incidents. At that time, milk came in bottles instead of bags, and there was still a milkman making deliveries in Ramat Gan.

"One morning I left a note that I needed ten bottles of milk. When I heard the clink of the bottles, I opened the door in my housecoat to bring them in. He had apparently decided that I didn't deserve ten, and had left only five.

"Now believe me, I am not the sort of person who shouts off balconies, but I had four small children, and five bottles of milk was just not enough. I couldn't run after him because I wasn't dressed. Feeling that I had no choice, I went out to the balcony and shouted after him, '*Chablan! CHABLAN!'*

"All up and down the street, windows were raised and women ran out onto balconies. Seeing that I was the woman shouting, they called to me, 'Where? Where?'

"Not yet realizing that there was something wrong, I pointed to the harmless old man with his horse and wagon and said, 'There!'

"The ruckus continued to spread, until a young schoolboy came into the yard and said, 'Lady, a milkman is not a *chablan*, he is a *chalban*.'

"When I realized that I had just accused this poor man of being a terrorist, I went indoors, closing the curtains and shutters after me, to be alone with my mortification."

Miriam shuddered. "I hope nothing quite so awful ever happens to me. I would shrivel up on the spot."

"From what you tell me, you seem to be over the last of three hurdles," said Rivka, as she nibbled one of Miriam's cookies.

"You make it sound like an obstacle course," observed Miriam.

"There was a whole burst of *aliyah* from America after the Six Day War, when we came. Personally, we never had a moment when we considered going back, but we knew many people who did, and I kept tabs of why. The first obstacle was just surviving the hassle of the first year: dealing with the bureaucracy, finding a place to live, choosing suitable schools for all the children, and so forth. The second stage involved finding a job or jobs, and in particular, the husband finding a job at which he felt he was needed and appreciated."

Miriam nodded. Each of those had been its own struggle and they had gotten through them. "And the third obstacle?"

"The people who gave up at the third stage were the most frustrating cases, because it really seemed unnecessary. It was a matter of social adjustment. For one reason or another, they had bought an apartment in a community where they had little in common with their neighbors. They didn't feel at home, failed to strike roots, whatever you want to call it, and decided to go back to America. Often there was a nice community only a few miles away where they would have been perfectly comfortable."

"That's certainly not my problem. I've made oodles of friends since I came here. I even have a part in the Chanukah skit, and I never used to act in school plays back in Boro Park. I think I'm better adjusted here than I ever was in America."

"I'm very glad to hear it," said Rivka. "Just as the second problem is usually one for the husband, this third one is usually a problem for the wife."

"You sound as if you're working for the Jewish Agency," teased Miriam, "trying to keep other immigrants moving along in the right direction."

After Rivka left, Miriam was thoughtful as she straightened up the house. Something in Rivka's analysis bothered her. Was she haunted by Trudy and Michael, who in some sense had never made it over the first hurdle, much less the second?

She was still mulling it over when Binyamin arrived home from work. He dropped his briefcase and laptop in the front hall and sank down wearily on the couch.

"Tough day?" asked Miriam sympathetically. He'd been having a lot of those recently.

Binyamin nodded. "Another flare-up with Rami. Both of us said things that would have been better left unsaid. How was your day?"

"Oh, fine. I managed to get all my charges safely to the park and back, except for one scraped knee. Also," she hesitated for such a short time that it was barely noticeable, "Rivka Weissman dropped by for a house-warming visit." She paused.

"That was nice of her," said Binyamin, glancing at her for the first time since he came in, "but why do you look as if you have some dark secret?"

Miriam giggled a little nervously. "You think we were conspiring against the Palestinian Authority or some such?"

"I have no idea what you were talking about, but of course if you don't want to tell me, you don't have to."

That was it, of course. She did not want to tell Binyamin about her conversation with Rivka, but why not?

At this point Shimmy walked out of the bedroom, discovered that his father was home, and squealed for Tami. Soon Binyamin's attention was entirely absorbed in playing with the children and hearing about their day. Miriam escaped to the kitchen to put supper on the table.

It was Friday afternoon as she was preparing for Shabbos that Miriam finally got the whole thing worked out in her mind. The problem, of course, was that she had adjusted socially, but Binyamin had not. She spent most of her time in a community where she had many friends of similar backgrounds, whereas Binyamin spent half his waking hours among people of very different backgrounds. Even when he came back to their own community he didn't have a strong sense of belonging. Ever since the class he used to give in Mevasseret had petered out with the phasing out of the immigrants' hostel, he had had a feeling of being superfluous.

She hadn't wanted to report the conversation with Rivka, because she hadn't wanted Binyamin to ask himself whether he had adjusted socially. They both continued to behave according to the decision they had made after Binyamin returned from the States last year: barring major crises, they would assume that they were staying. She didn't want to mention that some people found poor social adjustment reason enough to go back. She did not want to return to America, but now she was not so sure about Binyamin.

Chapter 26

Hungry Flames

T oday was the first day of summer vacation, and the family-care center had emptied out, as teenagers set up informal day camps or were drafted as baby-sitters. Tami, who had graduated to a regular *gan* at Pesach, would be home with her mother for the summer. She had enjoyed the relaxed atmosphere all morning, but by 11:30 she was starting to get bored, with no one to play with except Itzik and little Beila Landesman.

At noon, Terry called. "Malka and Chaya are going swimming this afternoon, and they're taking Yocheved with them, but they think she would have a better time if another little girl came along. My girls will take turns watching the little ones in the wading pool. Would your Tami enjoy that?"

"That would be terrific!" exclaimed Miriam. Yocheved, who was born with Down's syndrome, had been enrolled in the family-care center until today. She and Tami had always gotten along well together.

"It's really sweet of you to offer to take Tami," said Miriam to Malka and Chaya, when they arrived with Yocheved. She handed them the bag in which she had packed Tami's swimsuit, tube, and towel.

"It's really no trouble," said Malka, "and I'm sure it will make the trip more fun for Yocheved."

Miriam stroked Yocheved's hair and said, "I missed you today. I hope you have a nice time with Malka and Chaya."

"Why Mommy not coming?" asked Tami.

"I'd love to, sweetie, but I have to stay home with Shimmy and Itzik. Boys aren't allowed in the swimming pool during the ladies' hours. Another time, maybe I'll get a baby-sitter for the boys and come myself. I haven't been to a pool for ages."

When her neighbor brought Shimmy home, she fed him a quick lunch and put him down for a nap. Shoshy's toddler was the only child in her family-care center during the summer, and her father would come at 1:30 to pick her up. Miriam was almost sorry that she hadn't arranged a baby-sitter so that she could also go to the pool. The day was terribly hot, with a dry wind blowing in from the west, and a cool swim would have been very refreshing. She had just done a load of sheets and went to hang them out on the line. With a wind like this they'd be dry in an hour.

When Shoshy's husband came by for his child, he asked, "Have you heard about the fire?"

"What fire?"

"A forest fire that started out near She'ar HaGai, on the south side of the highway."

Miriam was instantly alert. "How big is it? Have they put it out yet?" That hot wind from the west no longer seemed so benign.

"The firefighters haven't managed to get it under control, and it appears that they're evacuating Shoresh."

Miriam's eyes widened and she gave a gasp of panic. "Oh, no!"

"I don't think you should be all that worried personally," said Mr. Landesman. "The highway is an excellent fire-break, and we're on the north side."

"You don't understand! Some friends took my daughter Tami swimming at the pool in Beit Meir, and that's on the south side, right after Shoresh!"

"That is alarming!" agreed Mr. Landesman. "I hope Beit Meir will be evacuated in time if the fire can't be controlled. I'll get out of your way in case there's something you can do."

Miriam closed the door after Mr. Landesman and tried to think. What could she do? She could call Binyamin, but that wouldn't do much good. He had gone by car-pool this morning and left her the car. If Beit Meir were evacuated, and the children were still at the pool, they would be evacuated with everyone else. But suppose they had already left and were standing at an exposed bus stop waiting for a bus that wasn't going to come?

She must try to go get them. Perhaps the highway would be closed, but at least she could tell the drivers of the emergency vehicles to look out for them. The next question was harder. Should she take the children with her or leave them with a neighbor, risking the possibility of an extended separation if she got stuck somewhere? Her panic at being separated from Tami pushed her toward taking them along, and that's what she decided to do.

She threw snacks and drinks and extra diapers into a bag and went to wake up Shimmy, whom she had just put down for a nap. She had been planning to take a nap herself, but it didn't look as if this would be an afternoon for relaxing. She scribbled a note for Binyamin and left it on the kitchen table. As soon as she walked out the door, with Shimmy's hand clutched in hers and the baby on one hip, she smelled the smoke.

As they climbed the steps to the road, she looked over her shoulder. The hillside on the other side of the valley was barely visible through the haze. Shimmy was rubbing his eyes with his fist, and hers were also beginning to sting. In order to get as little smoke as possible into the car, she pulled both children into the driver's seat with her and shut the door quickly. Then she plopped them into their car seats in the back, and bent over the back of the front seat to fasten the straps. She adjusted the air conditioning not to let in outside air.

Only as she was driving around the end of Telz-Stone, at a point where the huge pillar of smoke was already visible in the west, did she remember that she had called neither Binyamin nor Terry.

"Is this bus never going to come?" complained Chaya, kicking at a stone.

"You know what?" said Malka, looking down the highway in the direction from which the bus should come from Beit Shemesh, "I don't think it is. I haven't seen any cars at all coming from that direction. Maybe there was a traffic accident or something, and the road is blocked."

"I'm hot," complained Yocheved.

"I thirsty," said Tami plaintively.

"I think we should walk home," said Malka. "It's not that far. We've done it before."

"Not with two babies," objected Chaya.

"I not baby," asserted Tami.

"Of course not," said Malka. "You're a good, brave girl, and we're going to walk home together." She leaned over and whispered to Chaya. "If we have to, we'll carry them. It's better than broiling here in the sun."

The older girls slung the bags with their swim suits and towels over their shoulders, and each took one of the little girls by the hand. Together they set off along the gravel shoulder of the highway in the direction of Telz-Stone.

When they had been trudging along for fifteen minutes, Malka noticed that her eyes were stinging. She gave a quick glance over her shoulder, and it seemed that the air was a little hazy. She sniffed the hot wind and didn't like what she smelled. Had she made a mistake in having them set off on foot?

Binyamin was sitting at his desk, poring over a printout of the source file for his latest program. He had been taught that it was a good idea just to read the program occasionally. Here and there he made notations in red where a sequence of code seemed awkward, and at one point he noticed a bug.

Rami came bursting into his office. "Have you heard about the fire?"

"What fire?" asked Binyamin, looking up from his work. Would they have to evacuate the building?

"The fire in the Yerushalayim corridor. Don't you live around there somewhere?" Rami's concern sounded genuine.

Mitch came in through the door and stood next to Rami. "Binyamin, have you heard? They've evacuated Shoresh, and the fire is still moving east. Apparently there's a very strong wind pushing it."

A forest fire! And it was already east of Shoresh. Of course, Shoresh was on the south side of the road and Telz-Stone on the north. "Is it on both sides of the highway?" Binyamin asked. What sounded like a matter-of-fact request for information in fact covered a rising panic.

"You live on the north side, don't you? So far, the fire is south of the highway, and they hope that it won't be able to cross such a wide-open space. If you want to take the rest of the afternoon off to go take care of your family, you can have it."

"Let me call home first and see what the situation is." Binyamin dialed while the other men looked on tensely. For ring after long ring there was no answer at all. He glanced up at his coworkers. "No answer. She should be home at this time. Was anything said about evacuating Telz-Stone?"

"Let's go hear the latest bulletin."

"... Fire fighting units have been brought in from all over the area. The main highway to Yerushalayim has been closed off. Siryug helicopters are being used to spray water at the flames, but so far nothing has halted their advance. The evacuation of Shoresh is complete, and the residents of Beit Meir are now being evacuated."

Rami extended his hand. "Do you want to borrow my *pelephone,* so you can keep trying to reach your wife as you drive?" This was a very generous offer. Rami was quite possessive of his new cellular telephone.

"Thank you, I think I will. Unfortunately, I came by carpool this morning, so I'll have to get home by bus, and I don't think the public transportation system will be moving well." Maybe he should take a taxi to the highway and try to hitch a ride to Yerushalayim? He had always heard that in times of emergency, people were generous about offering each other rides.

Mitch looked unhappy. "I also came by bus this morning, so that my wife could have the car. Otherwise, I would lend you mine."

"I'll do it," said Rami to Mitch.

"Do what?" asked his boss.

"Drive him home. That is, if you'll let me off too." Apparently it was true. In times of emergency, people were generous about offering each other rides. This was a lot more than just giving a hitch. Rami lived in the Tel Aviv area.

"Of course, of course. Go, both of you." Mitch made a shooing motion with his hands. Rami went to get his briefcase. Binyamin just turned off his computer, put his small *Gemara* in his pocket and left everything on his desk. He wasn't even sure he would have a place to sleep tonight. He didn't need to take work home.

"This is really generous of you," Binyamin said to Rami, after they had gotten settled in the car and started on their journey.

"It's what I would want someone to do for me if I were in the same situation," said Rami simply.

Every few minutes Binyamin dialed home on Rami's *pelephone*, but there was never an answer. Rami turned off the main highway at Modi'in and set off along the road that entered Yerushalayim from the north. There was only one lane of traffic in either direction, acting as a detour for a three-lane highway, and cars crawled along. Binyamin was so impatient that he was ready to explode.

Miriam, too, was ready to erupt, and she wasn't the only one. Normal traffic to Tel-Aviv had been turned back or had taken a detour. All the cars lined up at the police barrier belonged to people who had family members in the path of the oncoming fire, and who were trying to get past to pick them up. An increasingly hot wind was blowing, and the smoke kept getting thicker.

The police officer in charge was bellowing through a bullhorn. "All traffic should turn back. Leave the road clear for emergency vehicles. The inhabitants of all the communities along the road are being evacuated. You can rejoin them in the city."

"How will we find them?" shouted one angry father in frustration.

"Where are you taking them?" asked another.

"The evacuees are being taken to Teddy Kollek Stadium in south Yerushalayim," shouted the policeman through his bullhorn.

Miriam pulled her car off to the side of the road, told the children to wait quietly, and walked the short remaining distance to the police barricade. "Could you please call the people in charge of evacuating Beit Meir and tell them to look out for two teenage girls with two small children? They were at the pool there, and may be overlooked in a house-to-house evacuation."

"I don't have direct contact with the crew in Beit Meir, but I can report them missing. A bulletin will be broadcast to everyone working there." That would have to do. He obviously wasn't going to let anyone past the barrier, and she could think of nothing else to do right now except follow instructions. She walked back to the children.

Miriam pulled her car out of line and turned back. She would go check with Terry, to see if the girls had gotten home somehow. If not, she would try to go to the stadium. The traffic was moving at a crawl because of all the cars traveling away from the fire. Miriam reached over and opened the glove compartment. When the traffic slowed even more, Miriam ventured a glance in that direction and saw a *Tehillim*. Once she had done everything she could think of to help Tami, she would say *Tehillim* for her daughter and all the others in the path of the flames.

"I tired," complained Tami. She was dragging her feet and pulling on Chaya's hand.

Malka cast a worried look over her shoulder. The smoke was getting thicker and thicker. She had long since realized that the traffic had stopped because of a forest fire, but she hadn't shared her knowledge with the other girls. She looked over at Chaya and saw the fear in her eyes. So Chaya had guessed, too. "Chaya, you pick up Tami and I'll carry Yocheved. We need to get out into the open." It couldn't be that far now to the point where the valley opened and the forest no longer grew right up to the road.

"Look!" shouted Yocheved, pointing ahead of them. Two fire trucks were screaming toward them, red lights flashing.

Desperately, Malka began waving. Chaya followed her lead, and even the two little girls waved their hands. Even if the trucks wouldn't stop, they might tell someone about the girls.

The fire trucks raced past without slowing, as did the car with flashing lights that sped after them. The girls were gazing back after the trucks in disappointment when they heard a screech of brakes. A second car came to a stop on the other side of the road and a man sprinted across the highway toward them. Malka felt a rising sense of panic. Had it been a mistake to attract attention?

"Quick, girls, follow me!" He took Tami from Chaya and started back at a run for his own car. Chaya and Malka, who was carrying Yocheved, did their best to keep up. The two little girls were whimpering. The man loaded them all into the car, and slammed the doors shut. The air was a little more breathable inside.

"Where are you taking us?" asked Malka breathlessly.

"There's a fire truck with a broken pump being pulled out for repairs. If we get there in time, I can put you four onto it."

"You hear that, Yocheved?" asked Malka in a tone of forced heartiness. "We might get to ride on a real fire engine. Won't that be interesting?"

"Wanna go home," insisted Yocheved.

The man put the car in gear and gunned the motor. The car zoomed westward toward the advancing front of the fire. When they came to a clear spot in the road that afforded a hazy view of the mountain ahead, Malka saw flickering tongues of flame.

At the entrance to the city, the traffic was barely crawling. Rami listened to the latest bulletin: "Contrary to the expectations of the firefighters, the fire has crossed the highway to the north side, and is moving up to Neve Ilan. The inhabitants of Telz-Stone will be evacuated as soon as transportation can be made available."

"That's where you live, isn't it?" asked Rami.

"It sure is," said Binyamin grimly.

They heard a description of the destruction in Shoresh, where more than thirty homes had been burned completely, while another thirty remained almost unharmed. In some part of the forest, the destruction was total, while in others, the fire skipped from tree to tree or from bush to bush and leaving some of the vegetation unharmed.

Rami's car finally reached the main road into Yerushalayim and swung out onto the highway. Since most people knew it was blocked, there was little traffic, and they began to make good time once again. Soon they were laboring up the long hill near Mevasseret.

"Rami, I really appreciate what you're doing for me. I know relations between us haven't been that hot, and quite frankly, I wouldn't have expected this help. Neve Ilan is pretty close to Telz-Stone, and if the fire reached there already, there may even be a certain amount of danger in going on."

Rami dismissed that idea with a brief wave of his hand. "I'm a tank driver in the army," he said.

They pulled off the highway at the entrance to Abu Ghosh. A steady stream of cars drove past them toward the overpass leading to Yerushalayim. Walking down the middle of the road was a group of yeshivah boys in Chassidic garb. Each boy carried in his arms a bundle wrapped in a *tallis*.

"What are they doing?" asked Rami, perplexed. "Why aren't they in buses or cars like everyone else?"

"Those are boys from the Belz yeshivah. They are evacuating the Torah scrolls, and I suppose their rabbis thought it would be more of an honor to the Torah to rescue them on foot."

Rami glanced once more at the small black-and-white group among the multicolored cars. He said, "You know, I have friends who would have gotten angry just to see them."

"Angry? Why angry?" asked Binyamin, puzzled. He twisted around in his seat for one last glimpse of the small procession.

"Because they dress differently. Because they're walking when everyone else is riding. Because they belong to a world that is threatening our normal world."

Binyamin was silent. He was afraid anything he said might draw a yet stronger reaction.

"You and I have fought a lot about these things over the last year. You know that I'm no particular friend of religion. Still, much as I can imagine my friends' rage, I don't feel it myself."

This sounded a bit more promising, and Binyamin dared an answer. "Why not?"

"Because I think they—and you—are doing something for the rest of us, something we're not always quick enough to acknowledge. Our claim to be here in this land—to be here as Jews speaking Hebrew—is stronger because of you. The tradition you keep alive is our living link to the days when we first controlled this land."

To Binyamin's mind that claim lost a lot of its validity because of Rami's insistence on leaving G-d out of the matter, but he didn't interrupt.

"You wouldn't know about this, but about ten years ago a newspaperman wrote an article called, 'I Have No Sister.' A leftist, mostly Ashkenazi demonstration had encountered heckling and violence from a rightist crowd, mostly Sefardim. He wrote that he no longer felt a sense of kinship with the Sefardim, that the attitude of patronizing pity with which he had been force-fed was being replaced by anger and hatred."

"I doubt that the Sefardim would consider the patronizing pity to have been much preferable," said Binyamin, but realized as he said it that it had been off the subject.

Rami shrugged. "Be that as it may, I've often wondered that about myself and the *dati'im*. They get me so aggravated at times that I haven't been sure that I still felt a sense of kinship with them—with you. Today—today I see that I do. I guess if I'd be a writer my article would be titled, 'I Have a Brother.'"

Binyamin offered his hand and Rami shook on the deal. "Thanks, Rami. I need a brother today, and I left all of mine behind in America."

"Happy to be of service. Tell me what to do now."

They had reached the entrance to Telz-Stone. Binyamin directed him to the house and hopped out. The family car was not parked in the usual spot. "I'll be back as soon as I can." He raced down the steps. He didn't expect to find his family there, but he did hope to discover where they had gone. He pulled out his key and fumbled trying to get it into the lock. "Steady. You need a cool head," he told himself.

He got the door opened, and looked around. There was no evidence that Miriam had made a hasty departure. Everything was in place. Binyamin took Miriam's jewel box from her drawer and his strong box with the deed to the house and a few other valuables. He went to the kitchen to get a bag for the items he was taking and saw the note on the kitchen table.

"Dear Binyamin, I have gone with the children to Beit Meir to get Tami."

Beit Meir! Tami! He glanced out the window at the smoke wafting past from the west. What was Tami doing in Beit Meir?

Binyamin went to the refrigerator and grabbed something to drink, some fruit, and a bag of cookies, which he stuffed into the extra bag. He stopped at the door and took one last look at the house. The next time he walked through this door the house might be an empty shell, with all the furniture reduced to ashes. At the fuse box in the front hall he paused. Finally, he threw all of the switches except the one providing electricity to the fridge and freezer.

Rami was waiting where Binyamin had left him. The atmosphere in the street was one of confusion and distress. Those who didn't have their own cars were carrying bundles out to the street, waiting to be evacuated. Mothers were running around looking for children, and children for parents.

Binyamin climbed in and handed the bag of food to Rami. "Here, I brought this. My wife left a note that she went to Beit Meir to look for our three-year-old daughter."

"Beit Meir? Why there of all places?"

"That's what I can't figure out."

Rami pulled out of the main gate of Telz-Stone, but where all the other cars turned right toward Abu Ghosh and Yerushalayim, Rami turned left toward Neve Ilan and Tel Aviv. He turned, in short, straight toward the fire.

"I doubt the road is open," said Binyamin. "Remember that my wife left before the fire had gotten so close."

"We'll feel better if we tried, won't we?" asked Rami.

The car snaked along the winding access road, once the main road to Yerushalayim. They came around the last bend and ran directly into the fire! It had leaped over the asphalt and was now burning on both sides of the road. On their right they could see it stretching back to the hills in the west. To their left, on the Telz-Stone side, it was burning the grass as it raced up the hill toward the first row of houses on the brow of the hill. Rami slammed on his brakes and Binyamin shouted, "Turn back, Rami, turn back!" Rami made a sharp U-turn, and soon they were part of the caravan of cars snaking slowly through Abu Ghosh on its way to safety in Yerushalayim.

"How many do you have?" Rami asked.

"How many what?"

"How many brothers?"

"Three brothers and three sisters, *bli ayin hara.*"

"And your wife?"

"Two sisters and four brothers."

"You know that that is one of the reasons we feel threatened. I'm an only child. Most of my friends have at most one sibling."

"It all depends on that first question, whether we are your brothers or not. We think we are, and we think we are helping you by having large families. After all, the Arabs have big families too, and this is a democratic state."

"We agreed that we are brothers, but ... it's hard to imagine what this state will look like in fifty years."

"G-d willing that we should get that far."

When they reached the overpass, there was a woman standing and asking passersby if they knew where the women of the convalescent home for new mothers had been taken. She had gone into Yerushalayim in the middle of the day, leaving her baby with the nurses in the home, and now she was desperately trying to locate her newborn.

Binyamin rolled down his window. "Do you know where the other people went?" he asked.

"Most of the people were evacuated to Teddy Kollek Stadium in Talpiot," she told him.

"All right, let's give it a try," said Rami.

The media were interviewing two boys who had taken a familiar back trail to get near the excitement and were caught by the fire. "The grass was burning under our bike tires." They had made it out to the highway and pedaled in panic all the way to Yerushalayim.

Using Rami's cellphone, Binyamin spent the trip contacting friends from their former neighborhood, in the hope that one of them had taken Miriam in, but she hadn't been in touch with any of them. They threaded their way once more through the traffic jam at the entrance to the city and then headed south. When they got to the stadium, Binyamin suggested that they cruise through the parking lot.

"There it is!" shouted Binyamin in triumph. He pointed to their car, parked not far from the entrance to the stadium. "Okay, you can let me out. Thanks for everything, Rami."

"Call me later and let me know if your wife found the little girl," Rami said.

"I will," promised Binyamin. "Give me the number."

"Take this," said Rami, handing back the bag of food. "Your kids are probably starving."

They shook hands again and then Binyamin set off at a run for the entrance to the stadium. Once inside the walls, he began scanning the bleachers in search of his family. He found them sitting with a group of friends and neighbors. As far as he could tell, Tami was not with them. They hadn't noticed his arrival; after all, they weren't expecting him to appear. As he drew closer, he saw that Miriam was cradling the baby, and Shimmy was leaning against her. Both looked tired and dejected.

"Abba!" called Shimmy, when Binyamin had almost reached them.

"Binyamin!" Miriam breathed with relief. "How did you get

here?"

They spent the next half hour filling each other in on their adventures, while Shimmy munched his way through most of the cookies. The stadium was awash with rumors about the progress of the fire, and Binyamin's report that he had seen it advancing up the hill toward Telz-Stone's houses passed from huddled group to huddled group. Miriam expanded on her attempts to locate Tami.

"The police reported that one of the emergency vehicles picked up a group of girls on the main highway," Miriam explained, "but no one seems to be able to tell us where they were taken and whether or not it was really our group. Terry and I take turns calling the police every fifteen minutes."

"Miriam, look over there!" That was Terry, seated slightly below them, pointing to the main entrance. A tall policeman had stalked through, followed by two teenage girls, each holding a small child by the hand. The two families began waving frantically. Malka and Chaya scooped up Yocheved and Tami and sprinted across the grass toward their parents.

At dusk, the wind changed and started blowing away from Yerushalayim. The fire stopped short of the houses of Telz-Stone. It advanced up to the clothesline of one of the first of the houses, and scorched the hem of a child's dress hanging out to dry. That was the only direct fire damage that the community sustained.

Late in the evening, tired, hungry and thirsty, the reunited Lerner family turned the lock on their own front door. Binyamin switched on the electricity, and they tumbled the children into their beds without doing more than taking off their shoes. Binyamin and Miriam sat down at the kitchen table for a cup of coffee and a belated supper.

"You know," said Binyamin, "it's possible to be too self-reliant and independent. You could have called me for help."

"If you had had an obvious way to get here, I would have. Anyway, next time ..."

"Let's hope there won't be a 'next time.'" He looked around at the familiar walls and furnishings. "I feel as if I just moved in."

"What do you mean?"

"Well, when we bought the place, my head was elsewhere. I was worried about my father, I had problems at work and my *shiur* was floundering. Somehow I never felt that 'click' into place that usually comes with buying a house and moving into a new community.

"Today, when I heard that the fire had crossed the road, my main fear was for my family, but somewhere underneath I also understood what I had to lose if the house and the community were destroyed. It was those hours of fear that really made it mine." He stretched and finished off his coffee. "There is a nursery near work. I think that tomorrow I'll stop off on the way home and buy that fig tree that I used to dream of."

Chapter 27

Homecoming

Miriam Lerner was on her way back to New York for her brother Reuven's wedding to her young friend, Sarah Dina.

Miriam would have liked to stretch her cramped muscles, but there was no way to do so. Tami was asleep in the seat on her right, with her head in Miriam's lap. Shimmy was asleep on her left, his head against her shoulder. Itzik was in the basket hung from the bulkhead in front of her. He was definitely not asleep, but she was resisting picking him up.

She checked her watch. They were due to arrive in New York in a little under an hour. She would have to wake them up to get them ready for landing, but she was putting it off as long as possible. It had taken so very long to get them to sleep.

Traveling with three children, without Binyamin, had made it a grueling trip, but she had agreed that he had fallen too far behind in his vacation days to be able to afford another trip right now. Reuven would just have to get married without him.

The lights came on, the pilot announced that they were beginning to descend, and everyone began bustling about. Her ears were hurting from the change in pressure, and she hoped that the children were not too uncomfortable. Miriam felt her sense of anticipation growing. Binyamin had been back twice to visit his father, but this was her first trip to America since they had moved to Israel two years ago.

The plane banked to the right, and Miriam looked across the aisle, toward the window. Now that they were at an angle, she could see the bright lights of the city sprawling below, the city that had been her home for most of her life. "Shimmy! Tami! Wake up! We're almost home!"

Shimmy rubbed his eyes groggily and asked, "Telz-Stone?"

"No, Shimmy, Brooklyn."

"That not home," objected Tami.

"For Bubby and Zeidy it is. It's the only home they've got."

Miriam pushed the baby's stroller back and forth. Of course, the baby couldn't get to sleep with those loudspeakers boom-booming at full volume. She would gladly have left him at home in her parents' house with a baby-sitter, but there were too many people here at the wedding tonight who would have no other opportunity to see him.

"*Mazal tov*!" There was Ella, looking much more vivacious than she had the last time Miriam had seen her in the airport one year ago.

"Ella!" They embraced. "I didn't know if you would manage to come."

"I couldn't stay away. After all, Reuven was my brother for four years, wasn't he?"

That statement echoed in Miriam's head. What kind of a sister had she been to Ella for those four years? A pretty unwilling one. She pushed the thought away. "Come meet the *kallah*. I hope you will love her the way I do."

Sarah Dinah was being photographed with the two mothers and the women at the various tables. Miriam caught her in passing from one table to the next. "Sarah Dinah!" she said, twining her arm around Ella's waist and pulling her forward, "I want you to meet my good friend, Ella Wahrhaftig. She lived with us for four years while we were in high school."

"Oh, yes," enthused Sarah Dinah, flashing a brilliant smile, "Reuven has told me all about you. He told me you were a real big sister to him."

Miriam felt an all-too-familiar pinch of jealousy. She, Miriam, hadn't been a good enough big sister? For once, however, she tried to face the feeling squarely. Was it fair? It was Miriam's help that Reuven had wanted in finding a bride. It was Miriam's presence in Israel drawing him to Yerushalayim. How much of her resentment of Ella had simply been her own low self-image?

Miriam was taking a vacation. The *sheva brachos* tonight were being hosted by the *kallah's* relatives out on Long Island, and she felt that she could miss the affair. Leaving Tami and Shimmy with her mother-in-law, she had gone by train to visit Ella. It was a luxurious feeling, traveling with only an overnight bag and the baby.

"Next stop, Winston!" called out the conductor.

Miriam put down Itzik on the aisle seat, stood up, and began struggling to get her bag off the overhead rack.

"I'll get that for you, ma'am," said one of the other passengers. Miriam had gotten so used to being independent that she almost told him not to bother, but then her better judgment told her to accept the offered assistance gracefully. The helpful passenger actually carried the bag out to the platform at the end of the train, and the conductor handed it down for her. Ella was waiting for her outside on the platform with her own one-year-old. Each woman took a strap, and together they carried the overnight bag to the station wagon.

"How does it feel to drive again?" Miriam asked.

"The whole thing was a big nuisance," declared Ella. "I had let my license lapse while we were living in Israel. It took me a while to get up the gumption to get a learner's permit and take the test again, but eventually I got tired of being dependent on Chaim Ozer and my friends to chauffeur me around. You can't get anywhere in a place like this without a car."

The idea of Ella lacking the gumption for anything at all seemed strange to Miriam.

It was in the early afternoon, while the younger children were taking a nap and the older children were still in school, that they finally sat down to talk over a cup of coffee. "Of course, I grew up under the same system," Ella said, "but by now 8:00 to 4:30 seems like a terribly long school day. That's the price we pay here for having to teach them to read in two languages at once. If I had been involved in the decision making, I don't think I would have put Shloimi, who isn't even six, into first grade, but he was all psyched up to learn *Chumash*."

Again, the idea of Ella not being involved in the decision making did not seem to ring true to Miriam. This time Ella caught her puzzled glance and answered it.

"After the baby, I suffered from clinical depression. It was very severe and lasted for nearly three months. It took another six months until I shook off most of the after effects."

The pictures flashed in Miriam's mind unbidden. Ella lying, pale and wan, in her bed in the hospital. Ella sitting off to the side in the airport, clutching her newborn daughter. Miriam slamming down the receiver on their telephone. Miriam sat for a while in silence, stirring her coffee.

"Ella," she said at last, looking up at her hostess, "if that argument we had was a factor, I apologize once again."

"We've both apologized twice already. That's probably enough. There were plenty of other factors. I was already feeling low about leaving Yerushalayim. Finding out what we were really arguing about just gave me the last little push over the edge."

Ella reached over and put her hand on Miriam's. "People need space to make their own decisions, and, if necessary, their own mistakes. I had to learn that the hard way. It was much better to have you teach it to me now, than to have to learn it from one of my daughters-in-law in twenty years."

The baby had been put to sleep upstairs, and Miriam was sitting in the living room, admiring the stained-glass window and waiting for Ella's friends to arrive. Tonight was the organizational meeting for the Outreach Banquet in the fall, and Ella was chairwoman of the organizing committee.

"Bringgg." Miriam jumped up to answer the door. Standing on the doorstep was a woman wearing a nicely styled *sheitel*.

"Hello, you must be Miriam. I'm Devora Rothman."

"Pleased to meet you. Ella is upstairs putting the children to bed. You know how they can tell when you want them to fall asleep."

"I understand that you've taken Ella's place in Yerushalayim."

"I think that would be a task a little beyond me, but we are living there, and very happily."

"Well, we're glad to have her here. We have to stretch to cover all the jobs, and an addition like Ella is a big help."

"Bringg." Miriam opened the door again. This time it was a younger woman in a floppy, wide-brimmed hat.

"Hello, my name is Daisy. I live just down the block." She said it with pride, as if it were an accomplishment.

Two of the *rebbetzins* from the yeshivah arrived, and Ella came downstairs to call the meeting to order. "Before we start," she said, "I have a treat for you. My friend Miriam has just told me a wonderful story of Divine Providence, how the fire in the Yerushalayim corridor stopped just when it got to the first Torah community, and how her own children got out just before the flames. I'm going to ask her to tell it over to you."

Miriam, startled at being promoted to the position of speaker, stumbled at first in her story. However, as she began to relive the events, the words tumbled out. Her listeners listened tensely until she got to the point where they were reunited with Tami, and then they visibly relaxed.

"*Gevaldig!*" said Devora, when she finished.

"Thank you for bringing us some of the spirit of Eretz Yisrael," said Rebbetzin Feldman.

Daisy just looked at her with admiration.

Miriam got back to her mother's house by five o'clock the next day. She fed the children supper, read them a bedtime story, and then got dressed up again. Tonight, her mother-in-law was making *sheva berachos* for Reuven, and since she was the one who had brought Sarah Dinah into the family, she wanted to be there on time to help.

When she got to the Lerners,' Miriam took charge of setting the table for the women. She was just crossing the hall back to the kitchen with an empty tray when a young girl entered. Her light hair was pulled back in a simple ponytail, but she was wearing a very dressy suit, with a gold necklace and matching bracelet. She looked around the foyer as if she had never been in the house before and didn't know where to go. Then she glanced down the hall and her face lit up with a broad smile. "Mrs. Lerner! I'm so happy to see you."

Miriam glanced over her shoulder, convinced that her mother-in-law must be standing behind her. Though the voice had a slightly familiar ring, she was tolerably certain that she had never been introduced to this girl. The space behind her was empty. Miss Unknown came forward, seized Miriam's right hand, and shook it vigorously. "I really don't know how to thank you."

Miriam, of course, smiled back, but her thoughts were racing. Which was better, to admit straight out that she didn't recognize the girl, or to play along for a few minutes in the hope that something would jog her memory? If she played along but didn't remember, it would be very embarrassing to admit later that she didn't know who this was. She was about to opt for full disclosure when she heard her mother-in-law, who now was standing behind Miriam, exclaim, "Oh, you must be our new *kallah*! I'm so pleased you could come," as she rushed forward and kissed the stranger.

Our new *kallah*? Had Zevy gotten engaged without anyone telling Miriam? Of course, she had been off at Ella's. It wouldn't have been so surprising if she had missed something.

Mrs. Lerner led the girl into the dining room. "You must be exhausted," she continued. "You only arrived this morning, right?"

"I'm sure that jet lag will hit me soon," said the *kallah*, "but right now I am too excited to feel it."

Jet lag. So she probably came from Europe or Israel.

"I'm so sorry that I couldn't be there for the *lechaim*," apologized Mrs. Lerner. "I had this party to organize, and just couldn't get away."

All right, so it wasn't Zevy. There is no way that Mrs. Lerner would have missed the *lechaim* for one of her own sons. Miriam retreated to the kitchen. When her mother-in-law came back in, she would ask for a full explanation.

Unfortunately, when Mrs. Lerner reappeared in the kitchen, she was accompanied by the new guest. "It's so kind of you to let me help," the girl was saying. "It will make me feel as if I am already a member of the family."

"You are a member of the family," asserted Mrs. Lerner.

Miriam was in despair. It would have to be full disclosure, embarrassing as it was. "Excuse me, you seem to know me, but I don't seem to remember where from."

The girl opened her eyes wide. "You don't remember when Rina

Schneider got appendicitis?"

Well, of course, she did remember that, but this was neither Rina, who was short and dark, nor Pessie, who was tall and blond. "Yes?" said Miriam tentatively.

"I'm Bitya Cooper, Rina's counselor."

Now it all came back. The girl who had come in while Miriam was bending over the groaning Rina. Bitya volunteering to accompany Rina to the hospital. Pessie collecting ice from all the neighbors. Packing the two girls into the Hatzolah car for the trip to the hospital. "Of course! Now I remember!"

"You called me up several times the next week to find out how Rina was doing."

"Right, I did." That's why the voice had been more familiar than the face. "I still don't understand what you were thanking me for when you came in."

"Why, for making my *shidduch*!"

"Now wait." Here Miriam was sure that she was on firm ground. "I know that we talked about Rina, but I am absolutely positive that I never suggested any kind of a *shidduch* for you."

"I'm sure you were the one. My housemother even had your address and phone number. She said that you were definitely the person who called up with the suggestion."

At the word "housemother," something began to stir in Miriam's memory. "Your housemother said that I called her?"

"Yes, she said that you were the person who suggested Elisha for me!"

"But … but …" Miriam sputtered. "I thought nothing came of that suggestion. Aunt Toby never got back to me about it."

"My mother probably asked that she not speak about it. Because of this," she bent her left arm at the elbow and held out her artificial hand, "we have to make compromises, but Mom didn't want all the compromises we ever agreed to, piled on top of each other." The hand was similar to that of a mannequin in a window display. Miriam was not surprised that she had noticed nothing the first time she had met Bitya.

The front door burst open and Reuven backed in, holding the handles of Elisha's wheelchair, which he had pulled up the steps, with Elisha's brother Motti helping from the other side. Reuven spun the chair around. Elisha had just a brief moment to register the presence of his *kallah* and smile broadly when he and Reuven were ushered into the living room to the tune of "*Od yeshama, b'arei Yehudah, u'v'chutzos Yerushalayim ...*"

Sarah Dinah, Reuven's *kallah*, and Motti's wife, Shaindy, followed closely behind. They had all come straight from Elisha and Bitya's *lechaim*. After greetings all around, the women adjourned to the dining room, where Miriam had set up the table for them. After she had shown everyone where to wash and everyone was seated, she headed back to the kitchen to get the first course. Bitya jumped right up and followed her. Although she wouldn't really need help until the second course, Miriam understood that Elisha's *kallah* wanted the chance to get to know her.

"Can you manage these?" Miriam asked, pointing to a tray of fruit cups.

"Sure," said Bitya. She held her artificial hand at the level of the counter and slid the tray onto it, holding it in place with her right hand. "I'll be right back."

Miriam was, in fact, quite curious about the plans. The Sheinfelds had bought a double apartment that had required few alterations beside a ramp. Elisha and the Millmans had moved in a few weeks ago. They had held a housewarming ceremony, which the Lerners had attended. Miriam remembered thinking at the time that Elisha's half was quite large for an unmarried *bachur*. Now it appeared that Mrs. Sheinfeld had been hopeful that Elisha would soon find a match.

Her mother-in-law was at the other end of the kitchen. "What's next?" Miriam asked her.

"Egg rolls from the oven for a first course. Put them on small plates." Miriam set out the plates on trays, and had just gotten the cookie sheets of egg rolls from the oven when Bitya returned.

"What will be the arrangements with the Millmans?" asked Miriam as they set out the egg rolls with tongs.

"They'll continue living in the other apartment, and he will help Elisha in the morning and evening, just as he's been doing up until now. In return, they won't have to pay rent. I met Trudy just before I left to come here, and I think everything will be fine."

Miriam handed over a large tray to Motti, who was serving on the men's side, and reached out to pick up the tray for the women.

Bitya put her hand on Miriam's arm to hold her back for a

moment. "I wouldn't want you to misunderstand what I said earlier, Mrs. Lerner. All my life I've been thinking in terms of making compromises, but now that the time has come, I don't feel that I compromised at all."

Miriam pulled her into a hug, partly to hide the tears in her eyes. "Oh, Bitya, we're cousins now. Please call me Miriam!"

The oven was warming Miriam's back. The aroma of cinnamon and vanilla filled the kitchen. Mrs. Adler had been baking all afternoon for the family members who would drop by this evening to say good-bye to Miriam and the children.

It reminded Miriam of another afternoon spent in her mother's kitchen, more than two years ago. Then she was eaten up with guilt that she had not yet said anything about the possible move. Now ... she was sorry to be parting from her mother, but ready to take up the threads of her own life again.

"It's been so wonderful having you here," said Mrs. Adler with a sigh, as she pulled a cookie sheet covered with cinnamon-nut rolls out of the hot oven.

"I was so glad to be coming for such a *good* reason. You'll see, Mama. Sarah Dina is a lovely girl and will make a terrific daughter-in-law."

"From the other side of the ocean," said Mrs. Adler with a second sigh.

Their Yerushalayim family was indeed growing. Next year they would have not only Reuven and Sarah Dina, but Elisha and Bitya as well. Benny would have to figure out some way to make their house more wheelchair accessible.

"Brinnnggg!" The doorbell rang, but before either of them got up to answer it, they heard the sound of a key turning in the lock.

"That must be Malka," Mrs. Adler guessed.

Her guess was confirmed as Malka walked in and slid into an empty seat at the table. "Well," she said, "I see that you're getting ready for Mimi to leave. It looks like you've baked enough for an expedition to the South Pole."

"You never know when they'll forget to take kosher meals onto the plane," said Mrs. Adler defending herself. "Besides, I thought people might be dropping by this evening,"

Malka turned to her sister. "Well, Mimi, let me tell you the truth.

When you and your family left, I didn't think you'd last out the year. I'm proud of you for sticking it out."

"I admit that there were some rough times," said Miriam. She thought of the day she had come to pick up Shimmy and found the *gan* locked, and of her subsequent humiliation in the *ulpan*. "I suppose, if you go through difficult times and survive, you come out stronger."

Malka gave her an assessing, older sister look. "Our new sister-in-law calls you 'Miriam'," she commented.

"That's what people call me over there," agreed Miriam.

"Then I guess that's what we'll call you over here, too," said Malka. She gave her a kiss on the cheek. "Have a good, safe trip, Miriam."

As the mountains came into sight, Miriam heaved a sigh of satisfaction and glanced at Binyamin in the driver's seat beside her.

"Feel like a pioneer approaching the Great Divide?" he asked with a smile.

Miriam's forehead puckered. "What's the Great Divide?"

"It's in the Rocky Mountains ... the ridge separating the streams draining into the Gulf of Mexico from those flowing into the Pacific Ocean. Crossing the Divide was a big moment for pioneers on the Oregon Trail."

"We also had a 'divide' to cross, didn't we," said Miriam. "But now I think we're over the ridge."

The car entered the Yerushalayim corridor.

Miriam gazed wide-eyed at the burned-out hillsides and the charred stumps of the once verdant forest. "Oh, Binyamin! How awful!" When he had driven her to the plane, it had been dark outside and she hadn't seen the swathe of destruction left by the fire.

"Since I drive through here every day, I've gotten sort of numb to the sight, but it really is painful to see."

At places the destruction was only partial, with green trees standing next to blackened spars. In others it was total. Miriam was glad the children had dozed off. When they got to the stretch after Beit Meir, Miriam shuddered at the thought of Tami and the girls walking along the side of the road with the fire closing in on them. The fire truck that had rescued them had been only slightly ahead of the flames.

They came to the open stretch before Telz-Stone and saw the prow of their community before them, lightly scorched but otherwise unharmed. Miriam had trouble controlling her impatience as they waited for a chance to make a left turn across the three-lane highway. As soon as they rounded the bend and the access road began running along the length of the community, the last vestiges of the fire vanished. Miriam reached over the seat back and gave Shimmy's shoulder a light shake. "Shimmy, wake up. We're almost home. Here's our backyard."

She looked out the window again just in time to see the stone walls of their building framed through the stand of pine trees in their backyard. Binyamin's new fig tree was still too small to be seen from the road, but the pomegranate tree was visible. She remembered the day two years ago when she had described Binyamin's dream of stone and pine to Reuven. It was now her dream too.

"Here we are!" announced Binyamin, as he parked the car. "Tami, Shimmy, wake up!"

Miriam opened the door, stood up, and drew in a lungful of mountain air. Binyamin unloaded one of the suitcases and took Shimmy's hand, while Miriam took hold of Tami and Itzik. When she got to the set of stairs, she stopped in surprise. "Who did that?" she asked, pointing to the ramp that now took up half of the wide staircase."

"Mr. Wechsler," explained Benny. "His mother is coming to live with them, and she's in a wheelchair."

Before going down the stairs, Miriam paused to look out over the hills, still covered with the green haze of their spring foliage, not yet burned brown by the dry summer. The fire had not reached the slopes that formed their view. But why linger here? She could see them as well from her own living room.

"How are you feeling?" asked Binyamin.

"How am I feeling? Glad to be home!"

ABOUT THE AUTHOR

Rachel Pomerantz was one of the first writers of *chareidi* fiction for adults. Her earlier books, *Wildflower, A Time to Rend, A Time to Sew, Mountains Around Jerusalem,* and *Cactus Blossoms,* dealt with the adjustment problems of *baalei teshuvah* and converts who have joined the *frum* community.

She also wrote a short history of the Holocaust, and a book of true stories of survivors selected to cover various periods and geographical areas, *Wings Above the Flames.*

By profession, Rachel Pomerantz is a research mathematician and thus travels professionally all over the world, which has given her the chance to visit many different Jewish communities.